Praise for Linda Broday and
Knight on the Texas Plains

"Ms. Broday is a bright and shining new star in the publishing world."
—Karen Kelley, author of *Bachelor Party*

"Ms. Broday...will easily capture your heart."
—*Old Book Barn Gazette*

"Heartwarming characters weave a story no reader will forget."
—Jodi Thomas, *USA Today* bestselling author

"A strong new voice."
—Helen R. Meyers, author of *Final Stand*

Also by Linda Broday

Texas Redemption

Bachelors of Battle Creek
Texas Mail Order Bride
Twice a Texas Bride
Forever His Texas Bride

Men of Legend
To Love a Texas Ranger
The Heart of a Texas Cowboy
To Marry a Texas Outlaw

Texas Heroes
Knight on the Texas Plains
The Cowboy Who Came Calling

The Cowboy

Who
Came
Calling

LINDA
BRODAY

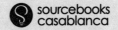

sourcebooks
casablanca

Published by Sourcebooks Casablanca, an imprint of Sourcebooks, Inc.
P.O. Box 4410, Naperville, Illinois 60567-4410
(630) 961-3900
Fax: (630) 961-2168
sourcebooks.com

Originally published in 2003 in the United States by Leisure Books, an imprint of Dorchester Publishing Co., Inc.

Printed and bound in the United States of America.
OPM 10 9 8 7 6 5 4 3 2 1

To the pioneers who settled this great land with grit, blood, and tears. And to the lonely cowboys who thought they had nothing worth loving, and the women who showed them they did.

One

OFTEN THE ELDERS SPOKE IN HUSHED WHISPERS ABOUT A long, painful night of the soul. How the wind visited, carrying problems as thick as a biblical plague. It's also said that impatience dries the blood sooner than age or sorrow.

Surely this must be such a time.

In twenty years, Glory Marie Day had come to know more about injustice and patience than most women twice her age. She hadn't asked for any breaks, only a fair shake, and fate hadn't seen fit to deliver even a sliver of that.

Truth of the matter, she hadn't overly complained of the lousy handout she'd gotten. She made her own luck and became tougher for it.

Whatever it took she'd do. Though the difficult task at hand might scare off a person of lesser grit.

Glory's fists curled in a ball. Somehow. Someway.

Reverend Matthews's sermon yesterday merely gave her added determination. "When Saint Peter marks against your name in the great Hereafter, you'd best make sure you have enough scratches on the plus side."

Papa always bragged about her being whip smart. Good thing, because she'd need everything she had to solve this problem. At least more pluses than minuses at the end.

Snooty Bess Whitfield's snickers brought her thoughts back to the present. For a Monday afternoon, Harvey's Emporium held a good many patrons. Across the room, Bess gave Glory's faded breeches an imperious frown, then whispered behind her hand to her companion, Amelia Jackson.

Though not close enough to hear, Glory knew the slurs by heart. "Poor homely Glory. Dressing like a boy, she'll never have a beau. Her father's a rotten jailbird. Better stay clear of those good-for-nothing Days."

A woman's voice interrupted her thoughts. "Here you are, Glory."

"Thank you, Aunt Dorothy." She accepted the box of cartridges she'd requested. Except for her aunt, Uncle Pete, and a few others, she would've compared life in the Texas town of Santa Anna as something akin to hell.

"Going huntin'?" The woman she loved as a second mother propped an elbow on a big jar of pickles.

Glory's mouth watered for one of the juicy pickles. Lord knew she loved them better than candy. The sign read five cents. Cheap enough, she reckoned, if a body had a nickel in her pocket. The eggs, milk, and butter she'd just sold her aunt barely covered the ammunition for her Winchester.

"Yes, ma'am. Better see what game I can scare up for supper." Without a doubt, if she hadn't stepped up to fill her father's boots… Well, she didn't want to dwell on that.

"You're the strong one, Glory. Your ma, God bless her soul, is too frail to see to the needs of you children. I love my sister-in-law to death, but Ruth wears my patience down to a nub. Right alongside Pete Harvey. I swear, those two were carved from the same block of wood."

Allowing a half smile, Glory slipped the cartridges inside her pocket. "Where's Uncle Pete today?"

Although the man suffered from flights of fancy, what the polite ones called it, Glory worshipped him. Pete Harvey's eccentricities added a certain flavor to her existence. She had to marvel at anyone who marched as he saw fit, taking whatever paths his imagination led to. If ever she should be so free.

"The fool is out dowsing for water. Cut himself a peach tree limb as a divining rod and declared he'd find water or bust a gut trying."

"This drought has everyone in a bad way. Paying Mr. McConley twenty-three cents a barrel is highway robbery. If Uncle Pete can truly find water, he'll have every family in Coleman County bidding for his services."

"Hmph! If is a big word." Aunt Dorothy straightened, reached for a long feather duster, and flicked it over the nearly spotless counter. "I'm mighty thankful I don't have to depend on his crazy notions to put food in our bellies."

Depend on Dorothy Harvey to look on the bright side.

Bess and Amelia sauntered to the counter. From the way they brushed tightly against Glory, the aisle might well have become a narrow strip of dry ground in a mud pit.

"Afternoon, Mrs. Harvey."

Did they speak in unison like that just to irritate a body?

"Girls, what'll it be for you today?"

Glory headed for the door but stopped when Aunt Dorothy called, "Oh, wait a minute, I have a letter for you, dear."

"We'll take one of these new toothbrushes and a jar of this paste to go with it." Bess gave Glory a sidelong smirk.

"Clean teeth is as important as bathing regular."

The implication that she did neither had Glory fuming. A daily rubbing of soda powder kept her teeth shiny and clean enough. Thank goodness proper customs weren't limited to those who could afford it. But, it sure seemed as if good manners ran in short supply.

Amelia plopped down a bar of perfumed toilet soap. "Can you put these on my daddy's bill, Mrs. Harvey?"

"I suppose I can. Will this be all?"

The Persnickety Twins nodded their heads again in unison.

While Aunt Dorothy wrapped the items in brown paper, Glory cast the jar of luscious pickles another longing stare. Even should she suddenly by some miracle possess a nickel, her sense of honor would kick in. She didn't want anything if her sisters couldn't have the same. Just wasn't right.

All of a sudden, the pickle jar doubled. And tripled. Then her vision dimmed as if someone had extinguished the oil lamps hanging on the store walls. She shook her head, closing her eyes for a minute. When she opened them, she could make out her aunt's form, a decided improvement.

Perspiration dampened her palms. This loss of vision had come and gone over the last few weeks. At first the episodes had been shorter and farther apart. Now, she experienced two or three a day. Still, she refused to let her worst fears take root. Nothing worse could happen…could it?

The tinkle of the bell over the entrance seemed far in the distance. It was the deep tenor that broke her trance.

"Afternoon, ladies."

Bess and Amelia tittered, nudging each other. Curious, Glory turned to see the cause of such a stir.

The tall stranger smiled and sidestepped past. He'd not paid her any attention. No, the two girls bedecked in fine dresses took his eye. No reason in the world why he should notice a girl in faded britches and mule-eared boots. No reason whatsoever.

She watched him head for the coffee grinder. Hmm, coffee beans. Yep, the brown strands nestling against his collar were the exact shade of those beans he poured into the grinder.

Nice.

From beneath lowered lids, she took in the rest of him. The dark-blue shirt added breadth to his shoulders. The polished silver buttons on the cavalry bib spoke of pride. Slim waist, long legs that stretched from here to yon, and a finely shaped behind. A figure that could easily climb atop a horse—or a…

A flush crept from her toes upward. Where had that thought come from? Her mind deserved a good scrubbing. Besides, he'd never give her the time of day.

For a split second, bitterness bubbled to the surface like

fermented yeast. She didn't want to be the provider, the strong one, the head of the family. For just one day, she'd like to worry about her teeth instead of feeding hungry stomachs. She'd like to wear dresses and act a lady. And for once, she'd like to have a man look at her with warm desire in his eyes. Someone besides Horace Simon, who was jeered for his childlike ways. Horace moon-eyed over her each time she went near, but she saw the loneliness inside and counted him a friend. She'd just like to have the attentions of a man like this stranger for once.

"Here you are, girls." Aunt Dorothy handed over the wrapped parcels before turning to the stranger. "Can I help you, mister?"

"Yes, ma'am."

Glory knew a moment of jealousy when he nodded and cast the fashion queens a brief smile. "Ladies."

Still, she quickly averted her gaze when he swung back to her aunt. She watched Bess and Amelia sweep regally toward the door, all the while whispering behind their hands and giggling. Prim and proper as they pretended, they sure acted stupid.

"I'll take some of this coffee and a bag of flour. Throw in beans, some jerky, and cartridges. That'll do it, I reckon."

"You passing through or plannin' to stay awhile?"

The paper Aunt Dorothy bundled his purchases in rattled loudly, forcing Glory to concentrate to hear his answer. Not that anyone would speak her name and busybody in the same breath. Mere interest—a slight but distinguishable difference.

"Depends, ma'am. I'm camped just outside town for the time being."

The length of his stay in the area probably depended on whether the Miss Prisses invited him home to meet their daddies.

Besides his being easy on the eyes, the man's polite ways fit snug about him. His resonant voice created tightness in her chest.

Her own papa had such a way of speaking. The lump in her throat refused to budge. Would she ever get to hear that sound again?

She quickly ducked when the man favored her with a glance and became intent on a handbill lying on the counter. Now that the store had emptied, she couldn't remain part of the woodwork. Being noticed was one thing, pitied another story altogether. For two cents, she'd not wait for the letter Aunt Dorothy mentioned.

She forced her mind back to the crisp paper in her hand. *Hell's bells!* The words leaped off the page. Mad Dog Perkins, a five-hundred-dollar reward for his capture. Why hadn't she paid attention to it before? That was enough to hire a real lawyer. Not one of the shyster varieties.

"Oh, yes, your letter." Aunt Dorothy reached into a wooden slot and handed her an envelope.

Worry forced all thoughts of Perkins from her mind as Glory recognized the flowing script. They'd received similar ones from Dr. Fletcher, the physician who treated Jack Day at the Texas State Penitentiary at Huntsville. Each one had brought pain and made her ever mindful of the racing clock.

Terrible foreboding knotted her stomach. Dark smudges stained one corner. Blood? Her chest constricted. Her daddy's?

"Hope to goodness it's not bad news, dear," her aunt remarked, noticing her reluctance, and then her eyes lit on the handbill. "You know, this very morning, Mr. Harvey told me over his cold eggs and burnt biscuits that he got a gander at a man lurking around Bead Mountain. That man's cooking is worse than his forgetfulness, if that's possible."

Glory tried to curb the impatience others had warned would dry the blood. Truth or not, she darn well knew it didn't help her nerves. "What did he say about the man he saw?"

"Swore he resembled Mad Dog Perkins. Course, that old coot sees things few other folks do. I think his mind's took to wandering worse than ever."

The stranger's head whipped around. The new

pocketknife he'd admired must have lost its shine. Glory caught the slight shift in his feet as he leaned forward. Maybe she was a bit hasty in bestowing attributes he didn't possess.

A lower tone of voice and turning her back would fix him. "Too bad we don't have a sheriff either here or in Coleman City. Not enough pay to develop a fondness for bullets. Did he mention his suspicions to the U.S. Marshal in Abilene town?"

"No need. Everyone from here to the Mississippi knows my Pete. Say he's tetched and don't pay him no more mind than if he was a flea."

Bead Mountain. The old Indian burial place would provide excellent cover for a wanted man, since most folks shied away from there. Haunted, the rumormongers whispered. Not that she believed such herself. Nothing but the howling wind could make her bones shiver.

"Thank you for the letter, Aunt Dorothy." She kissed the woman's cheek, slipping the letter next to the box of cartridges. "I have a hundred things to do and I'm wasting time."

She whirled—right into a rock-solid chest. The collision sent the handsome stranger's purchases flying.

"Sorry, mister." Mortified, Glory snatched up the items from the floor and stuffed them back into his arms before he had a chance to blink twice.

That's when she made her second mistake. Both steamy and dark, his gaze pulled her into a murky pool where she foundered helpless as a scuttled ship.

"No harm done, miss." The twinkle and lopsided grin held her spellbound. "Name's McClain. Luke McClain."

Tongue-tied under his scrutiny, she couldn't make a squeak. Before she made the worst mistake of her life, she fled.

ॐ

The sun beat down as Luke crept silently in the tall grass. Beads of sweat ran into his eyes, burning worse than an eyeful of cayenne. Momentarily blinded, he wiped his face with the sleeve of his shirt.

With sight restored, he spied his prey.

The figure squatted on his haunches just ahead. Mad Dog Perkins, as he lived and breathed. After months of looking, he'd finally found the slippery man. Before the day ended, he'd learn who and why someone had stolen his life.

Perkins knew—Luke bet on it. He eased his Colt from the holster and inched close enough to spit on the man who'd holed up at the foot of the small mountain. Thick brush at the base of a natural overhang offered an excellent hiding place. Destiny must've put that girl in the emporium that morning. Otherwise, he wouldn't have found the man so soon.

Luke crouched, ready to spring into the camp. But before he could make his move, a slim figure appeared from nowhere.

The newcomer yanked the lever of his rifle down and up in a snapping motion, startling Mad Dog Perkins.

What the...? Luke watched the scene with a knot in his belly. Who had beaten him to the prize? He shrank into the tall brush.

"Don't even think it, mister." The shadows of a floppy hat concealed the wearer's face, but the voice sounded way too young for this dirty business. "Throw your pistol over here nice and easy. No tricks."

Perkins growled like the rabid animal his name implied and tossed his weapon within inches of the rifleman.

Unable to watch someone steal what was rightfully his, Luke scrambled to his feet and into the small clearing. "Just a cotton-pickin' minute."

He skidded to an abrupt halt when the slim figure swung the lethal rifle his direction.

"No, you wait. Mister, I don't know what your business is here, but you're lucky I didn't part your hair."

Surprise curled inside him at sight of those delicate-shaped eyes. Those didn't belong to any boy or man.

Ricocheting surprise gave him a pleasing taste. A cajoler at heart, he figured taking candy from a babe couldn't present that much of a challenge.

"What're you doing? If I'm allowed to ask, ma'am?"

The Winchester remained pointed at his heart while she nervously eyed Perkins. A streak of dirt across her nose and cheek added grit to the stubborn tilt of her chin.

"Stay out of my way. I'm taking this man to Abilene town and collecting the reward."

His breath caught at the back of his throat. The unusual blue gaze seemed lodged in his brain. Her eyes reminded him of polished stones worn smooth by the timeless flow of water. That was exactly what they resembled— stonewashed. Yet, his memory of their meeting refused to yield the place.

"It's my duty to take charge of Perkins. No job for a lady." If he gave her the wrong impression, wasn't any fault of his. Didn't need a tin star when the callin' pumped in a man's veins as thick as life-sustaining blood.

"Over my dead body! I captured him fair and square."

Mad Dog shifted his stance from one side to another, seeming to gauge the distance to the rifle. The young woman sensed his movement and swung sharply.

"I wouldn't, Perkins. It would be a mistake to test my temper." She clearly meant business.

But so did Luke. He wasn't about to relinquish the desperado now that he'd found him. And not before he had a chance to get those answers he desperately needed. Yet, how could he make the interloper see she'd stepped in the middle of something where she had no right?

"Weeeell, I do declare. I must be sumpin' to have folks fightin' over who's gonna fetch me to the marshal." Perkins grinned, giving them both a good view of his brown, rotted teeth.

"Begging your pardon, miss. Tackling wanted criminals is a man's job." Luke used his most reasonable tone, the one he used when cajoling troublesome fillies. "Not meaning any disrespect, but I've dogged Perkins's trail for the better part of two months."

Her chin jutted farther. "I saw him first and he's mine."

"Y'all mind if I sit a spell while you dicker over—"

"Keep standing!" he and the woman answered together.

"Move one muscle and I'll shoot you," she added.

Luke didn't know which of them she meant. Judging from the fire-breathing glare, Mystery Lady might shoot both simply for the heck of it.

Although she was a tad on the slim side for his taste, he admired the way she filled out those britches. His gaze traveled upward to her heaving chest. Yep, her curves were certainly in all the right places…and then some.

By some quirk of fate, her hair chose that particular moment to spill from beneath the floppy hat. He could only hold his breath at the spectacle and watch the glimmering strands slip one by one from their hiding place. They teased, they dallied, taunting him in a slow, sensuous dance until the golden mass caressed her back and shoulders.

Have mercy! For a moment, he was afraid the thick lump he'd swallowed had been his own tongue.

Then it hit him. Harvey's Emporium in Santa Anna. His thoughts had been more on the handbill than who held it. No mistaking though—this was the girl who'd knocked the supplies from his hands. No one else in the whole state of Texas had eyes that color.

"If you're through staring, cowboy, you can holster that pistol and ride back where you came from."

A hot flush rose and crept toward his hairline. "I'm not going anywhere, miss, except to take this man—"

Perkins chose that moment to jump, knocking the girl to the ground.

Luke renewed his grip on the Colt, springing forward to help. Midair of his leap, an orange flash spat from the end of her Winchester. A deafening blast followed.

The bullet tore through flesh and muscle. A white pain enveloped Luke as he fell. Through the dizzying haze, he watched helplessly as the man who'd helped destroy him vanished from sight into the brush.

Now, someone's plan to ruin him was complete.

He might never again be this close to the truth. Despair twisted in his gut. His hand went limp. The revolver made a quiet thump as it fell.

Two

GLORY PULLED HERSELF SLOWLY TO HER FEET. THE DRY brush crackled in the wake of Perkins's escape, seeming to mimic her crumbling hopes and dreams. Sick at heart, she glared at the meddlesome stranger who'd thwarted her plans. If he hadn't interfered, she'd be well on her way to town, along with the means to solve all her problems.

The man sprawled, clutching his right leg. Despite deep aggravation, her stomach plunged when she saw red oozing from between his fingers.

"Dear heavens!"

"You shot me!" He struggled to sit up.

She pulled a kerchief from her back pocket as she ran to him. "I didn't mean for that to happen. You saw it, didn't you? Perkins, I mean. It just went off."

Kneeling, she tied the kerchief high on his leg above the wound. That meant working awfully close to his...uh... unmentionables. Her hand trembled so badly she could only hope her jerky movements would limit the blood loss.

"Why did you let him grab your rifle? Blew half my fool leg off here."

"Oh, and I guess you'd have done any better?" If he could complain, he wasn't hurt too badly. She hid her relief behind a frown. "Besides, you're exaggerating. The wound can't be all that serious. Now, if you'd have been closer, and

I hadn't loaded this Winchester with buckshot, we might've been contemplating amputation, McClain."

"How'd you know my name?" Luke grimaced as she gently eased the afflicted limb back to the ground. "I don't rightly recall the introduction."

All manner of strange pinpricks mocked her outward calm as she tried to avoid the face that stirred her fancies. The stranger could certainly charm the pitchfork from the devil himself. Fighting the war on both fronts, she focused on putting from mind the firm hardness of his leg and the close proximity of the other...part as she worked. Wild flutters of panic beat their wings against her rib cage.

A deep breath might steady her nerves. Yet, when she managed to gulp a large portion of the heady air, it merely made her realize nothing short of putting distance between them would solve the problem.

His name? Truth told, she didn't seem prone to forgetting it.

"You made your acquaintance to my aunt, not me directly, this morning. I may be a lowly female and therefore unworthy of capturing a wanted criminal, at least in your estimation." She gave the kerchief a yank, tying the knot a teensy bit tighter. "But I am not the least bit deaf."

"Ow! Damn, lady." The pasty white of his face warned that he teetered on the brink of blackness.

"Sorry. I need to get this down to a trickle or there'll be no need for me to haul your carcass anywhere. Else, might as well let the buzzards have you."

"A man truly lives for the moment when he can place his life into the hands of such a caring, compassionate woman." McClain's words came from between clenched teeth.

"I suppose you'd have better luck with the Miss Prisses then?" The sting of remorse came instantly. Rudeness went against her nature. She treated everyone with kind respect, even poor Horace Simon.

It boiled down to letting the answer to her desperate plan slip through her fingers. Her father depended on her. The whole family looked to her for their needs, and the question remained as to how long she'd have before she lost the skill to do so.

"Am I delirious? Who, pray tell, are the Miss Prisses?"

"Forgotten so soon? You certainly ogled them this morning in the emporium."

"Oh, those ladies. I was merely being polite. Nothing wrong with that." He cocked his head. "Do I detect envy?"

"You'd be wrong if you did." His assumption hit a layer of hard rock. She wasn't jealous of what Amelia and Bess had…it was more the things they could have that bothered her.

When she risked another fleeting glance at McClain, she fell headlong into that smoldering gaze. To say she became taken with him would've been an understatement.

"Not fair, Mystery Lady. I still don't have your name."

Glory blew a tendril of hair that'd fallen close to her mouth and wished the day hadn't turned so blasted hot. Or that the curve of his mouth that accented a white scar just below his bottom lip didn't make her heart race. Or that his arresting brown eyes didn't make her wonder what secrets lodged behind them. Although for the moment, a grim line held the lazy grin at bay.

And furthermore, she wished his study of her didn't turn her legs to jelly.

"It's Glory…Glory Day," she murmured.

Before he could further wilt her self-confidence, she stood, retrieved her Winchester, then scanned the rugged brush for signs of McClain's horse.

Common sense told her she was obligated to take him home with her. After all, she did shoot him and couldn't just leave him hurt, however much she so desired. But, once there, she'd turn over his care to her mother and sisters. Her duty done, she'd make certain she stayed well beyond reach of any magical spells the charmer tried to weave.

A horse's whinny off to the left alerted her. She pushed through the tangle of briars and thistle.

"An Indian pony. Might have known he'd not ride

a nag." She untied the light-colored paint, admiring the ripple of muscle beneath the tan-and-white hide. Good horseflesh. She doubted any in the area could rival it.

The stranger's face brightened when he spied her leading the animal.

"Saints be praised! The thought crossed my mind you'd left me for buzzard bait." McClain tried to pull himself up, but pain clearly evident on his face sent him back to the hard ground.

"I have to admit, the plan had merit." She bent and, trying to keep his nearness from her mind, slipped an arm around his holstered middle. "If you grab around my neck and push up with your good leg, we might get you on your feet."

"I'm game if you are, Miss Glory."

The man's solidness surprised her. For all his lean, lanky build, it taxed her strength to raise him. His body pressing tightly against hers sent rampant thoughts of the entirely inappropriate variety swarming through her head like flies to hot apple pie.

Her pulse and ragged breath were neck and neck in a horse race. Which one would win? And in what shape would it leave her?

By the time she got him vertical, she knew she probably would never be the same. Then came the job of boosting him into the saddle. One slight problem—where was she supposed to boost him from?

A quick survey up and down his trim form left few options. She'd simply have to put her hands on his backside and imagine pushing Bessie from a mud pit. She looped the paint's reins around her arm.

It wasn't as if his finely sculpted behind was bare. No sirree, his britches covered it, outlining it perfectly.

"When I count to three, pull yourself up, Mr. McClain." Why in tarnation did her heart pound like this?

"I'm hardly in any position to object."

Glory stooped slightly to give herself leverage. "One." Her hands rested on each side of his posterior. "Two."

"You know, I don't mind getting shot quite so much," he murmured.

She closed her eyes. He surely didn't feel much like the milk cow. And it hadn't rained in so long she couldn't even remember a mud hole.

"Three."

Up he went, sliding onto the horse.

"Don't mind my saying so, Miss Glory, but you sure have a heck of a system." He flashed her a crooked smile as he reached down to give her a hand.

"No, thanks, I have my own mount. I hid him down in a little wash not too far from here."

A rush of excitement swept over her when his grin slipped. Obviously he'd expected her to ride behind. Even anticipated perhaps? Who was she kidding? A man with heart-stopping grins wouldn't be interested in a pants-wearing female.

Jumbled thoughts clouded her head as she led the paint to the gully where she'd stashed her mule. Once the glow of besting him faded, disappointment set in. McClain's trousers resting snug against the inside of her thighs might not have been so bad. She'd never know now.

When she gave a fleeting look back, it was merely to see if he still sat anchored in the saddle. For no other reason, she assured herself.

Old Caesar brayed loudly when he saw her. Though the white mule had serviced the family well, for once Glory wished the animal were a horse. Nothing, except a donkey maybe, spoke of worse circumstances than a mule.

No sooner had the wish formed than her conscience berated her. She should consider herself mighty lucky to have what they did. Her poor father struggled for a bite of bread.

And at least she owned a saddle. The animal skittered as she placed her foot in the stirrup and swung onto the leather.

"Are you all right, Mr. McClain?" The man's ashen color didn't reassure her.

To his credit, McClain sought to put on a brave front. "Fine as frog's hair. Where did you say you're taking me?"

"Didn't say." She lifted the paint's reins.

"Well, if you don't mind, would you like to share that piece of information? A man has a right to know."

"You're a mean-tempered old cuss."

"Well, pardon me for breathing. Hobbling around with holes in a fellow's leg tends to sour a man's disposition. And what did you mean by old? I'll have you know I'm far from ready for an undertaker yet."

She thought it strange that the part about his age drew the biggest objection. "I'm taking you home."

"Sounds good to me—if I knew where home was."

He slid sideways. Glory grabbed him before he fell and pushed him back in the saddle.

"Hang on, cowboy. I'm taking you to our homestead."

"Don't wanna be a bother. If you'll just point the way to Santa Anna, I'll head over there."

"Too far, and besides, they don't have a doctor. Guess it's me or nothing."

"If'n you say so." His trailing voice warned her he was slipping close to unconsciousness. Blood now stained the right leg of his soft denims a dull red from thigh to knee.

Damnation! The wound might be worse than she thought. Here she was gabbing with the man when she should be more concerned for his welfare. She flushed. He'd tangled her emotions worse than a slipknot. The harder she struggled to get loose, the more bound she became.

She gripped the Winchester tighter and urged the animals to a faster pace, keeping an eye peeled for a possible ambush. Though she assumed Mad Dog's first thought would be to hightail it out of the country, she also knew he would be after revenge.

Tumbleweeds blew from the west like silent, gray ghosts spooking the animals. She dodged what she could while toying with the idea of resuming the search for Perkins. The likelihood of sneaking up on him a second time would increase the danger tenfold. Dare she let that stop her?

Their destination rose into view while she weighed the pros and cons. Mama topped the con list. That she'd raise a fuss was a given. And who would see to putting food on the table?

They waded into the Red Bank Creek, which meandered through the Day property. The con side grew longer. Glory couldn't shirk her duty. She sighed. Going after Perkins again was out of the question. Their means for survival had vanished into thin air. And she laid the blame on the stranger slumped in the saddle. No choice but to take him to the Day household, dearly as it galled her. Caesar plodded up the slope on the other side.

From a distance, there was something majestic about the stone house where she had come into the world. A body couldn't see the missing porch step, the hole in the roof, or the tear in the screen door. This far away, the tangle of wild honeysuckle covering the entire east side gave it a stature worthy of a castle. Her grandfather had constructed the dwelling half a century ago from natural limestone he quarried and hauled down from the mountain. The durable structure had withstood Texas twisters, drought, and spring floods. She tried to wet her dry mouth, but nothing came— not enough moisture for spit. The godforsaken heat had sucked the life from the land. Nothing thrived but tumbleweeds, wild honeysuckle, and broken dreams.

She patted Caesar's neck and gave him a nudge with her knee. "Get along, you flea-bitten bag of bones. We're home."

Her youngest sister came flying out to greet them, letting the screen door slam shut behind her.

"Glory, guess what!"

The ten-year-old's enthusiasm evoked twinges of jealousy. Patience didn't have to worry about food supplies or meeting the payments on the banknote. In fact, the pigtailed youngster had few things to disrupt her sleep. Like it or not, Glory meant to keep it that way for however long she could.

"What, Squirt?" She halted at the stone fence that surrounded the house and dismounted. "What happened today?"

"Miss Minnie had kittens. Four of 'em. They're so cute." Patience squinted against the sun. "Who's the stranger, Glory?"

"Name's McClain. Don't rightly know more than that."

"He's bleedin'. How'd he get shot? Huh? Stage robbers shoot you, mister?"

"Patience Ann Day! Where are your manners?"

McClain roused. "This jabberjaw your sister?"

"Afraid so. Can you get down?" Oh, Lord, she hoped so. She didn't need to get close to him again. He'd ruined her breathing and turned her brain to mush once already.

"Think I can make it. If nothin' else, I can fall—"

Before he could complete the sentence, he slid from the paint and crumpled to the ground in a heap.

"Go get Hope." She pushed the girl toward the house. "I need help."

"Hope, come quick!" Patience shrieked as she ran to the house. "Glory's brought home a man."

The statement brought a fluster on which she had no time to dwell. She touched his forehead. Cold and clammy.

"What's wrong?" Hope's hurrying stride whipped the skirts about her ankles.

Glory met her middle sister's worried gray eyes. "Please help me get him into the house. I think he's in shock."

With McClain between them, each draped an arm around their neck. He roused again and helped relieve their burden somewhat by hobbling on his good leg. Patience held the door and they maneuvered him inside.

"Where's Mama?" Glory peered into the tidy parlor.

"Lying down. She had one of her headaches."

"In that case, let's put him in my bed." She shifted the weight, ignoring sharp needles that shot through her neck. "I'll sleep in the barn."

"You can share my bed." Hope panted under the load. "We'll worry about that later."

Half dragging him, they dropped McClain onto the bed in a little alcove off the kitchen. Glory exhaled sharply.

"Who shot him?" Her mother's voice came from the doorway. Ruth Day leaned against the wall, holding one hand to her forehead. The ruckus had evidently awakened her.

Not sure what or how much to tell, Glory stared silently at the circle of faces.

"Sorry for the noise, Mama," she said gently. "Go lie back down. We'll take care of him."

"Who is he and what is he doing in my house?"

Her mother seemed determined to have answers despite her frailty and ill health.

A wince and a deep breath later, Glory wished she could soften the blow. "Name's McClain, and I shot him."

Shocked gasps flew around the small, windowless cubbyhole.

"You what? Why on earth?"

"An accident, Mama." She rubbed her eyes wearily. "Mad Dog Perkins grabbed my Winchester and it went off."

"Mad Dog Perkins, the outlaw?" Her mother struggled to comprehend. Worry creased Ruth's forehead. "Glory Marie, I think you'd best explain yourself."

The man called McClain groaned and opened pain-clouded eyes. "Mystery Lady?" he asked, his voice soft as a whisper.

"I will later, Mama. But first I need to tend to our guest before he bleeds all over my feather mattress."

"It's not proper to have a strange man in our house." Ruth twisted her hands nervously. "Whatever will folks say now?"

"Sorry, ma'am. Don't mean to cause no harm." McClain tried to sit up. "I'll just be on my way."

"No, you won't." Glory held him down firmly. "I shot you and I'll patch you up." She gave her mother a clipped answer. "Besides, since when did it matter to us what others say?"

Hope quietly added her opinion. "I don't think they can spread worse rumors than they already have."

"Elevate the man's legs. I once saw a doctor do that," her mother cautioned, swaying and holding her head in both hands.

"Patience, take Mama back to her room, then put some water on to boil." Glory lifted a pair of scissors from a sewing basket beside the bed before turning to Hope. "We need bandages."

"What're you planning to do with those, little missy?" McClain's eyes held more than a hint of nervousness as his gaze centered on the scissors.

"I can't pick out these pellets through your clothing. Now lie still."

"But…but, you can't just strip a man of his pride without a never-you-mind. Don't I have a say-so in the matter?"

"No." She snipped the material while he continued to object.

"Ain't there any other choices here? Can't I—"

"No."

She kept her mind on her task, ever mindful of the closeness of the wound to his important…stuff. Bothersome thoughts tripped over each other inside her head. Things like how firm his flesh was and how the muscles twitched just beneath the surface. The downy hair on his leg brushed against the back of her hand and she jerked back.

Dear Mother Mary! Her palms grew sweaty and her pulse raced as if she were running for her life. Or in this case— away from trouble in the form of a stranger on a paint horse.

"I did what you said, Glory." Patience skipped into the room, her reddish-gold pigtails bobbing.

"Asked. You did what I asked," she corrected, quickly jerking the sheet over the man's naked leg. "You don't need to be in here right now. Run along. Go see what's keeping Hope."

"Oh, phooey. I'm not a baby, you know. When I grow up—"

"Scoot!" This time Glory added a firmer tone and reached for the tweezers, ignoring the familiar pout.

"Anyone ever tell you what pretty eyes you have, miss?" It seemed as if McClain willed her to meet his gaze, for he stole her power to do otherwise. "Your ma's right, me being here is gonna cause…"

Inky-brown depths pulled her into a place of mystery and odd contentment. Breath left her in a sudden rush.

Three

"LET ME WORRY ABOUT THAT. YOU FOCUS ON BREATHING."

Buckshot had peppered his thigh. Engrossed in her task, Glory lost count of the small pieces of lead she coaxed from the soft tissue. An eternity later, she wiped her brow and dropped the tweezers into the metal bowl, satisfied she'd gotten them all.

McClain's closed eyes gave her hope he'd drifted into oblivion again. A blessing for sure.

Not that she knew firsthand, but having metal fragments dug from your flesh must severely test a body's courage and will. From what she'd seen, McClain wasn't short in either department. He'd handled the ordeal with considerable fortitude.

Lord knew her own had been severely stretched.

A rustle in her pocket reminded her of the letter she hadn't had time to read. She finished binding the wound and adjusted the sheet over the man's long form.

With as much quiet as she could manage in light of her clumsy boots, she tiptoed out of the alcove and into the kitchen. Patience sat cross-legged on the floor, trying to tie a frilly piece of cloth on Miss Minnie's head for a bonnet.

"Hi, Glory," the girl said, looking up. "I'm making Miss Minnie real pretty. Hold still, you darn cat."

"No swearing in this house. You know Mama would have a conniption fit if she heard you."

"I only said darn. An' it ain't cursing. Uncle Pete says it all the time."

"Isn't. It isn't cursing," she corrected automatically. "And 'darn' is not ladylike language. You can't repeat things that Uncle Pete says. I've heard him cuss a blue streak."

She watched her little sister play with the cat and four new kittens. It wouldn't be long before the girl would have each newborn wearing tiny doll clothes. Much to Miss Minnie's irritation, Patience had dressed her in all kinds of garb from the moment she showed up on their doorstep. Not that the scraps of fabric stayed on long. Somehow, the calico always found ways to get the ruffles and bows off.

It wasn't right that Patience had to resort to playing with animals instead of children her own age or even dolls. And it didn't sit well in Glory's mind that her sister should suffer the sting of the town's rejection.

A precious thing, a child's innocence. Too bad the loss of it had to come at any point in life, but far better when one was older and equipped to deal with hate and prejudice. The townspeople's taunting and ignorance had been harsh taskmasters for Glory and her younger siblings.

Hope struggled through the kitchen door with a bucket of water from the creek. "We used all the water, so I went to refill it before dark. Sorry to leave you to finish by yourself."

"That's all right. It's over and he's dozing."

"Glory, have you thought about supper?" her mother asked, joining them.

"No, Mama. I've been pretty busy." She tried to keep the annoyance from her voice. There was only so much she could do by herself. And there was still the matter of the letter.

"Well, I'm sure you'll think of something, dear." Ruth Day plopped down in a chair at the kitchen table. "Don't think I've forgotten the explaining you owe me either.

Bringing a strange man into our house. What do you have to say for yourself?"

Hope set the bucket of water on the sideboard and took a chair beside Glory, an expectant look on her pretty features.

"Not much to tell, actually. It began with a handbill I saw at Aunt Dorothy's this morning." Glory related the details of her confrontation with Mad Dog Perkins, and the wounding of McClain.

Patience came to her feet, her eyes wide. "You really tried to bring in a wanted outlaw? He could've killed you!"

"I don't ever want to hear of you trying anything that dangerous again." Ruth's anger ended any thoughts of resuming the chase. "Do you hear me, young lady?"

"I think we should commend Glory for what she did." Hope cast her older sister a look of admiration. "Had it worked, it would've answered all our prayers. Just think, we could've brought Papa home to be with us before..."

The miserable catch in Hope's voice rekindled Glory's frustration. McClain had ruined everything. He'd stolen her father's last chance to die in his own bed on the land where he had come into the world. She pulled the soiled envelope from her pocket and handed it to her mother.

"Aunt Dorothy gave me this letter today. Never had time to read it."

"Oh my." The woman's slender fingers trembled as she held the news from her husband. "I know your father will be home soon. I just know it."

Though Glory ached to tell her mother that it was hopeless, that Jack Day would die far away from them in a hateful, forbidding place, she held her tongue. She couldn't bear to snip the one thread of hope that kept the woman from slipping forever into her own world. Ruth had always hated Texas. Said the hot sun drained a person's soul.

Not that Mama hadn't hit upon a vein of truth. The unrelenting heat had surely withered her hopes, dreams, and lost innocence, turning them to parched, dry dust.

Patience and Hope sensed their mother's fragile state, for they both put a protective arm around her shoulders.

"Read it to us, Mama. Tell us the news from Papa." Hope laid her cheek softly against her mother's.

"Dear Mrs. Day, I regret to inform you that your husband has taken a turn for the worst. He asks for you every waking moment. Is there any way you can see your way clear to coming? Time is short and swiftly fading. Your humble servant, John Fletcher, MD." The letter dropped from lifeless hands while a quiet sob broke from Ruth's lips.

"It'll be all right, Mama. That doctor's wrong. Papa's gonna be well soon. You'll see." Tears filled Patience's blue eyes. "Glory can fix it. Can't you, Glory?"

Glory kicked a rock and sent it skittering. "Glory can do this, Glory can do that," she mimicked. "When are they going to see I can't solve all our problems?"

Cursing the sickening whirl in her stomach, she shook her head impatiently. "I have needs too."

The underbrush rustled to her right, bringing her attention back to the task at hand—supper. Could be an animal. Or it could be Mad Dog Perkins. She gripped the rifle tighter. Thank goodness she'd pumped a cartridge into the chamber right from the start, because she dared not risk making noise. The importance of stealth lent quietness to her feet.

Before she crept a couple of yards, a wild turkey took flight, landing on the low branch of a post oak tree. The succulent meat would sit mighty nice on their table. She held her breath and took aim, the bird clearly in her sights.

Then a second away from squeezing the trigger, her vision blurred. Now two turkeys sat on the branch and she couldn't distinguish the real from the illusion. She took her best guess and shot. The frightened bird skimmed just above the ground and over a small rise out of view.

Her heart sank. Two months earlier, she'd had no trouble with accuracy. Today, she couldn't hit the broad side of a barn.

The thought niggled her brain as she hurried after their escaping supper. Two months back seemed about the time a cougar had scared Caesar, causing the mule to kick Glory's head. Gave her a powerful headache, though she recovered after a day in bed.

"I wonder if that had something to do with…no, it couldn't. Not possible," she muttered to herself. Whatever the reason, she wished to high heaven it'd go away. Her shoulders weren't broad enough to deal with any more complications.

About an hour later, approaching darkness forced her to trudge home empty-handed. The turkey that had teased her taste buds had vanished. Two hawks, a porcupine, and a puny prairie dog were all she'd seen.

The fact that they had another mouth to feed further weighed on her heart as she pushed through the kitchen door.

Patience chattered like a magpie from the alcove where they'd taken McClain. Hope glanced up from her task of making biscuits. It brought an uncomfortable lurch to her chest. They could blame her for a bare table.

"Did you…?" The light from Hope's face left as she quickly read Glory's dejected posture.

"Nope. Nothing. Guess it'll be whatever we can scrounge from the garden or root cellar." She hung her serviceable hat on a peg beside the door. "Lord knows there's pitiful left. This heat's burned up everything. Including our will. Mama's right. Maybe there's no use."

"Don't say that, Glory." Hope wiped the flour on her apron and gave her sister a hug. "We'll manage. We've had hard times before and lived through them."

Glory envied her sister's eternal optimism. Their parents couldn't have bestowed a more appropriate name on her. Unlike her own. Glorious? Far from it. The Greek name Hydra would fit better. The name of a dragon killed by Hercules.

"Besides, what choice do we have?" Hope added softly.

"None, I suppose." She took a ragged breath. It'd been a long, disappointing day all around.

"Rest for a bit. Sit down and I'll see what I can find."

Too tired to resist, she let Hope push her into a chair. "Mama still lying down?"

"No, in fact, Aunt Dorothy stopped by. The two of them are in the bedroom talking."

"Wonder what about."

Hope disappeared out the door without answering. Whatever it was, Glory prayed it brought Mama out of her doldrums. Busy sorting through the list of possibilities, she overheard Patience from the next room.

"My sister didn't mean to shoot you, Mr. McClain. She's truly a nice person. Even when she yells at me sometimes, I still love 'er."

"I'm sure you do," Luke said.

"Doesn't it hurt something awful to get shot?"

"All in a day's work when you're a lawman, little 'un."

A lawman, huh? He'd not so much as breathed a word of this to Glory and he'd had ample opportunity. She smelled a rat.

"My name's Patience. How many times have you been shot?"

"Reckon if you count arrows and bullets both, might near ten or twenty times."

Glory shamelessly listened. You could learn a lot about a man not so much by what he said, but how he said it. Not that she cared a piddly poo about unearthing personal details. Other than making sure he wasn't the sort to kill them all in their beds, that is.

The braggart truly didn't suffer from shyness. His exaggeration—and she had no doubt that described McClain—was a feeble attempt to glorify himself in a little girl's eyes.

Well, that sure fit what she knew of him so far. Plus, his drawling slang spoke of rustic living. Most likely, he didn't even know his letters or how to cipher.

"Where'd your sister go?" he asked.

"Which one?"

"The crack shot. Miss Glory."

Her heart seemed to stop when he spoke her name. Evidently, neither had heard her come in. She should put a stop to his meddling. Still, she wanted to eavesdrop a little while longer.

"She went to find us some supper. Glory takes care of us since our papa got put in prison. She can shoot real good."

"I've gotten a taste of her shootin' skills." McClain's tone rivaled the dry Texas wind.

The nerve of him! She hadn't shot him on purpose.

"My sister can kill anything if she wants. That's why you're not dead, mister."

Hurrah for Patience. Glory almost wished she had put the braggart out of his misery. Or else have shot a different part of his anatomy. Now there was a tempting thought. An inch or two higher would've changed his deep baritone to a soprano.

"Appears I owe you an apology, Miss Patience. Didn't mean to hit a tender spot." Did her ears deceive her? McClain almost sounded sincere. "Why's your pa in prison? That is, if you don't mind my asking."

"Wasn't his fault. Glory calls it a case of ignorance on account a ol' lady Penelope being blind as a bat. She says that old sow cain't find her backside with both hands."

Glory leaped to her feet, shocked at her baby sister's language. It never entered her mind that Patience would repeat her rantings. Didn't matter that hurt and disappointment had driven those words from her mouth. The damage had been done. She had to stop this conversation and silence Patience.

The house filled with McClain's laughter. A step from the alcove, she paused when her mother appeared with Aunt Dorothy. Ruth's chalky face set off alarms.

"Dorothy's brought some news from town."

"What is it now, Mama?"

Ruth Day pursed her mouth, trying to form the words. Finally, she said, "Mr. Fieldings at the bank might call in some of the notes he holds."

"Aunt Dorothy?" Glory swung, fixing her aunt with a stare.

"I'm sure it's just a baseless rumor, dear. Might not be a smidgen thing to it."

"You must have thought different, to come all the way out. Did you hear how soon or which property?" Hell's bells! Maybe she'd been the one to take a load of buckshot the way she hurt inside. Despair riddled her thoughts. Losing the land—their home—would be the final straw.

"Are you behind on the payments?" Dorothy was asking Ruth as if her mother had an inkling of their financial state.

"I don't know." A blank look swept over Ruth. "Glory?"

"We're a little past due, but I was hoping to catch up come next week." She sank into a chair at the table.

"Well, perhaps it's merely harmless speculation. You know how folks get in a tizzy over the smallest whispers. And even if it turns out to be true, I'm sure he wouldn't take this farm." Dorothy gave them a helpless smile. "Oh, dear me, look at the time! I must get home before dark."

"Yes, Jack will be home soon too. He always comes riding in after dusk." Ruth's childlike statement startled both Glory and her aunt.

"No, Mama. Papa won't be coming home. Not now, not ever." She refused to let her mother think anything but the unvarnished truth. But the facts wouldn't keep insanity at bay. Ruth appeared to be slipping further from them.

"Yes, he is! I don't know why you want to hurt me."

Aunt Dorothy caught her eye and shook her head in warning. Pain and remorse played hopscotch up Glory's spine.

"I'm sorry, Mama. Why don't you go lie back down so you'll be fresh as a daisy when he gets here?"

"I'll put Ruth to bed," Aunt Dorothy told her. "Then

I'll let myself out. If you need me...if your mother gets worse, send Hope for me."

"Thank you. I will." At least she had her aunt and uncle to depend on. They weren't entirely alone.

Through a haze, she watched Aunt Dorothy steer her mother toward the bedroom.

What else was going to happen? She couldn't help her father, couldn't put food on the table, and couldn't save the farm if there was no money to pay the banknote. What else? Oh, yes, she couldn't half see and her mother was losing her mind. Heaven forbid if her plate overflowed!

In the quiet stillness, Patience continued to chatter up a storm to their wounded guest.

"Papa's not well. The doctor don't give him much time. That's why Glory tried to capture that mean ol' outlaw."

"You don't say."

"And, she could've, too, if you hadn't stopped her. With the reward money, we could get Papa outta prison and he could come home, and then Glory wouldn't have to be the man o' the house."

This time nothing would deter Glory. Patience seemed intent on airing their family laundry as well as her lungs. Four purposeful strides took Glory to the door of the small bedroom.

"I like you," Patience said. "For a stranger, you're awfully nice. Would you marry my sister, Mr. McClain?"

Four

"PATIENCE ANN DAY! DON'T YOU HAVE ANY SHAME?"
Glory's face flamed with pure mortification.

"I was only—"

"Letting your mouth gallop at full speed," she finished
for her. "Put a bridle on it. Mr. McClain doesn't need
pestering."

The fact that the man tried to hide a broad smile behind
his hand did little to dampen the heat rising from her toenails.

"I'd be obliged if you'd call me Luke."

There went that killer grin. The one that turned her
knees watery. Darn her fickle limbs for betraying her.
Ignorant of his letters or not, McClain had ample expertise
in the lady-charming department. That scared her.

Her tongue worked inside a suddenly dry mouth.
"Entirely out of the question."

"I insist. No more of this 'mister' business."

The man took extraordinary delight in watching her
squirm.

"Are you afraid of saying my name…or more of getting
to the altar?" A merry glint twinkled.

Patience piped up, saving her from a reply. "Glory's real
nice if you don't get on her bad side. An' she hardly ever
yells, 'cept if you make her mad."

Oh Lord, she felt ill.

"Get your little fanny out! Now." The idea of socking her definitely had merit. No telling what else the pip-squeak would yammer next. "I think I hear Hope calling."

"No, she's not. You just say that when you don't want me around."

Though not always biddable, Patience had never shown outright defiance. Why today of all times?

"Just because you've never had a beau don't mean you can't wed if a man asks you." Chatterbox blurted Glory's worst shame.

A few months shy of her twentieth birthday and not one boy had ever come courting. Nor had anyone so much as stolen a kiss, not even in her kid days when a group of them played hide-and-seek on a moonless night. He must think her terribly flawed to have never captured a man's roving eye. For God's sake, Gwennie Gabriel managed to snag a husband and she was certainly no prize. Glory wasn't even snaggletoothed or knock-kneed. If she wasn't quite so busy, she could get one, she told herself.

"Our...my state of affairs doesn't concern him. Now, I want you to march, young lady. Help with supper."

"On the contrary, Miss Day," Luke broke in. "I find your sisterly fuss refreshing. An entertainment I've missed. I haven't seen my family in a coon's age and this is mild compared to us. When we get together, we're a downright rowdy bunch."

Glory failed to see the humor. She pointed sternly to the open doorway. "Scoot."

"You're not the boss o' me. You're not my mother!"

The gibe hurt all the way down to the quick. Little did Patience know. With their mother becoming more distant, Glory could be the closest the girl had to one.

A creak of the screen door announced Hope's return. "Patience, come and get these cats. They're in my way."

"All right. I will." The younger sibling made a face that said she was going only because Hope asked and for no other reason.

"I apologize for my sister, Mr. McClain. Patience isn't always like this. Things aren't easy for her."

"Luke. You agreed to call me Luke. And you don't owe me any amends." He rose to lean against the iron bedstead.

Silver buttons shone against the dark-blue background of his shirt, stars shining in a midnight sky. His coffee-colored hair went in all directions, as if he'd run his fingers through it a hundred times. She sucked in her breath sharply. Each strand stood on end, lending a wicked charm to his devil-may-care features.

"I agreed to no such thing. Just wouldn't be proper." She turned on her heel.

"And you never do anything that's not." His soft, seductive tone toyed with her senses, brushing against her face and neck, stopping her in her tracks. "Explains why you've never had a gentleman caller."

He'd poured salt in the wound. Leave it to a stranger to home in on the obvious.

"Patience was wrong. I've had my share. Simply had no interest in pursuing them. I have far better ways to fill my evenings."

"If you say so. Luke McClain never disputes a lady's word."

Time had come to bury this particular topic. "What's this about being a lawman? You never uttered a word to me."

"You're mistaken."

"Patience only dreamed that up?"

The man shrugged. "Like you said, she's prone to stretching the truth a bit."

Appeared he shared that with her sister. She recognized sealed lips when she saw them though. Best to let him think he'd won. She'd keep her ears open for further slips. She suspected he was more likely an outlaw than a lawman. "If you don't feel up to coming to the table, I'll have Hope bring you a plate. Other than that, I don't think we have anything else to discuss."

Just what did that little grin mean?

"I think I can hobble that far. Holler when you're ready."

Lord knew that'd be years from now, centuries even, before she'd be up to facing him after Patience's embarrassing revelations. Not daring a glance his way, she merely nodded.

"Wait. Please?" A slight quaver in the plea halted her escape. She paused in the doorway. "I'm sorry for messing up your plans. Didn't know how important that reward money was to you. If I'd only…"

The sincerity took her aback. One minute the man joked and ridiculed and the next he spilled true feelings all over the place. A mixture of hot and cold.

"Don't worry about it. We'll survive. We always do."

Luke pondered her parting statement. Tough lady, that Glory Day.

From what he'd seen and heard of their situation, much of which he owed to Miss Chatterbox, they were in dire straits.

Clearly, Glory stood at the head of the family as provider. That explained her manner of dress. Not that he had anything against the men's britches. Quite the contrary. They revealed fascinating curves and a waist so narrow he could probably get his hands easily around it.

Now there was a delicious thought. If he dared be so bold, beyond a shadow of a doubt, she'd break his fingers in half without so much as a fare-thee-well.

A worn, faded dress hanging from a nail on the wall pounded home their dour circumstances. Somehow, he knew it belonged to Glory and he also suspected it was the only dress she possessed. Strangely, the wish to see her clothed in it became an intolerable desire. Her rich, blond hair cascading down her back, loose and flowing, would be well worth broken things—fingers or dreams.

Chatterbox's question about marrying her sister skittered across his mind, coaxing a wide grin. A tempting proposition.

If he was in the market for a wife, that is.

Which he wasn't, he quickly added.

The beauteous Jessie Foltry had smitten his heart. He couldn't imagine feeling about anyone like he did her. Too bad his older brother had made her his wife instead and she happily rode herd on a mess of little ones.

Still, a lady with stonewashed blue eyes shouldn't have to do a man's work. When he got up and around, he'd make himself useful before he took off again after Mad Dog Perkins. Kill some game to last a while, make some repairs to the place.

And it was a pure sin to Moses for a girl to never know the thrill of a first kiss or the advantages of a little caressing. Those fine, capable hands could soothe the wildness out of a whole pack of coyotes. No lye soap he knew could wash off the remembrance of her accidental touch where it came in contact with his thigh.

He listened to the three sisters in the next room, easily distinguishing Glory's disarming, refined voice from Patience's pouty tone and Hope's calm, easy way.

"You're a jewel, Hope. I don't know how you can make a meal from so little," he heard Glory say. "I think we can fill our stomachs quite well, despite me coming home empty-handed."

Guilt had a way of kicking a man in the gut. She had evidently spent the day locating Perkins, and partly thanks to him, lost the man. Then she'd toted his carcass home with her and saved his leg from amputation. He shuddered as he remembered her wielding the scissors. A woman with blood in her eye could do nigh most anything. He'd been briefly worried about her amputating another part of him altogether. Almost involuntarily, he lifted the sheet to make double sure he was still in one piece.

Relieved, he returned to his conscience. He'd kept her too busy to hunt meat for the table.

They had barely enough food for the four of them, yet stretched what they had to include him. Yep, that was true charity. He mentally kicked himself again.

"I found a few squash and collard greens that hadn't shriveled to nothing in the garden. Those with the dwindling stock of sweet potatoes in the root cellar will go fine with hot biscuits. I even fished around in the pork barrel and came up with a nice hunk of sowbelly to season the greens with."

Luke salivated at the mention of hot biscuits. Hadn't had a decent one since those Jessie made. Collards weren't his favorite, but he'd try to pretend—for the ladies' sake.

If you don't feel up to coming to the table, I'll have Hope bring you a plate. He'd seen more than a glimmer of expectation in Glory's gaze when she uttered those words.

Small chance. No one was going to bottle-feed him—despite the fact that Glory obviously preferred he stay in bed.

That was when he spied the sewing basket beside the short bed from which his feet dangled. The blue-eyed vixen had slit the right leg of his britches from stem to stern. Necessary, she'd said. Likely story. She'd seemed to derive just a tad too much satisfaction from the act. But, he'd better get busy sewing.

Hobbling into their midst half-naked would surely have Mrs. Day in a fine state. Might throw her into one of her conniptions Glory spoke about. He allowed a few things he lacked education in, but when it came to temper fits, he knew both the ins and outs.

He slid out of what remained of the trousers, and hastily threw the sheet over his bare legs before someone passed by the open door. Then he lifted the sewing basket.

Fixing the pants shouldn't pose much problem. After all, he'd sewn up a rent in the seat of his long johns once. Of course, he refused to dwell on how many times he stuck himself with the needle. Or how it looked when he got done. Didn't really matter that it more resembled a cat's cradle or a crazy spiderweb. Wasn't anyone going to see it but him. No sirree. He could sew with the best of 'em.

Black thread already stuck through the needle's eye. Good enough. He reckoned any color would work. Laying the two cut pieces together, he started at the ankle. The first rattle out of the box, he punctured his thumb.

Criminy! After sucking the blood off, he bent again to the task.

At twelve, he lost count of the sticks. How did women-folk manage to get anything accomplished with an imple-ment as sharp as a cactus needle? Pure torture.

Not only that, but he had more blood on his pants from the sticks than he did from the load of buckshot.

"Ouch!" This time he couldn't keep silent. It hurt like hell. With speed that made him suspicious, Glory appeared in the doorway.

"What's wrong? Is your leg hurting?"

"Not my leg." Luke held up the needle and thread, bloody fingers and all.

"Whatever are you trying to do?"

"Fix my blasted pants so I can be decent for female company."

Chuckles tumbled from her curved-up mouth. The sight almost made him forget his hunch that she'd been listening from the next room.

"Not a darn bit funny."

"I'm sorry. I can't help it."

The girl looked young, carefree, and utterly breathtaking when she abandoned the frowns. He decided holes in his fingers were worth seeing this lighthearted side.

"Go ahead. Laugh at a foolish, almost-naked man. Reckon I'll have to take my supper in here after all."

"Wait. I'll be back." In a flash, she grabbed his trousers and disappeared, leaving him wondering what on earth she was up to.

As if he'd go anywhere bare-legged. Unease gripped him. He had made her mad as hell. Enough for revenge?

He stood, yanked the sheet off, and tucked it around him. He was about to give chase when the sound of her boots struck the wooden floor. He admired the easy sway of her hips as she moved toward him.

"Here. Put these on." She handed him a pair of home-spun woolen britches. "My papa's," she explained.

Only after he assured himself she didn't lurk outside the door for a peek, he pulled them on, careful of his wounded leg. The girth of the pants swallowed him, but he was a man with few options. He peered at his achy hands. Might not be able to hold a knife and fork, but at least he could join the ladies around the table.

◦◦◦

Supper was quite an affair. Patience chattered nonstop, asking questions and keeping them thoroughly entertained.

Mrs. Day didn't appear as harried as Luke recalled her from earlier. Still quite lovely with her peach coloring and pale-blue gaze, the woman must have been a beautiful belle in her younger years. Only the few strands of gray streaking her hair and the wrinkles lining her mouth told the secret of her age.

When he compared the four faces staring over the sweet potatoes and collard greens, he marveled at the resemblance. In all of Coleman County there weren't any prettier ladies. He'd heard it rumored that the Misses Alice and Jennie Caperton claimed the titles of most lovely in the county. Yet, he begged to differ. Perhaps others might attribute their allure to a shortage of the opposite sex since they were the only two ladies in the town of Coleman City. Surely, they couldn't hold a candle to this household.

"My Patience tells me you're a lawman."

Damn! The lie.

Under Mrs. Day's matronly stare, he had a devil of a time swallowing. The woolen pants gouged like hundreds of sharp prickly pears in places he'd rather not think about. Squirming certainly didn't help. Of all things for the woman to bring up. He had no desire to discuss that topic. Most of all why he was no longer with the Texas Rangers.

A swig of fresh milk helped Luke down the big bite he'd just taken.

"A simple misunderstanding, ma'am." The falsehood clogged his throat worse than week-old corn bread. He quickly gulped the rest of the milk.

"My compliments, Miss Hope, on these biscuits," he said, hoping to change the subject. "Can't tell you how long it's been since my mouth's had such pleasure."

A pink blush rose to tint Hope's cheeks. The girl would make someone a happy man if her biscuits gave any indication.

"So, you was after Mad Dog Perkins too, Mr. Luke?"

"He's Mr. McClain, Patience, dear." Ruth Day dabbed delicately at the corners of her mouth. "We must have our manners if we have little else. And, it's 'were,' not 'was.'"

"It's quite all right, ma'am. My fault."

"If you insist." The woman's tightly drawn lips voiced clear disapproval. "Though I object to overfamiliarity toward strangers." She halved her biscuit and buttered both sides slowly. "I've tried to teach my girls proper decorum."

No doubt. Still, no mother would have her oldest daughter carrying such a load. Couldn't she see the years it tacked on to Glory's life? Not that he didn't admire the golden-haired beauty for accepting the responsibility. Her spunk amazed him. Going after Mad Dog Perkins took a sight more than courage.

"And a wonderful job you've done, ma'am."

The woman glowed under his compliment. From where he sat, the fragile woman was incapable of managing their daily affairs. She should thank her lucky stars for her three strong daughters.

Patience rested her arm on the table and shot him a grin. "Have you ever killed anyone, Mr. Luke? I mean when you were tryin' to capture them, that is."

He'd never considered wool breaking a man out in a sweat like this. Silence would've been a blessing.

The smattering of freckles that marched across the smaller girl's nose and cheeks reminded him of his nephew, George. But the endless questions exactly matched Luke's sister, Victoria.

"A time or two, Punkin." Luke didn't know why the word slipped out. Except it fit. He cast a sidelong glance for her mother's disapproval. None came, so he reckoned she'd not toss him out on his ear just yet. Maybe she allowed for all the blood on him.

"Where are you from, Mr. McClain? Do you have any family?"

This time, the quiet, angelic Hope entered the conversation. He wondered what thoughts went through Glory's mind. She'd not said four or five words thus far.

"My folks hail from Tranquillity, down on the Colorado. You might've heard tell of it?" He lobbed the inquiry toward Glory. Yet, he shouldn't have bothered. She focused solely on the meager bit of food on her plate, oblivious of the conversation. He wondered if she mulled over her afternoon's failures. Or what she'd overheard.

He cursed himself for the slight fib he'd told Patience about being a lawman.

"I've heard it mentioned," Mrs. Day said, wiping her mouth daintily again. A faraway stare appeared in her eyes. "My Jack is in Austin. He's on a business trip, you know."

Luke caught Glory's quick, darting glance that showed she feared what her mother would say. He wanted to tell her he already knew about her father's imprisonment. Despite apologizing for getting in the way and spoiling her plans, he wished he could do something, anything, to make it up.

"Do you think they worry about you, McClain? If it's been a while without word…what with your dangerous profession and all." Glory's studied gaze bored a hole into his soul. He wondered what she saw there to cause her eyebrows to knit.

"Profession? Just what would that be, Miss Glory? I'm no lawman."

"I know what I heard." Glory met his gaze. "You're still denying it?"

"Yes." Double damn! If only he'd held his tongue.

"Would you like to tell us what you are and why you would chase a wanted criminal? Are you a bounty hunter then?"

"I'm just a plain. ordinary man who wanted Perkins for the same reason you did."

"Fair enough." She lowered her stare at last. "Then I suppose your family, should you truly have one, misses you."

"Reckon they do for a fact. It's been way too long since I laid eyes on them." He had heard about the Spanish Inquisition but had never been subjected to one. Before now.

"Not that it matters. I only asked in case there was anyone we might need to notify—should you meet with an untimely end." Glory's quiet tone tickled the hairs on the back of his neck. "A wife or children perhaps?"

He'd had no inkling what pond the girl had dropped her hook in. Now it dawned. The fishing expedition brought a twinge of joy. Though why, he couldn't quite say. His heart didn't have room for two women, and Jessie currently occupied it.

"Just a father, brother, and sister is the sum of it." And Jessie and a little girl named Marley Rose. But Glory didn't have to know about them.

She stopped the beginning of a smile. But not before he saw the flash of relief. The wrinkle in her forehead smoothed.

Glory turned her attention to the others. "Mama, would you like another spoonful of squash? It's your favorite. Hope made it especially for you."

"I don't think so, dear." For the first time that night, he saw a sparkle in the matron's eyes. "I'm saving room for some of that hot molasses gingerbread."

All of a sudden, a solution hit him. He'd track Perkins to the end of the earth if necessary. And after he beat the information he needed out of his mangy hide, he'd hand the reward over to Glory. That'd go a long way to making amends. He only prayed it didn't take too long. Punkin spilling the beans about their father's health made haste crucial.

A teasing smile graced Hope's face as she rose. "How

did you know I made gingerbread, Mama? I wanted to surprise you."

"My darling girl, no fooling your mother. The smell is unmistakable. I can eat my weight of that cake."

So could he, Luke decided. He hurried to finish his second helping of everything, even the collards he wasn't fond of, so he could partake with the rest. He'd just finished shoveling in the last bite when Hope delivered the warm cake to the table.

The remainder of the meal passed without further sweating. Then, each girl carried her plate to the wash bucket. Patience eagerly added his to her stack. The worship in her eyes made him fidget.

"I'd be obliged if you'd join my daughters and me in the parlor."

Mother Day's request appeared to put the invitation more in the ordering category. Should he have such an inclination, which he didn't, he couldn't refuse. Being a guest and all.

Spending too much time alone made a man crave stimulation. He grinned. This promised to go above and beyond that.

Despite the throbbing pain that persisted in his leg, he moved as fast as he could to help Mrs. Day out of her chair. Quite a feat considering he dared not release his grip on the pants, for they'd surely fall around his ankles.

"Please," Patience begged with puppy dog eyes.

"Shush, dear, it may be too much for him. Losing blood weakens a man. We don't want him overdoing it."

He tried to read Glory's mind, whether she voted yea or nay. And though her brief glance made the homespuns itch twice as bad, her thoughts on the matter remained shrouded in mystery. Mischievous fancies he couldn't deny took root.

"Glory reads to us from Louisa May Alcott's *Little Women* when Mama has one of her headaches." Patience grinned. "It's the best time of the whole day. Do you like that book?"

The oldest Day sister looked ready to throttle Patience.

"Punkin, I've never been one for reading. Occasion for it don't come often." He looped an arm around the girl's shoulders and turned to the lady of the house. "Thank you, ma'am. Wouldn't mind staying up for a spell. Haven't had the company of so many charming ladies at once that I can remember."

Patience took his hand and led him to the biggest chair in the parlor. "This is my papa's. I don't think he'd mind you keeping it warm."

"It'll be our secret." Ah, he could finally turn loose of the pants as he settled into the haven. His wounded leg burned with the heat of a smithy's forge. Some choice cuss words crossed his mind while he endeavored to find a comfortable spot.

Then he watched what he suspected formed a nightly ritual. Mother Day took the seat opposite him while Glory lifted a book from the mantel over the hearth. Patience dropped cross-legged to the floor at her mother's knee and Hope slipped into a high-backed rocker.

"Mama, I'm too tired. Would you mind reading tonight?" At her mother's nod, Glory put the open book into her hands before she took the other vacant chair.

"Let's see, where were we? Do you remember, Patience?"

"Jo had just sold her hair to get money for Marmee to travel to see their sick papa."

"Oh yes." Mother Day began to read with lyrical refinement.

Luke closed his lids for a moment to soak up the sounds and images that sprang to life from the pages of the book. Strange that the story bore such similarity to the current household.

When he opened his eyes, Glory had lifted an article of clothing to her lap and begun to sew. His trousers! She was repairing the ruined pants in front of the whole clan.

Heat spread and not from the woolens. But soon a pleasant tranquility replaced his discomfort. The intimate sight brought a glow inside. One that rivaled the brightness of a lighthouse on the darkest, most stormy night. He rested his head against the high back. A king couldn't have found better lodging.

She caught him staring. For a split second, he spied honest desire in her features. Then it left. Must have been simply a mirage in the flickering light of the oil lamp.

She had let him know in no uncertain terms what he could do with such speculation.

Still...when did he back down from a challenge?

Five

GLORY WOKE THE NEXT MORNING TO A CHORUS OF BRAYS, moos, and rooster crowing. It took a full moment to remember why she slept in the barn loft. She rubbed her eyes and sat up. A book fell off her stomach to the hay.

Her journal was the one luxury she allowed herself. Jotting her innermost thoughts on paper gave her a sense of companionship, of having help in her struggles.

She barely recalled having written in it before she dozed off.

Curious about her last entry, she opened the page. *Hell's bells!* She'd written *Mrs. Luke McClain* several times in flowing penmanship. Something for lovesick schoolgirls, not old maids.

She slammed the book shut before the crowing rooster above her head saw it and blabbed her foolish scribbling to the world. Her face burned and it wasn't from the newly risen sun. If anyone—most of all Luke—were to see what she'd written, she'd die. She'd just dig a hole and bury herself.

She slid the book beneath the hay, hiding it from prying eyes.

"Cock-a-doodle-doo right back, you silly."

The bird flapped his wings and flew down to roost on the pitchfork handle near Bessie. He opened his beak and set up an awful racket as if telling the milk cow what he'd seen.

"Shush, you big mouth. I've a good mind to pluck and boil you for supper."

She pulled on the britches and tucked in her shirt, releasing a sigh. Only four more days until she could wear her dress.

On Sundays, she could be a lady.

But this was Wednesday, and though the day had just dawned, she already ran two hours behind.

While she tugged on the mule-eared boots, a heaviness landed square in the middle of her chest. Money—or rather the lack of it. Mr. Fieldings could surely take their land. Then she also had other considerations—her father's dilemma. If she poured all her efforts into getting money for her mother to be with him, they'd lose their home. Besides, in her present state, her mother couldn't withstand the rigors of travel. Glory knew she had to choose between the two.

Jo March sold her hair so her mother could go to her father's side. An excellent idea, except no one in Santa Anna, not even in the whole county, had a use for shorn hair. Nope, she'd have to think harder.

Her sisters stumbled half-asleep through the barn door.

"Good morning." Hope yawned, lifting the milk bucket from a nail.

Glory climbed down the ladder to the barn floor. "What's the matter, Squirt? Jabber too much yesterday?"

"Don' know what's good about it. When I get big, I'm not gonna raise any chickens." Patience snatched the egg-gathering basket. "An' I'm gonna sleep till noon."

"Don't worry. When you get grown, you'll have to do the same chores, like it or not. That's life." Hope put the bucket beneath Bessie and plopped onto the milking stool.

Glory suddenly decided she'd grown rather fond of eating. And keeping a roof over their heads took equal priority. Somehow, someway, she'd come up with two dollars by Saturday. Her mind eased with the choice made.

Papa, forgive me.

"I'm gonna have me a husband. One of those rich ones."
The little imp flounced over to the row of nests. "And I ain't
gonna live on no stinking farm either. I'll be a city woman
with pretty clothes. I'm gonna go to Paris like Amy March!"

That darn book had filled her with this nonsense.

"You'd best get those fancy ideas out of your head,
Squirt. Sometimes you can't help what you're stuck with."
Glory scooped up some oats. She merely prayed for a
break occasionally.

Luke's horse nudged her hand, almost knocking the
bucket to the floor when she reached over the stall. Lucky
for him, she had a firm grip or he'd be rooting on the
ground with the chickens for his breakfast. The pushy horse
appeared to have taken lessons from his master.

Their short feed supply called for scrimping. She'd considered putting the animals out to pasture. Except the sea of
dead grass changed her mind. And her soft heart wouldn't
allow it. They hadn't caused their circumstances.

Earsplitting squawks drew her attention back to the row
of hen nests. A brown leghorn took offense to being lifted
off her nest and flew into Squirt's face. Glory smiled when
the girl skittered back in alarm.

Her smile vanished, however, when Patience dropped
the egg she'd just plucked from the nest.

It spattered on the dirt floor with a squishy plop. Kind of
soft—the sound a breaking heart makes.

"Patience! Please be more careful. We need every one of
those." Mentally, she subtracted the egg from the dozen or
so she'd hoped to sell Aunt Dorothy.

"Don't know what difference one old egg makes."

"You will when you want me to bake another cake,"
Hope said.

That settled the girl down and she continued her chores.
Glory marveled at Hope's ability to calm ruffled feathers. She
lacked sorely in that area and came within a hairbreadth of
telling them both exactly what the loss of one egg could mean.

"At least I'm not gonna be some old maid like you,

Glory." The girl's one last parting shot stung. It hurt because she spoke the truth.

"Mornin', ladies."

The deep male voice startled Glory and she jerked, almost dropping the precious bucket of oats for Caesar.

Luke stood a yard or so inside the barn. Not close enough to account for this strange sense of suffocating.

He had a large presence about him. One she'd first noticed in the emporium yesterday.

She'd often heard Mama speak of how Jack filled every nook and cranny when he entered a room. Though she didn't think it applied to girth or height, she'd never known what Ruth meant before now.

Damn that accursed grin!

How could her heart beat so fast and stay lodged inside?

The man rested his weight on the gnarled walking stick they kept inside the kitchen door, her grandfather's from days gone by. The heavy way Luke leaned spoke of the deep pain he endured. A pure miracle he'd managed to walk from the house.

"Good morning, Mr. Luke." The pendulum of Patience's sour mood immediately swung the opposite direction.

A taunting gleam in the man's gaze disturbed her.

Glory wondered how long he'd been standing there... and what he'd overheard. She'd like to stuff a sock in Squirt's mouth. Preferably one with a week's worth of wearing.

"Figured I'd lend a hand with the chores. I'm used to rising at the crack of dawn. These ol' bones couldn't take a minute more of that bed. No sirree."

"Me too. I like to get up early." Patience skipped gaily down the length of the barn as if she did so each morning. She deserved the glaring darts Glory threw her way. And more.

Hope rolled her eyes and chortled softly without missing a stroke in her milking rhythm.

The humor escaped Glory. Then of course, the little chatterbox's statement didn't embarrass anyone else. Asking

Luke to marry Glory and calling her an old maid—what would come out of the Patience's mouth next? She shuddered to think, remembering her journal.

"Did you sleep at all, Miss Glory? I surely didn't feel right taking your bed."

"Nothing wrong with sleeping on hay." She grabbed the pitchfork and lifted a mound of the stuff. Anything to keep her eyes from straying to the mended denims that clung as sleek as cat's fur. "I do it every now and then to remind me where I came from, and where but for the pure grace of God I'd be."

Also where she—all of them—might be again should foreclosure occur.

Cleaning stalls was dirty and hot, but she wasn't about to hint that it bothered her. She could pull her share.

"Just the same, tonight we're switching." Luke hobbled along after her, holding on to the stick. "Anything a cripple can help you with? There must be something I can do."

Nothing except get himself back to the house and out of sight. How was she supposed to do her work with him shoving his devilish grin and his lean form in her face at every turn?

"Sorry I've added extra work for you on top of everything else you have to do."

Luke McClain made too many sinful thoughts swim through her head. She wondered if she was the only one who had trouble breathing. Recalling her own name seemed difficult enough when he was around. The morning had sure turned hot. Not a breath of air to be had.

"Staying busy keeps me from thinking about Perkins. And about how dearly I'd love to give you a piece of my mind." She swung to confront him. "We needed that five hundred dollars."

Her words slapped him.

Damn!

Luke cringed. Not that he didn't deserve it. He was no saint by a long shot.

But neither did he need reminding of the grief he'd caused. His conscience made sure he didn't forget.

For the thousandth time, he wished he could go back and undo it. He touched her arm, wishing to apologize. When they connected, a current crackled and he thought he'd grabbed the tail end of a lightning bolt.

"I'm going to make it up to you, I swear on my mother's grave. Put that in your pipe and smoke it."

❧

Idleness was a poor bedfellow. A couple of days later, Luke figured he'd recovered enough to make a few much-needed repairs on the farm. He felt obliged for the disruption he'd caused. Besides, if he didn't put his hands to work, he'd go stir-crazy.

Glory had ridden off on the white mule. Hope had Patience helping her with the laundry.

And Mrs. Day had taken to her bed with a headache. It seemed the woman's sole enjoyment in life was reading aloud after supper...except for last evening. Strange for the woman to not once poke her head out. Hope took a tray in and came out with a chalky face. Glory had read aloud instead. Sounded real nice in her smooth-as-thick-cream voice. She seemed to have some trouble seeing the words though. He'd made the mistake of asking about that.

"Nothing wrong with my eyes, McClain. Concentration is the problem. Keep losing my place is all." Then she firmly shut the book, her glare ending further discussion of the matter.

The answer merely aggravated his concern. He'd noticed other times when he could have sworn she had problems seeing, and the panic that had crossed her features.

Nope, Glory hid a secret beneath her stubborn pride. She had trouble. Something a pair of spectacles would help?

If only he could hang around a bit longer. The lady would deny it to her dying breath, but she needed him. Maybe after he finished with Perkins...

Evenings had become his favorite hours of the day. Glory could be the spittin' image of Jo March. Fact of the matter, he seemed to have landed smack dab in the middle of a real-life storybook.

Shoot! What was he thinkin'? Next thing he'd be spouting off a bunch of poetry or some such nonsense. Must be getting soft. He grinned. No, he took that back. Glory Day was the soft one—outwardly. He hadn't minded one bit when she'd accidentally bumped against him with those hips that drove a man wild. Lush, ripe curves.

Damn, she'd be the ruination of him yet.

Oh, but what fun if he could afford to let his imagination run rampant?

The stern features of Mother Day quickly stifled those visions. Her frailty could be an act. She'd probably have him strung up before he could whistle "Dixie." Suddenly, the image of a rope dangling before his eyes made him switch horses in midstream. He turned his thoughts in a more gainful direction.

Each day put more miles between him and Perkins. Being unable to ride didn't sit well. He'd give himself two days more, then he'd go whether up to it or not.

An object in his pocket poked, jarring his memory. He pulled out the tin star that said Texas Ranger and touched the metal reverently. He fingered the dent a bullet had left, recalling the time and place.

Grief, thick and overwhelming, squeezed his chest.

It'd belonged to Max Sand, his best friend and partner. A scorching day. Horse thieves ambushed Max and him near Chandler's Peak over by Goldsboro.

His hand trembled under the weight of the memory and he almost dropped the badge. It took six bullets to put Max down. He kept standing long after an ordinary man would've fallen. Max died in his arms despite his bumbling attempt to stanch the flow of blood. The tin star brought back all of his shortcomings and his promise to Max.

He squared his jaw.

Since then, he'd learned the killer's name.

A quick glance at the sky told him time was wasting. "Mad Dog, you'd better run like hell."

Hate left a bitter taste in his mouth. Luke dropped the star into his pocket. The reasons to get back on his feet had multiplied to three.

Irritated with the delay, he vented an oath. The walking stick protested as he leaned, taking stock of the neglected surroundings.

His energy would be better put to use doing needed handiwork. He limped to the barn for a hammer.

A few well-placed tacks fixed the torn screen door. He replaced a broken porch step and did half a dozen other small tasks. Grunting with pain, he managed to crawl onto the roof, where he patched a hole above the kitchen. Then, he turned his attention to the shabby barn.

"Patience Ann, put down those kittens and help me."

Frustration filtered through Hope's usual way. He'd not once heard her voice raised. He paused outside the barn door to watch the sisters. A familiar whine drifted on the slight breeze.

"Washing clothes is no fun. When I grow up—"

"I don't want to hear that babble. If you don't get busy hanging these clothes on the line to dry, you won't live past today. We all have to do things we don't like. But that's the way it is. Grin and bear it."

"Donkey head," Patience called her older sister.

"Mule breath," Hope threw over her shoulder.

Luke laughed. Normal behavior for siblings everywhere, it appeared. Squabbles he'd had with his big brother, Duel, swirled through his head. He'd not taken Duel's well-intentioned bossiness a bit better. Must be a law against accepting correction. Patience required a firm hand. She had a mite too much sass.

The girl needed her father. They all did. Glory's fierce determination as provider would put her six feet under without relief soon. He dearly wished for different circumstances that would prolong his stay. The family had a tough row ahead of them. Still, he reasoned, catching Perkins would help more.

Watching Glory work from daylight to dusk brought a hardness to his jaw. A trip to town before breakfast to sell milk and eggs; then she hauled water from the creek in a feeble attempt to keep the pitiful garden going.

Back and forth she went, almost dropping with exhaustion.

At one point, he'd grabbed the buckets from her, only to have them snatched right back, accompanied by a tongue-lashing.

"Kinda brazen for a man with only one good leg, aren't you?"

"You just can't abide anyone lending a hand, can you?" God, what a stubborn woman. Didn't make a lick of sense.

"Go sit down. You'll start your leg bleeding."

After she and the mule completed a dozen trips, he'd had enough. Despite her cussed independence, he led Soldier from the barn and tied two barrels on the paint's side.

"What are you doing?"

"Earning my keep." He tugged on his horse's bridle.

"We don't need you. I can take care of this farm." The fire flashing from her blue eyes had caught him by surprise. "We've gotten along perfectly fine without a man this far, and we sure don't need one now. So you can put your horse back up and get out of my way."

"Two can carry twice as much. I'm helping."

He had to strain to catch her muttered reply.

"If that's the case, you can do that by healing your leg and riding out of here."

Luke had scratched his head in confusion. "Didn't know my company was so dadblasted bothersome."

"Now you do." She'd kicked a clump of dried grass with her toe. "You're a bother, McClain."

Long into the afternoon, Luke still mulled over the words. He didn't think Glory meant to sound rude. The tone of her voice didn't mesh with the words. No hardness in the accusation. Her voice had been too soft. He suspected his bothersome nature wasn't solely due to the extra work he heaped on them. Could be his presence aroused womanly desires she'd buried deep beneath that gritty exterior.

Women. Trying to reason their ways boggled a man's mind.

He turned to go inside when he caught a flash of white from the corner of his eye. The mule rose from the creek bed with Glory astride.

"Have mercy!"

What he saw stepping from the incline wasn't a woman dressed in men's clothes riding on a white mule. A fairy princess on a snow-white stallion rode toward him. She wore a silk gown laden with pearls and rubies and emeralds.

Glory brought an ache in his chest, the kind that posed more danger than what came from her Winchester.

She held him mesmerized in the spell. Every intention vanished into the mist of the daydream he shamelessly created. Through half-closed lids, he watched her lift the floppy hat. At a shake of her head, the golden corn silk strands tumbled around her shoulders in a glistening swirl. Waning sunlight danced off the thickness. He imagined mischievous fairies cavorting in the field of spun gold.

The vision stole not only his breath, but his very thoughts. Surely he hadn't made that tortured groan aloud.

Rooted to the spot, he stared as she raised her arm and slipped her fingers through the silky mass. Blood hammered in his ears. His eyes widened to better catch the faintest details of her outlined breasts taut against the fabric.

Her proud carriage spoke of self-confidence that she could do anything she set her mind to. The strong spirit enveloping her settled around his shoulders.

While he waited for her at the barn door, he listed all the reasons why he should resist the one thing he most wanted to do.

His duty.

His purpose.

His secret devotion to his brother's wife.

The stabbing pain was red-hot and searing.

"I see the hunter gods smiled on you today." A tremor ran through him as he reached to help her down.

For an instant, she seemed about to hand him his head on a platter. Then almost shyly, she accepted his grip and dismounted.

"Pure luck, McClain."

He suspected she tucked that shyness behind the gruff exterior because it was easier than dealing with other emotions. Ones that scared the living daylights out of her. And him too.

Glory untied the legs of two large gobblers and let them fall to the ground.

"Nice shot," he said, examining them. "Punkin might have a point after all when she claimed you could shoot whatever you aimed for. Now, I'm not sure filling my leg full of lead was all that accidental. Could be—"

"Could be you talk too much." She probably meant the flippant tone as a warning. "As you said, you can't believe everything that impossible sister of mine says."

Luke should've let the comment pass, but he couldn't help stirring the boiling pot...even if he got scalded. Manure for brains, his father had said many a time.

"Like the part about you never having a beau? Or never lettin' a gentleman call on you? Or is it the part about never having been kissed that's bunched your tail feathers in a wad?"

A shocked gasp filled the space. "Mr. McClain! That's my business. What right—"

Before he realized his intentions, he slid his hand beneath her hair. With a tug on the back of her neck, he pulled her against him. Glory trembled under his touch, a fragile leaf in a storm's path.

Her soft lips parted slightly in anticipation as her eyelids fluttered down to hide the solid, blue gaze that rocked the foundation of his soul.

Sure as his name was Luke McClain, he knew he had to

kiss her. Knew he had to taste the forbidden nectar or die from pure want.

At that moment, he knew he wanted to be a bother more than anything else.

Six

"MR. LUKE, MR. LUKE." PATIENCE TRIPPED AND ALMOST fell over her own feet as she ran.

His slow advance toward moist, rosy promise came to a halt. Glory jumped back. Panic, and something awful close to fear, swept her face.

Cotton-pickin'!

He groaned, swallowing more than a mouthful of frustration. The girl ruined a perfect moment. Darn his hide, he might never find Glory in this receptive frame of mind again.

"Punkin, where's the fire?"

"Nowhere. Come 'ere." The girl grabbed his hand and pulled him. "I wanna show you some baby rabbits I found."

"Don't reckon it can wait a few minutes, can it? I'm talking right now." He tried to catch Glory's attention, to let her know he intended to pick up where he left off the next chance he got. But she snatched up the turkeys without a glance and made long strides for the house.

"Seems Glory's done talkin', Mr. Luke."

"Reckon she is at that." Regret covered him, scratching like those darn woolen pants. With considerably more pain than that in his busted leg, he let the girl lead him to her discovery.

Problem was, he hadn't found a woman he'd wanted to

kiss since Jessie. Not one awoke a flicker of response inside his lonely heart. None until he'd met the blue-eyed Glory.

Odd he didn't sense a betrayal to Jessie's memory. Not that she'd ever returned his sentiment. She hadn't. He'd kept his pining secret, not daring to allow a whisper of it to cross his lips. Only in the dead of night did he take her memory from the hiding place and hold her. Such as it'd always be. Jessie had eyes for no one other than his brother, Duel.

With his stare hidden beneath the shadow of the hat, Luke admired the sway of Glory's hips. Those britches outlined each curve of her willowy legs as she strolled toward Hope.

His swallow got stuck.

∽

Perspiration soaked Glory's shirt. She wished she could lay it in the sun's waning rays. Tiny trickles ran down the crease between her breasts. Boiling her in hot oil couldn't have made her skin more sensitive or more ablaze.

If beaus and courting did this to a body, she didn't know why anyone would seek the experience. Her stomach twisted and turned worse than a butter churn full of fresh cream.

She flopped a turkey onto the chopping block and reached for the hatchet. Suddenly the full import sank in.

Oh my! McClain had almost kissed her. Had it not been for Patience, she might've known the thrill of those taunting lips pressing against hers. A sudden giddy rush buckled her knees. She gripped the tree stump for balance.

"What's the matter, Glory? You're pale." Hope waited for her to chop off the bird's head so she could clean and pluck it.

"I'm fine." A quick flick of the wrist separated the dead turkey's head from his body. "Just fine."

"Well, you don't look it." Hope began her task of readying the big bird for supper.

Glory slung the other one onto the block. From the corner of her eye, she caught McClain's lean figure. Even at this distance, she couldn't miss the anguish that swept his face as it often did when he thought no one noticed. His leg hurt more than he admitted. Though he tried to fake everyone, he didn't pull the wool over her eyes for a minute.

He bent stiffly and made an agonizing attempt to squat for a better view of the rabbits to which Patience pointed. The trousers molded to the muscle and flesh beneath. She missed the second gobbler's neck by several inches.

"Your friend sure has nice manners. It says something about a man when he pays attention to a pesky chatterbox." Hope's observation made Glory wonder if she'd witnessed her shameful display earlier. "Yep, Mr. McClain is real nice. And handsome to boot."

"He's not my friend. He's a stranger." Impatience seeped into her voice. Not at Hope though. The irritation lay with herself for falling so readily into a perfect stranger's arms.

Perfect? *Dear heavens!* Even though she couldn't shake the nagging suspicion he kept a dark secret from them, she allowed there were one or two things that came awfully close to it. She supposed a body might call his white teeth surrounded by a warm, generous mouth and mischievous brown eyes as close to perfect as a man could get.

Nonetheless, she didn't have to become a mindless Amelia. She drew back the hatchet and this time cleanly whacked off the head.

Hope gasped softly, making Glory wonder if she'd spoken her thoughts aloud.

"Who do you suppose that is?"

She followed Hope's gaze to a horse and buggy turning onto the property. An unsettling hunch flickered through her mind.

"Guess we'll find out shortly."

Glory hurried to meet the visitor. Should this pertain to what she thought, she didn't want McClain to get wind. This was Day family business and none of his affair.

"Good Day, Miss Glory," called Alex O'Brien, a nice young man who worked at the bank. Seemed a pleasant enough sort and she didn't hold his pronounced limp against him. Can't help the way you come into the world or the things that happen once you get here. At least, most of the time.

"Afternoon. What brings you out this way?"

Alex wore a solemn expression. "Sorry to say it's business, ma'am." His gaze drifted past. "Howdy, Miss Hope."

Glory supposed it would be safe to say the boy was moon-eyed over her middle sister, though he hadn't yet gotten courage enough to come calling. Merely a matter of time.

"This isn't a proper place to discuss it." She cast an anxious glance toward McClain, who stood staring with something akin to snoopy interest. "Step into the house."

"Would you care for a drink of water or some fresh milk?" she asked after he seated himself stiffly in the parlor.

Alex licked his lips nervously. Her fear of impending doom grew at seeing him fidget with the hat in his hands.

"Water might be nice, ma'am...if it's no bother."

"Hope, please take care of our guest." Glory sank into her father's chair. O'Brien hadn't met her gaze since his arrival. That spelled trouble of the foreclosure kind.

"What can I help you with?"

"This is best discussed with Mrs. Day. Meanin' no offense, ma'am."

"My mother is ill and can't be disturbed. Besides, I handle Day affairs. Now what brought you?"

The boy took advantage of Hope's return. He accepted the tin cup, gulping the liquid. Glory waited while he wiped his mouth and returned the empty cup to her sister. The rocking chair creaked when Hope slid into it, smoothing her skirts.

"Mr. Fieldings sent me, ma'am." He licked his lips again, she suspected to bolster his courage. She didn't have to lay claim to mind reading to see that the bank employee hated his mission. "Aw, I wish I didn't have to do this. I'd rather take a beatin'."

A quietness spread through her body. A quiet that came in advance of a storm. She gripped the arm of the chair.

"It's all right, Alex. You have a job to do. Go ahead and spit it out."

"The bank is calling in your note. He's giving you two weeks to pay it in full or else this farm will become the bank's property…ma'am."

The news stole the air from her lungs. Her head rang worse than the time old Caesar kicked her. Two weeks. Aunt Dorothy's warning came true.

Hope's shocked cry jarred the silence. "No! What are we going to do? Where will we live?"

How could she have overlooked preparing Hope for this sickening turn of events? She threw Alex a look loaded with buckshot and hurried to her sister. He jumped to his feet. He wouldn't be wrong in sensing his welcome had expired.

"Don't worry, we'll think of something. We're not going to lose this house." Glory kept one arm around Hope's sagging shoulders and glared at the messenger. "Make no mistake, we're not going to easily give up this land that has supported two generations of Days."

"I'm terribly sorry." He inched toward the door.

"Not without one heck of a fight. Tell that to your boss!"

The screen door slammed behind the scared boy. It had barely stopped reverberating when Luke stormed in.

"What lit a shuck under that boy? I swear I've never seen anyone so hell-bent." Concern lined his face when he saw Hope's tears. "I'll kill him if he did anything…"

"Family business. Nothing more." She couldn't let him see their ruination. And she sure didn't want his pity. She could hear the buzz now—*Those poor Day girls couldn't even keep a roof over their heads. Poor as church mice.*

"All you have to do is say the word and I'll go after him."

In spite of the dread blocking her windpipe, she had to

smile at the picture of Luke dragging O'Brien back by the nape of his neck and the seat of his pants.

His solicitude almost made her feel…protected.

Almost special.

And if it were possible…almost loved.

The story of her life—everything came too late. She lived an almost life.

"I appreciate your offer, but we're just fine."

Luke didn't bat an eye. "Don't think Miss Hope shares that opinion."

Glory squeezed her sister tightly, willing the girl to reassure him.

"Alex was the perfect gentleman. There's no call for bloodshed." Hope wiped her eyes and smiled brightly.

"Now, if you don't mind, I have turkeys to pluck."

The strength came unexpectedly. They had more in common than she thought. At sixteen, the calm, easygoing Hope hadn't shown an inclination up until now for the kind of backbone it took to survive here. That she might share their mother's weak nature had indeed caused some sleepless nights. Speaking of which, she should check on Mama. She wished she knew the nature of Ruth's problem and what to do.

"Excuse me, McClain." She wasn't prepared when he caught her arm. Not for the warmth of his touch or the caring in his low drawl.

"I'm not stupid. Don't know what that boy said to rattle you, but I know trouble when I smell it."

His stubborn persistence didn't surprise her, but the tic in his firmly set jaw did.

"Let me help," he pleaded.

For a moment, he sorely tempted her. Even though he couldn't offer a solution, it would ease the burden a little to share it with a willing soul.

Even a perfect stranger who'd about swept her off her feet.

"You can't." The strangled words threatened to choke her.

Compassion turned the dusky gaze a deep, rich brown.

She barely felt his breath fluttering the hair at her temples, because she was too busy drowning with longing.

The slamming screen broke the trance.

Patience skipped into the parlor. "Mr. Luke, look what I found in the barn. What kind is it?"

Luke jumped back when the girl pushed a green snake into his face. "Fire and damnation, girl!"

Able to breathe again, Glory hastened to disguise the quivers that would expose her. "Not afraid, are you?"

"Not fond of anything that crawls on its belly." He edged toward the door for a getaway. "Snakes and I part company."

"It's harmless." She couldn't help tease. The petrified look on his face said McClain wasn't the tough, fearless man he tried to convince everyone he was.

Patience stretched it out. "Don'cha want to pet him?"

A forked tongue shot from its mouth.

"My father didn't raise any fool, Punkin. Besides, I don't think your pet likes me." With that, Luke bolted.

"Take the thing outside, Patience, then go pick us a mess of poke salad for supper. I saw some down by the creek today." She didn't wait for the girl to object. "After that, bring in the clothes hanging on the line. I'm sure they're dry."

"I'm just a little kid, Glory. I can't do all that."

"Sure you can. Now get to it." She walked to the door to her mother's room and knocked softly, praying she was lucid for once.

❧

A pleasant surprise came the following morning. The normal routine Luke had observed from the first day changed.

He did a double take, then backtracked when Glory came to breakfast wearing a dress instead of her usual britches. For a minute, he thought he'd lost count of the days and Sunday had snuck up behind his back.

The jolt damn near made him choke on the coffee Hope had poured.

Truth to tell, she looked beautiful in the faded flour-sack dress. Soft and feminine. Try his darnedest, he couldn't keep from staring at the snug cloth that molded, cradled each curve.

Luke set his cup down crookedly, barely noticing the hot liquid that sloshed onto his hand.

She'd twisted her hair into a loose knot atop her head. It added an elegant air. But it was the tiny gold ringlets framing her face that gave wings to the sensitive spirit inside. The part she tried so desperately to hide. She'd wrestle an alligator to keep anyone from thinking for one minute she had a hint of a chink in her armor. Not that she had to worry on that account. In his estimation, he figured Glory Day was the strongest, most determined woman he'd ever met.

But the sensitive part showed in the love she gave her mother and sisters. Even when they made her mad enough to spit nails.

"Mornin'." He hobbled around the table to hold her chair. "Didn't recognize you at first."

She accepted the cup Patience brought—"Thank you, Squirt"—then took a slow sip before answering. "You mean without my regular garb?"

Luke rubbed the sharp needles of pain from his leg, ignoring the pointed sarcasm. "I have to say you look fetching. Just wondered if I'd skipped a couple of days." His voice lowered to a whisper. "By any chance, is this Sunday?"

"It's Thursday. Just so happens I have business in town that requires me to look my best."

"Oh?" His brow shot up; then he winked broadly. "Courtin' business?"

Bright spots colored her cheeks, rewarding his efforts. Truth told, he couldn't bear to think of other hands touching her.

"You have a lot of nerve!"

Her stare assuredly was of the defiant variety, sorta what Custer might have used when he met Sitting Bull.

"Mighty dressed up. Smell nice too."

"It's business of another sort, if you must know."

"Your father? Has he—"

"No."

Her clipped reply gave him to know it was her ball of wax, and he could peddle his nosiness elsewhere or she'd shoot the other leg.

Bank business, he reckoned. No other reason to get gussied up and head for town in the middle of the week. Plus, he'd seen her counting the coins in the fruit jar and the tremble of her fingers. Her eyes afterward had held a hint of moisture. Punkin explained that's where they kept the family's finances.

Hope picked that moment to plop down a big platter of flapjacks between them. "Don't let these get cold."

"Is Mama up?" Concern masked Glory's clear gaze.

"She hasn't come from her room yet. I sent Patience to wake her."

"I did like you told me." The littlest Day brought the jar of sorghum to the table and slid sideways into her seat.

"Yes, but did you make sure she heard?"

A sharp edge had crept into Glory's question. Things were getting to her.

"Mama opened her eyes. What more do you want?" Patience glared from one sister to the other. "You always blame me. It's not fair."

"If you weren't such a lovable kid, we'd leave you on the reverend's doorstep with a note." Glory pushed back her chair. "Only he's too nice for that."

Hope stopped her. "I'll see to Mama."

"You wouldn't dare get rid of me. If you did, you wouldn't have anyone to push around," Patience argued.

Luke stepped in quickly to forestall the murder about to take place. "Hey, Punkin. Wanna go fishing after breakfast?"

"Just you an' me?"

"Yep."

"Oh boy. I know a good place to dig for worms."

Hope returned. "Mama's getting ready."

Thick tension swept the table. Why, he didn't know,

but his gut told him it involved the unwanted visitor from last evening.

He returned Punkin's grin. The day was young yet and he had the little darling all to himself. It wouldn't take much prying.

Seven

LUKE'S EYEBROWS ROSE WHEN GLORY TOOK ADVANTAGE of her mother's tardiness and asked him for a moment alone.

Outside at the wagon, a mockingbird flew past with a grasshopper in its beak. That something so ungainly could provide food for a predator gave her nerves a start. It took a good minute before she managed to gather enough grit.

"I have a request, actually a proposal."

"A proposition, you mean?"

His knowing grin made mush of what grit she'd plucked. *Hell's bells!* He'd turned her simple appeal into something indecent. Trying to salvage her pride, she weathered the irritating smugness. Yet, she'd rather dance a jig with the pitchfork man himself.

"Will you be quiet until you hear me out?"

"Proposing can be sticky. You certain you're ready to take this step? You seem to have left out the courting stage."

The devilish smile reinforced his similarity with Lucifer.

"You know very well I'm not referring to a match between us. It's not that sort of…arrangement." Heat flooded her cheeks. If her situation weren't so desperate, she'd leave the insufferable man standing neck-deep in his own egotistical mess.

"I see. Now it's an arrangement...of sorts." Mischief created twinkling stars in his brown stare.

"It's no use." She'd had enough of his foolish drivel. "You're clearly bent on twisting my words and I can see Mama's ready to leave for town. Good day, McClain."

"Wait." Luke caught her hand. "I'm sorry."

Delicate, fleeting strokes on her skin gave birth to a mass of unsettling tingles. Her heart pounded. A lowered glance found the source. Luke slowly rubbed his thumb back and forth over her wrist with the excruciating ease of a musician strumming a viola.

"Forgive me? Please?" His husky murmur only served to increase the sound of the waltz only she could hear.

Without meaning to, she raised her gaze...and once more fell into his trap. A rabbit caught in a snare. She found herself encased in the handsome trickster's genuine caring. Her parched mouth replicated the godforsaken land on which she stood—land she'd make a deal with a perfect stranger to keep.

"You clearly have a problem and I made light of it. If I promise to be good, will you tell me what you have in mind?"

Heaven help her. He beckoned toward a tempting path. The roguish glint in his eyes promised she'd have no regrets. Ha! She already did. Her hands remembered a nicely shaped behind and the solid muscle of a bare thigh. She recalled the soft breath of his mouth against her cheek in the almost-kiss that had found a home in her soul.

No regrets? Only of the worst sort.

Glory wet her lips, willing back the purpose that had brought her to seek him out. "I know you'll be leaving here in a day or so. Will you pick up Perkins's scent again?"

"Yep."

"I wish to make a deal with you." She twisted the handle of her threadbare bag, aware that the contents would not save them from destruction. A silver pocket watch and an emerald brooch couldn't buy a farm...or a pig in a poke.

"I'm listening."

The screen door closed. Her mother. She had to hurry, for what she had in mind didn't call for an audience. Especially when that audience forbade it.

"Let me go with you after Perkins and we'll split the reward fair and square."

"No."

Luke's blunt refusal pricked her heart. The rogue meant to have the entire reward for himself.

"I'm merely asking for halves. Don't make me beg." She struggled against rising panic. Her pride wouldn't allow weakness. Tears were for people with no backbone.

"Now there's a tempting thought." His low voice made her heart thud against her ribs. "Having it in my power to make you beg. Hmm. Might be worth reconsidering."

A quick glance saw that her mother had stopped to talk with Patience, buying her a few extra seconds.

"I'll agree to anything you want. I need that money."

Ruth finished her conversation and came toward them.

"Anything, huh? Know what that means?"

The lump stuck in Glory's throat. She stared at the dust swirling around her worn high-topped shoes. Should a woman feel this breathless when she'd sold her soul to the man who made her hope?

"Yes, I know." The words came no louder than a whisper.

But she wished she didn't. Wished she didn't yearn for his touch as only an old maid could. And wished she could accept that which he hinted at for all the reasons she'd listed in her journal.

"We'll leave tomorrow at first light."

She almost swooned. "I'll be ready."

"Morning, Mr. McClain. Fine day, isn't it?"

Her mother appeared in better spirits than she'd expected.

"Yes, ma'am. Right beautiful." Luke helped Ruth onto the wagon seat. "Damn near perfect."

The scintillating gleam in his dark eyes made it clear he didn't refer to the weather.

She ignored the irritating grin and flicked the reins, urging Caesar forward. "Giddyup, boy."

Luke's whistling followed until they turned onto the main road to town, taunting her with the melody of "The Battle Hymn of the Republic." It didn't take a man of science to get the message.

"That's a nice young man, don't you think, Glory?"

That wasn't *exactly* the word that came to mind. She must've lost what little sense she possessed. Very likely she'd set a path down the road to perdition with her bargain.

∼∽

"Grab that pole, Punkin, we're going fishing." Luke swung into step, matching his stride with the girl's.

"Can we take Miss Minnie, too?"

Patience cradled the mama calico. The affection the girl bestowed on the cat and her babies clearly came from being starved of companionship. From what he could gather, the children in town shunned her.

"Reckon so, but don't you think the kittens'll miss their mama? What if they get hungry?"

The girl skipped into the barn and over to the box where she'd corralled the babies. "Okay, Miss Minnie. Be a good mama to your children." She set the calico down and watched the kittens squirm over to nurse. "I'll give you a nice bowl of milk when I get back."

Another cat, one he'd not seen before, jumped from the loft and over into the box. The straggly animal sported one green eye and one blue. Strangest thing he'd ever seen. Reminded him of the three-legged dog who'd taken up with him once. Felt sorry for the darn thing.

"Mornin', Mr. George. You come to see your babies?" Patience cooed and petted the pitiful yellow cat.

"Mr. George?"

"Miss Minnie's husband," she stated matter-of-factly. "Ain't he the prettiest cat you ever saw?"

Her proud grin made him shake his head. Only Patience
would see the beauty in such a sight. She gave credence to
all mothers who thought their baby the most special, even
when their infant was as ugly as a bar of lye soap.

"Come on, girl. We've got us some fish to catch."

A short time later, Luke sat cross-legged beside Red
Bank Creek.

"You don't hafta put my worm on," Patience informed
him, copying his every move. "I can do it myself."

Watching her study the can of wiggly bait brought puz-
zlement. At first, he blamed her hesitation on a squeamish
nature, but he changed that assumption when she reached
in and pulled out a juicy one.

"Sorry, Mr. Worm, I hate to kill you. I hope you don't
have any children. But we need to catch some fish for
supper so Glory won't have to worry."

Her apology touched him in places he hadn't visited in
a while. She'd tried to find the one who'd be least missed.
Like he'd done when his father gave the ultimatum that he
could keep only one in a litter of pups. He'd looked into
the mother's pleading eyes, then chosen the runt because
she wouldn't mind losing that one quite so much.

Such a long time ago and yet it seemed like yesterday.

Without contemplating the worm's family, Luke selected
one, threaded it on the hook, and dropped the line in the
water.

Patience followed suit and leaned back on her elbows. "I
like fishing with you. Ain't this fun?"

"Yep." He stuck a matchstick in his mouth and let it hang
out the side. Funny how the girl's language switched. In her
mother's company, "ain'ts" automatically became "isn'ts."

"I noticed you and Hope don't go to school in town."

"They don't want us. Ol' Miss Goodnight said we
couldn't come." The girl squinted when she raised her face.
"Mama teaches us cipherin', readin', an' writing when she
don't have a sick headache. She used to be a schoolmarm
before she married my papa."

Wasn't right to blame the children for the sins of the father, either real or made up. It was the townspeople's attitude that was the sin, surely.

"It's a shame Glory had to go to town or she could've come with us." He gave the girl a sidelong glance, keeping his tone casual.

"She an' Mama had business to take care of."

"Business, huh?"

"But Glory wouldn't have come anyhow. All she does is work, work, work. An' when she ain't working, she's bossin' me around."

He jiggled his pole up and down, ignoring the bossin' part. From watching the family, he reckoned Patience wouldn't have suffered any from a good deal more scolding than she got.

"Couldn't have anything to do with the visitor last evening, you don't suppose?"

The girl copied his movements, jerking her pole. "Mr. Fieldings at the bank sent him."

He shouldn't have pumped Patience for information. But after Glory's desperate deal-making attempt, he'd suspected as much.

"You don't say."

"He's callin' in the note on the farm. Glory says we have two weeks to pay what's due or we hafta leave."

"Two weeks? Not much time."

Little wonder the blue-eyed beauty had resorted to begging. In comparison to the Day family's plight, clearing his name seemed minor. This new development put a rush on his plans.

"Glory'll think of something. She said not to worry." Big tears welled in the girl's eyes. "But I still do anyway."

Her shoulders seemed too small when his arm slid around them. "Punkin, I'm going to make sure you keep what's yours. I promise."

❧

"Mama, how are you today?" Glory asked the question she'd put off since Ruth climbed into the buckboard. She must judge her mother's state of mind before they faced the banker.

"Fine, dear. Why wouldn't I be?"

"Sometimes you scare me. I don't know how to help. And the things you say don't make sense." That wasn't the half of it, but she couldn't just come right out and voice her suspicions.

"Not to worry, dear. I'm perfectly well." Ruth smoothed her hair back with long, slender fingers.

Glory persisted. "You understand why we're going to town?"

The clop of the mule's hooves on the hardened ground couldn't override Ruth's loud sigh.

"We're going to talk to Mr. Fieldings, silly goose."

"You remember what about, don't you?"

For a second or two, Glory could tell from her mother's expression that confusion fought with reality. Glory wondered which side of Ruth would win. She crossed her fingers.

"Of course I do." Impatience echoed in the sharp tone. "Don't speak to me as if I were a child."

"Sorry, Mama. I need to make sure you grasp the situation."

"I don't care for your sassy tongue, Glory Marie Day!"

"You're right. I apologize." Feeling rotten for overstepping her bounds, she quit probing.

Rampant thoughts of the deal with McClain swam in her head. She couldn't bear to remember the scandalous declaration.

I'll do anything you ask.

A desperate bargain for a girl who'd never kissed a man, much less given him leave to have his way. Without a doubt, he thought her bolder than a scarlet woman.

Hundreds of tiny prickles marched to the tune Luke had chosen. All the way to the meeting spot in her belly. The chance of what would happen if Fieldings turned down her offer created the maelstrom. She sucked in her breath. She'd have to keep her word.

Then again, could she endure the disappointment if he didn't hold her to it? Now where in blazes had that thought sprung from?

Only the incessant creak of the wagon wheels and the mule's noisy rumblings broke the silence.

Besides, if things went accordingly, she'd have no need for such ridiculous speculation.

"I know we need money." Ruth's childlike statement came from the blue.

"In the worst possible way, Mama."

"Mr. Fieldings will give us a loan."

"No loan. Time is what we're asking for if we can't persuade him to take the watch and brooch in trade. A few extra months should help us catch up so we won't lose our home."

"Oh." Ruth shrugged her shoulders.

Glory had the answer to her question. Ruth's mind drifted aimlessly toward no particular shore. She wouldn't get much support from her mother today.

"I need you to stand with me, Mama. I'm depending on you to stay focused." She couldn't do everything by herself. Heaviness sat on her chest.

Sometimes she needed a parent. Sometimes she needed Papa.

The buckboard turned the corner onto Santa Anna's main street. All of a sudden, everything blurred. She descended into a gray, thick fog.

Not now. This couldn't...she didn't have the strength to fight this enemy today.

Strange how her vision had remained crystal clear the whole of yesterday. In fact, after shooting the two turkeys, she believed the problem had passed. Now, it returned with a vengeance.

Glory gripped the reins tightly, trying to salvage her mangled nerves. *Don't panic. Calm down. Take a deep breath.*

Then, as quickly as the thick grayness had swooped over

her, it left. The release of her pent-up air gave a good imitation of an overboiling teakettle.

Old Caesar appeared to sense their destination, for he made a beeline for First Bank and Loan and stopped before she could say whoa.

The establishment bustled with business. Glory wondered how many others stood in the same shoes as the Day family. Other families probably faced eviction too.

She captured Ruth, who had wandered to the dry goods store next door. When she entered the bank, she steered them to the nearest window. "We'd like a word with Mr. Fieldings, please."

Alex O'Brien peered through the black iron bars separating him from the patrons. "Good morning, ladies. Nice to, uh…see you. I'm sorry. He's, uh, busy right now. If you—"

"We'll wait," Glory interrupted, regretting her curt tone. No one could blame the young man for another's greed.

Her grip on Ruth's arm loosened a bit as she maneuvered them through the busy crowd to the bank proprietor's closed office door.

"I'm sorry, there's nothing I can do." The banker's flint-hardened refusal drifted through the partition. "You failed to uphold your part of the deal. I have no choice."

Glory could plainly hear crying of the feminine kind mixed with low, deep mumbling. Her hopes dropped faster than the level of Red Bank Creek. Another family reduced to pleading. She met her mother's troubled gaze. At least she could be thankful Ruth finally appeared to grasp their dilemma.

The door flew open and out stomped Helmut Volker. The German immigrant ushered his sobbing wife from the bank.

"Next!" Fieldings's stare drilled a hole in Glory.

She never twitched an eyelid. But she did clutch the bag that contained their sole valuables tighter to hide her shaking hand.

Her heels pounded the wooden floor when she marched in. If it reminded anyone of a firing squad volley, she couldn't help that. She perched stiffly on a chair. Following her, Ruth did the same.

"Let's cut to the chase, Mrs. Day." The portly man squeezed his girth into his protesting chair. "I know why you're here."

"How can you when we haven't said?" Glory demanded.

A snort shot from Fieldings's huge nostrils. His piggish breathing filled the room. She'd heard quieter hogs rooting in a favorite mud hole—or a slop pen.

"You're here same as the others, trying to beg, borrow, or steal their way into my good favor. Won't work."

"If you had a good favor, no soul would know it. I wouldn't steal or beg for a crumb of food. I'd rather starve to death. As for borrowing…that's a mistake my father already made." She glanced at Ruth and wished her mother had some gumption about her.

"I told Jack Day he'd rue his lack of judgment." The chair screeched as he leaned back in satisfaction.

"My Jack's an honest man! If we could get him home, he'd set things right and make you eat your words."

A brief flash of fire shot from Ruth's eyes. But before the sign of life took root, it vanished, and a dull pallor took its place. Glory wondered if it'd ever been there at all. "Mama's not well."

"My condolences."

The overstuffed feather mattress didn't appear a bit sorry.

"Sir, I have a simple request. We've brought some family valuables that we're offering in exchange for the balance of the note. Or to buy us a little more time." She fiddled with the strings, trying to get the cloth bag open. "These heirlooms mean everything to us. If our circumstances hadn't gone past the point of no return, we'd keep them under lock and key."

He leaned forward, a greedy leer in his beady eyes. She prayed he wouldn't notice a few flaws—the missing emerald from the brooch and a broken watch stem. Perhaps he wouldn't look close. At last the knot yielded. She reached inside.

"My grandfather's silver pocket watch given to him
by Sam Houston himself and Mother's emerald brooch.
Handsome, aren't they?"

She stilled her trembles as she handed them over.

～⌇⌇～

Luke returned their fishing poles to the barn. His mind
whirled with purpose.

"Come on, Soldier." He led the paint from its stall.

"I never knew your horse's name. I like it."

Patience glued herself to his side just as the strange-eyed
Mr. George padded imperiously in her footsteps.

He didn't relish his task. It was going to be hard for her
to understand, and no amount of explaining would soften
the blow.

"You never asked me." He grabbed the saddle blanket
and spread it over Soldier's back. "Punkin, you wanna go
help your sister in the house now?"

"Aw, she don't need no help." The girl flipped her pigtails
in true Patience fashion. "You goin' somewhere, Luke?"

Her mother would skin her alive if she heard her omit
the "mister."

"Yep." The saddle seemed to weigh a ton when he lifted
it up and adjusted the cinches. He couldn't bear to see the
hurt he knew he'd find in his fishing buddy's innocent gaze.

"Where you goin'? Ain't you gonna wait for Glory?"

"There's things I have to do. Stuff that can't wait. I have
to go today…now."

A sniffle tightened the pain in his gut. The girl didn't
know how this ripped his own heart out. Punkin deserved
a better hero than a man like himself. She needed someone
with honor who didn't resort to shameless deceit and trickery.

And Glory? She'd be a mad hornet. Thank goodness he
wouldn't be around to catch her temper.

"Don'cha like us anymore?"

He stopped. Her quivering chin made the lump in his

chest more uncomfortable. Leaning down, he took her face
between his hands. With his thumb, he wiped away a tear
that inched down her cheek.

"I'll be back. It's not forever."

"You promise?"

"Cross my heart and hope to die." Solemnly, he made
an X on his chest with his forefinger.

If dying came first? Well, he'd just cross that bridge when
he came to it.

Eight

"You have only one item that might interest me, Miss Day." Fielding's slack mouth glistened with unswallowed spit. "And I don't think you'll part with that."

Livid, Glory jumped to her feet, snatched up the valuables, and stuffed them into the bag.

He chuckled. "Should you change your mind, you know where to find me."

Confusion swept Ruth's face as Glory grabbed her hand and yanked her from the office.

Before the door slammed, she heard the fat pig snort, "Two weeks. Not a day more."

Shaking, she didn't stop or take a breath until they reached fresh air outside.

"He said we had one thing to bargain with, whatever he meant. Think of your father."

Glory's thoughts stumbled. For a brief moment, her mother had stood with her. Though wobbly at best, a post to lean on. Now, in the wink of an eye, she'd slipped back into confusion, jerking away that brief support.

"No, Mama. I'd do almost anything to save the farm, but I'm not going to let him touch me. Not for anything."

"Oh, I didn't realize." Ruth put her hand over her mouth. "Thank goodness you're taking care of things until your father gets back from his trip. He should return any day." The vacant haze they'd grown accustomed to of late had returned.

"I know." Glory patted her hand and helped her into the buckboard. "Let's go sell the eggs and milk we brought."

Unusual activity took place at Harvey's Emporium. The group of men congregating in front appeared awfully agitated. She pulled the brake, tied the reins to it, and hopped down, beating Horace Simon. He arrived nearly out of breath, a huge grin stretching from ear to ear.

"Howdy, Miss Glory." He took the basket of eggs from her while she helped Ruth from the seat. "Been hopin' to see you. I'm still your beau, ain't I?"

Innocence glowed in the boy's face. Unlike Uncle Pete, whose head clicked, whirred, and jangled with constant noise, Horace's inner workings appeared quiet and unmoved. In a way, she envied that. No pressure, no worries. Simply happy to be alive. At this moment, it seemed like pure heaven.

He might be slow-witted, but he had a heart as big as the sky. More than she could say for the majority of Santa Anna's citizens, lumping a good many of them with that overstuffed feather mattress Fieldings.

Glory patted his arm. "Of course, Horace, you'll always be my beau."

"Okay." If he'd been a dog, he'd have beat her half silly with his wagging tail.

She nodded toward the men. "What's going on?"

"Pete Harvey's a-tellin' about treasure."

"What kind?"

"The buried kind." Horace scurried to hold the door for Glory and her mother.

Uncle Pete noticed them and waved. Though short in stature, he made up for it in tall tales. Most of the townsfolk had long ceased to listen to his ramblings and it surprised her now to see their enthusiasm. She did admit that talk of buried treasure made her ears perk up though.

Aunt Dorothy greeted them. "Is that old coot still out there spouting his mouth?"

"Afraid so." Glory set the bucket of milk on the counter.

"I told him to shush up about it. But he never listens to a word I say."

"Here's some eggs Glory done brung you, Mrs. Harvey." Horace handed over the basket, his feet moving in constant motion. If the rest of him had followed, he'd have found himself five miles down the road. Anxious to get back outside to the man talk, she supposed.

"Thanks for your help, Horace." Glory cringed when he tripped over an uneven place in the floor. "You are quite thoughtful."

"Okay. I gotta go hunt for treasure." The door banged, setting the bell in motion.

"How you doing, Ruth?" Dorothy led Glory's mother to a seat at the back of the store where the men gathered to play checkers on rainy days and Saturday mornings. With nary a teaspoon of rain in the last four months, the area saw little use.

"Why does everyone make a fuss about my health?" Ruth's argumentative tone had her aunt raising an eyebrow.

"We've been to see Fieldings. Things look pretty bleak," Glory explained.

"Let me get your mother a cool drink of water and we'll chat a bit. Not often I have company. At least the sort who stops in for reasons other than to spread rumors or ask for advice."

Glory could comfortably say neither applied to them.

She had just finished relaying the eviction news when Pete Harvey shuffled inside.

"There's my Glory girl." The dapper man removed his derby hat when he noticed his wife's silent scolding. Glory smiled at his customary red garters that anchored white sleeves. To her knowledge, he'd never stepped outside the upstairs living quarters without red garters on his upper arms that shortened the length of his long sleeves. She'd always wanted to hide and watch what happened when he removed them. A giggle rose. She could picture the sleeves striking him about the knees.

Pete Harvey put her in mind of a Mississippi gambler. Only his bowed legs, curved in a perfect circle, ruined any misconception one might have of that.

Not that she had any idea of the characteristics of a Mississippi cardsharp. None other than the description in the dime novel Aunt Dorothy had loaned her that she'd read three times. Yet, she felt almost positive they showed no affinity to any kind of regular horseback riding.

"Morning, Uncle." She returned his infectious good humor. "Having a meeting of the minds out there? They want to elect you mayor or something?"

"Pshaw! The 'or something' would be more like it, gal." He drew her away from the other two women and lowered his voice. "Was tellin' the boys about runnin' into Sam Sixkiller."

"That old Indian who comes into town occasionally?"

Everyone in the county put old Sam and Pete in the same looney category. They could truly hatch some good stories when the two of them got together. Two peas in a pod.

"Yep." Uncle Pete's eyes sparkled with excitement.

"You two weren't drinking cactus juice, were you?"

"Not particularly at the time. You wanna hear or not?"

"Horace mentioned something about buried treasure."

"Shh." He drew her closer, casting a suspicious glance around the store. "Keep it down."

His logic escaped her. She didn't point out the fact that he'd already told half the town and by now the tale had spread to every home and prairie dog hole in the county.

"Sam said when he was a young brave, his tribe ambushed a group of prospectors somewhere in this area coming back from gold country in the Rockies. They had a powerful lot o' pack mules and burros with ever' one loaded down with gold nuggets."

"So the Comanches took the gold?"

"That part's kinda fuzzy." Uncle Pete pressed his mouth to her ear. "Sam thinks they only had eyes for the animals and scalps. Didn't know nuthin' about yeller rocks. To the best of his recollection, they emptied the bags onto the ground. Or they might've dug a hole and buried 'em."

"Uncle Pete, you've got to quit listening to every fanciful concoction. Sam's probably laughing his head off for pulling your leg." Glory gave him a peck on a grizzled cheek that sported at least a week's worth of bristles. "If there truly was gold, don't you think Sam would've taken it by now?"

"Nope. That ol' Comanche can't rightly recollect the spot. Been a lot of years and the land changes."

She'd learned from experience if you didn't work for anything, you didn't deserve it. Could'ves and maybes, or the dreams of an eccentric uncle, wouldn't keep the wolves from the door. Though for all her struggles, nothing but hard times seemed destined to fall in her lap. Who was to say if one was better than the other?

Unless…

The proposition with McClain shot into mind. Given the man's skill, they'd have no trouble apprehending Perkins. Her portion would see them debt free and she could concentrate on her father.

One question nagged at her conscience. At what price? Beyond a doubt, he'd hold her to the promise.

A delicious shiver wound around her heart like a clinging wisteria vine.

❧

Jack Day lay bathed in his own sweat. Not that he minded. It was a welcome relief from chills that normally rattled his bones. He welcomed the pain that came with each breath, for it assured him he hadn't yet departed this life.

"You awake, Jack?" Dr. John Fletcher laid a hand on his forehead. "Fever's broken. For now, anyway."

"Any visitors? My wife…" He asked the same question every day, except the days when he'd been delirious. Lately, the latter descended on him with increasing frequency.

Dr. Fletcher didn't meet his gaze, but paused before pressing a stethoscope to his chest. "I'm sorry."

"Just as well." He sighed wearily. "Wouldn't want them to see me like this."

"They'll come. You have to hold on to that thought."

"Yeah, for Ruth. She'll be here. Someway. Somehow."

The beautiful vision floated into place in his mind. Fragile Ruth. She despised the harsh Texas land with a vengeance, the howling winds, the dry heat, and the blue northers. It stole her spirit little by little, sinking her into a hell of her own making.

Here lies Jack Day, the soul killer. The epitaph carved on his tombstone would surely speak the truth.

He figured killing a person's soul had to be the worst crime a man could commit. Breaking your lady's heart, destroying her faith—those were the kinds of deaths that lasted forever.

"Tell me about your girls. You rarely speak of them."

A coughing spasm suddenly engulfed him. He gasped for air, tasting the sickening blob that stuck in his throat.

"Spit it out, Jack. Just relax and let it come up." The doctor lifted him to an upright position and wiped the bloody phlegm from his mouth.

"Don't have much time left, do I, Doc?"

"The good Lord hasn't seen fit to give me your departure date, son. Guess when He gets ready, He'll take you home."

"Reckon so." Jack leaned weakly against the pillows. "You asked about my girls. Still want to humor a dyin' man?"

"An old sawbones like me always loves hearing about pretty little ladies."

"Glory, Hope, and Patience—my pride and joy. Each is special in her own way. Glory is strong of mind and spirit. She's the provider now. Underneath Hope's calm sweetness lies surprising strength. And Patience, my baby daughter, took her time comin' into this world. Twenty-one hours to be exact. But don't let her name fool you. That little girl can put a Texas whirlwind to shame. Curious and full of excitement."

The prison doctor patted his shoulder. The touch of human kindness brought a measure of warmth to his cold fear.

"If I was a bettin' man, Jack, I'd lay odds you'll see them all soon."

A hopeless sigh escaped his lips. The dice he'd rolled had come up snake eyes. Thank the Lord the doc hadn't put up a stake on his prediction.

Jack's despair wore like a pair of long johns—clinging and personal.

The state of Texas served him an unjust fate. A higher power robbed him of ever setting eyes on his loved ones again this side of the shore. And cruel destiny made certain he would die alone inside these dark prison walls.

❧

Twenty-five cents jingled in the pocket of Glory's dress. That's what a dozen eggs and a gallon of milk fetched. A mental tally of their finances now had them within eighty-one dollars and fifty-seven cents of their goal.

Two weeks, and then the bank would put a no-trespassing sign on the farm, making it a crime to step foot on their land. Her grandfather had fought Indians, pestilence, and outlaws to settle there.

To lose it now would mean she'd failed in every single way.

Glory left her mother visiting with Aunt Dorothy and strode purposefully toward the *Santa Anna Gazette*. Charlie Gimble, the paper's editor and her only true friend besides Horace Simon, usually lent an ear no matter how much type needed setting.

The onslaught of a dust cloud swirled in the wake of three horseback riders who galloped past. She fanned the air to keep the grit from her mouth and tried to separate the yelling from the jangle of noise.

"They robbed the stage! The driver's been killed!" The men jumped from their saddles almost before their mounts stopped. A crowd quickly assembled.

"What's that you say?" Glory heard a man ask as she drew closer.

"Over by Post Oak Springs. A gang of masked, murderin', thievin' outlaws robbed the stage and shot the driver. Blood 'n' guts everywhere."

"Joseph, ride over to Abilene town for the marshal. Quick," Fieldings ordered, waddling from his bank doorway.

"What this town needs is a sheriff," a woman piped up.

"Why, even if Coleman had one, it'd help," whined another.

"With a whole cavalry at Fort Concho practically camped on our doorstep?"

"The cutthroats haven't let that little item stop them, now, have they?"

"Go peddle your notions elsewhere, Mrs. Woody. This is man's work."

Glory watched the woman flounce up the street in a huff. Though suffering from a self-righteous disposition, Mrs. Woody had a point. The robbers' boldness had everyone asking questions, including Glory. She couldn't shake the suspicion that McClain might be involved. Perhaps he considered Perkins the gang's ringleader. That could explain Luke's obsession with the man. After what he let slip to Squirt, only to deny it, he hid more than he told. Why say he was a lawman if he wasn't? It certainly made a person suspicious.

The next thought brought nausea. Was he with them or against?

"Another stage holdup." A man she recognized as Henry Sackett spoke to Cap Bailey, shaking his head sadly. "What's that make now? Seven, eight in the last two months?"

"Yep." Cap released a stream of tobacco juice. The hardened earth greedily accepted the brown blob as if grateful for whatever form of moisture came.

Glory turned back toward the paper office. At least no

one could blame this crime on Jack Day. Though they would dearly love to try. Maybe her father's situation had a bright side. He'd never fully know the hate this town harbored.

Charlie peered over his horn-rimmed spectacles when she opened the door. "What's all the ruckus?"

"Another stage robbed and driver killed. Makes you wonder what this world's coming to."

"Whoever is behind these keeps me in a helluva lot of printing material." He shifted the short stub of a cigar to the other side of his mouth, pushed back the bill of his green visor, and wiped the back of his neck with a handkerchief.

She didn't bother to tell him about the ink he smeared on the side of his temple. A waste of good breath. Ink and Charlie went together and she accepted that as gospel.

"Timmy, get your tablet, boy!" At Charlie's beckoning call, his young apprentice ran from the back room. "This is your chance. Get out there and get the lowdown on this stage robbery and murder."

"Yes, sir, Mr. Gimble." Timmy tucked a tablet under his arm and grabbed a pencil. He paused for a second at the door to jam a hat over his bright-red spikes.

Glory suppressed a grin. She'd never seen the twelve-year-old without them. Even in church, his mother's efforts failed to slick the rebellious mess into neat order. All the spit and hair tonic in the world couldn't glue it down. Unhindered, the spikes sprang back like toy soldiers on a march to save Texas from combs and spit.

"My name's Charlie, not Mr. Gimble. Make me proud, boy."

The shine on Timmy's teeth matched the sparkle in his eyes. "Okay, Charlie."

He tripped over his own feet and fell against the counter before he made it through the door.

Charlie groaned. "I'm training the lad. If he don't kill himself first."

"You're a saint. Not many in this town would give him a chance to learn a trade."

"Timmy's a good lad." He pulled out a chair for her. "Wonder why the criminal element picked Coleman County to terrorize."

"It's a shame law-abiding folks have to risk life and limb to travel through these parts."

"Yep. Can't complain too loud though. Sure makes interesting reading. My sales have shot up."

"Guess they get tired of reading about Uncle Pete's latest debacles and the dry spell."

"That's the honest truth. Why, I haven't even had to resort to filling space with Elmer Knox's hog farm or the perils of Josephine Baker's scandalous bloomers in the last three months."

Glory smiled at the mention of Josephine Baker. The rough-and-tumble woman owned the only boardinghouse. A freethinker, she stayed in hot water with the townsfolk for shedding dresses in favor of baggy bloomers and tunic shirts. Though she'd never had the pleasure of the rebel woman's acquaintance, Glory admired her spunk just the same. It took courage to swim upstream.

"Speaking of old Pete, what's this newest rumor?"

"He claims Sam Sixkiller babbled about some gold his tribe lifted off some prospectors. Between you, me, and the fence post, I'm pretty sure it's simply liquor talk."

Charlie squinted over his horn-rims. "I wouldn't be too quick to toss it out the window with the bathwater. Isn't the first time I heard such."

"From who?"

"Newspapermen never tell." He gave her a sly wink.

"And I know my uncle. I don't have enough fingers and toes to count the stories he's spouted. I love him dearly, but he's a big bag of wind." She sighed.

No, bad as she could use a hole full of gold, she'd have to rely on a more stable means…

The skills of a certain mischievous stranger would do for starters.

There went her stomach again.

Nine

"THAT DOUBLE-CROSSING, YELLOW-BELLIED FOUR-FLUSHER!"
Glory kicked a bucket. The tumbling crash made Caesar
skitter.

Patience quickly grabbed Miss Minnie, who'd come to
rub against her legs.

"I told Mr. Luke you'd be mad at him leavin' that way."
The girl flipped her pigtails and sniffed. Injured innocence
shielded her about as much as a tattered, moth-eaten cloak.

"How long has he been gone?" She'd ride after him.
With the bank painting them into a corner, she had
nowhere else to go and nothing to lose. They'd struck a
deal. They hadn't shaken on it or anything, but it'd been a
firm proposition in any event.

"How long?" she asked again through gritted teeth,
taking a step toward her sister.

Hope intervened with an outstretched hand. "He's gone.
There's nothing we can do about it."

"Like hell." She unhitched the mule from the backboard.

"Glory! Watch your mouth."

"Not my mouth I'm worried about, it's the knife in my
back." Instant remorse for her temper flitted like an antsy
butterfly, refusing to light. But McClain made her mad
enough to eat a sackful of rotten apples and she wasn't about
to apologize. Not yet.

"Why? I don't understand."

Hope's wan face mirrored not only confusion but alarm that came from intuition that a storm cloud poised above their heads and nothing whatsoever could avert it. Glory swung the saddle onto Caesar's back, then drew her aside out of Patience's range.

"McClain and I had an agreement of sorts. I would help him catch Perkins in exchange for splitting the reward. We were to leave in the morning."

"Mama gave strict orders to forget that crazy plan!"

She gave Hope a quick shake. "That was before the bank called in our note and Fieldings thought more of scratching his itch than granting more time."

Should necessity force her into accepting such attentions, she'd choose better. She had her principles. And if she had to degrade herself, she wouldn't do it with a stuffed mattress. Even a low-down cheat like McClain would be better than that.

"But—"

"Besides, Mama's not thinking clearly at the moment. This is the only way."

"Still—"

"Do you want them to turn us out of our home? Where do you think we'd go? Mad Dog Perkins can save us. Can't you see?"

"Surely, there's something else…"

"No." She turned back to the task of saddling the mule. "Only the double-dealing scoundrel snuck off when I turned my back for a few hours."

"Could you have been mistaken in thinking he intended to let you go along?" Hope chewed on her bottom lip. "Much as I love you, sometimes you assume a person says one thing when he means the opposite."

The roguish-eyed Romeo leaped from memory's shadows. Her whispered vow lingered plain as day. *I'll agree to anything you want. I need that money.*

And his questions. *Anything, huh? Know what that means?*

Painfully well. If she lived to be a hundred, she'd not forget Luke McClain's taunting grin that set off every bell, bugle, and whistle.

Sudden tightness caught in the back of her throat. Maybe he didn't consider her offer good enough. Maybe he'd spoken words he hadn't meant. Or maybe he thought her too plain for his taste. He did seem more taken with the fashion queens.

We'll leave tomorrow at first light. The lie returned to haunt her. He never meant to stick around.

She pulled the straps under the mule's belly and cinched them tight. "No. I didn't imagine our deal."

❦

The best way to catch a man is to backtrack. Return to the point of origin, where the knowns merge with unknowns.

A westerly wind kicked up a fuss as Luke slid from his horse at the base of Bead Mountain. Dust swirled, stinging his eyes—an avenging angel out to punish those who dared reach for justice. He held little hope of finding any tracks. A week's worth of wind would've blown away what Perkins might've left.

Still, dogged persistence brought him. It'd always gotten him what he needed. Wiping the blinding grit from his face, he knelt on the sunbaked landscape. Pain knifed through his right leg as the muscle flexed. It was a reminder of just how much he owed Perkins. Repayment would bring great satisfaction.

But you wouldn't have met the golden-haired woman who's turned you inside out. The small voice in his ear whispered gospel truth. Getting shot had certain merit.

He figured Glory would be mighty put out with him when she returned. Didn't matter that his intentions were purely of the honorable sort.

Well, maybe not that pure.

Please don't make me beg, she'd said.

At least part of his aims had square shooting in mind.

But, the other half?

Ah. He entertained no doubts that he would have taken great pleasure in picking up the gauntlet.

If he could've stayed longer...

Under different circumstances, he'd have kissed her until he softened that iron will, turning that stonewashed glare into the midnight blue of a stormy sea. He wished he could've quenched the longing in his belly that called out to a certain sharp-tongued woman.

Such things made it hard for a man to remember his purpose—and that he had more in the end to lose than gain.

A tumbleweed rolled end over end, lodging finally in a thorny agarita bush. It called attention to the trampled broom weed beside it. He pushed aside the broken stems. A clear hoofprint. The brush had protected it. Closer examination of the hardened imprint revealed a broken horseshoe. Couldn't go far without turning lame.

Perkins's horse? His best guess. Not Soldier and certainly not the Days' mule.

He straightened, picking cockleburs from his pant leg. The denims attracted the dadburned things worse than a widow woman to a perfectly contented bachelor. With the last of them off, he squinted into the sun.

North, south, east, or west?

"Which way did you go, Perkins?"

He sniffed the breeze. It seemed to him that a man as rotten as Mad Dog should leave a stench in the air.

The Colorado lay south, Post Oak Springs north. His gut pointed him northeast toward the city of Coleman and the abandoned military fort—Camp Colorado.

Before he yielded to that hunch, he'd first make a wide circle to see if he could locate any more clues to Perkins's whereabouts.

Soldier whinnied when he reached for the reins. "Come on, boy. We got us a coyote hunt."

❧

Glory adjusted herself in the saddle, glad she'd exchanged the cumbersome dress for britches. She gazed in all directions from atop Bead Mountain. Separated by eight miles as the crow flies from the Santa Anna twin peaks, the height afforded an unhindered view for miles. Little wonder both elevations provided the Comanche with an excellent communication system. Smoke signals may have proved invaluable against army troopers and unsuspecting settlers.

Now she hoped the height would aid her as well in outsmarting a tricky cheat. When she caught him, she'd ask about his involvement in those stage robberies. His quick disappearance threw more than a little suspicion on him.

A speck to the northeast aroused her curiosity. She pulled her father's spyglass from a knapsack.

Before she got it to her face, the sun disappeared into a black void. In an effort to force panic back into its lair, she shut her eyes and pictured pleasant things. A cool, clear creek on a hot day. A blue sky dotted with fluffy clouds. The teasing lips of a renegade…

Her lids popped open.

How did McClain get into her daydreams? Wasn't it enough that he filled her nights with tossing and turning?

She blinked several times, rubbing away the cobwebs.

Then as quickly as the blindness came, it left.

Raising the spyglass once more, she held it steady.

A paint all right. Couldn't make out the rider from this distance, but she recognized Soldier. None in the county bore a speck of resemblance to that horse.

They were at best a good mile away. She should catch him by nightfall—the perfect time to waylay someone.

A grim smile stole over her face and she patted the Winchester that stuck from the scabbard.

The sidewinder would learn a valuable lesson before the morning.

❧

Luke ate the last of the cold beans and hardtack that Punkin had insisted he take. He took a swig of water from his canteen and leaned against the smooth leather of the saddle he'd propped against a big rock. He assessed the rope with which he'd carefully encircled the camp. He sure hoped it blocked the path of cold-blooded, slithery creatures.

A family of warblers chirped loudly from a nearby live oak as they settled around their young.

The sounds reminded him of a similar night when he had camped with Jessie. Arresting his brother's wife had tested every belief in upholding his duty as a Texas Ranger. Escorting her back to El Paso to stand trial for the murder of her former husband had made him question the commitment to his job.

In those moonlit nights, when the silvery rays shimmered off her auburn hair, he fell in love with Jessie Foltry. Perhaps it had been the possibility of the hangman's noose that created the strong bond between them. He didn't stop to ask.

Her quiet spirit and determination to face what she had done and right the wrong of it, regardless of the outcome, taught him the meaning of courage. But her unwavering love for his big brother, Duel, should have nipped his desire in the bud.

Except it hadn't. Not after the jury acquitted her and she returned home with her husband and little Marley Rose. Instead, Luke's love burned brighter, if that was possible.

The ache of hiding his feelings from the world became as much a part of him as the wart on his right elbow.

Both he'd carry to his grave.

Off in the distance, a single coyote howled. Luke's heavy sigh blended with the mournful sound. For a second, he pondered the wherefores of the wild animal. Did he call to his ladylove, waiting night after night, and she never came? Or like his case, had Miss Coyote chosen another?

"I know your pain, boy."

He tucked his secret feelings back into the niche he'd built for them.

Eleven months ago, his conscience had warred with family obligation. Now guilt for the mess he'd created riddled the part of him he'd always considered decent and moral. He was no longer a lawman, but he still strove to be a good, honest man.

Partly because of his hasty actions, the Days stood to lose everything. They needed him. And whether or not they admitted it didn't relieve him of his duty, he reasoned. He would do whatever he could to help them.

The wind shifted to a more southerly tack and hand-carried the scent of wild honeysuckle to him. It brought to mind the fresh smell of Glory's hair. Did she miss him? Or did she breathe a sigh of relief to finally be rid of the bother? More likely the latter.

It surprised him to realize Glory Day had the power to make him forget Jessie. Or at least dull the memory.

Suddenly, a covey of quail took flight from a cluster of sumac and wild thistle. Soldier pricked his ears, stomping the ground nervously. The hair bristled on the nape of his neck.

Someone lurked out there. He'd faced danger too many times to ignore the warning. The Colt slid easily into the palm of his hand. Quickly, he rolled, stealing into the thick brush.

The fingernail sliver of moonlight suited his purpose fine. Hidden by dark shadows, he waited for the skulking varmint.

A needle jab in the fleshy part of his arm turned his blood ice cold. The roar of panic filled his ears as he listened for the distinctive rattle of a venomous variety. Nothing came.

He peered behind and saw he'd settled in a mess of juniper and prickly poppy. Thank God!

A slight rustle of coarse fabrics rubbing together slid the bloodsucking plants to the back of his mind. Luke pivoted his attention back to the campsite in time to see a black figure creep into view. It was too dark to see the face. The extra light of a fire would have helped him. But he hadn't wanted to announce his position with Perkins in the vicinity.

The intruder poked at the vacant bedroll with the tip of a rifle.

Luke crouched, biding his time.

At the right moment, when the culprit turned away, he jumped. They went down in a heap, jarred by the unforgiving ground. Off flew the intruder's hat and a cloud of sweet-smelling hair blocked his view. No hard muscles—just soft, womanly curves.

"McClain!"

"Glory?" He blew away the tendrils of hair that swarmed up his nose. The fresh fragrance attacked his jangled nerves.

"What are you doing? Get off me."

"Me? You're the one who skulked in here like a common thief."

No, he took that back. There was nothing common about Glory Day. Stretched out firmly atop her, he felt her racing heart. His toes curled from the sizzling current. Her heaving breasts cozied up against the hardness of his chest like a saloon girl looking to make a bit of change. *Have mercy!*

"Get off me, you lousy double-crosser!" She beat against his chest.

Christmas could've come and gone in the length of time it took to pry his fingers loose and lift himself. He battled with the need to hold her close. The bold way her body fit against his made him long for her.

With the deepest regret, he rose, letting her up.

She brushed off her clothes in a huff. Her withering glare might've killed a less hardy soul. For him, it would take more than that. Nothing short of death could wipe the grin off his face.

The evil eye she shot him when he didn't cower under the glare assured him she'd most certainly oblige if given half a chance.

He quickly plucked her Winchester from the dirt where it'd fallen in the scuffle. He wasn't taking any chances.

"Miss me, huh? Couldn't stand not having me around?"

"You're a cheat and a low-down liar."

"Whoa, there. I'm wounded." He'd reckoned she'd be mad enough to swallow a horned toad backward, but to come chasing surprised the hell out of him. Didn't she possess any sense to keep out of harm's way?

"I don't suppose you remember we had a deal? It simply slipped your mind that you agreed I'd come with you?"

The rise and fall of her shirt set his imagination ablaze. All that velvety skin lay beneath there. Soft swells he ached to touch. Nipples that begged for attention.

Damn! The honeysuckle still swimming up his nose must've pickled his brain.

How could a man fight against something he so desperately wanted? He struggled to pull his stare from her beckoning mouth and lost.

"If I recall, you promised you'd do anything I wanted if I brought you along." He meant his softly spoken reminder as a warning. The lady trod on his territory now.

She crossed her arms, gifting him with more of those looks that could hard-boil an egg in nothing flat.

"Foolish drivel. Doesn't matter now. You broke your word."

He edged closer. He wanted to *bother* her as much as she did him. And fire and damnation, did she ever!

"Are you quite certain?"

"I'm not bound—"

"Ah, but that's where you're mistaken." Luke's words came out smooth as velvet. The attraction between them was far more binding than any hastily spoken agreement.

Panic colored her stonewashed gaze.

"I declare our agreement null and void." She stepped back.

The rifle dropped from Luke's hand. He barely heard the thump of it hitting the ground over the racket inside his head.

"Too late."

A soft gasp came when he brushed her arm with light fingertips. It didn't take tugging or cajoling, she melted into his arms. Her surrender spoke of a need that equaled his.

Anything to oblige a pretty lady.

Tenderly, he caressed her lips with his tongue before he

allowed himself to partake of all she gave. He paid no heed to the fact that however much that was, it would never be enough. He'd learned a long time ago to collect each drop of rain. Sooner or later, it'd fill your bucket.

Ten

"Have mercy," Luke groaned.

He'd released his hold, yet his touch lingered, binding her more securely than the strongest steel.

Glory gasped. It hurt to breathe; it hurt worse to think. In one fell swoop, the cheat had managed to turn the tables on her again. He'd reduced her right and proper anger to nothing more than milk-soaked bread.

Dear Mother Mary!

The toe of her boot connected with his shin.

"That's for breaking our agreement, you double-crosser!"

"Ow. Let me explain, will you?" He rubbed his shin, giving her a wary glance. "And I'm not sorry for kissing you either."

"Conniver. Cheat." She jabbed a finger into his chest.

She seethed. Pure stupidity to think she could out-manipulate him. He'd shown exactly how unschooled she'd been in the art of deal making.

"My, my, such language," he chided.

Bless the clouds that drifted across the thin moon, blocking what little light it shed. It wouldn't do for him to see how his kiss had affected her, to witness the silly smile that insisted on covering her face no matter how hard she tried to wipe it off. Damn her lips anyway for their stubborn streak.

"Come here and sit down before you beat me half senseless."

The wounded sniff she borrowed from her sister. The song in her heart was all hers. Ducking her head, she didn't object when he took her elbow.

"I don't want the reward. My involvement with Perkins pertains to another matter."

He plopped on the ground beside the rock onto which she'd lowered.

A dull ache snuffed out the ecstasy of her first kiss. Hearing Luke admit what she'd suspected all along brought more anguish than she could stand.

"Why? Because you have enough with the stage robbery loot?" She hadn't wanted him to be anything but honest and good. And still, a part of her yearned to hold on to hope, however fragile. His hardened stare made it difficult.

"Robbery?"

"Masked gunmen robbed another stage today. Riders brought the news while I was in town."

"Are you accusing me?"

"I'm asking. You owe me."

"I swear I had nothing to do with those."

Was his sincerity simply another ploy in his arsenal?

"Then, why did you sneak off earlier today? Explain why you left me behind—if you dare."

"I can't."

She folded her arms across her chest. "I'm not budging until you do."

Not a wise move on her part. She eyed the Winchester he'd placed out of reach. Then she faced harsh reality.

She'd been woefully unprepared from the minute she first met him.

"You don't know what you're opening."

"Are you or are you not part of the stage robbers?"

"It's not that simple."

"Yes or no?"

"Damn you…no."

"Then why?" A weakness shook her.

If he didn't run out on her because he wanted to hog the reward, and wasn't one of the outlaws, there was only one other explanation. Jagged pain shredded her heart.

"For the reason of what just happened, that's why."

Why couldn't he have lied? She should've known he couldn't have any interest in someone like her. But darn it, he could've spared her feelings. For all her tough skin, she bled when pricked.

The moon's thin light cast shadows about the cowboy who had come calling, bringing promise into her lonely world. His features hardened. The dark brown of his hair blackened in the blending of the night with the mysterious gloom.

She realized she knew little of this man who made her pulse quicken with a mere thought. And even when she feared him dangerous, she trusted him with her life. Didn't make sense, and she couldn't explain it.

He hadn't apologized for kissing her. He said he wouldn't. Indeed, she'd ignored the warning he tried to send. The fault was hers. From the outset, she knew he'd take what he wanted without a second thought.

Stepping further into that pit of hell, she realized he'd made do with what was available—

A lesser choice…a discard.

Shame flooded her face. She'd brazenly flung herself on him in desperation to have one moment of passion, to know what transpired between a man and woman. And she'd pushed him into something he clearly hadn't wanted… because having his lips on hers was the only way to stop the raging inferno. But strangely, it had made the fire more hot, her body more achy.

"Damnation!"

The oath exploding from Luke made her jump. Lost in her own private misery, she'd grown accustomed to the quiet and the sound of his breathing.

"The true reason I didn't wait for you… I knew what would happen if you came. Didn't trust myself." Luke ran his hand wearily across his eyes. His voice lowered several notches. "I had to taste you or go crazy with want."

Agony cloaked the barely audible words. For a second, Glory thought she'd imagined them. Only she hadn't. She had tempted him. He just confirmed it.

She'd dangled the fruit in his face…a rotten, worm-eaten apple, and forced him to eat it.

No one had need of a woman who traipsed about in men's clothing, cursed at the drop of a hat, and when her vision was good, could shoot the ears off a wild pig at fifty yards. His words more than verified that.

"I'm sorry." The flint in her tone came from her damnable, wretched pride. Facing facts did that to a person. "Believe me, I came solely because we had a deal. I didn't mean…"

Lying came easy when a heart broke. But he didn't need to know that either. Or that she welcomed his touch in the way a daisy welcomed sunshine.

Or that he filled her world with color—and the musky scent of shaving soap.

"Reckon a piece of me hoped. So it was the money?"

"Yes." The lie was necessary. She'd not open herself further.

"Patience told me about the bank. No time to waste."

"You left because you felt *sorry* for us? Because we're losing our home?"

"Criminy cricket! Regardless of my own problems, I'm going after Perkins for the five hundred dollars so you can pay the damn note. Isn't that what you want?" His voice held bitterness she didn't understand.

"Yes…no." Her body stiffened. He could stuff his everlasting charity back into his meddling heart.

"Which is it?"

"I won't take a cent more than what we agreed. Another thing, if I can't earn it, you can keep the whole blessed reward."

He swiveled, disbelief written on his face.

"That's a fool thing to say."

"May be. Can't help my upbringing." She noted the stubborn jut of his chin and stuck out her own.

"You're going back. This is no place for a lady."

∾

With her mother already in bed and Hope doing last-minute chores in the kitchen, Patience tiptoed into Glory's alcove.

Her oldest sister's secretive attitude toward a certain brown book whetted her curiosity. She'd watched Glory scribble in it, wondering why she slammed it shut when she caught anyone looking. Must be something awfully important.

Though she loved Glory dearly, she hated the way her sister shut her out. Treated her like a baby. They all did, but Glory was the one she most wanted to be.

She pursed her mouth as she glanced around, checking for possible hiding places.

Why, she was damn…darn near grown. In five more years, she'd be old enough to find her a rich husband and move off to the big city. Far away from this stinky town and its snooty people.

If Glory did hide something, where would she put it?

Without a sound, she dropped to the floor to peer beneath the bed. Too dark. She looked longingly at the oil lamp on the small bedside table. Couldn't risk it.

A loud clang from the kitchen startled her. Hope would throw a fit if she found her going through Glory's things. She'd better hurry if she didn't want to get skinned alive.

She ran her hand along the floor, relying on touch. Nothing but dust. Disappointed, she lifted the edge of the feather mattress, sliding her hand between it and the sturdy rope frame.

Pay dirt, as Uncle Pete would say! Taking her prize, she slid the book under her nightgown.

"Patience Ann, come and dry these dishes."

Hope's order raised first panic, then her dander. One of these days they wouldn't boss her around.

When she got big…

"Don't pretend you didn't hear me."

That loosened her feet. Wouldn't do for anyone to come looking. She hurried from the room.

Hope turned and almost fell over her. "Mercy! Don't you know better than to sneak up on a body?"

"I came like you said."

Hope cast a suspicious eye. "From where? I didn't hear you. Nearly scared a year's growth out of me."

"Bare feet don't make noise." Patience gave her the most innocent expression in her arsenal, hoping she wouldn't notice the bulge or the protective way she folded her arm.

"Dry the dishes so we can go to bed." Hope pitched a cloth at her.

Quick reflexes and a left-handed catch saved the floursack towel from landing on the floor. The action jiggled the book. It slid slowly down, gaining momentum.

"Wait a minute. I hafta do something first."

"Hurry, then. I'd like to get some sleep before the sun comes up."

She captured the escaping prize as she sped from the kitchen. Hastily, she shoved it under the covers of her bed. That'd do for now, she reckoned.

"When do you think Glory'll be home?" she asked when she returned.

"I wouldn't know." Hope glanced up from her mending. "Why?"

Patience evaded her look, putting some elbow grease into wiping a plate. She strived for a casual shrug. "I miss her, that's all."

"Oh, yeah? About like a dog misses fleas."

"I'm not dumb, you know. She went after Mr. Luke 'cause she wants his help in capturing Mad Dog Perkins so we can keep our farm and so we can get our papa out of prison."

"Guess you overheard, huh?"

Patience gave a practiced righteous sniffle. "No one tells me anything. I'm not wet behind the ears. I've been dry back there for a while and I have a right to know what's going on."

"Sorry." Hope bit a length of thread with her teeth and held it to the eye of the needle. "I guess you have a point, but we do it to shield you. Because we love you."

"Well, I'm tired of it. I'm almost old enough to marry."

A smile brightened Hope's face. She put down the much-repaired petticoat and rose to embrace her. It felt nice. Real nice. Patience couldn't remember the last time her mother held her close. She missed that.

"You know, for a kid you sure grow on a person. Definitely too big to leave on someone's doorstep. Guess we'll have to keep you. And yes, you are becoming a young woman a lot faster than any of us realize." Hope kissed her forehead. "I'll try to remember in the future. In the meantime, we have to stick together. All for one and one for all."

Patience closed her eyes, savoring the closeness. If only Glory would do this. She worshipped her oldest sister.

Why, Glory could do everything. Could damn...darn well whip the biggest, meanest bear if it needed doing. And, she was pretty to boot. Patience envied her silky hair. So different from her own that looked as if someone had poured strawberry juice over her head and it left...a permanent stain.

"But do you think Glory'll be gone a couple of days?"

"Given her stubborn streak, I can't see her coming home until she gets what she went after."

She breathed a sigh of relief. She'd have the mysterious book back in place before Glory got home. Right after she read it. But she had plenty of time.

∽

"Wet your whistle?" Luke passed the canteen. The fact that he didn't drink first caught her notice.

Good manners marked a man worth knowing. So did the depth in his eyes. She respected a man whose gaze held substance. Even if she could never expect to be anything more than a passing fancy.

"Thank you." A full swig moistened the dust in her mouth, including the whistle to which he'd referred. His long, capable fingers brushed hers when she handed it back.

Her gaze flitted over the bleak camp and lit on the rope laid carefully in a circle around his bedroll.

"You don't seriously think that works?" She motioned to the folktale repellant.

Luke gave her a sheepish grin to go with the mulish tilt to his chin. "Haven't been bit since I started doing that."

"I suppose you did before?"

"No…"

"Then how do you know it works?"

"Just do, Miss Know-It-All." He slapped at a pesky mosquito. "Go ahead, make fun of me. At least I'm not twenty and never been kissed."

Heat flooded her face. "I have so. Lots of times." He didn't need to know those were *almost* cases. The taste of him lingered on her tongue. As for how many—it never paid for a man to get a swelled head.

"That's not what Patience claims."

"That sister of mine colors things with shades of her own choosing." Thank goodness for the night's cover.

Moonbeams bounced off the silver buttons on his shirt. He'd left the top closure open and the bib folded over, making a flap. To allow some cool air, she supposed. Or perhaps because he favored the rakish appearance it gave?

Truth to tell, the open collar lay just right to expose a powerful neck. Fine hair at his throat lay wistfully, seeming to beg for a tender touch.

He looked like a man who'd just paid for his pleasure and stood on the verge of plunder.

A heart-stealing cowboy.

A dangerous, forbidden attraction.

A double-crosser.

She reined in pestering thoughts, reminding herself such

fancying would get her nowhere. McClain had no interest in her, leastwise none of the lasting kind.

"You better head for home. It's getting late." His low drawl carried the same subtle warning.

She wiped damp palms on her britches and swallowed hard. She couldn't go back empty-handed. No matter what. Too many people depended on her.

"I never agreed. I'm coming."

"Oh, but you're wrong."

The announcement closed the door and locked it on any discussion. No mincing his words. Luke's deep sigh sprang like a bubbling well, escaping with a loud noise. Caesar had competition in the mule-headed department.

She could dig in her heels as well. "Only one way you'll get rid of me. Give me some answers."

Exasperation riddled his stare. "This ain't a bargaining table, but I reckon swapping a little chapter and verse in exchange for peace and quiet might be a fair trade."

She winced at the reminder that he counted the seconds until she left. The questions almost stuck behind the lump in her throat.

"What are you hiding? Why do you want Perkins so bad?"

The silence was deafening. He fished something from his pocket and stared out over the dark landscape. She grew more curious as she watched him clench the item. When he opened his palm, she saw it.

A tin star.

At last he spoke. "He has something I want."

"You mentioned you have just cause. Did he steal something from you?"

"Only my reason for living." He picked up a rock and threw it with force. Somewhere in the darkness, she heard it fall.

"I don't understand." Whatever happened ate at him. It put a hardness inside where there hadn't been. Having her father sent to jail had taught her all too well how much it crushed everything inside for someone to steal another's life.

"I didn't promise to make sense."

"Try."

"Perkins helped someone frame me for a crime that took my job as a Texas Ranger. I need to know who set me up and why. I'm assuming Perkins can fill in the blanks. When I catch up to him, I mean to ask. If I don't beat him to death first."

Now the purpose for his obsession made sense. She didn't have to see his face. The grit in his tone betrayed him.

"You're truly a lawman?"

"Not anymore."

Suddenly, he pulled himself to his feet as if the ground had become a bed of hot coals. He stalked a few feet and stopped. His intent gaze into the unknown made her shudder. A fortune-teller could look into a crystal ball and read the future. Perhaps in a way he could as well. She wondered if he saw her somewhere in there. Perhaps in the worm-eaten apples section?

"Forgive me. It's none of my business." Glory stood. She should head Caesar back to Santa Anna. Luke didn't want her here. He'd said so. She reached for her rifle.

"Wait. You should know the ugly truth. Then I won't have to run you off. You'll go of your own free will and ask yourself why you ever got tangled up with a man like me."

The heavy pall froze her breath. Strange how she didn't want to know more. His painful secret bore tremendous weight. She felt responsible, as if she'd conspired in the dastardly deed.

"I'm nothing but a miserable nobody." He whirled and the torment in his face stunned her.

She realized the instant he clamped onto her arm she should've run. His grief became hers, for it swept over her with the urgency of a wall of floodwater.

"Did you hear what I said? And I shade the truth. Can't even own up to what I've become. I had rather you and your family think the worst of me than see me for what I truly am. I'm a nobody. I have nothing. I am nothing."

"Don't say that…" She tried to close her ears, to block out the noise of his shattering soul.

Luke released his grip. "You deserve to know after patching me up. The moment I watched John Wesley Hardin in a duel with a U.S. Marshal, I found my calling. Then and there on Main Street in Waco I decided to become a lawman. But not just any—I wanted to be the best…a Texas Ranger, part of a special breed. I was fifteen years old at the time. Until a few months ago I lived my dream."

He shook with deep-seated anger. "They stole that. Some low-down coward planted a stolen army payroll in my saddlebag, framing me for a bunch of stage robberies."

"Couldn't you explain what happened?"

He continued as if she'd never uttered a sound. "I'll remember my commander's disappointment long as I draw breath. He kicked me out." Luke traced the tin star with loving fingers. "I'd rather be dead than not be a Texas Ranger. Lawin' has been my purpose for crawling out of bed. It's kept me warm in the rain and snow. I was… I am nothing without it."

She ached for this proud man who had given everything and asked for pitifully little. "There has to be a way to get it back."

"Only when, and if, I clear my name."

"Then that's what we'll do."

"You got a mouse in your pocket?" He put the badge away. "I go alone. This is my fight. Besides, you have enough to do. The farm, your father, not to mention your mother and sisters depending on you."

His dark stare made her dream of impossible things she had no right to even think. It should be a crime to arouse this flurry swimming in her veins.

Ha! She tried to imagine locking up a man for having overmuch charm and magnetism.

Luke touched her jaw lightly with a knuckle. A blaze flared among the simmering ashes.

"You'd best go. It's dangerous here."

For a moment, she thought he wanted to say more. Then he stepped away and made long strides until he vanished from her circle of vision.

Disappointment sent her muddled brain gallivanting in forty different directions.

One thing stood out in unmistakable clarity. He had it backward about her not having a reason to stay. She could name a dozen reasons against leaving.

Eleven

"THE GOOD BOOK SAYS, 'AND I LOOKED, AND BEHOLD A
pale horse: and his name that sat on him was Death, and
Hell followed with him.'" Reverend Matthews paused, his
gaze sweeping over the half-dozing congregation.

Movement out the open window caught Glory's attention. Quickly covering her mouth, she hoped to stifle the
gasp before anyone heard. Hope nudged her with an elbow
and cast her a puzzled glance. Glory gestured toward the
moving object.

Luke rode past the side of the church on Soldier. *The
man on a pale horse.*

Cold chills raised the hair on her arms.

Strange the way the reverend picked *that* scripture to
recite at *that* exact moment. McClain and death? She shivered. Too coincidental.

Then she glimpsed the limp body strapped across the
horse's rump and a sickening lump settled in her stomach.
A dead man. It could be none other than Perkins.

Reverend Matthews slammed his hand on the pulpit,
making her and the first ten saint-filled rows jump in alarm.
Those sleeping came awake, darting red-faced looks around.

The preacher pointed a bony finger toward the door.

"I saaaid, 'Aaand Hell followed with him'!"

Glory had never seen the usually mild man this aroused,

not even when his daughter ran off with a gambler. Some unseen hand had reached down and sizzled the reverend's hair, standing each strand on end. With scarlet cheeks, his eyes alight with a strange glow, he resembled some terrible demon.

Prickly claws inched up her back.

Knowing Luke's circumstances, she figured hell could very well clutch at his coattails. She shuddered to think of the horrible significance of the dead body. For them both.

"Good people, the time is here to guard against that pale horse. Death rides silently, a thief in the night." The reverend's clothing dripped with sweat. "It rides looking for you…and for me. To steal us away to everlasting hell and damnation."

She squirmed uncomfortably. If the preacher hadn't pierced her with his stare, she'd have bolted for the door.

Finally, he arrived at the end of his sermon. The strange being returned the meek servant it'd held hostage. "Before we go, I respectfully request that each of you make welcome our newest citizen, Dr. Ted Dalton. Will you stand, Dr. Dalton, so folks can take a gander at you?"

Glory jerked to attention. Santa Anna had gotten a doctor and no one bothered to tell her? But then, she hadn't been to town since she came to speak with Fieldings three days ago.

The newcomer rose. He stood tall, perhaps a tad taller than Luke. His dark coloring gave him an assured air. A quick smile. Nice. But not nearly as startling as Luke's.

"And also, don't forget to welcome Mr. an' Mrs. Sagen and their sweet little daughter, Josephine." The reverend pointed out the family who'd arrived within the month.

Glory hadn't met them yet, although they were neighbors. The girl looked about the age of Patience. She hoped the two would strike up a friendship. At least the family hadn't been in the community long enough to develop an aversion to the Days. Leastwise, she prayed not.

Speaking of baby sis, she had acted strangely ever since Glory walked into the kitchen yesterday morning after leaving Luke. In fact, Patience stared as if she'd seen a ghost. Now in church, Glory caught the girl's amused smirk.

She wound her way through the milling congregation toward the doors, wondering what mischief Squirt had gotten into. No telling. Right this minute, she couldn't worry about that. She had more important business.

Two more pews and she'd have clear sailing. Only she hadn't counted on the new doctor standing with his hand out.

"Nice to meet you, Miss…" His dark eyes reminded her of chimney soot. Soft and sort of clingy.

"Day. Glory Day." She found her hand lost in his firm grip. "Welcome to Santa Anna. I'm sure the community has duly expressed gratitude for your arrival."

His name escaped her. Walton? Walston? Oh Lord, why hadn't she paid attention? She returned his agreeable smile.

Before she could engage in further conversation, someone shoved. Luckily, the back of an empty pew kept her upright.

She might've known. Bess and Amelia giggled, each capturing an arm of the new doctor.

"Dr. Dalton, you must have Sunday dinner with us. We've brought enough food for an army." Amelia flashed her dimples, batting her eyelashes in some sort of secret Morse code.

"Yes, you simply must tell us all about life in New Orleans. We hear it's quite sinful. And we packed the most scrumptious fried chicken you've ever eaten."

Glory moved down the church steps and watched Bess tug Dr. Dalton in the direction of a shady elm her family had staked out.

During the summer months, Sundays were always dinner on the ground, literally. Custom dictated everyone bring plenty of food, and once the sermon ended, spread cloths on the grass. The gala occasion to eat and socialize broke the monotony of their mundane lives.

The varied shapes and colors reminded Glory of the friendship patchwork quilt Grandmother Day left behind when she took up residence on the other side.

Except the friendship part would've been misleading. The social circle shunned the Day family.

Glory hurried to their spot, apart from the others to help her mother unfold their best damask tablecloth. A lump stuck in her throat to watch her mother take great pains in hiding the hole at one end. Apart from the others, her mother unfolded her best damask tablecloth, taking great pains to hide the hole. Hope carried the lunch basket from the wagon while Squirt bossed. Glory had much more pressing things in mind than feeding her stomach. Besides, with panic whipping up a froth inside, nothing would stay put anyway. She headed down Santa Anna's main street.

"Where you going?" Patience caught her arm. "Ain't you gonna have lunch? Mama's got it all spread."

"'Ain't' isn't a word. You know that. You're getting too big to keep spouting poor English." She deliberately lengthened her stride.

"Other people say it." Patience skipped happily along.

"Mama doesn't allow it. You should know better."

"You're just being a meanie or you'd come sit with us."

Goodness gracious. She ground her teeth to keep from saying something she'd regret. "I'm not interested in eating."

"But where you going?"

"Crazy, that's where I'm headed if you don't quit pestering me. Now get your little self back to Mama and Hope."

"I bet you're gonna go see Mr. Luke. I saw him ride by the church. You're sweet on him. I know you are."

She froze in her tracks, glaring at the pigtailed pest.

"Why you would think that, I've no idea. I'm merely taking a walk and it's none of your business where." Anger that Patience hit on the truth made her lash out. "For the last time, please do as you're told. I'll see you later."

There went that pout.

"I'll tell Mama on you."

"I don't care. Just scat."

Tears sparkled in her baby sister's eyes. Darn! She'd only meant to be insistent. She draped an arm around Patience's neck and kissed her cheek.

"I'm sorry. Hey, you know what? I'll bet that new girl, Josephine, would love to be your friend. Why don't you invite her to eat with you? Maybe she'll come play sometime if you tell her all about Miss Minnie, Mr. George, and the babies."

"You really think so?" The girl wiped her face.

"Sure do. She'll see what a fun playmate you are."

"But will you be back soon?"

"I promise." She kissed the freckled cheek. "I won't take long."

Truth to tell, it would take only a few seconds to have their hopes and dreams turn into a wisp of smoke. One glimpse of Perkins's dead body and everything would crash around them.

Patience skipped toward the church. The poor darling was starved for a friend her age. Glory hoped the new girl took to her. Being an older sister, in addition to mother and father, sure carried a lot of responsibility—most of which she failed miserably at.

Unease clutched her when she turned back down the street.

How did Patience know she had feelings for McClain?

She'd dared write those secrets in her journal only after everyone went to bed. Her heart skipped a beat.

Come to think of it, she hadn't seen the book since getting home at daybreak yesterday morning. The chores hadn't given her a chance to look though.

Sweet on him? She had fought tooth and toenail against leaving Luke. She could help him if he'd let her. If he couldn't rejoin the Rangers soon…

You take away a man's purpose, you take his soul, leaving an empty shell. Purpose and soul went together.

Even though she told herself he hadn't meant to kiss her, she couldn't stop the glow the remembrance brought.

The moonlight.

The man of her dreams.

The magic of his touch.

Then, as now, her lips ached for more. He'd almost given in a second before he helped her onto Caesar's back. Temptation lingered in his eyes until his good sense took over and he realized whose favors he'd sampled. Didn't take a genius or the light of day to see the mistake on his face. Night couldn't hide that.

Good heavens! She couldn't believe she had kicked him.

She groaned aloud. Despite ignorance of the fine art of courting—not that she'd call what happened courting, mind you, and not having knowledge of the etiquette involved in such—kicking the suitor had to rank close to the top of the list of worst possible blunders.

He must've thought her the most priggish woman ever born. *Blast!* A second chance might never come again.

If it didn't? How could she make that one kiss last for a lifetime? And how could she pretend it hadn't meant so much?

At that moment, she spied Luke's horse. Worry multiplied. She set a pace to match her pulse.

◆

Luke squinted into the bright sun. It figured Glory would waste no time.

Stabbing pain returned with the knowledge she'd trailed him to the campsite for monetary reasons alone. Nothing else. She'd made it clear. Even so, he understood. Desperation tended to harden the softest heart.

She now marched as if Glory-bound and daring Satan to step into her path.

Dread swelled in his belly until it squeezed out room for hope or dreaming. The taste in his mouth reminded him of the nasty doses of Professor Low's Liniment and Worm Syrup his mother used to poke down him. Only that would be an improvement over this.

Damn! He'd rather face the business end of a forty-five than the bitter pill he had to force her to swallow.

It didn't matter what this had done to his plans. He reckoned he could live without the job he'd give his right arm for. Glory and her family's needs far outweighed his. And on the bright side, at least Max could rest easier in his grave.

By the time he entertained the notion of hiding, she'd already reached the stables. The sharp snap of her skirt against those long legs mimicked the sound of gunshots.

He prayed for a whizzing, deadly bullet to fly out of the air and end his misery. He wasn't that lucky. Suddenly, the honeysuckle-and-deep-regret posse surrounded him. No escape.

"I watched you ride past the church." Raw fear probably made her voice husky, her words cracked.

Just like his heart.

Glory glanced toward the body on the barn floor and clutched her mouth. "Who? What?"

"Howdy, Miss Glory." George Simon waved from a stall near the back. Rarely did Horace's father, the town's blacksmith, darken church doors. The man worked seven days a week.

"Afternoon, George."

She turned a sickly green.

Luke took her elbow. "Let's go outside."

The shade of a live oak beckoned. A breeze cleared his nostrils of manure and decaying flesh. Of course, that merely left him open to the fresh assault of a different nature.

"That's Perkins in there…isn't it?"

He worked his tongue, hoping for a bit of moisture. Sweet-smelling flowers and stonewashed eyes. A lethal combination.

The panic sitting in them now made them more blue than the deepest ocean. And a thousand times more unsafe. A fellow could drown in them if he didn't watch out. There had to be worse things that could happen.

"McClain?"

He hauled his thoughts from the danger.

"I wish... Damn!" He stared miserably at the toes of his boots.

"You didn't have to kill him. You knew we had to bring him in alive to collect the reward. How could you?" The quiver in her voice amplified her disappointment.

Reproach sat heavily between them. He couldn't look at her, couldn't bear to see the defeat in her pretty eyes.

"If you think I'd do that, then you don't know me very well." Luke lifted his hat and ran his fingers through his hair before jamming the sweat-stained Stetson back on his head. "Found him hanging from a tree, the body still warm. He hadn't been there long when I cut him down."

"I didn't mean what I said. I'm just so tired of carrying this load."

"If only I'd gotten there a few minutes earlier." He jammed a hand into his pocket and gripped Max's tin star. Though he tried, he couldn't keep the anger or the sarcasm from charging in. "That's the story of my life. Always too late. Never there when it counts."

Doomed to be second best. Not only to his big brother, Duel, not only to law work, but second to love as well.

Glory touched his arm. He dared a glance and found the forlorn sadness he'd expected. But not defeat. Pride and more than a glimmer of determination blazed. A marvelous thing had the situation not been so grim.

"Seems I'm forever accusing." She swung away.

The soft swish of her faded Sunday dress and the brilliant gold of her hair caressed by the sun's rays worsened the ache that ran all the way down to his boots. What he wouldn't give to make her his own. But what could he ask her to share? Disgrace and poverty didn't entice too many ladies.

"What do we do now?"

Her murmur almost got lost before it reached him.

He left the hunk of metal in his pocket when he withdrew his hand. He shrugged his shoulders, afraid to trust his voice.

Glory answered her own question. "You know, we'll survive. Don't have an inkling how, but we will. It's you

I'm worried about. How can you go on without your
North Star to guide you?"

His North Star? That she would be more concerned
about him than where her family laid their heads renewed
his faith.

If Glory could see a speck of hope in the situation, he
could rise above despair as well. One man had the information he needed; surely there were others.

And he didn't quite know how, but he'd darn well make
sure she kept her home. Some way.

"Reckon I'll just follow the sun and the moon until I
find it again. Shouldn't be too hard. Besides, I'm used to
things not being the way they should. Wouldn't know any
other way."

He edged toward her until his boots brushed the hem of
her dress. Her eyes widened, yet she didn't move a muscle.
The heady scent of her might as well have been hot lead.
Her nearness rendered him incapable of hearing the warning his heart tried to send.

This light-headed, woozy sensation mystified him. Not
possible. He didn't love anyone but Jessie. He'd sworn it
beneath a moonlit Texas sky after he'd carved her name on
a tree trunk.

But yet, he had this strange yearning to taste another's
lips. The pestering thought held on, refusing to let go. He
lowered his head into the scented, silky web.

Never had he thought he'd fall into a snare so willingly
or with such pleasure.

Patience hollered from across the street. "Glory! Mama
said for you to get your fanny back to the church."

Twelve

GLORY SILENTLY CUSSED A BLUE STREAK. A FLY IN THE OINT-
ment again. Patience couldn't find an end to her meddling.

"Yoo-hoo, Mr. Luke!"

Squirt skipped toward them, her arms flapping. A
thousand wonders she didn't take flight. It wasn't from
lack of trying. Glory decided the girl with glossy brown
curls keeping pace beside her had to be none other than
Josephine Sagen.

Luke's breath tickled her ear.

Mere inches away, a wry grin flitted across his features,
revealing his white teeth, before vanishing. The day-old
stubble and the smell of campfire lingered much too close for
comfort. Her stomach lurched with the same bittersweet pain.

"A smudge on your face."

He brushed her jaw with the lightest of fingertips before
stepping away.

Embarrassment crawled up her spine. His sole interest appeared relegated to a blob of dirt she'd managed to
collect. Simple as that. Humiliation penetrated her poor
befuddled brain. She must've sat through church with a
grimy spot shining away. Proud as punch. Folks probably
thought she hadn't washed in God knows when.

Heat stung her cheeks. No wonder Bess and Amelia had
given her a shove. An inward groan rumbled in her throat.

Hellfire and damnation!

The new doctor probably thought her the town's poor chimney sweep. What an impression she'd made, including just now.

Remembering the tears her hasty words had brought to her sister's eyes earlier, Glory softened her admonishment. "I asked you to leave me be, honey."

Patience shrugged. "Just doing what Mama said. Cain't blame me."

"Hey there, Punkin. Who you got with you?" If Luke wasn't so friendly to the chatterbox, she'd quit being a bother. Didn't he know Patience took his warm smile as encouragement?

"This is Josie. She's my new best friend."

"Glad to meet you, Josie." He offered his hand to Patience's friend. "You just move here?"

"Yessir."

Just when Glory thought the emotions twisting this way and that couldn't get any worse, a glow slowly rose from her chest. That Luke could make even small, lonely girls believe he'd been waiting in this spot just to speak with them complemented his character. How could she have thought ill of him?

Sudden tears hovered. She would never let him know she misinterpreted his friendly nature as anything else. She turned to take her battered dignity back to the church and ran into Charlie Gimble. The rumpled tablet in his hand played tag with the wind.

"Afternoon, Glory. Young ladies." The man cast them an ink-stained smile. Glory grimly thought if he'd arrived a few minutes earlier, they could've compared smudges.

With pencil poised, Charlie turned to Luke. "Are you McClain?"

"Could be." Luke walked toward the stable.

"Wait. I heard you have a story."

"News travels faster'n a herd of young cow ponies. Reckon you'd be the local newsmonger."

Charlie remained unfazed. "In the flesh. This ol' nose can smell a headline a mile away."

"Do tell." Luke arched an eyebrow. "I'd hate like heck to disappoint you. Nothing to report."

Patience giggled. "Oh, Mr. Luke. It's all over town how you brought in Mad Dog Perkins." The girl favored Charlie with elevated importance. "I know it's true, Mr. Gimble. He told me he's a lawman. Mr. Luke could've captured Perkins a lot sooner if Glory hadn't shot him in the leg."

Glory dodged the startled glance her longtime friend lobbed her way by finding that her shoes needed a good dusting and couldn't wait another second.

Murdering would be too good. The meddling child stuck out her tongue, completely unconcerned.

No doubt Charlie would want full details of her accidental debacle at the earliest opportunity. Something she wasn't ready to divulge. If those facts came out, she didn't see how she could keep Luke's secret. The newspaperman had the skills of a bloodhound.

"Mad Dog Perkins, eh?" Charlie eyeballed Luke over the top of the horn-rims perched on the end of his nose and scribbled something on the pad. "You kill him, McClain? And for the record, what kind of lawman are you?"

Luke's anger flashed. "You tell me, since everyone seems to know more than I do."

That sister of hers had opened a can of worms. How to put the lid back on without spilling them would take fancy footwork.

"Just doing my job. Folks look to me for information."

"Charlie, all you need to know is that McClain found Mad Dog Perkins strung up in a tree. As the Christian thing to do, he cut him down and brought him in. That's every bit of his involvement." She accepted Luke's silent thanks for attempting to lure the editor down another path.

"Kinda cut-and-dried, isn't it?"

"That's the way of it. I hope you're not one who shades the truth to peddle your papers."

Luke had added flint to this warning.

Charlie blustered. "I take offense to that, mister. I'm an honest newsman. Don't have any need to print lies."

"He didn't mean you'd stoop to that, Charlie," Glory said hurriedly to soothe his ruffled feathers. "Whoever helped Perkins meet his Maker is a mystery to us. Not that it should shock a body. Half the folks in the county would love to take credit. The rotten man gave skunks a bad name."

"I agree. No one should raise objections to making sure thanks go to the right person." Like a dog after a bone, Charlie wouldn't let go. "What kind of lawman are you?"

Patience opened her mouth, but before a word could spew forth, Glory gripped her arm.

"Ow!"

"He's the sort you don't want to mess with." Glory slipped her arm through Charlie's, ignoring the fact that her dress swished against a streak of ink on his britches leg. A little more dirt wouldn't hurt her, she reckoned. She'd already ruined what little reputation she had. "It's not important. You know, I'll bet you haven't eaten lunch. Mama and Hope have brought a whole basket of food."

Gimble tried to swivel back to Luke. "McClain, would you know anything about the rash of stage robberies?"

Glory tugged him toward the throng at the church. "I know you're dying for a piece of Hope's mince pie."

"Mince pie?" Charlie's eyes sparkled like fool's gold.

Thank goodness. He was the only man in the county who could be bought and sold with a piece of pie.

Not chattering like a magpie for once, Patience and her new friend Josie walked beside Glory.

Though she didn't dare glance back, she suspected Luke wore a relieved look. She'd hide his secret. The least she could do for a perfect stranger whose sinfully divine kisses gave her pause to consider certain advantages of wanton behavior.

In fact, she was so eagerly engaged in contemplating the unlikely that a light touch took her by surprise. Patience had slid her fingers inside Glory's. Her inquiring gaze met a happy smile. Warm affection sneaked past and over the wall. The squirt did have a lovable side. Glory returned the light squeeze. Maybe her sister didn't mean to get on her nerves.

"All right, Glory, what's this I hear about you shootin' McClain? Sounds like a juicy tale to me." Charlie's pointed squint made her fidget.

"She—" Patience began, only to be squelched by a hand over her mouth. "Ow. You're mean." She jerked away. "Come on, Josie. I'm gonna tell."

With a stab of remorse, Glory watched the two girls run in her mother's direction.

"Now, what was that about?"

"Nothing, Charlie. You know Patience."

"She claims you shot McClain. Come clean."

"Again, a dead-end trail." Innocently, she jiggled her hooked fish. "Mince is the only thing that nose of yours smells."

He glared. "But after the pie, I'm gonna insist on a few straight answers."

The dark smudge across his cheek was too tempting. She pulled a handkerchief from her pocket and wiped off the ink.

"Wouldn't have it any other way, Charlie Gimble."

For good measure, she rubbed her own face. Just in case.

   ⤳

Luke found himself staring after Glory and company. That she wiggled in the most interesting way didn't escape his notice. Everything about the eldest Day sister appealed to him.

Take how she wrapped Gimble around her little finger. The man never stood a chance.

Speaking of which, he pondered the likelihood of wrapping her in his arms and charming away the wrinkles that marred her smooth forehead. The faint smell of honeysuckle still wafted in the air, a haunting reminder of her presence.

As if he needed his memory refreshed. Ever since he first met her, he only had to close his eyes to sketch every detail of her face.

Yep, every last indentation and freckle.

Were things different…

But he couldn't change the events.

Or the fact that he'd done nothing to deserve her loyalty. Since Glory had opened up her family's home to him, he'd heaped more problems on her. That she protected his ego… Well, he could never repay that. One word would've hammered the last nail in his pride. Whoever framed him had knocked him to his knees.

Resolve tightened in his chest. He stared hard down the wagon-rutted street. No one would ever do that to him again.

Damn if they'd steal his right to defend himself.

Footsteps approached. He recognized George Simon by the rank odor.

"Shore is a mighty fine-looking woman."

He fought the urge to warn the blacksmith to keep his eyes on his horses' rumps and quit admiring the shape of Glory's backside.

"Got an undertaker in this town?"

"Cap Bailey. He's the town barber, dentist, undertaker, and spittoon cleaner."

"Know where I can find him?"

"Reckon he and the missus is down at the church."

That figured. Half the whole darn town was.

Rather than shock the ladies' sensibilities by carrying a dead body into their midst, he'd best bring Bailey back to the stables. Without another word to Simon, he strode toward the noisy gathering.

A quick glance located the Day family. He fully meant to avoid their spread, since the nosy editor had plopped down in the middle of the damask tablecloth, ink and all. But the sight of Glory standing apart with a stranger changed his course. The man held her hand much too boldly for his taste. Besides, he had no idea what this Bailey fellow looked like. More the reason to interrupt.

"Miss Glory, may I have a moment?" He gave the stranger the same frown he reserved for outlaws, horse thieves, and ones he most took exception to.

She jerked back her hand, breaking the conversation in midsentence. "I'm sorry, we'll have to resume this later."

Over Luke's dead body, she would. The stranger clearly encroached where he wasn't wanted. And Luke didn't like the blush on her cheeks one bit either.

"Mr. McClain, how nice of you to join us. Meet Santa Anna's newest, Dr. Ted Dalton."

He grudgingly gave the man's outstretched hand a mere brush. "Welcome to the community. Perchance is there a Mrs. Dalton?"

"Luke, how rude!"

Dr. Dalton chuckled. "Afraid I haven't been that lucky."

Luke bit back a curse. How could he match up against a man of learning? He watched the competitor tip his hat in Glory's direction. Why it galled him he couldn't say.

Maybe because she deserved the best, which might not include a nobody, but it also left out dandies too.

"Miss Day, drop by my office the next time you're in town and we'll see about…er, that matter we were discussing."

Glory's small hand on his arm prevented him from blurting out what the doctor could do with his offers.

"What was it you wanted, McClain?"

He didn't speak until they were well out of range. "May I inquire as to the nature of your business with that man?"

"You may not! It's private."

"Just asking. No need to get persnickety."

"What is so urgent that you'd risk another run-in with Charlie?"

Her nearness banished all thoughts from his head. He wanted to remember nothing except her lips and the rare occasion of a bright smile.

"What's wrong with you?" she whispered.

"Oh, uh...the blacksmith told me I'd find the undertaker over here. I don't know him from Adam."

"Cap Bailey is with his family near the church steps. You don't think it can wait?"

"It's better to get this distasteful business over with."

"I suppose." Doubts hid beneath her tone. "I have to get back to the rest now. Can we talk about this later?"

"Depends on your idea of later." He hated to break this piece of news, but had no choice. "I'm leaving at first light."

Her brow wrinkled in surprise. "You're coming back though?"

Mere folly to take the question at more than face value. Other than making her mad enough to eat tacks when he left her behind, Glory had shown little interest. And only then because she'd needed his help to solve her problem—something a nobody was good at.

Disappointment lodged inside, making sure he didn't forget.

With Perkins dead, it suddenly occurred to him that he had nothing left to bargain with. No proposition, no arrangement.

Movement a few yards away caught his notice. The good Dr. Dalton smiled and eyed them from the blanket on which he'd settled.

Luke's gut twisted.

"You can't get rid of me that easy." He forced a light tone, trying to ignore the avalanche the pieces of his heart created. "Can I ask a favor? Keep my leaving under your hat."

Thirteen

LATER ENDED UP BEING RIGHT AFTER SUPPER, TO WHICH Luke had wrangled an invitation. That Glory didn't deny his request for a walk afterward tied his tongue in knots. The dying twilight created its own brand of magic in her beautiful features.

"I'm going to miss Hope's cooking," he managed weakly.

"Does your leaving have anything to do with the people who might've framed you?"

"I'd rather not say."

"Can't or won't?"

"Can't for certain reasons."

"You said you'd be back though?"

"Would it make any difference?" Luke watched her closely. Dare he construe the slight pause, as if breathing had become a command rather than a reflex, as proof?

"Just asking. No reason."

This bouncing-ball exchange appeared to have more of a dodging nature. He wished for courage to ask the direction of her desires. Except he couldn't bear spoken aloud what he already knew. She didn't desire him in the same way he desired her. And should he not return? His heart pounded, protesting the thought of never seeing her again.

He propped his boot heel on the fence rail and stared

up at the North Star. He'd found his, but notwithstanding some miracle, he couldn't tell her so. She didn't feel that way about him—and he had nothing to offer her.

"I delivered Perkins's remains to Bailey. He asked more questions than your newspaper friend."

"Folks are bound to wonder. Can't fault them for that."

"I can when they base the opinions they've already formed about me on mere speculation."

"Human nature, I suppose." She grew pensive. "Hanging must be a terrible way to die."

"I've seen plenty enough to know I never want to find out firsthand." Including some near rope parties in his sister-in-law's case. Duel's appearance that night saved him from having to put some lead into half the town of El Paso—at least the part intending to lynch Jessie.

Glory lifted Miss Minnie, stroking the soft fur. "I sometimes think about what happens when a body reaches the end of his life."

Did she refer to herself or her father? It frustrated the hell out of him that he couldn't make all her worries disappear. At least he had it in his power to help with one small thing after tonight. The sacrifice would end everything. So be it.

"Do you ever give any thought to what you'd want as an epitaph, Glory?" Saying the name that occupied his waking moments more and more gave him pleasure. If she noticed he'd started dropping the "miss" of late, she hadn't objected.

"Hell's bells! What a morbid subject!"

"I take that as a no." He settled his shoulder against hers, enjoying the intimate touch. "Don't tell me you haven't at least considered death when you're lying in bed at night with nothing but the sound of your own breathing for company."

"My day is filled with too much work to waste with idle thoughts."

"But what about the nights?" He let his tone drop to a bare whisper. "Are they filled as well?"

She tensed and Luke kicked himself. That was something no gentleman should ask a lady. An apology formed in his mind, but never reached his lips. Glory jerked away and kicked a clump of dead grass with her toe. The rising full moon behind framed her livid features.

Her angry words were clipped. "She lived. She died. End of story. That's all."

Despite knowing trouble when he saw it, he pressed. "You don't expect anyone to care, do you? Or is it you're too afraid to find out there's more?"

The tremble of her chin sent jolting pain through him. He wanted to hold her in his arms and prove life held passion and happiness and time for laughing. Ha, such boldness for a man who could offer nothing other than wispy daydreams. He couldn't even bring Perkins in alive.

He leaned forward and clasped his hands together to keep from reaching for her. "This is what I want—*Here lies Luke McClain, he was one hell of a lawman. He fought injustice and crime wherever he found it. He gave generously of himself to make the world a safer place. He lived well and loved hard. He will be missed.*"

"My stars, Luke! A tombstone only has so much room. You can't write a darn book."

That didn't matter a hoot to him. He had her smiling again. Did she realize what she'd said? He liked the sound of "Luke" on her lips.

"It is a little long-winded, isn't it? How about just the 'lived well, loved hard, and will be missed' part?"

She shrugged. "Don't make any difference to me. It's your epitaph."

Her brusque tone didn't fool him. He began to suspect a thing or two about Miss Glory Day.

"You won't miss me even a bit?"

"Oh my goodness, look how late it's getting. I'd better go in before—"

"Wait." His plea stopped her. "Please, a minute longer?"

"Make it quick, McClain." She turned to face him.

"Do you have a problem seeing?" he blurted.

The sharp intake of breath told Luke he'd hit a sore spot.

Her voice was tight. "I would think a fellow in your shoes would keep his nose from where it didn't belong."

Luke grinned. "Actually, I'm not as curious as my sister. Victoria can ask more questions than anyone I know. And then there's Bart, a good friend down El Paso way. He's a regular—"

"It isn't any of your business if I am...which I'm not!" she spat.

"Mind if I see for myself? Bet you can't nick that chopping block over there."

"I can too." She accepted his Colt, tested the weight, took aim, fired.

And missed.

Luke lifted an eyebrow. The unfamiliar fear fanning out in his chest was different from the way he had felt when he had to arrest Jessie for murdering Jeremiah Foltry. In what manner he couldn't tell. Though he'd watched Glory stumble on occasion and have trouble reading, he laid it to a number of reasons.

He hadn't wanted the confirmation.

One more thing he couldn't fix.

"If I had my Winchester...if it wasn't almost dark."

The door to the house flew open. Hope and Patience stood on the porch.

"Glory, did you have to go and shoot him again?" Squirt called.

He glanced at his flustered companion. "I'm all right, Punkin. She was only practicing so she could do a better job next time."

"Go back inside. If I decide to put another hole in him, I'll sell tickets," she told her sisters.

His grin died a quick death when she cocked the hammer, lining up another bullet in the chamber. He held up his hands. "Hey, hold it. I'm an unarmed cripple."

In reply, she steadied her arm and sent another chunk of lead toward the offending target.

And missed again.

"You want me to move the blasted thing closer?" He tried to joke away the look of devastation that reminded him too much of his father's grief when he laid their mother into the ground.

The withering glare left no need for words.

"How long did you think you could keep this secret?" he asked quietly.

"Long as I had to. I hope you're satisfied." She handed the weapon back to him, the quiver of her chin betraying the struggle for control.

"It's all right if you cry." He prayed his calm gentleness soothed her in some way.

"Tears are for weaklings, a luxury I can't afford."

Luke pulled her against him. "I wouldn't want it getting around, but I've been known to shed a few on occasion." Hell, he'd cried when Jessie rode off with his brother. He sure felt like it again right now. "Despite saying the only reason you tracked me was the reward—"

"I admitted nothing of the sort. And supposing I did, would it alter anything?"

That settled it. She had no use for a man without means.

"Probably not," he said low.

"That's what I thought."

"But if I could change… Marry me, Glory. Let me take care of you, of your family."

Shocked silence. Not a good sign and not something he expected to his first proposal of marriage. It made perfect sense though. She didn't exactly have anyone knocking down the door to help. Unless you counted the new doc.

She leaned back to look up at him. "Why? Because you think I can't see good enough? Damn, I can think of better excuses to marry someone."

"I'll take your load if you'll let me." He traced her proud jaw with a fingertip and lifted a silky strand of her hair.

"And what happens when you get tired of being saddled with a useless wife and three extra mouths to feed?"

"How do you know how much I can handle?"

"I'm not about to find out. And that's final. I won't let you smother your lifelong ambitions…not for me, not for my family, and not because I'm going blind."

"A man's destiny can change." His gentle rebuke fell on deaf ears…if he'd even spoken the words aloud. Could be his heart voicing the need to switch directions. "Anyhow, you don't know you'll lose total sight. Maybe a pair of spectacles would fix you right up." Besides, he had trouble picturing proud, stoic Glory Day as useless. It'd never happen.

"I won't speak of this again."

"I'll keep the offer open should you reconsider." He launched the request toward her backside, for she'd moved in the direction of the house.

"I won't." Glory stopped and turned. "If you have no place to bed down for the night, you're welcome to use the barn."

❧

"Here she comes." Patience let the curtain slide into place and scurried into the parlor a split second before the back door opened. "They didn't kiss or anything."

"Patience Ann! It's none of your business. And you don't have to sound so heartbroken."

"He wanted to though."

"He wanted to what, Squirt?" Glory asked innocently, closing the door.

"Kiss you."

"How would you know anything about that?"

"Mr. Luke is your beau and that's what beaus do." By her slowly measured words, Patience let Glory know that only someone who arrived on a broomstick from the moon would be so ignorant. "Besides, you're sweet on him."

Glory stared. "You're fibbing. Take it back."

"No, and you can't make me." Patience squealed, running when Glory leaped for her.

Hope blocked her way. "Quiet. You'll wake Mama."

"Tell that to our little sister."

❧

Through the first rays of dawn, Luke paused on a little knoll. He glanced back at the darkened Day house, which loomed like a silent, gray ghost by Red Bank Creek. The idea of the overstuffed banker taking the one thing the family had left filled him with rage. He meant to keep that from happening by whatever means necessary. The way he saw it, only one answer came to mind—he'd have to take matters into his own hands. No other way. He couldn't break his promise to a little girl.

Or the one he made silently to himself.

Foreboding threaded a trail from his gut, stopping only when it wound itself around his heart. Glory could barely see to the family's basic needs now. How long did she have before blindness stole it all?

At least he could do this one last thing.

He wheeled toward his destination and that's when he first saw the gaping holes every hundred yards or so.

"Damn! Soldier, I'm glad we waited for light or you'd have broken your fool neck falling into one." He smoothed the ripples in his faithful companion's neck. "Can't be gophers. Never saw one that could make a hole that big." He edged closer. Shovel marks. "Nope, a man dug these."

If they were fresh graves, someone intended to bury half of Texas and was working on the other half. Luke carefully guided Soldier around them. Just beyond a clump of scrawny post oak trees he discovered the culprit in the act.

"Mister, digging all these holes is dangerous, not to mention a lot of work." Luke made sure he had a clear path to his holster in case the lunatic attacked him with the shovel. He didn't trust anyone crazy enough to dig up half the countryside.

"Morning." The man wiped his brow before resting on

the shovel handle. He squinted up at Luke. "Tolerable hot day to be so early. Say, ain't you that young feller been staying over at my sister's? The one who got hisself shot?"

Cotton-pickin', the whole blamed state appeared to know about his accident.

"Are you referring to the Day family?"

"Ruth Day is my sister. Them nieces o' mine are pretty girls." The hole digger winked as if they shared a confidence. "Don't believe I've had the pleasure. I'm Pete Harvey."

"Luke McClain." He leaned down to shake the man's hand.

"I seen you riding into town with Perkins. You the one what stretched his neck?"

"Nope." He glanced curiously at the field of holes. "Mind if I ask what you're doing, Pete?"

Glory's uncle swung his gaze right and left to make sure they were alone, then whispered loudly, "Looking for treasure."

"Ah, I see." Luke didn't need a second opinion to confirm that the man had bats in the belfry. He whispered back, "Having any luck?"

"Ain't no need to lower your voice, sonny, not a soul out here but us. Haven't found anything, but I ain't giving up."

"That's the spirit. Don't want to keep you. Guess I'll mosey on." He ordered Soldier forward, muttering out of earshot, "Sure hope his brand of madness is confined only to the males in the family." What were the odds?

❧

The next few days brought a flurry of exciting changes. Alex O'Brien began calling on Hope, which brought a pleasing bloom to her middle sister's cheeks, and Patience found a friend in Josie Sagen. Yet, Glory could see little reason for cheer in her own world. Her missing journal hadn't jumped from its hiding place yet, the foreclosure date on the farm kept moving closer, her father continued to die, and…

It positively had nothing to do with Luke. He could go and stay gone for all she cared. She didn't give him a fleeting thought. Other reasons caused this black mood.

She jerked open the kitchen door, put a foot down as usual, and cleared all three porch steps before landing with a thud on the ground.

Hell's bells!

A mound of feathers wouldn't make her trip unless…

From her vantage point it resembled a big bird. Holding her backside, she got to her feet. Since her flight over the top hadn't budged the thing, it must be dead. She grabbed the feet and lifted. A turkey, sure enough. Puzzled, she glanced around for signs of visitors. Nothing but the sudden stirring of a barn owl marred the early stillness.

The bullet hole pretty much ruled out death from natural causes. Now who in their right mind would put a freshly killed turkey on their doorstep?

Her thoughts automatically flew to Luke. He did think them a charity case after all.

In his not-so-subtle attempt to take charge of the family's empty cupboards, he'd stolen her last shred of dignity. She shook her fist toward the road.

Just wait until Mr. Fix-It came back. Would he have a surprise!

Fourteen

"HAVEN'T SEEN THAT FRIEND OF YOURS AROUND LATELY, Glory." Charlie Gimble wiped away proof of the day's warmth with a soiled handkerchief before droplets ruined freshly printed copies of the latest edition. "Why is that, you reckon?"

"*Friend* is a loose term for McClain, if that's who you mean."

She'd rather not discuss that sore subject, not with Charlie. Not with anyone. In fact, she could scarcely bring herself to think about him. When she did, her stomach did funny things.

"None other, and you don't have to get out of sorts about it. Merely making conversation."

"I'm not in the habit of recording each stranger's arrivals and departures. How would I know?" She fiddled with the edges of the newspaper, keeping her gaze lowered.

It had been a week since Luke rode off on his mysterious errand. Since then, she'd found food on their doorstep three mornings. She tired of waiting to tell him where else he could put that charitable offering.

Plus, she couldn't get a blasted thing done for watching the road for a man on a paint horse.

"Folks whisper he's staying at your place."

"They'd be lying." Nerves skittered beneath her skin's surface. "He left. Said he had to take a trip."

"You know what I think?" He jabbed at the front-page

article. "These stage robberies, three in six days, that's what. Looks mighty convenient the way he suddenly appears and disappears. My smeller isn't wrong. The man's hiding something."

"Forevermore, Charlie. First you have him in my bed and now branded as a criminal. McClain is not an outlaw, a murderer, or a thief."

That he was a heartbreaker she quietly omitted. She only acknowledged that admission in the dead of night. When she couldn't sleep. When the night's heat rumpled the sheets. And when the sudden taste, smell, or sound of him reminded her that dying would be simpler than forgetting.

"You mark my words, a fellow harboring a secret is a terrible danger to us all."

Hell's bells! The only peril McClain presented was his knack for turning her knees watery. And although she didn't need his kisses to carry her into spinsterhood, they had been pretty memorable. For a fact. And, God help her, she thanked him for the marriage offer. Her one and only. At least she could savor the proposal even if he hadn't meant it. Nothing erased the fact that he didn't want her. He simply thought it was his duty to help her.

Charlie pushed back the green visor. "Something you need to get off your chest?"

"Nope."

Too many bothersome questions. She turned to the window in time to see the new doctor bound up the stairs to his office over Farland and Whitney Telegraph Service. No time like the present.

"I'll talk to you later, Charlie."

"But we didn't—"

Glory never heard the rest. She hurried before she could talk herself out of it.

The door squeaked, announcing her entrance. Ted Dalton glanced up from his desk.

"Am I interrupting?"

"Not at all." He stood and came forward. "Forgive me,

I'm the world's most forgetful at names. No excuse for so lovely a lady."

"Glory Day." Did the man have an eye impairment too? she wondered, glancing down at her customary britches. Or did he simply have a gift for flowery language and needed a willing ear to practice on?

"Ah! How could I have forgotten? I am at your service, Miss Glory Day. How may I help you?"

She suddenly lost her nerve. Now that she faced him, she realized the impulse had been a mistake. Besides, she'd not had a spell with her eyes in a couple of days—only once since the night McClain challenged her. Most likely it had cleared up by itself.

"My goodness, look how late it's gotten. Don't want Mama to worry. You know how mothers are."

Dalton laughed. "Indeed I do, happen to have one myself. Are you sure you have to leave so soon? It's not every day I get so pretty a visitor." He grabbed his bowler from the hook at the door.

She abruptly turned, seeking escape. The floor, the walls, the doctor's image blurred before dropping into blackness. She stumbled over a chair and fell into the open doorway. Dalton's strong grip steadied her.

Slowly, she got her bearings. She had to leave. "Quite certain. No need to walk me out. A man like you is far too busy." A keen sense of touch helped her onto the landing. She found the rail and inched forward.

He tucked her arm through his. "Why, Miss Glory, you mustn't deprive me. All work makes Jack a dull boy."

"Not necessary." First with dirt on her face and now she couldn't stand on her own two feet. Coming from the newspaper, she wouldn't doubt an ink stain somewhere. He must think her a senseless twit.

"I would be extremely remiss in my gentlemanly duties. Besides, I was on my way over to Harvey's Emporium." He bent to whisper, "I ordered a shocking pair of red galluses, kid leather gloves, and a silk ascot."

Those sounded like courting clothes to her, not that she would know. She briefly wondered to whom he'd taken a shine. Assuredly not her.

They neared the bottom before the murky veil lifted, allowing her to discern outlines. Peculiar though that the cloudy blur persisted. The returning clarity she'd had each time previously did not come. She let Dalton support her, praying he wouldn't think the tremble of her hand out of the ordinary.

"Yoo-hoo!" Patience yelled from across the street.

Oh, great. Now Squirt would think she had gone sweet on the new doctor. She should remove her grip and step away. Heaven only knows why she didn't. Perhaps she was tired of trying to be the strong one. It felt nice to lean for a change.

"Isn't that your sister?"

"What gave it away?"

"She's cute. You should meet mine sometime. Now, there's a corker. Maggie Mae can talk a gopher into climbing a tree."

Laughing melted her tension. "Thank goodness I'm not the only one whose life suffers from such an affliction."

They turned the corner and ran headlong into a gentleman emerging from the bank. The smile died on her lips.

"Luke?"

"Miss Day." The prodigal stranger tipped the brim of his hat, narrowing his eyes. "I see you missed me. In a general sort of way."

No mistaking the chill in the summer air or the rigid tone. She jerked free. "We were... I mean, Dr. Dalton and I had business to discuss."

"Funny name for it."

The man at her side appeared oblivious of the hostility. "McClain, isn't it? We met briefly at the church social."

Luke openly refused the doctor's outstretched hand. Glory must have turned three shades of purple. Just because McClain asked to marry her didn't mean he owned her or anything. She had a perfect right to step out with whomever she chose.

Giving Luke an eyeful, Glory slid her palm into Dalton's waiting grip. "Thank you for being such a gentleman and brightening my day."

"My delight. I regret to have to cut our visit short. As I mentioned earlier, I have business at the emporium before it closes. McClain, next time you take a load of buckshot, come see me." He patted her hand and murmured low, "Remember, I'm always here. Perhaps on a return visit you won't be afraid to trust me."

She lowered her eyes lest he glimpse her poor vision that would eventually render her useless. "You've been most kind."

Luke fell in beside her, fuming. He had a lot of gall. Her irritation outmeasured his by far. She restrained an outburst until Dalton moved from hearing range. "Your rudeness shamed and embarrassed me. There's no excuse for it. Generally speaking, of course."

And no accounting for her racing pulse either. The devil could take the man for all she cared. Dear Mother Mary, she'd not been the same from the moment he barged into her life.

"Hey, where are you going? Don't you want to know where I've been?"

"Not particularly." She set a fast pace. Then, she recalled the meat left on their doorstep. She whirled and jabbed his chest with a forefinger. "I'll have you know, the Day family may be poor as paupers, but we still have our pride."

"What are you babbling about?"

He had become an expert faker. The puzzled expression almost looked genuine. That wouldn't trick her, however.

"You can take your handout and drop it on someone else's porch. Stay away from ours."

Luke stood dumbfounded. The day had started out with such promise, only to have her toss vinegar over his news.

"Hey, wait just a cotton-pickin' minute!"

The thought had crossed Luke's mind she might be a tad upset, but she couldn't know about paying the banknote when the ink hadn't even dried yet. He jumped in front, forcing her to either stop or dust off the soles of her boots on his hide.

"I deserve to know what you're talking about. You can't throw rocks and think it's over and done with."

"I can and I will." She attempted to maneuver past him.

"I'm the one with a reason to get out of sorts." How was it the doctor, a brand-spanking-new member of the community, knew about his wound along with half the town? He didn't enjoy being made a laughingstock.

Her mouth formed a perfect O. Her eyes widened. "You disappear for days, leave food on our doorstep, insult an esteemed gentleman of the highest profession, and you have the right to get perturbed." She released an unladylike snort. "Figures you'd try to play dumb."

"Esteemed? Food? If I didn't know better, I'd say you tore a page from your uncle's book. I just rode into town!"

"Or so you claim."

She had to be the most maddening woman. The money might change her tune. Although he was still a nobody. Nothing he could do about that. At least not for a while.

"What was that crack Dalton made about hoping you wouldn't be afraid next time? Of what, pray tell?"

"Nothing you'd understand." She stomped on his toe.

"Ow!" He hopped on one leg after her, feeling like an idiot.

He finally threw up his hands in defeat. "I should've known this is the thanks I'd get for my trouble."

"Mr. Luke!" Patience waved her arms.

Horror kept him momentarily transfixed when the girl darted directly into the path of a freight wagon and a team of six. The hesitation lasted barely seconds. He sprang forward. Wooden spokes of the wheels brushed his leg a split second after he pushed the girl from danger.

Glory raced to her sister's side, kneeling beside her. "Are

you all right?" The tremble in her voice, the ashen face revealed the depth of her scare. For all Glory's fussing and fuming at Patience, she couldn't conceal her love.

Stunned for the moment, Punkin sniffled and wiped her nose on the handkerchief he handed her. Luke sat on the ground, his breath ragged and thanking his lucky stars.

Glory scolded her sister. "Are you crazy? They could've trampled you to death."

"She's all right." He stood, gave Patience a hand up, and dusted his clothes off before glancing toward Glory.

"And you? I can get Dr. Dalton." Glory hastily examined him for damage.

"No." That was the last person he'd want summoned. He wouldn't soon forget the way Dalton had held her arm. She'd not use him as an excuse for more carrying on.

"Patience Ann, don't scare me like that again." Glory kissed the top of her sister's head and hugged her close.

"I won't."

Dorothy Harvey arrived out of breath. "Is she hurt? I watched the whole thing from the window. I just knew they'd squish her. I swear. That freighter don't own this street."

Amidst Mrs. Harvey's tongue clucking, Charlie Gimble hurried from the newspaper office. The green visor had slipped down to his bushy eyebrows, giving him a comical appearance. Luke suspected the man paid no heed to things of that nature.

"What's all the racket?"

"A wild man almost ran down little Patience here," the emporium owner huffed indignantly, her hands on her hips.

"Anyone hurt?"

"It shook Squirt up but she's fine otherwise," Glory said.

"We need traffic laws. They have them in places like New York City, you know. If you break one, they levy a fine against you. Sure cuts down on riffraff."

"Oh, Charlie. Such things are for big cities. Santa Anna is a long way from that kind of progress. We've barely moved beyond open prairie and renegade Indians." Glory shook her head and aimed Patience toward Old Caesar. "Let's go home. We've had enough excitement."

"I left customers waiting." Mrs. Harvey bustled back to her store.

Luke stared after Glory. Things hadn't gone according to plan. He hadn't gotten a chance to tell her he'd solved part of her problem.

And there was still the matter of Dalton to set straight.

An abrupt swivel set the youngster's red braids swinging. Patience ran back and flung her arms around him. "I'll never forget how you saved my life."

"Any time, Punkin." He ruffled the top of her head.

"A bona fide hero…again? Seems this town can't make do without you," Gimble drawled.

Now what in Sam Hill did that mean? The newsman's eyes perked up as they had the day he hauled Perkins into town. Luke hated to give him reason again. But he had things to talk over with Glory. They hadn't finished until he got things straight.

"You should've seen how fast he ran in front of those horses, Charlie. The way he stood there shielding me, stopping them with his bare hands." Punkin paused to take a breath.

And slew the smoke-belching dragon with the jawbone of an ass would probably come next. Nothing like blowing the episode sky-high. He picked up his hat, acutely aware Glory had retraced her footsteps. No doubt to give her sister a stern talking-to.

"I think he's the bestest, bravest man I know," Punkin ended, favoring him with an uncomfortable measure of hero worship.

"I didn't do anything that anyone else wouldn't. Just there at the right time is all."

"How modest." Gimble leveled him with a sharp stare. "Heard you've been away. Mind telling me where?"

"No one's ball of wax that I can see."

"It is when high crime is being committed."

"Charlie, that's enough," Glory broke in.

Criminy cricket. He didn't need her defending him. What kind of man let a woman do his fighting?

"I can speak for myself." He thrust his hand into a pocket. The crinkle of paper reminded him.

"I beg your pardon?"

He regretted the instant flash of fire that turned her gaze every color in the rainbow. Brother, did he know how to arouse her anger! The toe of his boot found a clump of prickly poppy, startling a resting lizard. Damn, if only he had equal success with her gentler side.

"That didn't come out like I meant."

"Since I'm not needed, I suppose we'll go home and leave you be." She grabbed Patience.

The girl broke free again. "Will you come for supper? Please?"

"Don't think that's a good idea, Punkin."

"She won't stay mad forever."

"Come on, Squirt. I'm not waiting for you." Glory untied Caesar.

"Uh-oh, I'd better git."

"Hold up a minute." He marched beside her.

"But I'm not done with you, McClain," the editor snapped.

"Tough."

He caught Glory before she climbed up behind Patience. He pressed the paper into her palm. "This belongs to you."

She didn't answer, didn't even spare it a glance. She did, however, accept a leg up into the saddle. A start, he supposed. He grinned. Maybe he would claim that seat at the supper table. Couldn't blame a man for taking the bull by the horns. Not when someone waved a red bandana in his face.

With Perkins dead and Glory spurning his proposal, he'd not find much reason to hang around once he secured the Day farm.

That was before the other three Ds: Devilment,

Discovery, and Dalton—as in the most esteemed kind—and not necessarily in that order. The events of the day pointed out the advantages of switching horses in midstream.

Aware that Gimble watched from where he'd left him, he whistled the jaunty war tune that had been running through his head and turned in the opposite direction.

Fifteen

ONLY WHEN THEY WERE SAFELY FROM VIEW DID GLORY unfold the sheet of paper. She stared in stunned disbelief.

The deed to the farm! Free and clear. No turning them off their property now.

"*Dear Mother Mary!*"

"What?" Patience asked.

"It's a miracle." She squeezed her little sister tightly.

"What, Glory?"

"Wait until we get home." She tried to urge the pokey mule out of his slow meandering, but the stubborn cuss had set his speed and wasn't budging. "We have to share this with the others. Mama will want to get out the last of Papa's mulled cider."

Who? How? Questions swam in her head.

The who—obviously Luke. Her joy soured faster than a jar of dill pickles. He'd done it again…made her beholden. His meddling in their personal affairs obligated her.

She'd not stand for it!

Mr. Fix-It, Mr. Heart-Stealer, Mr. Meddler had stepped too far this time.

Food charity hadn't posed so large an obstacle she couldn't forgive him. Even though he denied having any knowledge, which she doubted. But after everything was said and done, she might have let that go.

Her mind drifted toward more tranquil waters as it was prone to do when she didn't keep a tight rein on it. The sound of his husky drawl lingered in her mind, a poignant reminder that being a lady meant much more than wearing dresses and possessing a real toothbrush. A whole lot more. She slid open the top two buttons of her shirt to allow a breath of air. She couldn't recall if ever she'd seen such a hot July.

No time for wool-gathering. She shook her head to get her thoughts back to the current dilemma. Rearranging things to suit himself and taking over a body's life didn't fit in the supplying-food category. It seemed unpardonable and downright audacious.

When would he understand he couldn't make everything go according to McClain law? He had a lot of nerve. Day family business meant hands off. Furthermore, she could walk down the street with whomever she pleased should she take a notion!

It appeared he didn't want her, yet couldn't abide seeing her with anyone else.

The reins slipped from her numb fingers. Paying the bank proved a willingness to give freely of everything except his heart.

Ol' Caesar turned onto the property by the time she came to the how of it all. Where did he come by eighty-one dollars and fifty-seven cents?

Charlie swore Luke played a part in the stage holdups.

She tried to make enough spit to swallow, deeming the dry dust as having more to do with her difficulty than the list tumbling crossways in her head…

He'd refused to tell her where he was going.

Three robberies occurred during his mysterious absence.

He returned with a pocketful of cash.

Damnable facts.

"Whoa." She slid from the saddle and froze when the next thought hit her like a load of double-aught buckshot.

He'd used blood money to buy back their land.

"Mama, Hope, come quick!" Patience flew through the door. "Glory done saved the farm."

"What on earth?" Somehow Hope managed to keep from falling in the collision with a Texas whirlwind.

"Mama, we have big news!"

Hope raised her eyebrows as Patience tore through the house. Glory couldn't speak. The ache in her chest went all the way to her ankles, taking root like stubborn broom weed.

Ruth Day emerged from the bedroom, holding her head. "I want to know what in God's name the yelling is about."

"Mama, Glory fixed everything. Ol' Mr. Fieldings can't kick us off our land!" Patience blurted.

"Is that true?"

Words failed her. She silently handed over the document.

"Hallelujah!" Ruth's face glowed.

Hope stared in amazement. "I can't believe my eyes."

"How?" the two women asked in unison.

Glory sank into a chair. Explaining that they couldn't accept the money—and worse yet, why—would test her limits.

"How is this possible?" Ruth's legs gave way. Thank goodness the rocker was handy or she'd have landed on the floor.

"Luke McClain, I'm afraid." Numbing cold seeped into her veins.

"But why?"

Because he took great pleasure in snooping around in other folks' lives? Because he thought nothing could flourish unless he had a hand in it? Or because he robbed for sheer pleasure? Which answer best suited?

Nausea whirled in her stomach the same way it had the day she watched her shackled father climb into the back of the prison wagon. McClain took her for an imbecile. That he misused her trust made the sickness inside rise, strangling the words.

Bless Patience for answering. "That's just the way he is. Mr. Luke likes to help people. Even saved me today from being trampled to death."

"Goodness gracious, what next?" Hope groped for the settee.

Ruth appeared on the verge of fainting. "My baby!"

"He sure did." Patience swelled with importance as she flipped her braids. "A whole team of horses could've sent me to my grave." She gave an exaggerated sigh. "I wish I could marry him. Especially since I saw Glory looking goggle-eyed at the new doctor in town."

"She what!" her mother exclaimed.

Oh dear, Mama had suffered enough shock for one day. Glory should've known the jabber jaws would waste no time. But not even the warning scowl Glory sent bought silence.

"Plumb shameful how she laughed with him, pretending she couldn't walk good. Batted her eyes like that feather-brained Amelia too."

Hell's bells! She reached for her loose-tongued sister, but Patience anticipated the move and scooted from reach. Who could predict what she'd say next?

Glory's face blazed. "I did not."

"Did too. I saw you."

Delighted to find herself the center of attention, the dope affected a flirtatious gesture with her hand. Wait until Glory got her alone. She'd give her reason to think twice about letting her mouth run away with itself.

Hope smothered a giggle. "I can't believe that. Not our Glory."

Patience went on. "Mama, I invited Mr. Luke to supper so you can thank him."

Glory's mouth dropped.

"Wonderful," Ruth said. "We have double reason to celebrate. Hope, dear, you'll have to whip up one of your special meals."

Patience wasn't finished. "Of course, he may not come. Said something about it might not be a good idea. Maybe because he caught Glory with Dr. Dalton. He looked awful mad." She shrugged her shoulders, the perfect picture of innocence.

Fire and damnation! No wonder McClain thought he could take charge of their lives with Patience being so free.

"My stars." Glory faked nonchalance. "You sure spin some mighty big yarns for Mama and Hope's benefit." She only prayed they'd take everything Squirt said with a grain of salt.

If not? The whirling twisted into a tight knot.

Though grateful McClain had pushed her sister from harm's way, she couldn't let them accept his generosity in paying off the bank—especially if the money had been stolen.

It was just too bad not owing the bank took a huge load from her shoulders. It was a weight she would have to bear again when she told McClain they couldn't accept his gift.

The Days were not a charity case and she would just have to tell him that. With Patience's revelation, perhaps the opportunity would come sooner than she anticipated.

"I've got to get a cake on." Hope bustled out.

"Whatever shall I wear?" Ruth sailed merrily for her bedroom, her headache evidently forgotten.

That left an edgy Patience, who judged the distance to the door with a wary eye.

"Go ahead, try."

Patience held up her hands. "You know I was only funning. Don'cha, Glory?" Squirt backed up. "'Cause I was. Funning, I mean."

"At my expense, which I'm not happy about." Glory stepped forward, blocking the path.

"I can trade something of yours if you'll let bygones be bygones."

She glared through narrow slits. "Is this a trick? What could you possibly have?"

"Something you want really, really bad."

"You're bluffing. I don't believe you."

"First you hafta cross your heart and hope to die that you won't get upset."

"I don't make deals with stealers."

"Borrowers." Patience licked her dry lips. "I only found it."

"Don't make deals with borrowers either." She tapped her foot, growing impatient. "What is it?"

"Promise first. And you have to close your eyes while I go fetch it."

"Forevermore! All right, you have my word."

"You promise not to chase or hit me or be mean?"

"Of all the things to accuse me of now." Glory had never hit Patience or been mean. She had chased her a time or two though. "I gave you my word, didn't I?"

"Are you crossing your fingers behind your back? Show me your hands."

Glory stuck them out. "Now, go get it."

"Shut your eyes and no peeking."

Through the teeniest opening she watched Patience inch toward freedom before shooting out. Glory went to the door. No sounds indicated that Squirt had gone outside. A few minutes passed. Just when she decided her sister had duped her, footsteps sent her racing back to her spot.

She lowered her lids in time. "Well, do you have it?"

"I'm gonna count to ten, and then you can look."

"I'm tired of playing your little game."

"One, two," Patience began counting.

On six, Glory's eyes flew wide.

Her precious journal lay on a table. She glimpsed a flash of skirts disappearing out the door. Glory lifted the book, cradling it against her chest.

"Patience Ann!" No doubt the girl had read every private thought she'd scribbled in it. Anger and betrayal churned.

Bad enough an outsider practiced a free hand in her life, but her own flesh and blood?

Heaven help her!

Nothing was sacred.

❦

Luke made a sweeping right turn onto Day land. He expected they'd shower him with appreciation for helping them keep it. On the way, he'd formed an acceptance speech for the occasion.

Their gratitude would lessen the sting of what he'd done.

Soldier's fussy snort jerked him from that memory. In his agitation, he'd brought the bit to bear a tad too tightly in the horse's mouth.

"Sorry, Soldier."

A soothing pat calmed the animal and he returned to his thoughts. Running into Glory while coming from the bank had given him an unexpected jolt. And he damn sure hadn't enjoyed the sight of her with the doctor all intimate-like. Time was, a fellow could respect another man's territory—that is if a body had one, which he didn't. He'd merely asked her to marry him because he saw no other way to help. But damn it all, she should respect the offer whether or not she could hitch up with someone like him.

The twang in his mouth had to come from the bite of licorice he'd bought at the emporium. He wouldn't allow any other reason.

Before the night passed, he'd get the scuttlebutt on Dalton. Even if he had to kiss Glory to pry it from her.

A grin stole across his lips and he sat up taller in the saddle at the thought of gathering that particular bit of information.

Patience ran from the house. "He's here. Mr. Luke, you came for supper!"

"Hey there, Punkin." He threw his leg over and swung down. "I see you recovered in fine fashion."

Patience wriggled her hand inside his. "I'm tough. I told Mama and she can't wait to thank you. And for saving our farm."

"She can't, huh?"

"Hope made a cake for you."

"That's good because I brought my appetite."

She squinted up at him. "Are you still mad?"

"Don't reckon I am. Why?"

"On account of seeing Glory with Dr. Dalton. She hasn't set her cap for him or anything. I know."

The matter-of-fact way she stated it took him aback. "You sure about that?"

Punkin glanced toward the door, then motioned for him to bend down. "She wrote in her private book that she's taken a fancying to you," she whispered. "I read it."

"Oh." He winked broadly, not daring to question how she happened across anything so personal. A few things were safer left unasked.

"Mr. McClain, don't let Patience keep you outdoors." Ruth Day stood, holding open the screen.

The greeting stole the words he'd practiced on the ride from town. Mother Day had scarcely shown polite tolerance since Glory brought him home leaking blood everywhere. Cordial and Ruth Day seemed an inappropriate marriage. He'd expected gratitude, but the change in Mother Day still caught him off guard.

"Mrs. Day." Luke removed his hat before stepping past. "I hope you don't mind me taking Punkin up on the invite."

"Not at all, I am pleased to see you." She hung his hat on the hook. For a moment, he thought the woman might hug him. Instead, she lowered her arms as if suddenly finding the appendages belonged to her. "I hear I'm indebted on several counts. Patience tells me you risked life and limb on her behalf this afternoon."

"I really didn't do all that much. She's prone to a child's imagination."

"And the deed to the farm? Surely we didn't dream that?"

"No indeed, Mama." Glory quietly entered the room. "McClain is exactly the one to blame."

He quirked an eyebrow, hoping to disguise the ruckus inside kicked up by the mere sight of her. The fragrance she'd brought with her settled over him in a fine dew, rendering him speechless. He wondered though at her dry, brittle tone.

"Good heavens, Daughter, that's not what I meant to say. We can't begin to repay Mr. McClain for his good deeds."

Glory flared. "Yes, let's not forget to appreciate how he stuck his nose into our business."

Cotton-pickin'! Luke scrubbed the back of his neck and forced a smile.

Mrs. Day's hand flew to cover her mouth. "I won't abide that kind of talk. You will be polite to our guest. Now apologize this instant."

Luke had a sneaking suspicion hell would freeze over waiting for anything so unlikely. And in a way, she had a point. He had overstepped his bounds just a hair this afternoon. But damn, he hadn't expected to see her on someone else's arm.

The alluring Glory had quite a temper!

His grin broadened.

Sixteen

BEWARE GREEKS BEARING GIFTS. OR STRANGERS IN THIS CASE.

Whoever said that must've known McClain, Glory decided. He'd no more than stepped through the door when he presented a bag of licorice to Patience.

"For me?" Squirt giggled, dancing in a circle.

Didn't the dopey girl know how silly she acted? All the more reason for her and Hope to refuse should he try to give them gifts as well.

"Miss Hope, for you a silk ribbon for your hair."

"Blue is my favorite color." Hope betrayed her by reaching greedily for the adornment.

"Mrs. Day, I have something here." He rummaged in the worn leather bag he carried.

Ruth put her hands up to her cheeks. "Oh my goodness, I feel like a young girl at Christmas."

"And look just as pretty." He pulled out a lovely tortoiseshell comb. "Something to help you stay that way."

"Young man, I don't quite know what to say."

A mist blurred Glory's vision worse than it already was. She didn't know when she'd seen Mama so happy.

In fact, she couldn't remember this much excitement in the Day household since Papa left. The miracle almost washed away the fact that McClain probably purchased the gifts with stolen money.

Still, she'd not accept anything for herself. He'd not sway her with mere tokens of friendship, even if he came by the money honestly. He seemed hell-bent on stealing what she worked her fingers to the bone to maintain.

She turned her back to the scene, anticipating her name any second. Just let him try to win her over with a present. He could hornswoggle the rest. Not her. She had her pride. Didn't matter. What she so desired he'd never give.

The seconds ticked by and nothing.

Did he possibly think to slight her? She frowned. Only the most despicable, high-handed man would ask for her hand, then trample on the feelings he'd stirred.

A sharp sting pricked her dignity. He considered her less worthy than Mama and her sisters.

The grandfather clock on the mantel, the wedding portrait of her parents on the wall became mere specks. Darn this sudden wrenching in her breast anyway!

A light touch on her shoulder gave her a start.

The hand surely belonged to Luke, for only he could loose this flurry inside. She blinked several times, cursing the inability to see what he held. At last the item came into view.

A toothbrush. A real one.

Glory whirled. Every well-planned, scathing remark vanished, not the mere footprint of one remained in her head. She cradled the treasure with wonder.

"You hankered for one of these the first time I saw you in the emporium. I also recall how you had to bite your tongue to keep from giving those girls their comeuppance." Quiet challenge lay beneath Luke's words. He dared her to refuse something she so desired. If she could.

Moral indignation that had burned so hotly before deserted her. "I thought you didn't notice me that day. You appeared quite taken with the…other patrons." She gave the turmoil inside a stern shake.

"Oh, I noticed all right."

In a Monday that held more twists and turns than a

dog's hind leg, his barely audible reply and intent stare added yet more bewilderment. Why did he have to go and make her forget her outrage? Awfully difficult to harbor a grudge when he seemed intent on filling her head with nonsensical things.

She stared at the object in her palm, afraid it would fade into thin air as the genie in the *Arabian Nights* had. Fairy tales were for children, not grown women who knew better. McClain couldn't be Aladdin—unless he whipped out a magic carpet. This night she wouldn't rule out anything.

"Say something, Glory." Hope gave her a sharp poke.

Patience grinned. "If you wanna kiss him, we'll hide our eyes."

Hell's bells! Patience had managed to give her one more reason for a good talking to. If Glory didn't die of mortification, it would be a sheer miracle. Everyone waited.

"I know you want to," Patience persisted. "Leastways that's what you wrote in your private book."

Let her kill the meddler now.

"What kind of fool would pass that up?" Luke raised her chin with the lightest of nudges.

Her legs threatened to buckle. Powerless in the spell of his gaze, she marveled at the rakish curve of his mouth. The essence of him wrapped around, over, and inside her as she gladly stepped onto his magic carpet.

One more kiss wouldn't hurt anything.

A sudden scurry of feet seemed in the distance. Glory's ears pounded. His frenzied heartbeat jumped through the fabric of his shirt. She sank into the curve of his arm because he stole her will to do otherwise.

The kiss that began with tender softness deepened. She shuddered under his caress, a piece of clay in the hands of a master.

Her feverish skin throbbed with some strange need she didn't comprehend. She only knew if she died in his arms this second, she would depart the world in a state of bliss.

When he lifted his head at last, she would have fallen

without his steadying support. She rested her face on his broad chest for a moment to still the dizzying whirl.

"Thank you."

His murmur came faint as a breeze through willows. Her hair ruffled in his ragged breath.

A few seconds later, she remembered where they stood and the liberties she'd allowed. Never before had she been so carefree. Or so warm.

"Good heavens!" She patted her hair, giving the room a sweeping glance, relieved to find it empty. "I don't know what came over me."

"Whatever it was, I hope it remembers the way back."

"Don't think this changes anything, McClain." She prayed the stern warning would wipe the pleased smile off his face. It didn't.

"Shoot, if I thought that, I'd have put my bet on the wrong horse."

"I'm still furious. You owe me an explanation."

"And yourself? Did the offer of my name mean so little?"

She groaned inwardly and lowered her eyes before he saw the answer. For the cost of a handful of wind she would stand before the preacher with him.

Darn him and his magic carpet!

Fact remained, no amount of wishing could erase the truth. Her father left...and so had her mother, though each in a different way. At the end of the day, she could put faith only in herself.

What hand of fate had flung him into her life? The man seemed to take extraordinary liberty in assaulting her with his presence at every turn with no intention of staying.

"I need to ask where you got the money to pay back our note and buy all this." The pain inside made her voice sound cold.

"Will it matter?"

Glory wished for things that could never be. To stifle yearnings that swept her along like a dandelion in a sudden gust would take more will than she possibly had. And even more impossible…blocking the knowledge that she could forgive all else as long as he promised to never leave. She gripped the toothbrush. It took every ounce of strength to remember the answer she must give.

"I must know."

"In my own time." He brushed her cheek lightly with a fingertip.

"Did—"

"Have mercy, woman! Did Gimble hire you?"

Only after she could do a sight more than melt did she dare raise her eyes. "You've involved us in whatever it is you do."

"Fair enough. First tell me what you were doing with your esteemed Dr. Dalton."

Anger put her on familiar ground. She rested her hands on her hips and jutted her chin defiantly. Magic carpet rides were for damsels without obligations and those who could afford to daydream. "He's not my anything. And I don't have to justify it."

"Then why are you trying to nail my hide to the wall?"

"McClain, you're bound and determined to stick your nose in where you have no right. Well, I won't stand for it. I'm the one running this household. So don't let us keep you from wherever it is you need to mosey on to."

"Fire and damnation! I'm trying to help."

"We don't need your brand of that."

Luke wished to high heaven he could make her understand that he had their best interest in mind. Unfortunately, logic and Glory would never wear the same shoes.

Hope chose that moment to step through the door. "I came to tell you supper's getting cold. Draw a truce and let's eat."

"After you." He offered his arm and was glad Glory didn't argue about it, because in the next instant she stumbled into the door frame. His heart lurched against his ribs. Her vision was worsening. *Damn!*

If he did get a bit high-handed now and again, he only did it because maybe he cared. Because maybe he worried about what would come of them if she went blind. Or

162   LINDA BRODAY

maybe it was because she helped him see what he wanted to be.

Luke couldn't tell her any of that though. She had enough doubts already. His conscience gave him hell for not explaining about the money. But he just wasn't ready to do that yet.

❧

Luke couldn't remember such an occasion. Everything a man could want—lively conversation, good food, and an audience other than Soldier for a string of stories he'd stored up.

Even Miss Minnie wore her best outfit of paisley and lace. She brought along her litter of kittens to join in the festivities. Discontented with Punkin's lap, they leaped onto the table, sloshing the redeye gravy.

"Patience, put those cats outside," Mother Day scolded. "I won't have them on my good china."

Luke contemplated the dishware while Punkin rounded up her brood. The set must've come from some war, maybe even the Alamo. His plate had more chinks and cracks than those walls after Santa Anna finished lobbing cannonballs at the Texans.

"Who wants dessert?" Hope rose. "Mr. McClain?"

"You betcha." He winked up at Glory, who had stood to make room for the butter cake he'd heard about. "Now I know two good reasons for a man to take a wife."

"You mean other than making her a slave to your kingly wishes?" she muttered.

He enjoyed the red flush. Raising her dander kept her blood pumping. At the very least he made it impossible for her to ignore him.

"Nope, that would make three. Glad you pointed that out. I'll have to add it to my list."

For a moment, the fine china appeared in danger of a few more cracks. If he meant to keep needling her, he'd better study up on ducking skills. After he left, though, he didn't quite know how he'd practice without her.

His senses still reeled from the kiss. No complaints from him that the attempt for a quick, lighthearted peck backfired. Keeping him awake all night would pose the worst ill effect. And if it prevented her from thinking about Dr. Esteemed, he'd declare the goal a victory.

"Mr. McClain, will you do us the honor of reading tonight?"

He tried to drag his admiring gaze from Glory's curves as she carried the dishes to the wash bucket. A pure sin for a woman to give a man these interesting thoughts.

Ruth Day cleared her throat delicately.

"Um...happy to read, Mrs. Day."

"Wonderful."

A proud glow covered Hope's face when she set the confection in the middle of the worn tablecloth. "Mama, I can't recall when I've seen you in such high spirits."

"Nor I." Glory delivered small plates and forks.

"We must celebrate like this when your father comes home."

"Papa's coming home?" Patience asked, returning from evicting Miss Minnie and babies. "When?"

A dark cloud squashed the joyous mood. Luke caught the hopeless stare Glory exchanged with Hope before she drew a curtain over her features.

"Patience, do wash your hands before you sit down," Ruth said vacantly.

"When, Mama?"

"Darling, your papa will be here the minute he finishes his shopping trip. And when he rides through our gate and climbs down, I can simply imagine the joy." Ruth Day dabbed at the corner of her eye.

"I'll make Papa's rice pudding, and we'll hug him and laugh. Yes, we will." Hope cut the dessert into portions.

An uncomfortable pall fell over them. The knife clinking on the plate seemed louder than a dropping anvil. Luke silently accepted the thick slice of warm cake.

"Mama, I heard you ask McClain something a few

minutes ago." Glory refilled her mother's glass with cider.

"He's agreed to read tonight."

Shocked panic hadn't exactly been the reaction he'd hoped for. He hid the ache it brought. He returned the startled look with another wink.

❦

Luke's deep baritone didn't surprise her, for Glory'd long known of that. It was his education. No mispronunciation or stuttering. He skimmed over the hardest words with ease. His voice lured her down a sinful path.

Glory rested her head on the high-backed chair and closed her lids, letting her thoughts meander.

The quick blaze of passion appeared to have knocked her moral compass out of whack. She couldn't distinguish up from down, left from right, or beginning from end.

Dear heavens! She wasn't some mindless Amelia.

Still, she couldn't stop herself from lingering over the episode like someone too long without food. This afternoon was one of those events divided by a before and an after—too innocent before and too hungry afterward to mend the errors of her ways.

The snap of the book yanked her back to the parlor. She jumped, wondering if anyone noticed her inattention.

"Ladies, I'd best make it back to town or I'll have to bed down on your doorstep."

"Aw, don't go," Patience begged. "You can sleep in the hayloft. Can't he, Mama? Please?"

Mother Day hid a yawn behind a lace handkerchief. "It seems a fair enough exchange for his generosity."

Just dandy! They'd never get him out of their lives if they let him keep hanging around. And when he left, which was an eventual reality, it would bring deeper pain than she ever could imagine.

"Glory, dear, will you see to our guest's needs?"

Seventeen

GLORY HAD TO SET SOME RULES. ESPECIALLY SINCE THE MAN spent every waking moment thinking up new ways to bother her.

August fireflies darted close to her head, mere specks against the darkness. Pretend everything was fine. Whatever she did, she couldn't afford to stumble over a rock, a sprig of dead grass, or step into a gopher hole. Luke would not use her problem to excuse his behavior.

She forced every ounce of concentration on the ground's shadows. And tried not to think of the man beside her.

It didn't take her memory's gentle prodding to recall how casually he'd draped Soldier's reins over one arm and how his saunter emphasized the carefree manner about him. Locked in a battle to preserve both her dignity and self-respect, she jumped when he suddenly burst into a whistle.

"Is that the only music you know?"

Luke stopped. "Does it irritate you?"

Everything about Luke McClain pestered her. Of a surety, his presence held the number one spot. Had she shown even a shred of inclination toward forgetting, the tenderness of his touch rekindled the fire. In another lifetime she could reach for what he offered.

"I can't see you have anything to be that pleased about."

"Depends."

He broke into a more lighthearted song and this time hummed instead.

Familiar agony pierced her soul. The melody was one her father used to sing while he did his chores. But that seemed eons ago...

When she didn't know about injustice or that joyous times could end in the blink of an eye.

When she clutched her childhood and entertained thoughts of being a lady.

And when she didn't know the bittersweet pain of true love and realize it came with a price.

"What'd I do now?"

"Papa...sang that."

"Didn't mean to dredge up sad memories. Have you gotten word from him lately?"

"I expect a letter any day informing us of his passing." She swallowed hard.

"Just tell me what and I'll do something."

"You can't! Stay out of our business."

A dozen more steps to the barn and she'd make it. Full of confidence, she advanced—and slammed into the corral fence post.

Darn, she'd forgotten the corner stuck out that far.

"Watch it, darlin'." Luke caught her before she landed in the dirt.

For a brief second, she let him hold her fast. A safe warmth engulfed her. So wonderful to rest. No need to struggle against the helpless fight. Locked in familiar arms, she could let go and relax for a moment.

"Let me help you," he murmured into her hair.

His tortured voice was strange to hear. No mistaking his message though. She steeled herself, retreating behind the armor that kept out hurt and betrayal.

"Help?" She pushed him away. "You've butted in enough."

"A little snippy, aren't you? What've I done?"

"Nothing." *And everything.* Rubbing her arms still aching for his embrace, she yanked open the barn door.

"Hey, what does that mean?"

Glory fumbled for the lantern that always hung from the nail inside. The darkness confused her memory.

"I'll do it."

Luke's arm grazed her breast as he reached past.

A sharp intake broke the silence. The sound didn't come from her though, for no air filled her lungs. Yearning and need had stolen the ability.

A match struck and the smell of sulfur drifted up her nose. She heard the globe slide into place. Strange how the dull glow of the lantern hid behind a thick veil.

"Soldier, let's get to bed," Luke said.

Icy fear gripped. How would she get back to the house alone? Territory she once knew like the back of her hand now became an awkward maze. Hope's milk bucket created a racket when Glory knocked it off Bessie's stall.

"You trying to wake the dead?"

Luke's quiet approach added to her fluster. Sulfur and shaving soap blended together. With an arm firmly about her waist, he guided her.

"Sit. And don't argue."

Glory found herself lowered. A bench creaked under their weight.

"Now, what in Sam Hill is going on?"

The more things changed, the more they stayed the same. Mr. Meddler could take a few shyness lessons. And she could take a page from Grandma Day's book: *Girl, the best people in our lives are like the best lessons—especially the ones we fight tooth and nail against knowing. Give 'em a chance and you won't be sorry.* Too bad Grandma Day never met McClain. His leg lying against her knee flung her once again onto the treacherous path she sought to escape.

"Nothing anyone can fix." Glory tried to regain control.

He pulled her face around. With her trembling lip anchored between her teeth, she could barely make out the features that filled her dreams.

"Not what I'm asking, lady. How bad is your sight?"

"I've had better days." She took a tremulous breath.

"You speak to Dalton about it?" The strain in his voice relayed anger at having to mention the doctor's name.

"No."

"Maybe some spectacles—"

"You don't understand, McClain. Nothing can change what's happening to me. Not one stinking thing." She ground out the painful words she'd dared not tell anyone, not even herself.

"Maybe if you try."

And maybe pigs could fly if she wished hard enough. Every instinct screamed permanence. She would have to learn to live in a colorless, sightless world. Somehow. Someway.

"Why are you fit to be tied? Why at me?"

She clenched her fists. "I'll not be helpless like my mother. I can't depend on anyone but me. You got that?"

"I haven't—"

"A stranger from God knows where, you come in here and take over our lives to suit your fancy. Doesn't matter what we want. Oh, no. It's got to be done Luke McClain's way. We're just a bunch of helpless females with half a brain between us. Don't know how we survived all these years before you rode in on your trusty steed to rescue us." She paused to catch her breath.

"So—I've done something wrong?"

"And then...and then when the thrill is gone, you'll leave just like everyone else," she finished in a breathless rush, suppressing the sob that lurked in her throat.

He'd leave and take a piece of her with him.

"That's what's bothering you?"

"Hellfire and damnation, yes!"

Among a few hundred other things in the heart department.

"Marrying me would solve most everything. I'll take your burden in the wink of an eye. Let me."

"Why would you want this? Tell me why." A flicker of

hope was the only thing that kept her rooted to the bench. Three words held the power to change her mind.

The tiny flicker went out in the silence that spun between them. She stiffened. He'd have to speak the truth aloud.

"Just say it."

A heavy sigh came while he apparently searched for a tactful reply. "Because you have no one, dammit!"

"A bit of candor at least. I see it clearly now. Out of gratitude for saving our home you thought I'd fall helplessly at your feet. Go ply your attentions on another. I'm no damsel in distress in need of saving."

"Don't know where you get these crazy notions, but you'll not make me your whipping boy."

The bench tipped when he stood. She grasped for something, not expecting to encounter his hand. She rose and jerked loose.

"I bid you good night, sir."

Luke felt the cool sting of her dismissal. Even so, he couldn't leave her to find the way back to the house by herself. Despite the pain her words brought, he moved silently in her footsteps. He cursed the cruel hand that would rob such a vital woman. She didn't know it, but she'd never be dependent on anyone. Still, he could understand the nature of the beast. Such a fear lodged in his throat, choking the life from him each time he happened to brush the tin star in his pocket.

Night swallowed her proud carriage when she edged from the barn. He moved swiftly, close enough to reach out.

In the next instant, a panther's cry rent the air. Glory bolted. *Damn!* His blood froze. Did she know she ran away from safety, not toward it?

Before he could reach her, she sprawled. Crumpled in a heap, she beat her fists on the drought-riddled soil. He knelt and cradled her. This time she accepted his comfort.

"It'll be all right. I'm here." He had to squeeze the words past the vise hindering his air passage.

"Luke, I'm scared. I don't know what to do."

"Shh. I'll help you figure it out. Just—"

"Accept your proposal?" She stiffened. "I won't be bought with thirty pieces of silver."

"I don't know where you get these loco ideas." He didn't stop her when she shoved him aside and struggled to her feet. "But I'm going to get you safely inside the house. After that…"

Another panther scream prevented further objecting. She meekly let him take her arm.

At the door, he lifted her hand. Opening the tight fist, he kissed the palm. "I'm not the enemy. Promise me you'll tell your family. If not me, let someone else help."

He released her hand and turned.

"Luke?"

He paused in midstep. "I'm here."

"Thank you for the gifts…and for keeping me safe."

"It's because I care." More than she'd ever know. He brushed her cheek with a light fingertip. "Good night, m'lady."

The lump in his windpipe grew as she felt along the walls to her room. This was a different hurt from any he'd ever suffered. More than when he watched his mother gasp for the last time. Glory went through the motions, yet she'd already resigned herself to a life of the damned.

He recognized that fact in her eyes. He'd seen that same resignation in others before her. And there wasn't a blessed thing he could do. She viewed marriage to him as something more distasteful than sucking a rotten egg.

Softly, he eased the door shut and stared up at the starlit sky. Leaving was the only thing left. But, before he rode off, never to look back, he had one other bit of business.

Clenching his jaw, he jammed his fists in his pockets and walked toward the barn.

❦

"Soldier's gone and so is Mr. Luke," Patience reported the following morning as though she was the town crier. "What's the rope doing stretched from our back door to the barn? And why are dead squirrels on our porch?"

Oh dear, food charity again. Always happened when Luke left. But rope?

Glory carefully reached for the handle of milk pitcher, praying she didn't misjudge the distance. "I don't know what you're referring to."

A chair scooted on the wood floor.

"Come here," Hope called. "You've got to see this."

If only Glory could make out anything other than shadows. The light of day revealed in full measure the face of horror she'd tried to ignore the last two months. Having disaster loom on the horizon differed greatly from having it knock you down and rub your face in it.

Her vision would not return.

Ever. She knew this to be true.

How much longer could she hope to hide her blindness? She pushed back her chair. Eight steps to the faint blurs at the kitchen door? Or ten? She took a deep breath and began counting off each one. Upon six, she collided with flesh and blood.

"Ow, watch it, Glory. Didn't you see me?" Patience whined.

"Guess I simply wanted to hear you complain, Squirt."

"You're just trying to be mean 'cause I found your private book by mistake."

"Oh, honey." Glory sighed.

The slamming screen announced baby sis's departure.

"What private book?" Hope moved briskly about the kitchen, readying for the day.

Funny how a few hours could change a person's entire life. What had been of extreme importance yesterday now seemed small and petty in comparison.

"My writing journal that I'd missed for the last week and a half. Quite mysterious how it fell into Squirt's possession. What did you want to show me?"

"Can't you see? The rope. Wonder who would've done such a thing. Or to leave a bunch of squirrels by our door."

Glory could hazard a guess.

"Come sit down. I have something I need to tell you. Quick, before Chatterbox comes back."

Glory followed the blurry figure to the table and fumbled into her seat.

"Is it Papa? Have you—"

"No, Hope, it's me. I've tried to shield everyone from the truth, but now you must know."

"What's wrong?"

Dread filled her heart. She hated bringing more troubling news on the ones she loved. They already had a mess load of disappointment to cope with.

"Promise you won't breathe a word of this to Patience or Mama yet. Swear?"

"I don't understand."

"I need someone's help and I pick you. We'll tell them when the time comes." Her matter-of-fact tone belied the churning that railed against fate.

"All right. I'll keep your secret if you say I must."

Before she lost courage, she bared the terrible reality.

"I can't distinguish anything beyond shadowy blurs," she finished. "And those will soon vanish too, I'm afraid."

Glory expected the silence. What she had thrown on her sister would change each of their lives in untold ways. Only in the days ahead could they realize the full magnitude.

Hope's voice trembled. "There are no words. What can I say? Except…"

Glory found solace in Hope's embrace. She touched her sister's face, detecting proof of her deep caring. Some things a person didn't have to see to know.

"I'm so sorry. I love you, Glory."

She cleared her throat. "I love you too."

"Now the tether rope makes sense. Mr. McClain knows."

"He found out last night."

"What did he advise? Did he offer…?"

That he'd give whatever she required—except his love.

"He thinks marrying him will set everything right."

"That's wonderful."

"It might be if I didn't object to being bought for eighty-one dollars and fifty-seven cents. My self-respect is the sum of all I have left. And that I'll not sacrifice."

"You desire him though," Hope said gently. "A yearning smolders in your eyes sometimes before you push it behind that curtain of scorn you erect."

"Blind or no, I won't settle for a one-sided marriage. It's all or nothing."

"How do you know he doesn't feel the same?" Hope softly challenged.

Her sister's delusions wouldn't make it so. Luke would never cherish her in the way a husband did a beloved helpmate. And he sure didn't see her as an equal—more like a helpless albatross.

"He doesn't feel anything but pity."

"You're quite positive?"

"For God's sake! A body can't compare the union of two people to an auction where a man can buy or sell animals. Suppose I accept, banking on his good intentions. What will happen should I prove more trouble than he expects?"

That terrified her more than anything.

Glory knew if she dared give him half a chance, Luke'd take her heart and run. But not before he destroyed the tattered remains of her dignity.

Eighteen

"OLD LADY PENELOPE IS DEAD? HOW?" THE NEWS STUNNED Glory, who'd ridden into Santa Anna this Saturday morning to sell eggs and butter. The entire Day family tagged along. Of the clan, Hope stayed by her side. They left their mother with Aunt Dorothy, and the Lord could only guess where Squirt hid out.

The furious clanking and banging of the printing press told her Charlie was in a lather. She waited for a lull, which didn't take long. Abrupt silence marked the time to talk.

"Someone hanged the poor ol' soul from a tree—three steps from her back door. They found her early this morning."

"Who would've done such a thing? At ninety and frail, she couldn't have harmed anyone," Hope put in.

"Except Papa, don't forget! Because of her poison, they sent him away." *And ruined our lives in the bargain*, Glory added to herself. Though she cringed at what fate had brought the gossipy woman.

"Where's your stranger, Glory?" Charlie asked.

Thick tension held them in a stranglehold. Unfamiliar distrust colored the question. In all the years she'd known the kindly editor, he'd never used that tone. Darn, if only she could see his eyes. Surely he didn't suspect she had anything to do with it. Perhaps his motives lay more or less in slinging a few other accusations Luke's way.

"I've explained this once before—McClain is not my stranger, stable hand, or sheepherder." She gripped Hope's arm for support. She didn't like the undertone her ears picked up.

The noise of the wind filled her head, a monster coming to destroy. She shivered.

Hope gripped Glory, her voice firm. "We haven't seen him in almost a week."

Dear loyal Hope. For someone who had amazing resistance to anger, she had Glory's hand in a powerful vise.

"He left your place?"

"Are you calling us liars? Hope just said he hasn't been around, Charlie."

"Well, he was in town yesterday!" The arm of the press lowered with a bang. "I saw McClain leaving ol' Penelope's, God rest her soul, yesterday shortly after sunup."

"You spied on him?" She knew he'd taken an instant dislike to Luke, but never thought he'd stoop to this.

"Sure the hell did. I warned you he was too close-mouthed for my taste." A screech came when he raised the top. By the soft squish, she knew Charlie had applied more ink over the letters with the roller. "The man ran from her house, jumped on his horse, and lit out. Left a lot of dust behind on his way out of town…and one defenseless dead woman hanging by the neck."

Air surged from Glory's lungs. After Charlie placed this edition on Santa Anna's streets, any explanation Luke had would fall on deaf ears. That is, if he hadn't disappeared for good. Had she driven him to the brink of desperation when they spoke of her father the last time?

She'd been quick-tempered and short, demanding he stay out of their business. By all rights he should've turned his back on her. Yet, he'd held her tenderly and kept her safe from the panther.

Her stomach lurched as the memory shamed her.

Charlie had the wrong man. Luke had scruples and integrity. Didn't matter how it looked. She trusted her instincts.

A killer couldn't make her feel the way he did.

"Ladies, hate to rush you off, but I have work to do to get this newspaper out."

"We've got to be going anyway. Coming, Hope?"

Glory let her sister lead her to the door, since Charlie wouldn't notice anything other than his precious news. Outside, she pushed away Hope's hand. She wished to hide her loss from everyone awhile longer. A stumble wouldn't appear quite so out of the ordinary, and she'd take that risk.

"Miss Glory, Miss Glory." In his exuberance, Horace very nearly knocked her over.

"Hello, Horace." She rescued her hat where it dangled precariously, scooped up her hair, and tucked it back underneath. "How are you today?"

"Reckon I got lotsa sunshine now. My eyes are glad to see you. I'm still your beau, ain't I?"

How was it she'd never heard the frantic tone submerged beneath the repeated question? Horace said the words exactly as he always had, yet she realized she'd never truly listened. In fact, her ears picked up sounds of late in a much different fashion. She seemed to hear thoughts behind mere conversation. Why Horace held this fascination with her or why it was so important to him remained a mystery. Some sixth sense told her she was his link to the real world. Perhaps if she broke the fragile cord, he might become even more lost inside his own head.

"Ain't I?"

"You surely are."

"Oh boy! I gotta run tell my pa. Goodbye, Miss Hope. Goodbye, Miss Glory."

"You probably shouldn't encourage him like that." Hope nudged her into the bright sunshine.

"I know, but we're about the only friends he has. I can't bear the way the town thumbs its nose at him." Glory sighed and moved forward with caution. "The zealous bigots. They won't tolerate anyone who dares to be different."

"Do you refer to our sometime guest?" Hope asked.

"Charlie has his bullets aimed in the wrong direction. He's no murderer."

"I agree." Hope's voice came softly. "A little bit farther, and there's a step from the walk to the street. Here's my hand in case you need it."

"Thank you, but I can manage." She hoped, grateful that faint shapes and blurs hadn't fled along with the rest of her sight. But she feared that soon they too would leave and plunge her into a bottomless pit. She'd have no choice in the matter.

A glacier slid down her spine and into her shoes. How would a life of darkness be? And when she had no one...?

"It doesn't look good for Mr. Luke. I wish Charlie hadn't seen him leaving the old woman's house. Step down now. And do hurry—there's quite a crowd at the emporium."

"I don't like this." The turbulence charging the air chilled Glory's blood. This was something that ate from the inside out, a hate she'd witnessed firsthand during her father's trial.

❦

Luke and Soldier rode as one with a single purpose. He'd settle one final score and then...then he'd make certain never to bother the golden-haired beauty again. Tightness in his chest grew and traveled to points south. She appeared to be lodged in his thoughts, and he didn't see any way of getting her out—should he even have a choice in the matter.

"Soldier, I hear a man can get lost down south of the border. Rancho Del Norte should be far enough, I figure."

Trouble would have to cut a mean trail to find him there. He unscrewed the top of the canteen, took a swig of water, and scanned the brush for his quarry.

Where had the slippery, murdering scum gone?

If he hadn't lost his two-fingered grip on the man's shirt, he'd have caught the fellow who'd hanged a pitiful old woman.

Much had happened since the morning he left the Day farm.

"A feller named Foster gave me twenty dollars to say I saw Jack Day rob that bank," Penelope Tucker had confessed three days ago. "Then he told me to keep my mouth shut. I did. Till now. Cain't live with the guilt of what I done, sending an innocent man to the calaboose. I'm not a spring chicken, you know. Reckon I'd like to clear the slate before I get called."

Luke left that day not dreaming they'd take her life before he returned. He'd ridden to Abilene intending to get the U.S. Marshal to come verify her claims. A day late and a dollar short on that account.

"Ambushed and kilt," a man told him of the marshal's fate.

Telegraphing for help left him the last card to play. But that, too, had been for naught. Someone had silenced Penelope Tucker by the time he returned. What had been the good of his efforts? The word of a nobody meant nothing.

Now he had no choice but to find the man who had murdered Perkins. "Can't believe I let the scoundrel get away."

Soldier perked his ears and bit off some buffalo grass. Good thing the stuff didn't need any water or it'd die right along with the other vegetation. Even the weeds seemed hard put to survive.

"I'm not giving up, you hear?" he yelled in frustration. "Better pick a big rock 'cause I aim to find you."

Heaven help him, he'd get Jack Day out one way or another. With blindness robbing Glory of the means to provide, Luke couldn't waste any time.

And since she wouldn't marry him...

Damn! But oh, what sweet lips.

Thinking of her sultry gaze raised gooseflesh the size of nickels. Such daydreams should be a sin, plain and simple.

On second thought, he reckoned they were.

~~~

Glory and Hope edged near the loud group in front of Harvey's. She yearned to block the ache in her breast and the hate she'd already heard.

"I say we form a posse. Run that no-good stranger to ground."

"Shoot fire, we cain't form a posse, don't have a sheriff."

Outrage burned in the back of Glory's throat. An angry mob was a fearsome thing. She groped until she found Hope's sweaty palm and held tight.

"All the more reason to form a citizen's brigade," came a surly roar from J. R. Fieldings. "Count me in."

"And me."

"I will."

Calm accented her uncle's voice. "Do you suppose we oughta see what the feller has to say first?"

Glory silently applauded.

"Oh, go fly your kite, Pete Harvey," the banker scoffed.

"Yeah, leave men's work to us. I think a bullet is all we need to wait for," Joseph Starkweather put in.

"Nah, waste of good lead. Get a stout rope like the one he strung around old Penelope's windpipe."

"Oh dear," Hope murmured. "I can't bear this. Let's get Mama and Patience and go home."

They had barely moved an inch when a volley of shots erupted. Hope shrieked, pulling Glory into a crouch.

"What is it? What's happening now?"

Dear Mother Mary, she wished she could see!

"Break it up. This meeting's adjourned."

She couldn't recollect the deep drawl or the steely warning that momentarily quieted the noisy rabble.

"On whose authority?"

"You folks need some persuading?" the mystery man replied. "I can just as easy put some bullet holes into a few of you."

"Who are you, mister?" Uncle Pete asked.

"Captain Dan W. Roberts, Texas Ranger."

Texas Ranger? Had he come to arrest Luke?

Fieldings hollered, "We've had a woman murdered. Is a little justice too much to ask?"

"More like vigilantes to me. Go about your business and let me do my job."

Good advice. She hoped the captain could restore calm and order, but when a town had a powder-keg frame of mind, the likelihood remained slim. Especially if this captain meant to bring more harm to Luke. The Rangers hadn't given him much of a chance before and most likely wouldn't now. Even while she hungered for his touch and couldn't bring herself to think about him leaving for good, she prayed he stayed far, far away. Out of the clutches of Santa Anna's upstanding and Captain Roberts.

"My stars, the entire town's in a fine uproar," Dorothy Harvey was spouting when they made their way inside. "Who would've thought that handsome young man had murderin' in him?"

"We don't know he killed anyone." Defending Luke came automatically. Glory fumbled for the wooden stool Hope brought.

"That's right, Apple Dumpling. Judge not ye lest ye be judged."

"What do you know about scripture quotin', Pete Harvey? Reckon you don't darken the church doors except for marrying and buryin's." Aunt Dorothy launched into a fit of harrumphing.

Glory smiled at their good-natured bickering. Her mama and papa used to do the same. Despite the hard twinge such memories brought, she welcomed the warmth.

"A man don't have to let a preacher put 'im to sleep to get religion," Uncle Pete said in his defense. "I have a sight mor'n some."

"Shush, you old galoot."

"Better watch it, Sugar. You know how frisky name callin' makes me."

"Pete, there's children here!"

"About time they learned something."

The bell over the door tinkled, interrupting the exchange. Though Glory had no reason, she suddenly shivered.

"Can I help you, Captain?" Aunt Dorothy asked.

That could only mean Captain as in Roberts.

"I'm looking for a man named McClain. Luke McClain."

Nineteen

A DOUSING OF ICE WATER COULDN'T HAVE MADE HER colder than the Ranger's statement. Glory tried to swallow. Nothing got past the grim dread blocking her throat.

"Last saw him three or four days back, Captain. My sister-in-law and her two daughters here might tell you more on account of he stays with them occasionally," Aunt Dorothy supplied.

"Why are you looking for him?" Glory blurted the question through stiff lips.

"Sorry, miss, but I really can't tell you. Now, is there any truth to McClain frequenting your home?"

"He's shown us extreme generosity with my Jack away." The cultured voice belonged to her mother. "We hold that man in the highest regard. I won't abide a slanderous word, understand?"

"Yes, ma'am."

A sound she couldn't quite place filled the store. Tilting her head slightly, she determined it came from the Ranger. Something striking against an object.

"For God's sake, Ruth. Far as we know, he ain't trying to accuse the feller of nothing. Are you, Roberts?" Uncle Pete asked.

"Not yet."

"We haven't seen him." Nor would Glory tell if she had. She adjusted her hat.

Though it galled to owe the man, and he made her so mad she saw crooked, she'd not offer him up as a sacrificial lamb. The debt she owed amounted to much more than dollars and cents. No amount of money could ever repay him for giving her a brief taste of things other young girls took for granted. Of letting her know how nice kissing felt, how her insides melted. And of the special quiver his mere presence brought. To her those things were worth a king's ransom.

"It's imperative I find him, miss. Or maybe you'd rather the group outside get him first."

Glory wavered. The man made sense.

Silent until now, Hope spoke up. "Luke spent the night in our barn Monday. He left by the time we woke the next morning. None of us have a clue where he went. That's the honest truth."

"Thank you, ladies, for your cooperation." The loud noise Glory recognized was leather slapping together. Probably gloves of some sort. Gauntlets maybe? "I intend to be in and out of Santa Anna should you remember anything else…or happen to see him. I bid you all good day."

By the time the bell announced the Ranger's leaving, her frayed nerves had come within an inch of snapping. She prayed they hadn't made things worse.

"Girls, I'm getting tired," Ruth declared. "Find your baby sister and let's go home."

"I'll get her, Mama," Hope said. "Be back in a minute."

The shadow Glory knew as Hope had no more disappeared when she felt someone tap her shoulder. She turned toward the source, not distinguishing the form.

"Can I talk to you a minute, girl?" Uncle Pete whispered in her ear.

She slid off the stool and followed the footsteps. "What is it, Uncle Pete?"

"Didn't want to spill this in front of the rest. Sam

Sixkiller told me your feller got in a scuffle with a guy named Foster over at the Oak Vale stage stop."

"McClain?" She didn't like the way her stomach flopped. More suspicion. A bigger wall of doubt. "When?"

"Day before yesterday."

Dear Mother Mary! A troubling stillness murmured that it had to do with the stage robbery. Or similar mayhem. Though she immediately ruled out Luke's involvement in Mrs. Tucker's murder. Whatever else, the man wasn't the cold-blooded, heartless kind. Still, she couldn't totally erase his sudden reversal of fortune. Too much money too fast.

Her uncle wasn't finished. "Also been meaning to mention I saw McClain riding from your house last week. Now that I recollect, it was the morning of those last stage holdups. Didn't see fit to share his destination, but he appeared to tote a powerful heavy load. Just thought you oughta know."

A fit of nausea rose. "I appreciate it." Whatever it meant probably didn't pertain to the good variety. Damn her luck to hell and back! All these years of waiting for kissing and romancing only to find her Prince Charming may have tarnished the princely part.

"Glory, girl, when did this other problem come on you?"

"I don't know what you're talking about."

"You can't see the hand in front of your face, that's what."

Hell's bells! Her playacting skills must sorely need improvement.

"No need for the whole wide world to know. Hope… and one other person are all I've told. How did you figure it out?"

"Didn't take no brains. You can't fool your old uncle." His hug relayed deep affection. "You and I know a little secret—that there's ways of seeing without looking through your eyeballs. We see things no one else does—we see with our hearts."

"Oh, Uncle Pete." She laid her head on his chest to hide the tremor of her chin. "I miss my papa."

"So true, girl. But I'm gonna shoulder some of the burden. The world is a lonely place when you're by yourself."

"You won't tell anyone else, will you?"

"They'll discover it eventually. You can't hide it."

Glory stepped from the comforting circle. "Just a little longer."

What sounded like wood scraping against the floor aroused her curiosity but she kept silent.

Uncle Pete placed a smooth walking stick in her hands. "Take this."

Dear heavens, no one but toothless old men and crotchety old ladies used such. She supposed virtue must come before pride, however. And if it staved off the inevitable a few more days, so be it. She'd have to become a better actress though.

"Put it out in front of you when you walk and you can find what's ahead. Keep you from falling and breaking your noggin."

"Won't it draw more attention to my problem?"

"Nah, just tell 'em you turned your ankle."

She didn't have the heart to debate the major differences between leaning on the stick to take the weight off a limb and wielding it as some sort of pointer. He wanted to feel useful.

"But I can't pay you."

"My gift." He cleared his throat. "Shoulda paid more attention to family 'stead of hunting for buried treasure."

"Stop it. I won't have you apologizing for being who you are and doing what you love. You're a rare jewel. Besides, you have always been near whenever we needed you."

"But I hafta do more. Bless your heart, you can't take care of Ruth and your sisters now that you can't see. You'll need help."

"I'll manage; don't worry. It's simply a matter of setting my mind to it." She'd never admit the task ahead broke her out in a cold sweat. She prayed for courage and stubborn will.

He leaned to whisper in her ear. "Your ma is up range without a horse. How long's she been like this?"

Glory took it he meant Ruth's wandering mind. "Awhile."

"Think it's a tad too much laudanum?"

"What are you talking about? Mama don't…" Her voice trailed. That could certainly explain things. "Uncle Pete, if you know anything, tell me."

"Thought I was helping her. Dorothy, me, and you girls are all Ruth's got. For months, I kinda been giving her bottles of the stuff. Only now she's drinking it faster'n I can say 'lickety split.'"

"You only did what you thought right. I don't fault you for that. But please don't give her more until I can ask Dr. Dalton."

"Wisht I'd knowed. Gave her a fresh bottle today. Could kick myself all over Georgia and into Mississippi."

"Don't worry. Hope and I will try to watch her."

The words came before she thought. Not very likely she could keep an eye on things. She'd have to get accustomed to life as it was and not as she wished it. If only she could. One thing about it—good, bad, or indifferent, changes came whether you whistled for them or not.

The door jangled the bell again and she cursed her shortcoming.

"Patience is waiting for us in the wagon," Hope called.

Glory gave the man a reassuring squeeze. "Thank you for telling me about Mama. I'll treasure the walking stick."

"Reckon I'll come calling in a day or so." He gave her a peck on the forehead. "Hold down the fort till I get there."

"Sure will." She moved cautiously toward the sunlight.

"Wait a minute, Ruth." Dorothy's heels clicked on the floor. "There's a letter from Jack."

"I'll bet he's coming home. I just know it."

Ruth's excitement colored the shadows about her a darker black. Glory thanked Providence that Caesar knew the way home. She untied him and climbed up, wondering how to break more complications to Hope.

Loud sniffling came from the bed of the wagon. Patience? The logical choice since she knew Hope and Mama sat on the seat beside her. Probably pouting again. She flicked the reins and they began their trip back to the farm.

"Patience, baby, what's wrong?" Ruth must have turned, because she exclaimed, "Oh, dear God, look at your face! Who did this?"

"No one." Patience seemed sullen and withdrawn, not at all her usual talkative self.

"Hope? Where did you find her? Do you know anything?"

"No, Mama. I saw her coming alone from behind the livery. She wouldn't tell me how she got a bloodied nose."

Unless Glory was ready to tell her mother about the vision loss, she had to wait until she could get Hope alone. Though the children in town showed a mean streak from time to time, they'd never actually harmed Patience.

She flicked the reins again. "Get on, you pokey old beast!"

No use. The mule continued at his sedate pace. Damnation, they should've stayed home today.

"Baby, tell me what happened this instant and who to blame."

"It's nothing, Mama. I fell, all right?"

"I'll put some liniment on your face the moment we get back."

The sniffs appeared to quiet a bit.

"Mama, I tore my dress. Are you mad?"

"Don't worry, dearest. Hope can fix that. You know how handy she is with a needle and thread."

Silence, broken only by Caesar's snorts and the familiar creak of the wagon, lasted until they reached home. The seat shifted when Hope and Mama climbed down.

"My poor baby. I'm puzzled how a fall could do this. Come, let me doctor you up."

Glory grabbed her middle sister before she could follow. "Tell me what happened."

"I think she got into a fight, but she denied it when I asked. Do you need some help unhitching?"

"Not today. I've done this so many times, I can do it with my eyes shut." And a good thing, she thought, feeling her way with the cane. The mule followed, his breath on her neck.

"Where did you get the walking stick? Uncle Pete?"

"He said it couldn't hurt anything."

"You told him about your eyes?"

"Didn't have to. Our uncle seems to have a sense about certain things." She lifted the bridle and rigging and threw it over a stall. "I hate to be the bearer of more bad news. Lord knows you've had it dumped on you by the bushel of late."

"What other kind is there?"

Hope's dejection almost changed her mind. "Uncle Pete confessed he's kept Mama supplied with laudanum and that she's become as dependent on it as drinking water."

Her sister gasped. "Doesn't he realize the danger?"

"Only occurred to him after he saw her today. He warned me that he gave her a new bottle. We need to watch her and speak to Dr. Dalton after church tomorrow. It could explain Mama's madness."

"Glory, what do you suppose will happen to us?"

"We're going to be just fine. Don't you worry."

Glory sank against Caesar's stall after Hope went inside. *You can always marry Luke.*

The thought flickered and died, leaving only ashes of a beckoning dream. If he hadn't proposed for all the wrong reasons…

Love seemed a small thing to ask of a husband.

Besides, it was obviously too late to accept his offer. Even if she wanted to consider it, which she didn't. She had enough troubles. Didn't need to take on his too. And he'd probably fled the country anyhow. Left her behind just like her father.

Well, she didn't need anyone with wandering feet.

McClain could peddle his sweet talk elsewhere. A pure blessing she hadn't married him.

All of a sudden, a figure dashed past. From the slight build, she gave the blur Patience's name. She followed to the far end of the row of stalls.

"Squirt?"

Sobs made finding her easy. Patience lay on a pile of hay.

"Leave me alone."

Glory sat down and rubbed the small shoulders. "What's wrong? You can tell me."

"Mr. Luke didn't kill ol' lady Penelope. I know he didn't."

"Of course not, honey." She pulled her sister to her. "You didn't fall today, did you?"

"Nope."

"Fight with someone?"

"I couldn't let them say those horrible things. Luke's my friend. He's not a murderer. Or a thief either. How come those kids are so mean?"

The thin girl snuggling against her aroused Glory's protective tenderness. She kissed the top of the pigtailed head. "I wish I could tell you justice and truth always won out. Only I'd be lying. Life isn't fair. People are quick to point fingers, especially if they're scared."

But wasn't that what she'd done from the first encounter with Luke? Fear, both then and since, had led to the final push that sent him away…maybe forever this time. It was her fault. She knew that. In fact, she took the entire blame for the family's present mess. He'd wanted to help and she gave him grief for his trouble.

"Why don't they like me, Glory?" Fresh sobs broke loose. "Am I ugly or bad?"

"Let me tell you something, Patience Ann Day. You are the prettiest, most special little sister anyone could have." Glory smoothed her hair. "Another thing—you have true courage, the kind I wish I had. You're ten times braver."

"I am?"

"You sure are. I'm nothing but a big chicken. And you know what else?"

"What?"

"I'm real lucky to have you for my sister." The truth of it hit her. The girl irritated her to death at times, but maybe little sisters came into a body's life for the simple reason to add balance. Like a pair of scales. Patience offset her sour disposition. A person needed excuses to smile occasionally.

"You're not just saying that, are you?"

"No kidding. Cross my heart and hope to die."

Patience gave a loud sigh. "I love you, Glory."

She gently ran her fingers over the puffy eyes, discovering scratches on baby sister's cheeks. Anger blazed along with self-loathing. She should've stood up for Luke, not left it for Patience.

"I love you too."

"You're not still mad about your private book, are you? I'm sorry about finding it."

Ha, leave it to Squirt to throw more whitewash over the truth. She gave her a fierce hug. "I've already forgotten the incident. But now that you refreshed my memory…" She held her down and tickled her until squeals filled the barn.

"I do declare, ladies! About time you learned the finer points of having fun. Can an outsider join in?"

The sensual drawl could only belong to one man. But was it real, not merely a trick her mind played?

Patience jumped up from the straw. "It's really you!"

"Is it too late for an invite?"

Excited tingles collided in their goings and comings along Glory's spine. And he hadn't laid a hand on her.

The charmer had returned. For the first time that day, Glory felt like smiling.

Twenty

LUKE PUSHED AWAY FROM THE TABLE, WONDERING HOW A MAN had room for all the food they'd piled onto his plate. Not that they had to work overly hard. No such thing as a decent meal and a certain pretty lady when a man lay low. Still, the chief excuse for the visit was to get the latest news, he told himself.

Why the hell had Roberts shown up? Just riding through? Should be Major Jones.

Luke desperately needed a plan to get out of this mess. No doubt his rope had knots in it to think he stood a hope and a prayer.

He could get caught in his own noose and end what he'd started...before he could free Jack Day.

He took a slow turn about the table. Deep sadness lay behind each smile, almost as if they mourned a loved one's passing. He reckoned they had ample reason for sadness. Not too many things ran in their favor these days.

When he saw the ribbon in Hope's hair and the comb in Mother Day's, his chest swelled. They evidently liked the small gifts.

The toothbrush he gave Glory crossed his mind.

Remembering that special night sent warmth flooding into his belly. An uncomfortable hunger rose that no amount of food could satisfy. No one had to twist his arm to call on the Days.

His gaze lingered on the woman across the table. Her face swam before him when he drifted to sleep at night and woke each day. He fancied her around every turn. Glory flowed in his veins as real as his blood. Watching the waning light brush her hair with some sort of reverence created a hollow crater inside.

She seemed to be in one of her quiet moods. A pure sin to Moses she couldn't see him, for he'd surely wink if for nothing more than to put some color in her cheeks.

He clenched his jaw until the pain matched that of his heart.

Of all the things in this world, he reckoned nothing would give him greater joy than to set to rights those beautiful stonewashed eyes.

Mama Day dabbed at the corners of her mouth. "Young man, what made you return? With the folks of Santa Anna and that nasty captain ready to shoot you on sight, I believe I'd have to say you're being awfully foolhardy."

"I reckon so, ma'am." He'd brave a hail of gunfire and walk over coals with his bare feet just to kiss his Glory one more time. But he wouldn't have good sense to tell Mrs. Day that. "I came back to get something I left in your barn."

Glory pushed the food around on her plate. "Must be all-fired important."

It was the first time Glory had spoken during the meal and she did it with a measure of stiffness he understood. Misery had a way of snuffing out tender feelings.

"It is." The words came out hoarse, not the lifeless tone he'd aimed for.

The way her head jerked around you'd have thought he slapped her. *Fire and damnation! Good going, McClain.*

"Enough to risk your life?"

A painful lurch made his reply no louder than a sigh through a field of cotton. "Yes."

Whatever she thought, her face kept the secret. She'd not given one measly sign that his risking life and limb pleased her. He even welcomed the hair-trigger temper that had come freely in times past. Anything to hint she hadn't died inside.

Patience interrupted his thoughts. "I'll wallop anyone who says you murdered ol' lady Penelope. Or stab 'em and feed 'em to the wild pigs. They'd best keep their traps shut."

He propped his elbows on the table. "I do declare. I might oughta take you with me to do my defendin'." He touched the bruises on the young face. "That's quite a shiner. Scratches too. Tangle with a bear or something?"

Patience bent quickly to stroke Miss Minnie. "I fell."

And his name was Dakota Kid.

Plain to see she didn't want to discuss it. He guessed some of the little darlin's in town had added the handiwork.

"My stars, I can't recall when I've eaten so much," Mama Day said. "The batch of fish was delectable."

He reckoned that must mean *good* in Ruth-Day English.

"How did you catch so many, Mr. Luke?"

"Well, Punkin, I smeared a little honey on the hook, dropped it in the water, and whistled for 'em. They pert near jumped onto the bank of their own free will."

He leaned forward and listened.

The sound of hoofbeats made his belly knot. He covered the distance to the window in three steps. One horse and rider.

"Expecting company?"

"It could be my Jack." Mama Day joined him. "Oh, I do hope so."

Hope crowded between. "It's Alex O'Brien."

"Who?" Luke asked.

"Her beau." Patience didn't want to miss out, scooting under his arm. "And he's wearing courtin' clothes."

"Mr. McClain, you can hide in the barn. We'll send word when he leaves." Hope swung around. "Quickly. Oh dear, someone take up his plate."

"I'll keep him company."

Glory's unexpected volunteering shocked him. Luke tried to stifle the promise of his good fortune.

He'd hoped merely to steal a few minutes alone.

More than that would bring unbearable pleasure.

❧

"You don't have any snakes in here, I hope."

Glory suppressed an urge to laugh, recalling the night she went after Luke when he broke his bargain with her. The mere idea of a poor little snake terrifying a tough man of his caliber still seemed a bit odd.

"We only keep the friendly type. Miss Minnie and family run off the bad ones."

"It's nice to hear you joke. Most times you're far too serious. Tonight, you seemed a million miles away." The heels of his boots scuffed against the barn floor.

The reason burdened her soul. She'd let her papa down. That fact made her own dilemma pretty trivial. Not a scrap of hope remained. Zero.

"Another letter from prison came today." The tremor inside broke through her armor. "I'm worried about Mama."

"Your father didn't…?"

"We haven't received notification yet but it's just a matter of time."

"Miracles do happen, you know. Maybe—"

"Stop! Quit trying to coddle me. My father is past saving." And so was she. Hard reality, but true.

Sniping wouldn't cure anything. He hadn't caused their misfortunes. She wished she could take it back. Silence weighed heavy before he let out a chuckle.

"Did I say something funny?"

"Didn't realize you can still shoot with both barrels and hit what you're aiming for. Happy to see you're not out of ammunition. Here I thought you'd all but climbed into the grave and pulled up the bedsheet."

"Hell's bells! I'm not dead yet!"

"I can see that. Yes sirree." He whistled in admiration.

The tingles she had had before seemed mild in comparison to the hum vibrating inside how. His drawl reminded her of a lazy cat, stretching from a nap. It stirred every emotion she'd ever known twenty times over.

Luke brushed her shoulder. "In case Romeo chances to glance out, we don't dare light the lantern."

She pasted on a wry smile. "No need to worry about darkness on my account."

"Damn!" He whacked something, the wall most likely, with his fist. "Let me bend over so you can kick the seat of my pants. But shoot, you can't see my rear end either."

"Please, I'll get used to it."

"Yeah, but will I?" he asked softly.

The hopeless undercurrent in his tone tugged at her heartstrings. Whether he sought reassurance or not, she felt drawn to reach out. The hard muscle of his arm gave her a jolt. "I know of worse things."

Like picturing his silly wink and grin when memory faded.

Like holding on to the feel of his embrace, his lips.

And like having to keep on breathing once he'd gone. Yes, many things numbered the list, each one pain-ridden.

"We might as well make ourselves comfortable while we wait." Luke's fingers brushed her face. "This courting business could last for hours."

A man with a magic carpet would know. His arm slid around her waist, igniting a heat that dampened her palms. She knew he led her down the row of stalls. Dankness, chickens clucking on their roosts, and the way the barn became cooler the deeper inside she went told her.

"What's the situation with your sister?"

"I take it you mean Hope." She moved cautiously, not yet familiar with the uneven slope of the floor. "I look for her and O'Brien to tie the knot before long."

Panic lodged in her throat.

One more person to walk out of her life.

They all would...leaving her alone with memories of useless dreams.

Caesar and Soldier snorted. Bessie kicked up a fuss when they moved past. Thirty steps from the door. She perceived them near the same place she'd located Patience earlier. The hay rustled when they sat down. His gaze, the rich shade of coffee beans if memory served, burned through the midnight of her soul.

His arm slid around her, the heat of his body arousing a strange hunger. Although he had a callus on his thumb, his touch was as soft as satin on her cheek.

Though he hadn't denied killing Penelope Tucker in so many words, his nearness didn't threaten her.

He wouldn't take her life—merely her heart.

Not much separated the two. Either way she'd lose. She smoothed the rough seam of her britches leg, then bunched it up before she straightened it again.

"Perhaps you'd better get whatever it was you left in the loft...that important item you had to return for," she suggested.

"Later."

Glory's pulse quickened when he tucked a strand of hair behind her ear.

"I merely want to look at you." He cleared his throat. "'She walks in beauty, like the night. / Of cloudless climes and starry skies.'"

"You know Lord Byron!"

She'd never have imagined. Luke was like a many-faceted diamond. Depended on the way the light shone and which side it turned as to what you saw.

Luke chuckled and drew her down onto the fresh hay. "I blame it on my mother's insistence. Truth to tell, those are about the only lines of Lord Byron I remember."

"But still...not many Texans can quote a single word."

"I didn't think poetry or reading mattered until I met you. Now my mind dwells on it." He tickled her neck with a piece of straw. "Do you know how pretty you are right now?"

His silky voice guaranteed mystery and excitement. She

skated on a frozen pond that disguised thin spots. Danger of falling through any moment terrified her.

"You're wrong, McClain. Hope is the comely one."

"Both your sisters are fine-looking ladies. But you're the real beauty. You have a glow that shines from the inside out. When you walk by, heads turn. People stare." His voice cracked. "You put thoughts in a man's head of everything he can't have and make him believe his notions aren't nearly so far-fetched. Darlin', you take my breath and steal my every thought."

"Thank you, but you don't have to say those things."

What effect did he think he had on her? Words held no meaning unless Luke spoke them. She moved through the days in constant disarray, conscious only of his presence… long after he was no longer there.

"Oh, but I do. They come from my heart."

He held a magnetism over her she couldn't shake. As she sat next to him now, nothing mattered, not even the arrogant way he tried to fix their problems.

She didn't give a hoot if he had turned scoundrel.

Or stage robber.

Or outlaw.

Or snake-oil salesman.

Long as he never left. A light caress of her wrist moved up her arm. Glory shivered…fearing she might die from want. Coaxed into the circle of his arms, she snuggled into that safe place where nightmares and dark beasts couldn't reach her.

For the moment, her world had no troubles.

No danger—only light. Where everything was perfect.

She felt the most fortunate of women.

His lips brushed the top of her head. "You give so much. I only wish…"

"Shh, no regrets." She leaned back. With tender care, she touched the face she could no longer see.

She traced his eyes that could twinkle with laughter, glow with excitement, or heat her with a mere glance. The nose that couldn't seem to stay out of her affairs. The high cheekbones and strong jaw that defined the man she knew.

Such a one could not willingly take another's life.

Straying to his sensuous mouth, she outlined it with the barest of fingertips.

"You never told me how you got this scar."

"You never asked." He nipped at her dawdling fingers.

"I am now."

"Mountain lion. I reckon I was ten at the time. Duel had just turned fourteen. We went hunting and got lost. From nowhere, this big cat jumped us. We shot, barely wounding it. The animal followed us all day, waiting for an opportunity. When night fell, it attacked. Nearly ripped Duel's damn arm from the socket. I tried to fight it off and that's when it ripped a big gash in my throat and caught my mouth."

"Dear Mother Mary! How did you get free?"

"Duel killed it. I'll never forget it though. That feeling of being stalked. Of not knowing when it would finish the job."

A faint tremor rippled through him, and she knew he walked the same path now, fighting for his life once more.

"I'm sorry."

"Don't be. It taught me a valuable lesson."

Luke shifted away, but she still felt his nearness.

"Come lie down and tell me what deep, dark secrets you have in that head of yours," Luke murmured against her temple.

Glory patted the straw until she found him, then lay back. "I hate to disappoint you. Nothing as bloodcurdling as your story."

"That bad, huh? Well, everyone can't be so lucky." He lifted a length of her hair, curling it around a finger. "Anything ever make you crawl under the covers and hide? Tell me something I don't know about Glory Marie Day."

That she'd never met a stranger like him?

That he gave her a reason to keep going?

Or that she cared for him with her heart and soul?

She took a shaky breath. "I used to have a dog named Max. We had a bond, he and I. Max took sick one day. He lay there and suffered over a week. I wanted Papa to make him well. Didn't understand why he couldn't, 'cause my papa could fix anything. Max died in spite of all my tender care. He left me. Then Papa went away. Mama has gone, too, though in a different way. Hope will get married. After her, Squirt will go off to find her big adventure."

And she'd be by herself. *Without the man called McClain.*

"You hide your scars on the inside. Don't know which is worse, darlin'. My experience has shown one day it's sunshine and roses, the next blustery and a passel of thorns."

Such a heavy sigh from a scoundrel who wore rakish grins the same way he toted his forty-five—never far from either. This more serious side took her off guard. She knew how to steel herself against a sweet-talking cowboy. Or almost anyway.

"I wouldn't have taken you for a philosopher."

"Do you know how long a second is when you're waiting for something important, and you can't swallow because it'll choke you? Then when you want the moment to last for an eternity, it passes in the blink of an eye." Luke's voice became hoarse. "This second is one of those."

The hay rustled again, and she sensed he rested on an elbow, watching her. She lay unmoving, waiting with bated breath. She'd take whatever he could spare and consider it a blessing. Beggars couldn't be choosers. Perhaps she'd used up her allotment of miracles.

"Lady, you're going to make me do something I reckon I shouldn't. But I never laid claim to good sense."

His touch threw her in disarray for it brought a yearning so powerful it could destroy. Her skin burned with a fever.

Feathery kisses had her head swimming. Luke nuzzled her earlobes, worked down her jaw, then her neck. The palm he laid over her breast trembled. His touch awakened exquisite, sweet torment. Tears formed and inched down her cheeks. He did things to her she hadn't earned the right for. That he would give this precious gift to a blind, destitute girl brought a bittersweet ache.

As he fumbled with the buttons of her shirt, she knew she'd stepped on that magic carpet again. Awareness brought paralyzing fear and a sense of crossing an invisible line. Once she let herself need, would she ever stop? And how many regrets would she have if she chose to live that way?

"Say the word and I'll quit. But this is all I've thought of since you hauled my shot-up carcass home that day."

"I want you, Luke." There was no going back.

Anywhere not touching him was too far. She clutched a handful of shirt and pulled him closer. His mouth found hers in the same instant the air fondled her, sliding across her bared nipples. They rose to aching, rigid peaks. Shivers ran the length of her.

Tongues could bring the most amazing pleasure, she learned. Every movement of his head left a moist, sinful trail behind.

A mass of tingles waltzed up her spine. Her breath became ragged as she slid her fingers into his hair. Luke took a nipple further into his mouth, creating a swarm of flutters through her. Her heart raced with the pleasure of his touch.

This cowboy moved confident and sure, though not in an arrogant way. A man possessing extraordinary magic, he knew which flick or brush would elicit the right response. He went lower, sliding down her flat belly. And yet she craved more.

Glory had never undressed a man before and scarcely knew where to begin. She'd never dared think of such things. Haste turned her fingers to all thumbs. Yet she desired to lie naked with Luke on a bed of hay and couldn't bear another second of torture.

A few seconds, a button or two more.

She gasped.

The hardness of his chest met with her tender skin. The delicious friction added another layer to the moment they'd carved from dead dreams and disappointment.

His heated, swollen need throbbed against her bare thigh. Luke's touch moved lightly across her stomach, down her legs, then into her wet opening. There he paused, letting her absorb the strange caress.

When he slipped a finger inside the tender folds, sensation pulsed over her in thick waves. She embraced each one and pressed herself tightly against his hand, praying the night would never end.

Dear Mother Mary!

Damp tendrils clung to her face. Something consumed her that she had no name for. She only knew she wanted more. She had to quench the flames that threatened to scorch her soul or else they'd not stop there, but engulf the whole of her.

"Relax and enjoy it," Luke whispered against her ear as he climbed on top of her and filled her with his hardness, stretching the walls of her body.

A burst of unimaginable pleasure rippled through her and she gasped with the unexpected joy the feelings brought.

Glory thrust her arms around his neck and arched to meet him. Salty tears and love married on her tongue in one crowning moment. A cry rent the air in the mating of her flesh with his.

She rose on the waves in a frenzy of heavenly heat and rapture. Higher and higher until the sensations gave way in an explosion of pure white light.

She found a way to put out the fire.

Luke rolled to the side where they lay quivering, gasping for air, perspiration creating a sheen on their bodies.

After several minutes passed, Luke raised to kiss her with gentle reverence. "Have mercy, lady! I ain't ever been to Glory Land, but I have now."

And in what a fashion, he might add.

Luke drew her against him and they lay, their passions sated, drifting in a sea of bliss.

Suddenly he raised his head, making sure he hadn't mistaken the noise. "Listen."

Unmistakable pitter-patter on the roof told him he hadn't taken leave of his senses. The rumble of thunder amid the deluge appeared out of place on the drought-stricken plains.

"I never thought…oh, blessed rain!" Glory laughed.

Her jubilance almost shrouded the wretched misery gripping his guts. Time to leave soon.

"Yep, a cloudburst all right."

"For two cents, I'd run out and stand in the middle of it. It's been so blasted long."

And he'd gladly get soaked with her for half of that.

"You'd best get dressed before Punkin comes barreling through that door." He hated the gruffness that snuck into the warning. His breath came ragged and harsh.

"Just think how her tongue would wag." Glory fumbled for her shirt.

"Yes, indeed."

Dim light through the loft door played across gentle features that had seen tender years cut short by too much work and turmoil. He'd give nigh anything to bring back the stolen smiles and laughter.

If his plan worked…

Twenty-one

A GULLY WASHER APPEARED TO HAVE PITCHED CAMP ON DAY land. It appeared the good Lord's wagon had overturned and the load of potatoes rolled out. Rashes of lightning through the cracks momentarily lit up the interior of the barn.

Luke tucked in his shirt and buckled his holster, wondering whether the crash truly came from beyond the doors.

Maybe it was the sound of dread lodged in his heart.

Trick yourself into believing it's nothing more than a mere storm. You have to or you'll go mad.

Another brief bolt gave him a glimpse of Glory. She dressed slowly, pulling on each item of clothing as if it were one more burden placed on her weary shoulders.

A cough dislodged the lump in his windpipe. "I'll climb to the loft. I should be able to find what I left."

She didn't need to know he'd already found it.

Nope. Because keeping her wasn't part of the bargain he made with himself. Watching and not being able to claim her for his own would…well, let him just say it wasn't something a man could do. Might as well yank out his innards and stomp on 'em. Hell, at least leaving might save something.

"Don't forget to watch for snakes," she called softly.

Feet of lead tended to move very slowly. Several feet away, he propped himself against a stall, staring at the vision of her. Far enough.

He'd lied, but Glory would never know. Each flash of light bought a second more of heaven.

Dressed now, Glory called, "Did you find what you're looking for?"

Everything and more.

Luke wiped traces of wetness from his eyes and retreated farther so she wouldn't guess he'd been watching.

"Yep. Sure did." Forced lightness didn't come easy. He'd need practice if he kept this up.

She appeared relieved when he dropped beside her. Luke reckoned she'd not grown as accustomed to the shadows as she let on. Or could be the storm created the jitters.

"I left before saying goodbye last time." He absorbed the fragrance of her to take with him.

"A bad habit of yours." Her composure showed signs of cracking.

Damn.

The important matter he'd forgotten, a bit of paper, scraped his palm even though he held it with great care. He lifted Glory's left hand.

"I meant to give this to you then but I was afraid."

"You, McClain? I thought only snakes scared you."

"A whole mess of things scares my socks off." Most of all riding off, knowing he'd never return. Either six feet under or making himself at home down Mexico way, this was the end of the trail.

He slipped the cigar band on her middle finger and laid her hand back in her lap.

"What is it?"

"A token to remember me by."

"You speak as though you won't be…"

The catch in her voice punched him in the gut. He shouldn't have come. No one would emerge a winner. Even as he whipped himself, he knew no power on earth could've kept him away. He found the frank assessment bitter. She'd pay the price for his selfish desires.

"Most likely I'll not see you again."

"Does it pertain to the robberies and Mrs. Tucker's murder? If so, I don't care. Whatever you are or have done can't change the way I feel."

"Even should you discover I'm guilty?" he asked softly.

"Nothing…on this earth can ever change my heart." Glory grabbed his arm. "Promise you'll come back. Please."

"Can't. What I do is too dangerous for you to know."

She bit her knuckle until Luke expected to see blood. Probably in desperation to still the tremble of her lip. Lord knew he fought the same band of steel that threatened to squeeze the life from him. He'd reached into the wretched depths of his soul, a place where nothing but truth dared enter. He found the harsh reality of what he saw a weighty cross to bear.

She felt her hand. "But what did you put on my finger?"

"A cigar band, a symbol of my feelings for you that you can hold. Shoot, maybe you'll even tell folks the cowboy who came calling wasn't such a bad sort after all…should circumstances take a turn."

How they could get much worse he didn't know, for surely death couldn't impose the type of misery gripping him now. He winced, forcing breath into his raw lungs.

"This danger…let me help you."

Luke chose to ignore the plea that shredded his control. He'd rolled the dice before he turned toward Day property and they'd come up double sixes. It was too late to change course.

"If I win, your father will be a free man."

"And if you don't?"

A jagged flash revealed her ashen face. He'd already lost what he spent his whole life looking for. Sucking what little air remained, he gathered her into his arms.

Then she tilted her face.

Have mercy! If anyone had said looking at someone through tears could form halos around their head, he'd have called them crazy fools.

He kissed the sightless, stonewashed eyes. Then the tip of her nose. Despite his intent to stop there, he could not.

A groan rumbled in his throat. Trembling under her spell, he teased the curved mouth with tiny flutters of his tongue before he feasted fully on the beauty.

Just then Patience bounded inside. "He's gone! You can come back inside."

Damn that girl! Luke raised his head. "Over here."

Best end it now. He moved back and let go of his hold before he took leave of the drop of sense he had left. Before he pulled her back to the hay. And before he forgot he had a long way to go before the dawn.

"Mr. Luke, you don't have to hide anymore."

Little did she know.

Puddles formed at the girl's feet as rain slid from the bright-yellow slicker. A similar one for Glory draped from her arm.

"'Preciate it, Punkin." He tweaked her nose. "Gotta make tracks."

"Ain't you staying the night? The storm'll drown you."

Under these circumstances, he considered drowning an improvement.

"Luke?" Glory's strangled cry almost broke him.

"Can't. It's gotta be this way, darlin'." He cupped her face in his palm. "Shh. Let Punkin take you back to the house. Don't worry about me. Just keep picturing your papa sitting in his own parlor. He will be soon. Trust me."

"But—"

His lips smothered her complaint. Slow and deliberate, he took everything she gave. And when her mouth parted, he thrust his tongue inside to savor one last taste. A man racked with guilt, he pushed her toward the door.

"Now scoot. I've got things to do." He turned, settled his hat firmly on his head, and took a final look around the place that would linger in his memory until he departed this earth. Then, he closed his eyes against the awful pain that dropped him to his knees.

The morning came much too soon to suit Glory. She drew herself into a small ball, cursing the day that saw fit to turn a deaf ear to her prayers.

She recognized the footsteps entering the alcove, choosing to ignore the intrusion.

"Are you sick?" Hope's concern filtered past the grief.

Glory lifted her head from the tearstained pillow. The feather mattress sank as her middle sister perched on the side. Ill? That didn't begin to cover this purgatory she'd fallen into. "Can't a body lie abed without everyone asking why?"

"You didn't come to the breakfast table and I wondered."

The thought of food didn't sit well. "Not hungry."

"Aren't you coming to church with us?"

Sitting through a sermon on varying degrees of sin held no appeal whatsoever. "I don't think so."

"You've been crying! Did something happen last night?"

"Luke's gone."

Despair crawled from that inner catacomb where shattered dreams went to die.

"He'll be back."

"No, not this time. He said goodbye."

"If it's only a quarrel, you can make amends."

Dear God, she wished it were that simple. Disbelief riddled her hope. It was a small miracle she could continue to breathe with a heart that had stopped beating. Her and Luke's disagreement? Only in the killing of two lonely souls. She fingered the cigar band he'd placed on her hand, the token of his caring.

"Nothing like that. Now, can you leave me?"

Hope lay on the bed and stroked Glory's back. "You're the glue, the driving force, that holds Mama, Patience, and me together. We can't let you give up on life simply because you got a raw deal. I refuse to do that." A quiver filled her voice. "If you're not strong enough to fight, I'll do it for you until you can get some starch back in your spine."

Patience spoke, throwing herself on top of both her sisters. "And me too."

How long Squirt had been in the room, Glory could only hazard a guess. Fresh hotness washed over her. She did need them. Family could give her something to cling to in this new place where cold was the temperature of pitch-black.

Not that it came close to filling the shoes of a charming scoundrel. Nothing could. Lord knew she'd need every scrap of help to ease the loneliness though.

Patience laid her cheek to Glory's. "Please, Glory. We can't bear it without you. If you don't wanna get up, I'll lie here with you. I don't wanna hafta whip those darn kids anyhow."

That decided it. A body couldn't be alone in her misery with a small crowd. She pushed them off.

"Hell's bells! You win. I may as well get dressed."

"I'll pour your coffee."

Quite a satisfied snap to Hope's skirts, Glory thought, swinging her feet to the floor. She'd make an effort, though she couldn't promise how long she could mask her desolation and loss.

A deep sigh later, groping for her Sunday best, she found it shoved into her outstretched hands.

"Who's there?"

"Only me." Patience sniffled. "I'm sorry you're blind."

"I asked Hope not to tell."

"She didn't. I knew it all by myself."

Did everyone in the whole blessed town know? Mama? "Will you keep my secret? Just for a while."

"I love you, Glory. I'd never hurt you." Patience launched herself into Glory's arms.

She pried the small arms from her neck. "That goes double for me. Now scat so I can have a minute's peace."

Only when she heard voices in the kitchen did she truly know they'd left her. She pulled the dress over her muslin petticoats and buttoned it. By touch alone, she found the cotton stockings, then her shoes.

Strange how much remembrance a person relied on. The comb on the stand, underthings in the top dresser drawer… and the reason why she'd grow old alone.

Just for today, couldn't she be a scared little girl? She squinched her eyes shut. *Please block the memories*, she prayed.

Suddenly, she bent and patted the floor beneath the bed until she located the empty seed box. She sat and held it on her lap.

Though old and useless, the wooden container held the greatest treasure anyone had ever bestowed. The top slid back easily and she reached inside. She unfolded the piece of faded tissue paper from around the prize—the toothbrush Luke had given her.

She cradled it to her heaving bosom.

Still brand-new, it represented something she thought beyond reach. It had taken a stranger on a paint horse to show her such trappings did not a lady make. True, she'd never be refined and wealthy in the way of Bess Whitfield. But Luke taught her a lady meant far more than that. She already had what she'd always desired.

Blaming her father for her perceived lack had been wrong. She'd dishonored him and now it was too late to beg forgiveness.

Fate had to strip her of so many things for her to see.

She'd asked only for one kiss and was given a love unlike any she'd dared imagine.

A pretty fair exchange, she reckoned. Except she wished someone had warned her how gutshot she'd feel at giving it up. The hand that reached through the mangled mess and ripped her heart from its mooring cared nothing for her survival.

"Are you dressed, Glory?" Hope called.

With tender care, she replaced the paper over the toothbrush. Then removing the cigar band from her finger, she tucked both precious items inside the box and slid it beneath her bed.

"Be right there."

A few calming breaths later, she slipped on a smile to mask her broken heart.

The rain-cooled day gave most of Santa Anna's faithful reason to rejoice. Everywhere Glory turned, folks spoke in shushed tones about the possible end to the drought. Perhaps fear that the heavens should get wind of their doubts and plunge them back into dryness kept their voices lowered.

Mama pleaded a sick headache this Sunday morn, refusing to rise from her bed. This made Hope's and her task imperative.

They stood at the bottom of the steps after the service.

"I see him," Hope whispered. "Dr. Dalton's coming."

"Is anyone with him?"

"He's alone for the moment."

"Good. It'll make it easier."

"Uh-oh."

"What?"

Suddenly, someone jerked Glory's arm. "I want to know what you think you're doing. We're not going to stand for it."

Bess's vicious attack left her reeling. Whatever did the snooty girl mean? Somehow, she had to keep her vision impairment from the town, for they'd only delight in using it against her. She turned her face toward the sound, staring as if she had perfect sight.

"Nice weather, isn't it, Bess?"

"Don't nice me, you…you farm tramp, beau stealer."

Stinging words for someone who had the wrong facts. Lightning must've struck the fashion queen's brain. Glory hadn't stolen anything that she knew of.

"What are you babbling about?"

"As if you don't know." Amelia joining the fray came as no surprise.

Uncle Pete once pointed out that if one half of the Miss Prisses came to an abrupt stop, the other's nose would be imbedded very far up a part of her indelicate anatomy.

"Would you care to enlighten me?"

"You probably thought you could get away with it, but we spied you walking arm in arm with Dr. Dalton."

Finally, it made sense. Luke hadn't been the only one to blow the episode out of proportion. She tried to ignore the torture that came when her mind spoke his name.

"For heaven's sake!" There went that unladylike snort she hated. "I'm not going to belittle myself justifying it."

"I don't know where you get the idea that you're pretty enough for two men to be courting you. You're as ugly as a fence post."

"That's about enough. Leave my sister alone." Hope's snarl shocked the daylights out of her. Glory had never heard her sister use that tone.

"Who's gonna make us?"

"Me, that's who."

If only she could see. She was missing out. Grunts and the swishing of air made her think of blows being exchanged for some reason. Fisticuffs in her defense?

"Ahem, ladies, is there a problem here?"

Despite having spoken with Dr. Dalton no more than twice, Glory recognized the distinguished baritone.

"Of course not." Bess couldn't have been sweeter. "We were simply discussing the virtues of respecting one's property."

"I see." He chuckled the same way he had before when he told of his sister. "Well, it looks like the discussion split your lip, Miss Whitfield."

"Hope?" Alex O'Brien arrived winded and puzzled. "Did I just see what I thought?"

"You sure did, and I'll give 'em some more if they don't button their mouths." First snarls and now smugness. What else would Hope reveal before the day ended, pray tell?

"I thought my imagination was playing tricks on me."

"It didn't. Did you want something, Alex?"

"I rented a buggy from the livery. I'd like to take you home if it's all right."

"We're a little busy right now. We have business of a personal nature with Dr. Dalton. If you don't mind waiting?"

Glory imagined a certain light in the boy's eyes at the prospect. How nice to be young and foolish. As she once was.

Before she learned everything came with a high price.

"I'll count the minutes," he said.

She died to know if Bess and Amelia had decided they'd bitten off more than they could chew and moved on. Fire and damnation, she cursed this blackness!

"Misses Hope and Glory, fortune indeed smiled on me this morn. What is it you wanted to bend my ear about?"

"A delicate situation, Doctor." Glory directed the answer toward her right, where she'd heard him.

"Ah, a professional visit. Then, in that case, I suggest we adjourn to my office."

Strength in the hand that took her arm gave her to know it most likely wasn't Hope. However, after the events of the last five minutes, she could be totally wrong. For the first time since awaking, she felt a smile form. Her sister had literally meant what she said about fighting for her.

"Dr. Dalton," came Amelia's whine. "Bess and I brought some of that fried chicken you love so well. Will you come eat Sunday dinner with us?"

"Later. Duty calls at the moment."

"I doubt we can keep it warm."

They'd certainly earn high marks in persistence.

Again, Ted Dalton chuckled. "Cold is my favorite, girls."

She felt him turn slightly.

"Oh, and, Miss Whitfield, you might put a damp cloth on that lip. I see the makings of an awful bruise."

Gasps filled the air behind them.

"Miss Hope, you've got quite a mean punch. Ever think of becoming a pugilist?"

"Oh no, sir; I'd never do anything like that."

The doctor's teasing and this new side of Hope had Glory's head whirling. She only prayed Squirt stayed out of trouble. She hadn't seen her since the reverend ended his sermon.

Defending principles appeared to run rampant in the Day family.

Twenty-two

THE STAIRS TO DR. DALTON'S OFFICE CREAKED. GLORY stumbled once when her foot failed to clear the upper step. His firm grip kept her from falling. The care he took of her stirred the dying embers of times past.

And yet, his presence jumbled her nerves.

If she couldn't trick Patience, what luck did she have with a man of learning?

Here she'd worked herself into a frazzle to stave off the inevitable and the effort could be for naught. She failed miserably in the pretending lessons.

The turn of the knob told her they'd reached the top.

"You ladies have a seat and tell me what I can help you with."

Locating the chair edge with the back of her legs, Glory sat down. "It's our mother. We recently discovered she's consuming an unhealthy amount of laudanum."

Hope took over. "Sick headaches consume her to such a degree she's grown dependent on the drug. Mama talks in riddles. Most times she can't remember that our papa is… away and has been for a long time."

"You are right to seek help. That addiction carries grave effects." The young doctor paused for a second, tapping his fingers on the desktop. "This clears up another puzzle though."

A curious thing to say. Glory tried to curb the peculiar pinpricks running the length of her spine. "A puzzle?"

"It pertains to your last visit, Miss Day. I couldn't quite understand why you're so desperate to hide your impairment. I didn't know about your circumstance and how your father's leaving dumped the family's entire survival on you."

"Don't sit in judgment, Doctor, until you've been there." Glory hadn't meant to spit the sharp rebuke from her mouth. Not in that way. But it irked her to see how fast a body jumped to the wrong conclusions.

"My sister didn't mean that the way it sounded," Hope apologized.

"No, the regret belongs to me. I should mind my manners. Will you believe I only wish to help?"

Those offerings were a dime a dozen. No one could return the thing she most needed. Still, he meant well even if he could use a bit more prudence.

"We both spoke before thinking." Glory allowed a wan smile. "A problem I have quite often."

"Getting back to your mother—how long has she taken the laudanum and how much?"

"Though we don't know for certain, we believe she began shortly after my father left," Hope said.

"That's when we started noticing she had trouble separating fact from fiction. Her headaches grew increasingly worse and kept her abed for days." Glory wrinkled her brow. The truth was there all along had they chosen to see it. She'd not filled Papa's boots very well.

Worry likely created the catch in her sister's breath when she helped complete the picture. "Yesterday, Uncle Pete confessed how he'd secretly supplied the laudanum for years. Could that account for the symptoms?"

"Absolutely." Dalton sighed heavily. "It's nothing more than a liquid form of opium and extremely hazardous when taken frequently. In large quantities, it kills."

"Oh dear!"

The gasp came from Hope and gave noise to the shudders inside Glory. "What can we do?"

"Taking it from her in one fell swoop poses an equally vexing problem. Many patients die in the throes of the horrible shakes that develop." The sound of him scratching his chin met Glory's ears. "The only thing you can do in my estimation is to wean your mother off it gradually. Hide the bottle and dole it out in small quantities. I suggest one spoonful a day for a week, then begin every other day, and slowly taper off."

"Thank you. It relieves our minds to confide in someone." She hated that the bulk of the task would fall on Hope's shoulders yet again. Hell's bells!

Dr. Dalton's next question came softly, but with the blunt force of a hammer. "Would you mind if I examine your eyes? Purely to satisfy my professional concern of course."

❧

Miles from Santa Anna, Luke sniffed the smoke of a campfire floating in the breeze...and coffee?

Just what he needed to drive the chill from his bones. Last night's storm had drenched him. Or maybe he'd died from longing and the good Lord hadn't told him yet.

Folks claim nothing but death creates such mind-numbing cold. He could put up an argument to the contrary.

He slid from the saddle for a look-see. Didn't pay to ride into a fellow's territory uninvited. These days especially. Luke didn't mind a trip to the Promised Land; in fact, he welcomed relief from the utter misery gripping his gut, he just didn't care to be helped there with a rope.

Rain-dampened grass silenced his movements. He pushed aside the low branch of a Texas redbud. Scents from the small fire had his belly rumbling. Not a soul in sight. Whomever it belonged to—

"Hold it, pistolero."

Someone cocked the hammer of a weapon. The metal

poking into the back of his head assured Luke the person wasn't asking for directions. The stranger took his Colt, slipping it easily from the holster. The hackles on Luke's neck rose. He never developed a fondness for sitting ducks. Especially if he was in the duck's shoes.

"Smelled your coffee. Didn't mean any harm."

"Turn around slow and easy."

Thank his lucky stars the man hadn't shot him on the spot. Luke swiveled and got his first look.

"Dan? You old son of a gun."

"That's Captain Roberts to you. You're getting sloppy, McClain." The Ranger handed back his pistol. "Time was you'd have snuck up on a man, made him eat some lead, and sent him to his Maker before he knew what happened."

That was in the old days when a certain lady hadn't occupied his thoughts.

"Care to share a cup of that brew?"

"Not if you don't mind shedding some light on the urgent telegram you sent. I met the necktie party when I rode in. Pretty riled up. You're in a mess of trouble, boy."

"Seems so." Luke rubbed eyes that burned from lack of sleep. Felt bloodshot and raw, just like his insides. A night of blinding rain and intolerable grief tended to do that to a man. He wondered how Glory fared this Sunday morn. Better than he had, he hoped.

"Anything to do with the gang robbing the stages you told headquarters about a week or so ago?"

"You guessed it. Only it's worse now. Where's Major Jones anyway?"

"He died last month. That's how I got your telegram."

"Sorry to get that news. None better than the major."

"Yep, mighty big shoes to fill. Don't know that I'm able."

"You're a good man, Dan. Don't sell yourself short."

"I'll do what I can. You'd best fill me in, I reckon."

A few hours later, Luke watched Captain Roberts disappear through the brush. Relief settled some of the turmoil knotting his belly. They'd arrived at a plan that could work, given that everything would go accordingly.

He scooped a handful of mud, smearing it on his face. His hair got a generous helping as well. Then, he took the black eye patch from his pocket and rigged it in place. A few tears in his clothing, a liberal splashing of rotgut, and he reckoned his own mother wouldn't have recognized him.

Soldier pawed the ground when Luke reached for the reins. He watched the animal's eyes grow wide when he climbed instead on the strange mount the captain had brought.

"Hate to do this, boy, but you'd give me away. Folks around here know I ride a paint."

Luke stashed the horse near a stream in a secluded spot where no one was likely to stumble across him.

At least he hoped they didn't. Soldier was family.

The broom-tail mare sidestepped when he headed for Camp Colorado. After scouting the area the last few days, he knew for a fact the gang made use of the abandoned military fort.

"Cotton-pickin', girl! What's the matter with you?" Luke scratched his head.

Crazy horse. He'd never seen an animal trot sideways.

The rolling motion made him think he'd go off any second.

"Where in hell did the captain find you—a reject at an animal graveyard?"

The mare tossed her head from side to side as if to say she was most proud of the way she walked. *Fire and damnation!* If he wasn't so hard up, he'd turn her out to pasture and walk. Course, that might get him tossed out of the hideout on his ear. No self-respecting outlaw went into a den of thieves afoot. Better a flea-bitten nag than none at all. He reckoned he was stuck with Miss Gut Twister.

Across Jim Ned Creek, he found a small wash and kept in it until he spied the old fort. Tall thistle would let him get within shouting distance before a lookout saw him.

With the land now officially owned by Henry Sackett, he wondered whether the man was in cahoots with the gang.

Regardless, his gut said Vince Foster led them.

The muscles in his jaw twitched. Nothing he could prove yet, but he meant to find out one way or another. The run-in he'd had with the man left a bad taste in his mouth.

"You have one hell of a nerve coming onto my property and accusing me of robbing stages," Foster had yelled, his face a mottled red. "And I damn sure didn't frame anyone."

"A very reliable person claims otherwise."

"Who would that be?"

"Why, so you can keep him quiet?" Luke had asked quietly.

The relay station owner had shoved him, then drew back his fist. "Get off my land."

"Or what?"

"Consider this a final warning," Foster had snarled.

The recollection of that day tumbled, dead weeds carried by the parched Texas wind. Luke hadn't figured on Foster silencing the woman to keep her from talking. Old Mrs. Tucker might still be alive if not for his own carelessness. He'd underestimated the man. But he learned fast, and he wouldn't make that mistake again.

Luke would bet everything he owned that either Foster or one of his henchmen did in the woman. Had to. Come hell or high water, they'd pay for that and the other crimes too.

"I know you framed Jack Day, and I aim to prove it," he muttered into the wind.

Glory would get her father back. He just prayed it wouldn't be in a hearse. It all depended on him. A weighty burden for sure. Still, he couldn't live with himself if he rode off for parts unknown before he tried. The tally of his losses made quite a list—his job, his reputation, the parcel of land he'd saved for, and...

He had trouble getting air into his lungs.

The biggest sacrifice of all—the woman who'd given him lessons in pride and strength.

His Glory.

Giving her up staggered him. The way he saw things, he had nothing else to lose. Truth to tell, he truly was second to Duel. A soul killer at best. Never mind the worst.

This would be the last thing he could do for her. He prayed it'd be enough.

A shot zinged past his ear.

"State your business, mister."

Luke put on his poker face and peered into the brush. He couldn't see anyone, although tiny movement gave away the man's position. "A feller over by Fort Concho said you might need an extra gun hand. I came to see if the job is still open."

"Your name?"

"Up in the Black Hills they call me Texas Kidd. Maybe you heard tell of me? Got a bounty on my hide from here to the Dakotas."

"Cain't say I have. What're you wanted for?"

"Robbing, horse rustling. Held up a bank or two. And stages."

What credentials did a hardened outlaw need anyhow before they accepted him into their midst? He hoped they'd buy it. For good measure, he adjusted the eye patch a little better. Fire and damnation, the nuisance sure hindered a man's sight!

"Ever kill anyone?" the man asked.

Luke rested a forearm on the pommel. "Well, not counting the six or seven I planted grass over on purpose, I kinda plugged a few accidental-like."

"Pass on through and ask for Lefty."

The jitters quieted a tad. The first hurdle always appeared higher.

"Giddyup, you gotch-eared thing."

A fine howdy-do for someone who was supposedly an expert horse thief to ride such a sorry animal. He hoped they wouldn't hold it against him.

Other than jackrabbits and flies, no sign of life moved.

The crumbling walls of the old fort hid their secrets well. Luke scratched his head, not relishing the dried mud that came off onto his fingers. He sure wished he could wind this up soon so he could take a bath.

Someone watched. The hair on the back of his neck twitched.

All of a sudden, the dirt floor moved. His one-eyed squint saw the muzzle of a rifle sticking out from the crack of a trapdoor.

"Move a muscle and you won't have need for breathing."

"The lookout told me to ride on in. Said to ask for Lefty."

"Got a name?"

"Texas Kidd. Maybe you've heard of me?"

"Mebbe." A man climbed from the hole. "Thought you was dead, Kidd."

Luke tried to work up enough spit to swallow. For God's sake, he'd made up the title. What were the chances of a real live one? The game could end before it started if he didn't resemble the man.

The rifle-toting desperado eyeing him wouldn't fall for just any cock-and-bull story.

Twenty-three

SILENCE STRETCHED.

Luke racked his brain before deciding a bluff remained his sole choice. "Dead? Naw. Got some folks to start the rumor. Pure necessity on account of the posse on my trail."

The man eased toward him, keeping the barrel trained.

He hoped Desperado didn't get nervous. That rifle would put a hole in his chest big enough to herd cattle through.

"You've changed, Kidd. Somethin' different."

Sweat trickled down his forehead. He tensed and dismounted, ready to pull and fire the Colt if the need arose.

"For a fact." Luke added an extra helping of boldness to the swagger he adopted. "'Sides, I took some lead and pert near bought a parcel of prime land on Boot Hill."

Would Rifle-Toter believe such a tale? He held his breath.

Even if he hooked the man, he couldn't land him. Not unless he found a name to call him pronto. Though he could think of a few, they'd most likely get him shot.

"Don't say."

The gamble could pan out. Lord knows he'd never been much good at cutting the cards, but it was worth a shot anyhow.

He prayed for an ace. "Hell, Lefty, we've all aged. You don't expect me to keep my boyish charm while you get uglier than a horny toad ever' time I see you. Shoot, I didn't even recognize you."

A chuckle opened Luke's squinched good eye.

"Ugly, huh? You always were too big for your britches. Your poor mama must've plumb tuckered herself out whooping you."

Whew, the hunch paid off. Relief rippled through him. Lefty almost knocked him down slapping his back so hard.

"Well, yours probably hid you under the porch when company came calling for fear you'd scare 'em half to death."

"Good to see you, Kidd."

He'd made it into the hideout with all his hair. Reckon the captain would be pleased. He'd wait to see if he kept it before he passed the music and dancing.

❧

"But why do I hafta do it?"

Squirt's whine said little sis hadn't stepped that far from the new one who'd surprised Glory of late. Not yet. It'd take more than a day or two, she supposed.

The Sunday afternoon clouds parted and let the sun peek through. She could feel the heat through the kitchen window. They had to sneak the laudanum from their mother's room before she did something they'd forever regret.

"Because I need your special touch with Mama if she wakes." Glory drew Squirt closer and kissed her cheek. "You're not a little kid anymore. From now on, Hope and I are going to treat you like a young lady. We're depending on you."

"Well, if Hope wasn't out gallivanting all over the country with Alex O'Brien, she could do it."

Glory tried to block the rhythm of the small heart beating against her. It spoke of a special kind of fright.

The way hers did since…

This called for focus. Calming the quivers inside would

take her mind off unpleasant, scary goblins. Soon nothing but ghostly images would replace what once filled her life.

"Honey, you're the only one who can wrap Mama around your finger. I chose you for this important task. You can do it, sweetie. Remember how brave and strong you've become."

"All right. But you'll wait outside the door?"

"I won't budge until you come out."

They stole softly to the bedroom. Patience turned the knob and tiptoed in.

Glory listened for sounds. No voices came. Good. That meant Ruth slept. A few seconds later, Glory jumped when Patience touched her arm.

"I can't find it," Squirt whispered.

"Did you look on the bed table?"

"Yep."

"Maybe the bottle fell under the bed."

"Nope, nothing there."

She went over all the logical places in her head. Mama had to have it in there. Somewhere.

"It must be in the bed then. The pillows?"

"Aw, don't make me look there. She's lying on one and her arm's on the other. I just know she'll wake up."

Damn this infernal blindness!

"Guess I misspoke about you being grown-up and thinking you could handle the job. You tried but it's too big for you. I would do it myself, only I'd fumble around and wake her."

If this didn't work, nothing would. They could wait for Hope. Except Dr. Dalton stressed haste.

Finally, Patience let out an exaggerated sigh. "Well, okay. I'll try again, I suppose. For you. I just hate sneaking into people's rooms."

Since when? Glory had to clap her hand over her mouth to hold the laughter. "That's my girl. Check in the bedclothes too."

The grandfather clock in the parlor ticked, counting off

one of the long seconds Luke spoke about. Minutes seemed to have passed. *Concentrate on other noises*, she urged herself. Still nothing. Her heart pounded.

At last came the faint click of the doorknob.

"Glory, you'd better come." Patience sniffled, her voice shaky.

The odd tone chilled Glory's blood. "Why?"

"On account of…"

"What? Tell me." She gripped the small shoulders.

"Something's bad wrong."

Oh, dear God! The wind flew from her lungs. She stumbled across the bedroom, not waiting for Patience to guide her.

"Mama?" She patted the length of the still form until she located her mother's face. "Mama, wake up."

Cold, lifeless skin.

She located Ruth's mouth. It gaped open.

Dalton's instructions should they find the opium-laced bottle empty whirled in her head—send for him immediately. Even then it might be too late.

"Patience, tell me if she's breathing."

No answer came. Panic swept Glory. "Answer me!"

"I—I can't—tell."

Dear Mother Mary! She put her face against Ruth's lips and detected the faintest of breath.

Mama, don't you love us enough to see how we turn out?

The sound of the pain-filled answer became as loud in her ears as the familiar gong announcing the hour. Yes, their mother would throw everything away. She'd toss Hope, Patience, and her aside as objects unworthy of a struggle.

Damn you, Ruth Day!

She blinked back hot tears. She'd not give in to them. Not today. Only in the dead of night could she allow such things.

"Patience, you'll have to go for Dr. Dalton."

"But—"

"No buts. Honey, you can do it. Hurry!"

The screen door slammed behind the youngest Day, leaving nothing but eerie silence in her wake. Sitting beside Ruth's bed, Glory cradled the thin, blue-veined hand, desperate to hold on to a shred of hope. She stroked the smooth fingers that had never known a callus or blister—the pampered skin of refined beauty.

A shutter suddenly banged.

Glory jumped in alarm before she realized the wind had picked up, gusting against the windows. Blood in her veins turned to ice.

The wind always carried problems.

Inside the house, spirits of long-dead elders huddled around. They spoke in hushed whispers of that long, painful night of the soul. She suddenly grew old and haggard.

Her biggest fear, the thing she'd fought most, had come to pass.

Useless.

Dependent.

Alone.

Glory rested her head on the sheets. She'd become the very image she so despised. The strength of the wind shook the house, a beast trying to get inside. For her, it already had.

Vague hoofbeats and voices reached her. Probably something her madness conjured. She was alone.

"Patience? Glory?" Hope called. "Where are you?"

She jerked up her head. "In Mama's room."

"Dear heavens! Oh no." The soft calico Hope wore brushed against her. Glory wished she could tell her she'd only dreamed the tragedy.

"We found her too late. I sent Patience for the doctor."

"Why did I have to go with Alex today of all days? Why couldn't I have come home with you?"

"Stop it!" Glory laid Ruth's hand on the sheet and rose. She shook her middle sister. "Stop that right now. You are entitled to a life of your own. You deserve any happiness you can make. Nothing you did would've changed a thing anyway. We found Mama like this."

"The laudanum bottle. How much…?"

"Patience looked for it."

"It has to be here."

A rustle of the covers grated on her nerves. She couldn't bear to know the answer, as it would mean their mother took the easy way out because she was weak-minded.

The shutter banged loudly again.

"Here it is." Hope paused. "Oh God!" came as a strangled sob.

Finding the truth would complete the numbness seeping over her. She had no room for warmth or love or tenderness.

That had vanished. All it did anyway was bring hurt.

"It's empty, isn't it?"

"Yes." Hope's shoes made a hollow sound on the floor when she moved to the window. "They're here—the doctor, Patience, and Uncle Pete."

❧

Twelve chimes of the clock announced the midnight hour, and Glory had yet to find her bed. Nor had anyone else. They all waited for God alone knew what, even Uncle Pete, who refused to leave.

"I'm scared." Patience threw her arms around Glory's middle. "Do you think Mama'll die?"

"The doctor has done everything to make sure she doesn't."

Though whether it would be enough or not only time would tell. For all intents and purposes, Ruth was dead when help arrived. She just hadn't stopped breathing yet.

Dr. Dalton came from the bedroom for a hundredth cup of coffee. Bloodshot eyes, rolled-up sleeves, and a wrinkled frown were what she pictured in her mind. He had proven his worth. She had no idea how they could pay for his services. It added one more person to whom they were beholden.

"Are you afraid?"

Arm in arm they turned into the parlor. Glory counted the steps to the rocking chair and pulled Patience onto her lap.

"Sure am, Punkin." Addressing her baby sis by Luke's nickname had slipped out. She gasped for air.

"I sure miss Mr. Luke. Wish he'd come riding up on Soldier. Don't you?"

Oh yeah. And a whole lot more. She would never smell fresh hay or hear raindrops on the roof without remembering a love that transcended the boundaries of time and space. It was endless and unconditional. She took him without judgment. However, whatever, whoever he wished to be would thrill her.

Please let him know I'll shrivel and die without him.

She wouldn't ask anything else—not even to get her sight back.

Safety amongst a band of cutthroats could be measured in split-second increments.

Luke kept a sharp eye out for slithery things that favored underground dens as he walked through the unkempt group. His nerves were stretched. Staying alert and ready could mean the difference in living and bedding down with the buzzards.

"Texas Kidd, huh?" The one doing the asking picked his teeth with a long Bowie knife.

The fellow's looks matched a garden slug's. Though Luke felt he owed the slug an apology for the comparison.

"That's what I said." Luke pulled up an overturned barrel and sat down with the six or seven men who half-heartedly played cards. Their bored expressions suggested they couldn't wait for the order to ride. "You boys sure have quite a setup here." He let out a long whistle. "Yep, the trapdoor above hides the whole shebang. Whoever thought of it has my admiration."

"Humph, if you say so."

So much for hoping they'd toss in a tidbit now and again. Offering a name would make his job a tad easier. No one had bothered with introductions.

"Ever run across any snakes down here?"

"When we do, we skin and eat 'em."

He hoped they were pulling his leg. Then he decided keeping an eye out might not hurt.

"By chance, you mind pointing me in the direction of who's in charge so I can find out when I can get to work?"

"You're awfully nosy, ain't you, Tex?" Slug flicked his wrist and launched the knife. The blade stuck in the table half an inch from Luke's hand.

"Just pays to draw a bead on how the operation's run."

"He'll send word when need be." Lefty shuffled the cards. "We sit tight and wait."

That meant the boss man stayed at another location. Either these men plain didn't know, or else they were awful dumb. Luke cast the Arkansas toothpick a cautious glance. Too many questions could get his teeth picked next. Might pay to become miserly in that department.

"Fine by me. Don't have nothing but time."

"Figure we'll have to lie low for a while on account of the law poking around." The man to his left spoke, then stuck out his hand. "I'm Bill."

"Glad to know you." Luke shook it, measuring the friendliest in the group.

"These others are Frenchie and Cuny. Creede was the lookout you ran into."

"Howdy, boys." Nary a one acknowledged him.

"We don't need no Ranger breathing down our necks. I say we kill the troublemaking weasel," said Cuny, the only red-haired one of the bunch.

Luke's blood froze. "Ranger? Here in Coleman County?"

"Yep. A Captain Roberts, I heard."

For a bunch of moles who only came up for air once in a while, they knew the state of affairs pretty well. Somebody kept them informed.

"Anyone know why he showed up?"

Cuny shrugged. "Could be on account of that woman who got herself hung. Be my guess."

Luke waded deeper. "Rumor has it they're looking to pin that on some fellow named McClain. Say, you despera-does know him?"

The man called Frenchie spoke up. "Only by the smell."

Now what the hell did that mean? Luke pretended unconcern as he met the surly glare.

"Don't say?"

"McClain's been spending a lot of time with that Day family. Saw with my own two eyes." Frenchie reached for the knife and flipped it end over end, catching it by the handle.

Slithers crawled up Luke's spine. Evidently, the man kept a close watch on the Day farm. For what reason? He didn't like any of the answers popping into mind.

"Yep, that Glory Day is one handsome woman despite the britches. Gives a man a powerful urge to settle between those white legs for a picnic lunch. Yep, one of these times I reckon I will."

Damn!

It took every ounce of control to keep Luke from reaching for his forty-five and blowing the ugly thought right out of Frenchie's head. He clenched his fists and remembered his purpose. The man had better beat a wide path around Glory though. Or else he'd throw caution to the wind and take great pleasure in educating the bastard on the finer points of anthill torture. He'd heard tell of a man staked out in one who lived for over a week.

"Hey, Tex, whatever happened to that wife of your'n? Now there was one pretty woman. The way she sashayed under a man's nose used to give me a bad case of the wants."

Lefty's question brought an unforgiving quiet. If Luke failed this test, it'd all be over.

"Fickle women. I swear they're all the same." He scratched the mud-encrusted stubble on his chin, adjusted the eye patch, and leaned forward. "She ran off with a Bible-toter. Said she wanted a man who'd live longer'n a gun hand. Can you believe the luck?"

Grunts swept the underground chamber. Luke reckoned he hit on something the gang agreed on.

"What was her name?" Lefty asked. "Cain't seem to recall."

Criminy cricket! Luke had no clue how to sidestep this hole. Well, gut instinct had brought him this far.

Luke laughed. "Hell, me neither. I've put a lot of whiskey and a whole passel of saloon gals between her and forgetting. And you yahoos said I asked a lot of questions!"

The trapdoor opened before anyone could shoot him. A man stepped down the narrow ladder.

❧

"That sister of mine has a powerful wish to pass on." Worry rode herd in Uncle Pete's voice. "I don't have no more sense than that white mule out there."

"No one holds you accountable." Glory considered that if she'd paid more mind to Mama's problem and had more compassion, it would've made a difference. Anger didn't serve much purpose.

"Well, it darn shore ain't your fault either, missy."

She wondered if he'd gone into the mind-reading business.

"How do you know so much, Uncle?"

"Had a whole lotta years to get smart. I done learned fear is in the future. Regret is living in the past. A body can't do either for long without going off his rocker. I'm guessing Ruth did both. But I sure didn't hafta rush her along."

No matter what he said, Glory hadn't helped the situation any. Fear and regret fit in both pockets…in large doses.

"Is Patience finally asleep?" she asked quietly.

"Curled right here beside me." The way Uncle Pete said it she knew he watched over them with a fierce protectiveness. He must be exhausted himself.

"I'm glad. Don't know whenever she cried so much." If Ruth died, it would affect baby sis more than any of them. Already their parents left a big enough hole as it was. What their future held only a soothsayer would dare predict.

She recalled Dr. Dalton's assessment upon completing the eye examination in his office.

"Bear in mind I'm certainly no expert, and I'd give anything not to confirm your suspicions, Miss Glory," he'd said.

"You can fix her, can't you?" Hope asked.

"Too much damage. The blow to the head restricted blood flow to the back of her eyes. The outcome looks bleak."

The words echoed in Glory's mind even yet. *No hope.*

Uncle Pete yawned loudly. "Yep, I figure life is a package. Comes with good things and bad. A mixture of storms and sunshine…"

His voice trailed, leaving deep snores to fill the room.

Glory contemplated those truths and silently agreed. She only wished the good would outweigh the bad for a change.

Twenty-four

By dusk Monday, Ruth Day appeared to have passed the worst.

Uncle Pete left. Dr. Dalton rode back to town, saying he'd call on Ruth the next day. Hope and Patience were busy with a multitude of chores they'd neglected during the vigil. That left Glory to sit with their mother.

Regular breathing indicated more natural sleep.

Relieved to have gotten through the crisis, Glory rested her head against the back of the chair. She contemplated her middle sister's news of this morn. That Alex had proposed didn't come as any surprise. Hope's glow only reinforced the gloom of her own situation. Soon Glory would know more about loneliness and heartache than she cared to.

A faint rustle of sheets alerted her.

"Mama? Are you awake?"

She located Ruth's hand by touch and lifted it to her cheek. So frail and dainty. The veins on the back stood out.

"Did I die?"

"No, you're very much with us in your own bed."

"Why do you insist on keeping me here? Why didn't you let me go?"

The thin, distraught plea whipped the air. Glory bit her trembling lip. Despite everything that had happened, Ruth persisted on the low road she'd chosen.

"Because we...because I need you." Because if she lost one more person she might give up herself.

She put her face on her mother's bosom.

"No. From the time you were born, you never needed me. You were always strong and brave. I can give nothing to you now."

"You're wrong, Mama."

"I watched you, you know. I envied your uncanny ability to do whatever it took to survive. You were the one person I most wished to be." Ruth's sigh seemed to come from the deepest part of her soul. "But you belonged to your father, not me."

A feeble touch smoothed back Glory's hair. She prayed for words to tell her mother things she never dared say.

"All the times when you hugged Hope, babied Patience, and wiped her tears, I tried to pretend you cared about me just as much, tried to tell myself it didn't hurt that you pushed me aside."

"Oh, my poor darling. I never shunned you. Not on purpose anyway. Your attitude held me at arm's length. I didn't know how to get past the fortress you erected."

She dared not put stock in the lie and lower defenses that saved her from ruin.

"Don't you care enough about us to live to see us grown, Mama?"

"I don't expect you to understand the kind of love between a husband and wife. When your father went away, he took everything good about me with him."

Ruth had no idea she'd described Glory's feelings for the man she called McClain.

Luke had left her world a desolate waste when he rode off into the storm. Suffering the same devastation created a tiny crack in the thick wall she'd built.

Yet as always, Ruth blamed her lack on others. She hadn't changed.

"Though I tried to excuse the circumstances truly beyond Jack's control," her mother continued, "an utter sense of betrayal made me angry and afraid. I didn't want to live without your father. But it was never, ever about the love I have for my precious daughters. Please believe that."

"I want to." Maybe the time had come to allow herself to feel compassion for her mother. Still, could she allow herself that weakness? Could she risk voicing her deep disappointment?

"Let me show you, Glory. Can you give me another chance?"

Glory managed a shaky breath. "I convinced myself I could be content with any scraps that fell by the wayside after you gave Hope and Patience everything else. But then I see how desperately you meant to rid yourself of us one way or another."

"What have I done! Can you find it in your heart to let me make amends?"

How could she not? Doing so would heal both their spirits. She could merely nod because of the lump clogging her throat.

"Does that mean you forgive me for being such a burdensome old woman?"

Glory wiped away a tear. "Long as you promise to keep living."

❧

The leader of the outlaw gang watched a lone rider approach. He didn't lift his finger from the trigger of his pistol until he recognized the man who'd come to report. He waited, his impatience growing.

The rider climbed down. While the man slapped clinging thistle off his britches with his hat, the leader scanned the brush.

"You sure no one followed you?"

"Yep. Kinda skittish, aren't you?"

"Careless can get a man killed. I worked too hard to get this operation to where it is. So far no one suspects, and I aim to keep it that way. No slips, understand?" He spat brown tobacco juice from the side of his mouth. "I ain't ready to call it quits yet. Anything new to tell?"

"We have a new addition to the group, boss."

"I warned you about letting strangers in. Too risky."

"Lefty vouches for him. A fellow by the name of Texas Kidd."

The hackles on the back of the boss's neck rose. He trusted no one. Not even his own mother if she still lived. Something felt wrong. "What does he look like?"

"A real ugly feller. Wears a black patch over one eye. Don't think he took a bath his whole life."

"Texas Kidd, huh?" His gut twisted. "Don't trust him."

"You want I should kill him?"

"Not yet. Watch him close and keep your lip buttoned."

"Already been asking a bunch of questions. Wanted to meet the head man right off."

"Did, huh?" He'd never known his gut to be wrong.

"Yeah, an' he's got a strange way about him too."

"Like I said, don't give him the time of day. Have you heard anything new on McClain?"

"No one's seen hide nor hair of him. Folks in Santa Anna took the bait just like you planned. They blame him for hanging that old lady."

"Good. Serves him right for what he did to my son. An eye for an eye is what I always said."

"He might've left the territory."

Damn! He hoped to hell not. Luke McClain hadn't gotten near enough grief. And he had a special treat saved for him.

"You've been watching that Day girl, ain't you?"

"Yep, just like you said. No sign of him."

"He'll turn up. Is that all?"

The rider lowered his eyes and scuffed the toe of his boot.

"Well?"

"A Texas Ranger showed up."

"You don't say."

"Feller by the name of Captain Roberts."

"Shit! Who sent for him?"

"Don't know, boss. Could be just passing through."

"We'll have to lie low for sure now. When a Ranger sinks his teeth in something, he don't let go. Put a man to watching him and be extra careful. Roberts is a tough hombre to tame."

The rider climbed back into the saddle and galloped back in the direction he came.

Boss slung his fist into the solid corral post. He'd just got wind about a shipment of gold ripe for the pickings. One of the biggest hauls he'd seen in a while and he couldn't do a damn thing about it.

❧

Glory came awake by degrees. The sound of her own heartbeat filled the little alcove, her sanctuary. No one stirred in the house. Mornings used to be her favorite time. She'd write in her journal or just lie and arrange the day in her head. Well, she wouldn't be doing any more writing. And the day's schedule? It remained pretty blank of late.

At least Mama appeared to be mending. The ordeal might have jarred her back to reality. Maybe she'd get her wits about her again for Hope and Patience's sake.

Uncle Pete hit the nail on the head. Life was a package of good and bad. Didn't come with any guarantees. You simply took what it gave and made the best of it. No whining, no excuses.

But wasn't that what she'd sunk to? a still voice whispered. Truth could make a body squirm.

Yet, she couldn't fathom how anyone void of sight could lead a productive life. At least not the kind she used to. For God's sake, hunters had to know what they aimed at to shoot a rifle! And while she could still saddle the mule, how would she determine directions? Just supposing there were other ways to kill game for the table, work the farm, how did one go about it?

Weariness washed over. She pushed the sheet aside and

slowly pulled on her clothes. It was a bit much for her at present. She'd mull it over for a few days.

The kitchen floor creaked in the usual places on her way through. She found the walking stick where she left it propped in the corner. The door swung open with ease.

Startled movements outside put ice in her veins. Someone or something was on their back porch.

"Who's there?" A racing pulse brought sharpness to her tone. She prodded the air with the wooden staff until it struck a firm object.

Kneeling, Glory touched animal fur. It didn't move.

Of a sudden, the faint rustle of clothing perked her ears.

"Someone's there. Whoever you are, speak up."

A voice cleared. "Uh…it's only me, Miss Glory."

"Horace?"

Sniffles preceded the answer. "Yeah."

Crying had an unmistakable sound. She knew it well.

"What are you doing here? Has something happened?"

Folks said his father beat him on occasion. She prayed the rumor hadn't come to fruition. No one deserved such treatment.

"I c–come to bring the meat I killed."

Ah, the mysterious leaver of food. Glory felt her way past the gift and down the steps. Horace reached out to help.

"But why?"

"On account of I knew you had bad troubles. I didn't want that you should starve. Or worry."

A little part of her couldn't help wishing the culprit had been Luke. Every nerve in her body yearned for his touch and when the smell of hay drifted in the breeze, she remembered their last hours with indelible clarity.

Hell's bells! Where had he gone?

For two cents, she'd saddle Caesar and hunt down the charmer who had the audacity to show her the way to the Promised Land and then leave her high and dry.

"Horace, what troubles are you talking about?" She touched his shoulder.

"I'm not stupid like everyone says."

"Of course you're not." She'd like to give a piece of her mind to the good, self-righteous busybodies who threw barbs with abandon.

"I followed you sometimes." Horace sniffed. "I saw you get blind. I only wanted to help. Didn't mean to do nothing wrong."

"No, please don't think that. Your generosity is a fine thing. I don't know of a more caring soul in Coleman County." She sensed his load becoming lighter.

"For true? Honest?"

"That's a fact. I'd rather stand shoulder to shoulder with you than any of the whole mess."

"Aw, Miss Glory. You mean you'll keep lettin' me do stuff?"

Though she didn't know exactly what that consisted of, she recognized his need. "You bet I will."

"I'm not your beau anymore. But can I still be a friend?"

Wetness filled her eyes. She recognized the spirit longing for acceptance. He'd settle for whatever she could spare.

"I'll take whatever you want to give me. Who put this notion in your head?"

"No one."

"Then you decided all by yourself you don't want to be my beau anymore?"

"I do, but I can't. Not anymore."

"Why?"

"Ain't right to have two beaus. Mr. Luke is the onliest one you need. I'll jus' be your friend. All right?"

"How did you know about Luke?"

"I just do. He has the key."

The boy spoke in riddles. "A key?"

"To your heart. He knows how to open the locked places. Whoever has the key gets to marry the princess."

Her breath caught on a jagged piece of her soul.

Horace expressed ideas with astounding eloquence. Luke had unlocked everything that she'd been too scared, and too angry, to let herself think about. Most of all, he'd shown her how to ride the magic carpet and gifted her with a great love.

And then he'd left in the middle of the rainstorm.

"No, he can't marry the princess. He's gone."

"But I know where he is."

"You followed him?"

"Just a little bit. Did I do wrong?"

That could only mean Luke hadn't left the country. All of a sudden, she had an urge to laugh—or hug Horace, which she did. "You are the most special of friends."

"Want I should tell you?"

The thrill vanished. It wouldn't do a bit of good to know, since Glory couldn't go to him, and her situation made that highly impossible. Better Luke stay hidden, however enticing the fruit dangled.

"I can't…" The thought strangled her.

"Because your eyes can't see?"

"A blind person has to accept that there are a lot of things she can no longer do. Better off to face the grim reality."

"But if you could see again for just a moment, what would you want to do?"

Dear Mother Mary! The mere thought of such a miracle raised goose bumps. She'd go after Luke and tell him how much she loved him. Didn't seem right for a person to never know of the tender feelings another had for him. Just not right at all. So much for ridiculous speculation. Eternal darkness had robbed her of confidence. She closed her mind to the wish that dealt added misery.

"Fact is, I will never see again and that's that."

"My grandma told me once that strength is found in hush. Only still water will let you see a picture of the sky. You can't see if it's storming, you know. Leastways that's what she said."

The statement fluttering no louder than a pair of hummingbird wings hit Glory with the force of a mighty wind.

Self-pity had deafened the tiny voice that told her to be free, creating this frightening noise inside her head. To look for inner peace would take shushing the storm. It required digging down deep inside. When she found it, it would reflect everything she could be.

"Your grandmother was a wise soul."

"I know. She said a bunch of other stuff but I can't remember it. Miss Glory, do you think Grandma can see me from heaven?"

"She's not merely watching over you, Horace, but she has her arm around you this very minute. Feel her?"

"I thought that was you."

"It's both of us." She found strange comfort in the boy. Perhaps she could find her worth again. Might take some adjustment and learning new ways to go about daily living. But she could. She could do whatever she had to. Somehow, she'd work her fingers to the bone to make the farm something to hand down to future generations.

A sudden thought left her dumbstruck. It had taken simple words from a simple mind to open her eyes. She hadn't lost her will, just misplaced it. No one could take that unless she gave it up.

You have every reason in the world to step aside now and let others take the reins. No one would fault you.

Heaven help her if she'd let someone else fill her shoes!

She just found that two cents she had yearned for earlier. "Horace, tell me where Mr. McClain is."

"Oh boy! I'll take you there. But you'll have to wait till I do my chores first. Pa'll skin me alive."

"We don't want that. Come back when you finish. I'll be here."

"Wait'll I tell Cleo."

"Maybe we should keep this a secret between us."

"Cleo won't tell. She's just a mouse. My bestest friend. Besides you, that is." He kissed her cheek. "Be back later."

The thud of his shoes on the ground told her he ran.

Glory cursed the blind thief who had robbed her of so much. "You can't have me. Not today. Maybe tomorrow, but be prepared for a fight!"

Twenty-five

GLORY PLOWED UP THE DEAD GARDEN WHILE WAITING ON Horace. Working the soil kept her mind occupied. Patience offered a tad too much helpful advice, but baby sis meant well. Together they planted cabbage, onions, and squash.

She'd always found a reverence in the miracle sprouting from the tiny seeds, and today that awe created a throb in her heart.

Of late, she'd been so overwhelmed with the big picture that she'd almost lost sight of the small things. Yet, it was those tiny details that added meaning to a life…

The beauty of a single drop of dew on a flower petal.

Dawn's pink tint that gave promise to a morning.

And…the twinkle in Luke's eyes when he dared her to spurn his attentions.

She sucked air into her hungry lungs. Some things a person couldn't forget, no matter how hard she tried.

A cooling breeze swept her brow. The day had turned cloudy with the fresh smell of rain drifting in the air. Another shower would give the newly planted seeds an excellent start.

New beginnings all around seemed the order of the day. A sense of pride radiated through her.

Though still in the figuring-out stage, she found she had a ways to go before she turned in the plow for a rocking chair. Doing something other than whining changed her perspective.

"Glory, someone's coming. You think it might be Mr. Luke?"

A flush rose at the mere idea. "I don't know, dear."

"Oh shoot, it's only Horace."

"You don't have to sound so happy about it. Horace happens to be one of my favorite people."

"I know. Horace is nice, but he's not Mr. Luke."

For a fact. Still, tingles camped out along the curve of her spine. With a little luck, she might soon know whether the next hours would offer success or failure. Her sole desire was simply a say in the matter. And to be able to tell McClain she loved him.

Glory tried to get the two worrywarts she'd left behind off her mind. Hope and Squirt had pitched a real fit. They didn't understand. Truth to tell, she didn't either. The logic of traipsing off after a dream defied logic. Yet, how could she not?

"Horace, where are we headed?"

"You know that place where the soldiers used to stay?"

"Camp Colorado?"

"I guess."

"You saw Mr. Luke there?"

"I think so."

Goodness gracious! What kind of star had she hitched her wagon to? Time to find out. She pulled up.

"Tell me one way or the other. Did you see Luke at the old fort? Think hard."

Animal snorts and the creak of saddle leather broke the moment of silence. At last the muddle in Horace's brain cleared. "Yep, I sure did."

The reassurance bolstered her. Caesar moved forward.

"Miss Glory, did you ever know my ma? I keep trying to see her face, but I cain't."

The wistful plea settled in the center of her breast. The boy had no one except a mean father. Even with Ruth's problems, Glory counted herself fortunate.

"I can't tell you, because I was only a little girl myself when she died. I'm sorry."

"Me too. Grandma said she was awful pretty."

"Only a beautiful mama could bring a special fellow like you into the world."

His sigh left room for doubt. "I suppose."

A peal of thunder startled Caesar. She leaned to pat the animal's withers, crooning encouragement. A soaking appeared in store. Hope and Patience would have more cause to worry.

They arrived at the juncture of Horde's Creek and Jim Ned before a drop or two fell. Camp Colorado's crumbling walls stood just ahead according to Glory's recollection.

Horace touched her arm. "We hafta get off here and walk."

"Why?"

"'Cause that's what Mr. Luke did."

Excuse her for asking dumb questions. She swung her leg over and slid to the ground.

"Wait here, Miss Glory. Might not be safe."

She hadn't set out to stay behind. "No, I'll come with you."

"Hold my hand then. Don't make noise."

The roar of wind, the kind that forever brought problems, drowned out her argument. She could only follow where his clammy hand pulled her. Though the request for quiet appeared a bit ridiculous with the sky falling down around their ears.

"Duck down. This is it."

The hurried squat made her scrape her knees against a rough brick wall. "What do you see?"

"A couple of lizards and a baby rabbit. It's real cute. Now it's hopping away."

She curbed her frustration. Under ordinary circumstances, she had no trouble allowing for the child's mind in a grown-up body.

"I meant any sign of Luke."

"Nope."

"You're positive this is the right place?"

"Think so."

Biting wind gave her disappointment free rein. They came on a fool's journey. She sagged against the mud brick. She should've known better than to pin her hopes on the impossible.

"I see him! The ground spit Mr. Luke out. It swallowed him, and then it spit him up."

"You're speaking in riddles again. The ground can't gobble anyone."

"Can too. And I think it ate his eye."

The mother tongue of Horace should've brought a smile to her. But her patience could stretch only so far.

"Quit making up stories."

"It must've because he's wearing a patch over it."

Hell's bells! If only she could see!

"Are you sure it's Luke?"

"Uh-huh."

Then why didn't Horace call to him? She tried to get to her feet, but his grip kept her anchored.

"We hafta hide. It'll eat us too."

"For goodness' sake. I'm going to Luke." She tried to rise one more time.

"Oops, it done spit out another one."

"One what?"

"A man."

"What's happening now? What are they doing?" Ice formed around her heart. Dark. Forbidding.

This cursed wind has brought this!

✧

Luke shrugged off the hand that spun him around. He gave the half-breed they called Creede an even stare. "Afraid I'm gonna tuck tail and run?"

"Boss don't keep anyone who won't follow orders."

"Fire and damnation! Anything wrong in getting a breath of fresh air? A man can only take so much of Frenchie."

"No one said you had to kiss him."

"A little rough around the edges for my taste."

"Rules is rules."

Those didn't pertain to anything other than him clearing the stench from his lungs to his way of thinking. "Gotta go to the bushes. Got a sour stomach. I'll check on my horse while I'm out."

"Make it quick."

Criminy! Luke didn't relish the ribbing he'd take. "Won't be long. Got an aversion to water."

And an aversion sure enough to dying. Too early yet to shed the disguise. He walked toward the wild plum thicket where they tied the mounts. The gang had to stash them aboveground because no one had taught their four-legged compadres how to climb down the ladder.

No one would find the horses in the thick growth anyway. Hell, he had trouble locating them himself. The stuff grew where little else did.

Just as Luke reached to push his way through, he heard a noise. Someone or something. No sentry tonight because the group decided only a fool would have the guts to sniff them out with a storm brewing. Maybe he'd only imagined it.

"Pssst. Mr. Luke, over here."

Someone used his name. He froze. "Who's out there?"

A swift touch located the smooth handle of his Colt.

"Hurry, before it swallows you again!"

Then came the voice he'd never forget. "Luke?"

His heart lurched against his ribs. Something bad must've happened. He couldn't think of any other reason she'd leave the safety of the farm to brave menacing weather.

Should they find Glory here… He couldn't bear to entertain that thought.

Heaven help anyone who laid a finger on her.

Arms grabbed him when he stepped over what remained of the fort wall, and he found himself face-to-face with the silken-haired lady. "What are you doing here?"

"I brung her 'cause she got blind."

A man couldn't make out much with a one-eyed squint. Didn't know how those pirates got by. At last Luke got things in focus. "Aren't you the smithy's boy?"

"Horace... Horace Simon."

"What's wrong? Is someone hurt...or dead?"

Glory frowned. "No. Don't get mad. I asked Horace to bring me."

"How on earth... No one knew..." The turn of events stole words from him. One part wanted to kiss the living daylights out of her while the other leaned more toward shaking her until her teeth rattled. Strange how both included touching her. "You know the danger you're in?"

"We sure do, Mr. Luke. What with the earth eating folks and spitting them back out after it steals your eyes."

"What is he talking about?"

"He saw you and the other man rise from beneath the dirt." She explored his mouth with her fingertips and moved up to the black patch. "Horace thinks it ate your eye."

The contact aroused all the things it shouldn't.

"You have to go. Pronto."

"Why are you wearing a patch?"

"That happens to be my business."

"Tit for tat, is that it?"

Have mercy! Given the rough lot a few yards away who shot people for sport, it wasn't time for chitchat. What he was about to do would most likely destroy anything that remained between them. Whether by fair means or foul, he had to get her away before...

"I'm busy, Glory. Besides, we have nothing to discuss."

Glory's lips turned white. Her chin quivered. "You're not curious about why I came?"

"When are you going to realize everything isn't about

you?" The callous question came from his lips but he didn't recognize the words. Still, he had to get her away from here.

God forgive him! Pain rippled across his chest. He'd just shattered the one woman who meant the world to him. He could barely see her pretty features through the mist in his eyes.

"I never thought... You're nothing but a deceitful, despicable coward. You're one of these murdering scum. You have joined them, haven't you?"

Luke winced. He deserved that and more.

"Go home where you belong, Glory. Horace, take her."

"Not until I say what's on my mind."

They'd been through this—that night he'd gone alone on Perkins's trail. She was as stubborn as the day was long. His glance flicked to the trapdoor. They'd come looking soon.

"Come with me. I'll give you one minute."

"I'll keep watch, Mr. Luke. I won't let the monster get you."

Shoving aside the plum thicket, Luke pulled her in after him, her walking stick banging his shins. They'd be safe enough in here, he reckoned. The horses snorted, pawing the ground. Startled, Glory leaned into him. His breath became labored. He struggled to adjust, cursing the fact that he'd forgotten she couldn't see. He couldn't get used to that.

"Don't be afraid. It's only the horses." A flash of lightning split the sky, allowing him to take in the breathtaking beauty he'd thought never to feast his eyes on again. He braced against all sorts of temptations. "Say what you came to say. The clock is ticking."

"You're scaring me. I've never heard this tone."

Her head came to below his chin. The heady scent of honeysuckle stuck in his throat with each gulp of air.

"Which one would you have me use? You're in danger here. You shouldn't have come."

"I've made a big mistake—I thought you were worth risking something for."

"Ah, now it's getting through to you. You see what I've become."

Glory's gasp overrode the clap of thunder. "Which is the real Luke? The framed Ranger or hunted killer?"

He winced, her cold anger cutting him to the quick. "Reckon you're glad you didn't take me up on my offer of marriage. Go home and forget you ever knew me. Forget everything."

All of a sudden, the bramble hiding them rustled. "Hey, Tex, you gonna take all night? Them cold beans didn't hurt anyone else's belly."

Luke's worst nightmare just came to life. He silenced Glory with a finger to her lips.

"Son of a dirt-eater, Frenchie! Didn't think you liked me. I wouldn't come any closer unless you have a clothespin—"

"You bastard, I'm just making sure you don't run out before I get a chance to kill you."

A rancid taste filled his mouth. "Well, you can see I ain't going anywhere."

"Me an' the boys'll give you to the count of five to get your butt back."

"Right behind you."

Luke waited, making sure Frenchie had left. "Time's up."

"Why are you doing this? It doesn't make any sense."

"Better you hate me." *And live*, he added. Lord knew she couldn't hurt worse than he did. There would be no forgiveness for what he'd done.

"Who is Frenchie? What are you doing?"

He set her apart and turned before desire to hold her, to kiss away her fright became stronger than his resistance. If he could be sure he'd come out of this mess in one piece... He didn't lay odds on that. Still, he had to warn her.

"One more thing, Glory. If you need help, run straight to Captain Roberts. He can protect you."

"Your concern is touching. Get on to your business, whatever that may be. I wouldn't want to keep you." Sarcasm didn't become her. If only it could be different.

"No matter your distaste for me, don't take my warning lightly."

"After the way I treated the man, I could sooner sprout wings and fly."

"Never sell Roberts short. Watch your back."

"Besides, why would I need... You're hiding something!"

Momentary weakness made him bite his tongue, for the urge to spill the truth came in overwhelming waves.

It would serve no purpose except to endanger her life all the more.

A deep ache shuddered inside. He hoped to cross her mind occasionally, and when he did, maybe she'd remember some good. That she'd look with favor on the man called McClain would be the least he could hope for.

How could a man who'd betrayed the love in his heart just moments before tell her to embrace each day with abandon because a body never knew when the curtain would fall on the last act? He could never take back the despicable things he'd just said to her.

She'd never know the wondrous gift she'd given him.

"I wanted to tell—"

Glory never got to finish. His kiss stole the avowal of love she'd braved all her fears to deliver. Luke staggered the senses she relied on to keep her world righted. That compass was more important now in the darkness that persisted even when the midday sun peaked. She simply knew his arms were the one place she always wanted to be. He brought peace to her wounded soul.

When his mouth left hers and he was gone, she felt alone on a wind-stormed desert.

"I love you, my stranger," she murmured into space.

Though people spoke of walking to the ends of the earth for someone, she had never understood the true meaning until now.

She'd go to the end and one step beyond for Luke McClain.

A sound alerted her, something different from the wind

blowing through the branches. Bands tightened around her throat.

"Horace?" she squeaked.

"Well, if it ain't Miss Glory Day in the flesh, as I live and breathe."

The heinous crackle awakened every hatred tenfold over.

Twenty-six

DEAR MOTHER MARY!

"What's the matter, girlie, cat got your tongue?"

Glory knew without a doubt she'd found trouble.

It was the fault of this damnable wind. It carried seeds of destruction, scattering them with abandon wherever it went. She strove for some measure of calm, knowing her wits would be all that would save her. Terror gripped her.

"I'm looking for Horace."

"Well, I can be whoever you want. Makes no never mind to ol' Frenchie. Horace'll fit the bill just fine."

Keep him talking. When she made a move, it had to count. It would be her sole chance.

"I'm afraid I've lost my brother."

"Who you trying to fool now? You ain't got no brother."

When the man touched her, she jabbed the walking stick into his midsection. He clutched her ankles on the way down. Loathing gave her courage to finish the job. She lifted the staff and drove it, bringing her full weight to bear. A crack and the loud oath that rent the air assured her she didn't miss. She made a mad dash for freedom, ignoring briars and brambles that grabbed her clothing. The sky opened up, drenching her.

"Miss Glory, hurry! Over here." Horace's shout guided her, a beacon on a storm-tossed sea.

He led the way to the animals, helping her onto the mule. In the midst of thunder, lightning, and the curse of evil, they urged the mounts toward Santa Anna. The downpour pummeling Glory's face and arms made it nigh impossible to hold the reins. At last Horace took them from her stiff fingers and led Caesar to some sort of shelter. While the noise of the torrent hadn't faded, it no longer pounded against her. She got down slowly.

"Where are we?"

"Under a rock shelf. We can rest here. I'm sorry, so sorry." Regret lay heavy in the air. The boy-man evidently assumed he'd failed and that their predicament was somehow his fault.

She laid a comforting hand on his arm. "Horace, you did real good. We're out of the rain. We can catch our breath here."

"But...but Mr. Luke depends on me. I'm supposed to take you home."

"You will after the rain stops." Glory took his hand. "You've done everything asked of you and more. No one but the good Lord has control over storms."

Relief filled his voice. "And I didn't let the ground eat you, did I?"

"You certainly spared me that all right." She couldn't hold back the tender smile. Heroes weren't measured solely by the size of their brains. The depth of Horace's heart more than made up for any lack. She'd sooner put her life in his hands than most anyone else she knew.

"Do you think Mr. Luke got swallowed up again?"

Bands around her chest squeezed, creating pain unlike any she'd known. Had the lovemaking been a sham? Had he laughed behind her back afterward? No, she would never believe that. He'd had a reason for what he'd done and said.

"I think he can take care of most anything, Horace." She blinked away the hotness lurking behind her lids.

"Yeah, but are you sure?"

"Yes."

For the sake of argument, perhaps he hadn't meant those words. Perhaps he'd had a perfectly logical reason. And perhaps he knew she wouldn't leave—unless he ran her off. The moment of passion could mean an apology. If she wanted to buy into that theory.

Luke's hints of a dangerous undertaking that last night popped into mind. He'd said success of his mission would grant her father's wish. He fought injustice and crime wherever he found it—the words in his proposed epitaph.

Did the fixer possibly think to set one more problem to rights? Yes, that's exactly what he'd thought.

Her throat ached from lack of air. What he'd done today came out of caring—to save her.

Luke wouldn't let anyone ride on his magic carpet who repulsed him, that much she could bank on.

Remaining doubt fled. But it let fear creep back.

Her stupid pride had placed Luke in unimaginable peril. What if he met with harm because of her? She might've gotten him killed. She couldn't live with his death on her conscience.

One thing for certain, men like Frenchie wouldn't think twice about ending the life of an infiltrator.

Unshed tears blocked her ability to swallow. Luke risked death to help her father—and her. If her surmising held truth, he was indeed a man of uncommon valor.

"I can almost guarantee he'll survive come what may." She patted Horace's hand.

One man against a whole den of thieves and murderers?

"'Cause he has the key. Anyone with a key has special powers. He could probably kill a mean ol' dragon even."

Yes, he certainly possessed abilities of few mortals. No argument there. Only a man like McClain could unlock bitter hurt and bring a smile. She'd never have found the tenderness she'd long buried had he not entered their lives.

Uncommon to say the least.

❧

Sheets of rain washed away the grime that Luke had carefully applied. With any luck, those yahoos below wouldn't give him a second glance. Leastwise, he hoped not.

The horses looked awfully inviting, and if he had a lick of sense, he'd climb on one and ride out.

Except he hadn't accomplished what he'd set out to do.

No one had ever given him a prize for being long on brains, but he was no quitter.

Jagged lightning struck an oak tree a few hundred yards away, close enough to raise the hair on his head and put a ringing in his ears. He gave one last yank to the ropes he'd hog-tied Frenchie with. The man lay unmoving.

His jaw tightened. Thank God he'd followed his instincts and waited or… He shuddered to think of Glory enduring one moment in the lewd outlaw's company.

The blow delivered by the butt of his pistol would keep the man out for a while, he reckoned. For good measure, he stuffed his bandana into Slug's mouth. Lord knows he wanted to give him worse than he had, make him pay for having to pull the legs from under the woman who'd shown him dreams didn't mean a thing unless you had someone to share them with. Just so much emptiness. No one had given him so great a treasure.

Shame and misery burned a path where his heart once lay.

He'd lost her.

Should another opportunity come down the line to add to Frenchie's grief, he'd damn sure grab it. Gut feeling told him the fight wasn't over.

For now, he'd consider it a blessing to get word to Dan where to find the outlaw. Slug wouldn't stay quiet for long. And though the man hadn't seen who hit him, he'd surely suspect. If he should get loose, Luke prayed he couldn't add two and two.

He gave the form a swift kick with the toe of his boot

before he covered him with branches and ran for the hideout.

Gale-force winds almost ripped the trapdoor from his hand. He lost his footing and tumbled down the ladder when it slammed.

"Hey, watch where you're slinging water there, Kidd," Bill complained.

"What's the matter? Don't take kindly to bathing?" He offered the sarcasm, watching the waterfall stream off his hat brim. It soaked into the dirt floor around his feet.

"Not the regular kind. I do get one on occasion. Mostly when it's accidental-like."

Figured as much.

Lefty's narrowed gaze gave him an attack of the jitters.

"Took you long enough, Tex."

Luke bent to brush his soaked trousers. "Thought you boys would appreciate me calming the horses. The whole herd had the walleye. Don't know how you do it, but where I come from we ride to a stage holdup."

"What did ya do, sing 'em a lull-ee-by?" Creede threw in.

"Nope, mine's more partial to 'Dixie.'" Luke took a seat by the ladder, thinking it prudent. Just in case.

"You happen to see Frenchie out there while you was serenading?" Creede smelled something and it didn't pertain to crusty underarms.

Stay calm, Luke reminded himself. He picked up a block of wood, opened his knife, and shaved off a pile of thin strips. "Nope."

"A mite strange, seeing how you come back and he didn't."

Luke shrugged. "You sure he's not on a bunk back there asleep?"

"I sent him to look for you," Creede snarled.

Luke shivered under the half-breed's glittery gaze. He plucked a matchstick from the ante pile Bill and Lefty used and stuck it in the side of his mouth. He regarded Creede's high cheekbones that called attention to the sunken face. He could remember only a handful of men who'd made his skin crawl all the way from his feet to his eyeballs.

"Nope. Didn't see him." Luke shifted the match from one side to the other. "Lightning could've struck him though. It hit a tree and about knocked me for a loop."

Bill scratched his head. A showering of white flakes fell to the poker table. "Reckon we oughta go look for him?"

Tension brought the whittling knife a shade too close to Luke's finger. He smelled his goose cooking. The second before a bullet pierced his chest wouldn't give much time to explain.

"Nah," Creede scoffed. "Wait'll the storm passes. I ain't gonna get wet less'n I hafta. 'Course, the rest o' you can if you got a mind."

"Tomorrow's soon enough for me." Bill headed to the bunks. "Never did like him no how. Good riddance. Too damn mean."

Their reluctance brought a wave of relief. Luke folded the knife and stood. "Think I'll turn in. Anyone else?"

Creede leaned his chair against the wall. Danger flickered in the thorny stare. Luke hoped he'd never have to cross him. The quiet ones always made the stillness inside sit up and take notice. Luke fought for enough spit to swallow but failed.

"Got some thinking to do first."

"Suit yourself."

Nothing made Luke more skittish than turning his back on an enemy. The bunks lining one wall of the underground den seemed halfway to California. His wet boots squeaked with each step. He tensed for the sound of a forty-five clearing leather.

❧

At last the storm showed signs of abating. Near as Glory could figure, the day had slipped into dusk. Hope and

Squirt probably grew sick with worry. Horace fidgeted beside her.

"My pa's gonna be real mad."

"I'll explain things to him."

"He don't listen. Pa never listens."

The sorrow she'd noticed before reappeared, thicker and more somber. George Simon's discipline bordered on cruelty. That much she knew. Small wonder Horace'd always had such an urgent way of speaking to her. He craved to belong, to someone, anyone who gave a damn. In his mind, he probably saw marriage as an escape. But it wouldn't accomplish anything, merely enslave another. Simon wouldn't turn his boy loose under any circumstances.

Funny how clear things had become since she'd risen that morning.

She reached for his arm and squeezed it tight. "Don't worry, I'll make sure your pa understands." And he'd better not punish the boy either. Glory didn't exactly know what she'd do, but she wouldn't stand idly by.

"It's all right. Honest. Pa's just making a man out of me like he says. 'Sides, my pa is all I got."

Her heart broke. How sad that he feared being alone more than the razor strop. But in a different way, so did she. Alone and blind.

Horace straightened suddenly. "Miss Glory, there's a man coming from the devil place."

"Can you tell who? Is it Luke?"

"Nope, ain't him. It's that other man I saw."

A painful jolt seized her. Frenchie? Maybe he'd followed. "Be real quiet. Has he spied us?"

"Don't think so. Some branches are sorta hiding us."

The horse's approach penetrated the hammering in her ears. She held her breath. The rider probably came within a stone's throw. She had to force air into her lungs when he galloped on.

"He's gone, Miss Glory. Where do you suppose he's going?"

A premonition told her Luke's life possibly depended on them finding out. She grabbed the boy's hand. "Come on, we've got to follow him."

By the wind direction, she believed they rode west. She estimated they'd gone around twenty miles when Horace stopped. A logical guess would put them in Bead Mountain vicinity.

"Get off now," Horace whispered.

"Where are we?"

"Oak Vale."

"What's the man doing? Can he see us?"

"Nah, he done went inside."

"Can we get by a window or something without being seen?"

He took her hand. "You'll hafta goose walk."

"Huh?"

"You know, wiggle-waggle."

She crouched and tried not to think about the pain the ungainly waddle cost her ankles.

"Shh."

Rough wood scraped her knuckles after a few minutes.

Thank goodness. They'd reached the building without a hue and cry sounding. Voices from inside the structure drifted through the chinks. Two men. She didn't recognize either.

"You're positive the new man is McClain?"

"No mistake. Even with the eye patch, I recognize him now that he don't have all that dirt on his face."

Glory's heartbeat stopped.

"Thank our lucky stars the rain came along before we let him in too deep."

"Boss, he may have waylaid Frenchie. The weasel went out looking for McClain and never came back." The man spoke in a deeper tone and had to be the one they'd followed.

"I may hafta give you a bigger cut this next time, Creede. You deserve it." Pacing commenced along the breadth of the wall. After a few minutes, the boss continued. "Hmm, this calls for a change in plans. I don't think we'll skip this next job after all. There's a gold shipment due through here tomorrow on the westbound stage. Just might be the thing."

"You got an idea, Vince?"

Huddled outside, Glory could barely contain her excitement. Vince? As in Vince Foster? Was Vince Foster the gang leader? This could put an end to all their problems. Most of all, McClain's. Sudden coldness seeped into her blood. The marauders had too much at stake to let Luke live. She pressed closer to the wood. Her beloved's life depended on what she overheard.

"Have something special in store for McClain. After tomorrow I figure I'll even the score once and for all."

"Why you got it in for him anyhow?"

"He shot my boy, Willie. Took his life and left him for the varmints to eat. I got him kicked out of the Rangers to start with. An eye for an eye, I say."

"That why you had Frenchie hang the old woman to make it look like McClain did it?"

"Yep. Besides, she was fixing to blab about the frame-up on Jack Day."

Glory gasped. Intense pain seared the long-present scars. Foster had stolen something precious from her family just because he so desired. An acrid taste filled her mouth. What had her father ever done to this man?

"I'm done toying with McClain. It's time he got his full punishment. He's gotta die." The pacing stopped and so did her breathing. "All right, here's what we're gonna do—hold up the stage tomorrow, steal the gold—and here's the beauty of the plan, during the robbery, you boys'll shoot the bastard and plant some of the gold on him. We'll make it look like the stage driver drew down on him."

"I'm worried about that captain in town. You think—"

"Nah, I can take care of one Ranger. No problem keeping him out of the way until the dust settles."

Captain Roberts! That's it. Glory had to get to him. She fumbled for Horace and whispered, "Let's go."

They didn't speak until they got back to the animals.

"What're we gonna do, Miss Glory?"

"Do you know where Captain Roberts is staying?"

"You bet. He's at the boardinghouse in Santa Anna. The Ranger boards his horse at Pa's stable."

"If you'll take me there, I won't ask any more favors."

"Shoot, I like being with you. Do you like me?"

"I think you're pretty wonderful."

Please let her stop this crazy scheme before she had to learn all over again how to go on without the charmer who'd taught her to love.

Twenty-seven

THE PLEASANT AROMA OF PIPE SMOKE SWIRLED ABOUT Glory's head in the small parlor of Mrs. Josephine Baker's boardinghouse. The captain's breathing came from behind. She surmised he stared out the window while he digested the information they'd brought. Horace sat quiet and unmoving beside her on the velvet settee. And even though she'd urged the boy to get home before his father became too furious, he insisted on staying.

Captain Roberts broke the silence. "All right, Miss Day. I have some things to set in place. We'll capture this bunch once and for all."

"And keep them from harming Luke," she said bluntly.

"That first and foremost, my dear." The man gripped her hands and softened his brusque tone. "I won't let anything happen to him. You can rest easy. Now, can you get home? I'm afraid I can't see to that."

Horace cleared his throat. "I promised Mr. Luke I'd keep her safe. Uh…if it's all the same to you."

"You're a brave woman, Miss Day. McClain is one lucky man." He released his hold and addressed Horace.

"Boy, that goes for you too. You make a fine tracker. Any time you need a job, come see me. We always need new recruits."

"You mean it, Mr. Captain?"

"Wouldn't say it if I didn't."

Glory sensed a bright beam radiating from the boy-man when he helped her on the mule. It didn't dim during the ride to the farm. The thought of joining the Texas Rangers filled him with pride. She found it remarkable, especially when George Simon kept trying to knock the stuffing out of him. A light finally appeared at the end of Horace's gloomy tunnel.

"You should have let me explain to your father. I don't want him punishing you when it's my fault."

A full minute passed before he answered, "He's asleep."

"All the same, I have a duty."

A change came over him when they arrived at the Day house. It came on silent wings and as swift as Miss Minnie's pounce.

"You think I can bed in your barn for tonight?"

Plain and simple, Horace was scared.

"I'd be proud. You've earned more than that after what you gave me."

"But I didn't do anything."

Though the hour had grown late, Hope came running. "Did you find Luke?"

"Yes, but I'm sorry we went."

"Why? What happened?"

A thickness welled in her throat and the pungent taste of fear flooded her mouth.

"Oh, Hope, I'm afraid I might've killed him."

❧

It was strange how many things a body never grasped when relying on sight alone. Glory contemplated this wonder at the kitchen table, where she sat throughout the night, too nervous to sleep.

She discovered something she'd never known before—each sound created its own distinctive music, told its own tale. And only by becoming still and quiet inside could anyone hear these beautiful harmonies. It suddenly occurred to her she was seeing the reflection of the sky on that glassy lake Horace spoke about.

The sun was just waking from its slumber.

Hope, Patience, and Mama hadn't stirred, but outdoors, the mockingbirds and squawking blue jays already busied themselves, rooting to find their breakfast.

Barn doors couldn't muffle Bessie's moos.

Water dripping from the pump at the sink spoke of needing a new washer. It had dried out and cracked waiting for the rain to fill the cistern again.

And her soul's hushed whispers played the haunting refrain of a tune too agonizing to bear. What had she done? What if her unthinking, selfish act caused Luke's death? She'd have to carry that to her grave.

A tremble shook her.

The chair protested when she rose and walked the dozen steps to the window. She gripped the rim of the wash counter.

Luke needed a miracle.

She wouldn't even ask for his return to the farm.

His continuing to draw breath would suffice.

The door opened. The smell of honest sweat preceded the visitor.

"You're up early, Horace."

"Been hunting. Left a mess of quail by the porch and here's the eggs from the barn."

"My goodness, you're going to spoil us, you know." She heard him lay each egg carefully in a bowl.

"Just helping. Do you mind, Miss Glory?"

She didn't have any say-so over the smile that came. Friends like him didn't happen around every bend in the road. When they did, you shouldn't refuse what they offered. Luke taught her that.

"Not one bit."

"One day I'll show you how to make animal traps. That way you can catch food for when I'm gone off to the Rangers."

Out of the mouths of babes. Now, why hadn't she thought of that? Traps instead of rifles. That would keep them fed.

"I'd appreciate that very much." She filled the pot with water and guessed at the ground coffee. "Do you have time for breakfast?"

She collided with him in a sudden turn to the woodstove.

"I done stoked the fire. Here, let me show you." The simple man took her hand. Heat from below rose. "Set the pot down real easy."

"Yes, I feel it. I don't know how I'll manage without you."

"You can do it."

Footsteps told her when Hope entered the room. The middle Day sibling had a quiet, firm step, whereas Patience trudged along with the ease of a plow horse. "Good morning, sister."

"My stars, you've already got coffee on. You should've awakened me. Morning, Horace."

"Beautiful day, ain't it, Miss Hope?"

"No need to rouse you. You deserve your rest." Glory tucked her hair behind her ears and slid into her seat. "It was late when I sent you off to bed. How's Mama?"

"Sleeping peacefully. She's going to be all right."

The lumbering stumble announced Patience. "I'd better gather the eggs."

"Uh, I already did," Horace said.

Patience whooped. "Yippee. Glory, can he come live with us?"

Horace spoke up quickly. "I can't on account of I'm joining up with the Rangers."

"Really?"

"Yep. Tell 'em, Miss Glory."

"Captain Roberts asked him last night. I heard him."

"Wow, I wish they'd take girls."

Glory didn't need eyes to see the dreamy expression on Squirt's face.

"But they don't." Horace hastened to add, "If they did, though, I'm sure they'd ask you." He made a scuffing noise on the floor with his feet. Glory recognized signs of duty over personal rathers. "I gotta be going. Pa'll be up."

"I'll get the mule saddled so I can keep my promise." The chair scraped the wood floor when she rose.

"No! I...I'll tell him for you."

The door slammed before she could reply.

"Oh dear. I hope he doesn't get into trouble," Hope murmured.

A pretty safe bet. Otherwise, the boy wouldn't be so terrified. Fear and dread sat in her stomach like a wagonload of wet laundry—for Luke and Horace. Hell, she might as well lump all the rest of them in there too.

A sharp jab brought Luke out of the bunk. Hair-trigger reflexes born from years of hunting down murderers, outlaws, and horse thieves had his six-shooter drawn and aimed before the person doing the poking could blink.

"Whoa there, Tex! Merely following orders."

Flickering light from oil lamps allowed a good view of hands raised high and the fear of God in Lefty's eyes.

Luke gave a noncommittal grunt and slowly holstered the weapon. "You have a death wish or something."

The man's Adam's apple bobbed. "Boss says we got a job to plan."

Since Luke had watched Creede leave twice yesterday, the last time after everyone else went to sleep, the half-breed must carry orders back and forth from the leader. Foster, he'd bet. Nothing had happened to change his mind on that. Should the next few hours prove his hunch right, he could rid the county of this hornets' nest.

And then he'd have a decision. Mexico or...?

Glory's upturned face interrupted his train of thought. Only someone with tender feelings would've risked what she did. But even if that was the case, his surly treatment had surely sent her away for good.

"A job, huh? Any idea what?"

"Have to ask him."

Luke collected his hat from the bunk and sauntered along the tunnel that barely accommodated his six-foot frame. Sure didn't allow any type of headgear, unless they were dwarfs. He ducked through the shored-up opening that led into the taller main room. Creede's gaze followed him when he entered.

"Lefty tells me we're about to ride. That true?"

No answer came.

"Am I supposed to guess? Or read your mind?"

"You talk too much." Creede crossed his arms.

Luke took a seat, picked up the cards, and shuffled. His growling stomach protested the meager pickings of late. The underground hideaway prevented cooking, not even a fire to boil coffee. The flue would send up a signal. They existed no better than rats.

The rest of the group straggled in a few minutes later. Creede drew the stage route on the planks and marked an X where they'd swoop down from the shadow of Bead Mountain.

"Anyone seen Frenchie this morning?" Cuny asked with a mouth full of jerky.

The half-breed's dark stare burned a hole through Luke. He did his damnedest to ignore the hackles rising on his neck. "I'll help look for him."

"No." The venomous explosion burst from Creede. Everyone swiveled to stare. "Me and Bill will go."

Yep, the man had something stuck in his craw. Luke hoped he'd hidden Frenchie good enough and that the wily outlaw hadn't managed to squirm loose. Dan would be waiting at the same place on Hord's Creek, if he found a way to get there.

Give him a whole lot of luck…and a few hours, preferably in that order.

A sudden rattling of the trapdoor yanked him from wishful thinking. The men scurried with weapons drawn.

Luke didn't budge from his perch. He had nothing to hide—unless...

"Where the hell that sumbitch go?"

Luke found breathing difficult.

Frenchie! In the flesh.

So much for the luck part he'd asked for. He'd just entered the music and dancing stage. Better get ready to do the hot-lead polka.

&

Around midmorning Glory sat in the parlor, keeping Mama company while Hope and Squirt did laundry outside. Listening for the slightest sound of horses prevented carrying on a decent conversation. Her nerves became more unsettled with each passing moment.

"You seem jumpy, dear." Ruth moved to sit beside her. She smoothed back Glory's hair with a tender touch. "Anything I can help with?" Glory didn't have to consult a crystal ball to understand her mother delicately referred to the vision impairment. Bolstered by Hope and Patience, she'd finally told Ruth that morning. Surprisingly, the Day matriarch took the news well.

"I'm a bit on edge. Nothing to worry about."

"You know, when I was a little girl, I used to fret myself sick. I would hide under the covers when it thundered until my father bribed me out with a piece of gingerbread or a promise to read me a story. Everything scared me to death."

Glory had never heard Ruth speak of her childhood. "And Uncle Pete? Did he share such fears?"

"My brother would stand in the middle of a lightning storm and dare it to strike him. He didn't have a brain in his head, not even then." Ruth's refined lilt swirled around the sitting room like rich, thick chocolate. "Pete promised Father he'd always take care of me."

And her uncle had kept his word. Even to the point of almost killing his sister. The still water reflected the picture. Especially her mother's mental decline after Papa went away.

Endless waiting and heartache had a way of eating every ounce of strength and purpose a body possessed from the inside out. Ruth had tried the best she knew to get through each day, however she could. Shame washed over Glory for the ill will she'd harbored.

The front screen door banged loudly. The unexpected noise lifted her a foot off the settee.

"Mama! Glory! We have visitors."

Dare she believe? Her heart beat wildly.

"Don't yell, Patience Ann. We're not deaf," Mama admonished her. "Who would come calling? I wonder."

"I can't tell yet. Some man and woman in a wagon though."

A buoyant flush that had risen faded as quickly as it came.

"Get away from that window! My heavens, we don't want them to think we're a bunch of heathens."

The scolding indicated Mama was well on the mend. The firm hand had been absent longer than Glory cared to remember. Ruth rose, straightening and plumping the cushions to receive visitors.

"I don't know how we can see who it is if we don't look out."

"Quit grumbling, dear. We'll know after they knock."

Damnation! The suspense was killing Glory. She got to her feet. If only she could see. Were that possible, she'd not sit around twiddling her thumbs, she'd be in the thick of things.

The whinny of horses, two by the sound, drifted through the open door. Voices accompanied them.

Not Captain Roberts. He'd ride horseback.

Unless he needed a way to haul someone injured…

…or dead.

Dear God!

At last the rap came. Mama's worn kid boots thudded against the hardwood. Another set of footsteps trailed, giving away Squirt's location. No helping the girl's nosiness.

"Good morning. Can I help you?" Glory didn't have to strain to listen. Something about the deep baritone had a familiar ring to it. Not Luke, but?

"I'm not sure. Are you Mrs. Day?"

"You have the right place. Please come in."

Flustered by sudden visitors, Glory didn't know whether to sit, stand, or hide in her room. Mystery and a sense of optimism swept over her. Whoever they were, they brought promise.

"Folks in town said my brother stays with you some."

Luke's brother? Could this be true? The man had the same commanding presence that filled every corner of the house.

"The only one who fits that description would be Luke McClain." Ruth ushered them into the parlor. "Care to sit?"

"Thank you, ma'am. I'm Duel McClain and this is my wife, Jessie. The children are Marley Rose, Lily, and baby Ethan."

Luke's family had come.

Excitement left Glory faint. Duel would help and surely no one stood a chance against two McClain men. Not even the devil himself. Or one Vince Foster.

"We're delighted to meet you. Mr. McClain spoke fondly of his family. My daughters and I owe your brother more than we can ever possibly repay."

"Mama, aren't you going to introduce us?" Glory gently prodded. Seldom had they a chance to engage in niceties.

"My goodness, I completely forgot my manners! These are my oldest and youngest daughters, Glory and Patience. Hope, the middle child, is doing the wash."

A heightened sense led Glory. She moved carefully but with deliberate steps toward the voices, her hand outstretched.

Patience whispered loudly in the vicinity of Glory's ear, "The man is in Papa's chair and the woman is on the settee."

"Thank you." How humiliating.

Then the girl announced to their guests, "My sister can't see anymore on account of she's blind. Mr. Luke asked her to marry him though. Even after she shot him. And that was when she still had good eyesight. She said she wasn't aiming to. I think it truly was an accident. It didn't even make him mad. He's awful nice."

Hell's bells! Give her something to stick into that big mouth! Heat flooded her face. She forced a smile and the brittle laugh.

"I do declare, Squirt. They didn't ask for our life history." She found her hand engulfed in Duel's. His firm grip unlocked the emotional dam she'd built. "You don't know how relieved I am you came. Your brother is in terrible danger."

Twenty-eight

OLD-TIMERS IN THE LAW BUSINESS TEACH NEVER TO UNDERES-timate an opponent. Luke wished he hadn't skipped that lesson. He took a deep breath and crawled from beneath the table.

Frenchie had blood in his eye and murder in mind, no two ways about it.

And his sorry hulk blocked the way to daylight.

"I swear to my time. Where the hell you been?" Luke poured his heart and soul into the playacting. He hoped it worked. "You had us worried sick. We wanted—"

"Why, you lying…" Frenchie's leap sent them both to the floor. The table turned on end with a crash.

Before the rest pulled them apart, Luke managed to add a few improvements to Frenchie's ugly face. Didn't matter he took some licks as well. The price of satisfaction.

Creede stepped between the pair and grabbed hold of Luke's clothes. "Frenchie, did Kidd waylay you out there?"

"Whoever hit me snuck up from behind. Never saw the skunk. But that's splitting hairs. I did run into him before I saw stars."

"Where?"

"Down by the horses."

Luke shook free of the grasp and wiped his bloodied lip with a shirtsleeve. "See? Told you I was going to check on the mounts and that's what I did."

Distrust and suspicion blanketed the room.

"How come you think he's lying?" Cuny asked.

"Because I know pretty boys like him. Don't trust 'em."

"For God's sake, you're not going to buy this, are you?" The staring clan seemed far more eager to begin the polka music. The gun hanging from Luke's hip brought a bit of comfort.

Creede snarled, "You see anyone else, Frenchie?"

"Only that girl, Glory Day. Was going to love her up real good." He glared at Luke. "Till *he* cracked my skull."

"You got anything to add, Kidd?"

"I didn't see anyone out there except Frenchie. Don't know nothing about a girl. Maybe she got lost in the rain and wandered up. Hell, I don't know. It's common knowledge she's sole provider for the family. Maybe she was out hunting. Those plum thickets are home to all kinds of wild game." *And ugly varmints like Frenchie*, he added to himself.

"All right, boys, we've got a job to do." Creede righted the overturned table.

Frenchie snarled, "Not until I get me some satisfaction. This ain't done."

"I say it is for now. Set your differences aside. After the business with the stage is over, you can beat him to a bloody pulp for all I care."

A sneer that would make any mother sorry she ever birthed such a miserable piece of humanity curled Frenchie's lip. The man shoved past, giving one last warning. "I'm gonna kill you, pluck out your eyes, and feed you to the crows."

Luke returned the level stare. "Name the place. One thing you're gonna find is…I don't die that easy."

❧

Jack Day gasped for what air the dank penitentiary offered. He vaguely heard Dr. John Fletcher enter the hospital ward. Few noises managed to be heard over the moans of other dying patients.

An occasional scream pricked his sanity and made him wonder if the sound came from him.

Chills shook him.

"Good morning, Jack." Dr. Fletcher put a stethoscope to his chest. "Nurses tell me you had a bad night."

"Doc, has my Ruthie come?" He could barely get the words past his chattering teeth.

Fletcher smoothed the quilt back over him. "She will. You can't give up hope. You hear me, Jack?"

"I don't know how much longer I can hold out."

"In all honesty, your strong will to see your family is all that's keeping you alive. You let go of that, you're a goner."

"Wonder what's keeping them. They should've come by now." Urgency swept through him. He grasped the doc's hand. "Are you sure you wrote those letters? You weren't just humoring me?"

"On my oath as a physician, I sent every one."

A fit of coughing left a trail of blood on the sheet.

Damn the person whose lies sent him here!

They'd robbed him of more than time. Keeping him apart from those he loved angered him most. Why the frame-up? Didn't make a lick of sense. He'd never wronged anyone.

"After I'm gone...will you please tell my Ruthie how much I loved her?" Defeat tormented him. He'd lost.

"You have my word."

Dr. Fletcher turned to his female assistant and spoke in a low tone. He concentrated on their voices. It was important to know the crux of things.

"He won't last the night, I'm afraid. A pure miracle if he does."

"Then we don't want to waste what food there is on him."

The doctor grabbed the woman's arm. "You give this man whatever he requires. Comfort him in his last hours, be it with drink, sustenance, or a kind word. That's what we do. If you can't do that, I have no need of you."

❧

Duel's galloping horse faded into the distance. Luke's brother had wasted no time unhitching the pair from the wagon after Glory sketched the details. Perhaps help had arrived too late, though she sensed a definite shift in their favor. In her heart, she knew this McClain would do everything in his power to make everything come out the way it should.

She formed a silent prayer he'd get there before Foster managed to carry out his dastardly plan.

Hope and Mama were out back finishing up the wash. A remarkable change had occurred in their mother, especially the surprising vitality that replaced usual apathy. Marley Rose's and Lily's squeals came from the next room where Patience entertained them.

Glory held the small infant and tried to imagine his face. But her mind kept wandering to places it shouldn't go.

"Don't worry." Jessie McClain patted her hand. "My husband won't let anything happen to him. Next to Duel, Luke is the toughest, most decent man I know."

The telltale break in the woman's soft voice said much about her feelings for both brothers.

"This is extremely hard for you. Despite my short acquaintance with Luke, I can't bear to think about the outcome. If something happens to him… Knowing, caring for both, I imagine would double the pain."

"I love them—Luke as well as Duel."

Pain radiated through Glory's chest. What if something happened to either man?

She gripped the sleeping bundle tighter. "You never said what brought you to Santa Anna."

"We came to tell Luke their father, Walt McClain, died."

"I'm so sorry." She remembered his pride when he spoke of his family. "How devastating for Luke."

How would news of Papa's death come? she wondered. Certainly not by anyone familiar or who would have great care of their feelings.

"Yes, it shocked us all. Walt slipped, fell down a ravine, and was crushed by falling rock. We didn't know Luke's whereabouts until we contacted the Ranger battalion in Waco. It seems Luke came through there a few weeks ago to empty his savings from the First Bank and Mercantile. He told them he was trying to clear up some things here in Santa Anna."

"His savings?" The weak question barely managed to get through her stiff lips.

That's how he paid the banknote!

It hadn't been blood money at all. A thick lump settled in her throat.

"Luke had been putting aside some money for his own plot of ground." The settee shifted when Jessie rose. Her footsteps moved toward the parlor window. "Whatever he needed the money for must've been mighty important to throw away his dream of owning a parcel of land. You know? A man doesn't think he's much of anything without property to call his."

He thought the Day family worthy of the sacrifice.

Love swelled side by side with the ache.

They owed him a tremendous debt. One Luke never meant to collect. His gift came with no strings. Glory knew all about shattered dreams. Men didn't have a monopoly on such. And that he gave of himself, willing to risk his very life, to make theirs easier, told the depth of his heart.

Why hadn't he explained? He'd let her think the worst.

"Did the men in Waco tell your husband that someone framed Luke and he lost his job as a Ranger?"

"No. Forevermore! How that must've eaten at Luke." Jessie paced back and forth along the length of the room. "I learned last year the true measure of his conviction. He believes he received a calling much like something religious men get from on high. Duty and honor for upholding the law flow in his blood."

Glory's thoughts whirled to that night he had shared his deep shame. "He was obsessed with clearing his name. I now know the one who did the framing and it may be…"

Jessie's fierce hug brought comfort and strength. "Don't even think that. It won't be too late. It won't."

"You're right. We must look on the bright side." A thin smile wavered on Glory's lips before it decided to stay. "I'm so glad you came."

"Me too."

Understanding filled the gap between them. The woman clearly couldn't disguise the love and admiration she had for the youngest McClain brother.

"Did Luke tell you how I arrived in the family?" Jessie asked.

"He didn't talk a lot except to say he missed you all very much and that it had been a while since he visited."

"I think his sworn duty to the Texas Rangers almost did him in when he had to arrest his own sister-in-law for murder."

"A mix-up, I'm sure."

"If only it had been." Heavy sorrow seeped between the words. "The fact is, I did shoot and kill Jeremiah Foltry, my husband at the time. It was no accident. Although he did unspeakable things, I didn't hold out much hope that a court would listen. Hanging appeared a sure bet. But Duel persuaded Tom Parker to help us and here I am. The reason I'm telling you this is—miracles do happen. Just when life looks darkest doesn't mean it'll stay that way. Duel and Luke are mule heads, that much I'm sure. They also have strength and ability like few men I've seen."

The startling revelation left Glory reeling. Although she'd only met the woman a few hours ago, she recognized a kindred spirit when one came along. Jessie could only have had provocation of the worst kind to have harmed any living soul.

And Luke? Arresting her must've torn his guts out. What a thing having to choose among family, duty, and honor. All three as sacred as breathing.

Her thoughts leaped to that night they'd spoken of epitaphs and tombstones.

He gave generously of himself to make the world a safer place. He lived well and loved hard. He will be missed.

Glory blinked back tears. He would indeed leave empty holes. More than he knew.

"What a horrible time. You must've been so scared." Her voice broke. Scared seemed too weak for the needles pricking her insides this day. She was downright petrified.

"That's all behind me now," Jessie said. "I have a love unlike anything I've known, the most wonderful husband a wife could ever want, and little ones to watch over and shape. I suppose I had to go through the worst to get to the best. At least that's my observation anyway."

Glory prayed for that same miracle here.

Baby Ethan stretched from his nap and made little mewling noises. She wished she might see him.

"Do the children resemble your husband?"

"Good heavens, I certainly don't see how they could. Our children, including the three oldest at home, are all orphans. Duel and I are unable to have babies of our own."

Heat rose to Glory's face. "Forgive me for prying."

A musical laugh sprang forth. "I've learned it doesn't make any difference who brings them into the world. What's important is the love you give them once they're here. I get immense satisfaction from watching them grow and learn, knowing I can help turn them into the people they become."

"Each of us has our own cross to bear, I suppose."

"No one is perfect. If they give such an impression, I remind myself it's only skin deep. Secrets lurk within us humans."

Glory contemplated her words. She'd been far too narrow-minded and prudish. And now stricken by blindness. The perfect stranger who'd appeared from the blue had irritated her with his meddling, but kept a roof over their heads anyway. It appeared that she might never get to thank him for his unselfish efforts.

Despair tasted like a mouthful of thick mud on her tongue. Ethan whimpered and a second later let out a lusty cry.

Jessie lifted him from her arms. "He's hungry. It's all right, my darling," she cooed.

"We have fresh milk from just this morning in the crock beside the sink. I'll show you."

"I hate to trouble you. I brought along a supply of canned to use. Ethan doesn't mind. He's not as finicky as Marley Rose, who drank goat's milk or nothing at all."

"It's no bother. Our Bessie gives the sweetest milk."

❧

Noon arrived with still no word. Glory tired of listening for approaching riders. They gathered around the table, feeding hungry stomachs. However, eating held no interest for her. She didn't care if she ever ate.

"I wish I had a little brother or sister," Patience whined. "Someone like Marley Rose or Lily. They're so cute."

"Mine sissie," Marley Rose stated emphatically.

The smaller girl jabbered, shaking her finger.

"Yes, darling. Lily is your sister, no doubt about it," Jessie answered.

Mama laughed. "You wouldn't think they were so much fun if you had to take care of them every day, Patience, dear."

"I would too. I'd never complain or get tired of playing with them. I'd take them for walks and fishing and even let them hold Miss Minnie's kittens."

"Mine kitty?"

"No, sweetie, the kitties belong to Patience," Jessie said.

"No. Mine." Marley let out a squall.

Patience gave a loud sigh. "I'll let you have one if you'll just be quiet. Okay?"

That's what Glory thought. Hadn't taken Squirt long for the new to wear off.

"I'm sorry. She's not normally this way. It must be unfamiliar surroundings. I think my husband would shoot us if we took another animal home with us. We have enough trouble taking care of the goat, dogs, horses, and the like, not to mention the snake Marley dragged home and made into a pet. Duel gripes that we have enough to fill Noah's ark."

Glory let a half smile settle into place. They'd best warn Luke about the snake before he went for a visit. He and slithery things had nothing in common. The memory created a thickness in her throat. That is, if he survived today. She'd give anything to lengthen the odds.

"Patience, why don't you take the girls to the barn when they finish and let them see the kittens?" Hope suggested, collecting the dishes from the table.

Ever the peacemaker, her middle sister.

Then, she heard the sound she'd been expecting. She never knew hoofbeats could be so sweet.

Twenty-nine

Damn this blasted heat!

Sweat dribbled from Luke's forehead onto his arm.

Hidden as he was from sight of the road at the base of Bead Mountain, not a breath of wind could reach him.

Or maybe he should blame it on jumpy nerves. The way Creede, Frenchie, and the boys looked at him when they thought he wasn't paying attention told him they had something up their sleeve. It couldn't be of the good variety.

He eyed the mare and wondered if he'd meet a hail of bullets if he hightailed it.

The idea had merit, as it promised to help him live to a ripe old age. That's when he heard the rumble of the stage.

Too late. Story of his life. Not enough time to get word to the captain...and most soul-wrenching of all, failure to take care of Glory and free her father. Too late. Everything too late.

There was nothing left to do but fight with everything he had. It was up to him to stop this bunch. Right here. Right now.

A Ranger never gave up, never shirked from a fight, and never gave less than he took. Such a vow would benefit everyone, no matter their persuasion. Yep, even with an uphill battle, he bet he could put these thieving murderers to bed with a pick and shovel if that's the way they preferred to go.

Bad seeds each and every one of them. A swift glance located the men who lay in wait.

All except Creede.

Now where in hell had he disappeared to?

Cotton-pickin'! No time to search. Luke pulled his Colt from the holster and checked the cylinder. Cartridges filled all six chambers.

Six chances to stop the group of bad hombres.

A gambler's odds.

He slid the Colt back into place and eyed the rifle in the scabbard. If he could keep it near, it carried a full load. From experience, a man in battle could lose sight of both horse and weapon. It was crucial to aim carefully and shoot well if he wanted to walk away from this. The mare skittered when he swung into the saddle.

Dust rose beneath the team of six. They'd rounded the last curve and headed into the narrow basin. He tensed.

Do or die, heaven help him, this was it.

Lefty rode out as planned, shooting into the air.

The driver sat rigid on the seat as did the passengers Luke glimpsed through the window of the carriage.

Double damn!

So much for hoping it carried nothing but payroll. The horses stretched out upon hearing the blast. They didn't stand a chance of outrunning the black-hearted bunch. The driver couldn't know about the stacked odds. Luke drew a bead on Lefty and watched the man tumble off his horse. He galloped toward the others.

A volley of shots burst from inside the stage as the remaining gang came from hiding with pistols blazing.

They raced alongside the speeding carriage.

Luke aimed and Cuny hit the dirt. Four shots left in the forty-five.

Then, things took a turn for the worst when the driver caught a bullet and flew from his perch onto the dusty road. Luke set his jaw, jerked his rifle from the scabbard, and opened fire on the murdering bunch.

Someone grabbed the rigging. He recognized Bill. The man would have the conveyance stopped in a matter of seconds.

Just as Luke took aim, a bullet whizzed past his ear, splintering the door of the carriage. Leaning from his saddle, Frenchie eyeballed him again and squeezed the trigger. The muzzle spat an orange flash.

For once, Miss Gut Twister moved as if she had a lightning bolt on her tail. A cluster of live oak shielded Luke. He jerked off the eye patch. From cover, he surveyed the carnage.

Shots continued to erupt from the coach interior.

Didn't make rhyme or reason the strange way they burst forth. Whoever it was didn't know beans about making their shots count.

Another bullet slammed into the tree beside him, sending a chunk of bark flying. He glanced over his shoulder.

Creede had the reins firmly in his teeth and a pair of pistols in each hand, riding directly for him. The black stare held an otherworldly glitter. The half-breed took dead aim.

Fire and damnation! Luke ducked and jumped from the mare's back behind a rock formation. He hunkered down, waiting for a break in the barrage. Then he rose ever so slightly. When the ugly face centered in his sights, he delivered a load of hot lead. Red oozed from Creede's shoulder.

The stage came to a stop.

"Hey, fellows, we done been tricked! Ain't no people in here. Just a bunch of straw. And firecrackers."

Luke couldn't stop the chuckle. He didn't know how the captain had found out about the holdup.

"Son of a bitch!"

"McClain, you're a dead man," Creede yelled.

Suddenly, a hail of gunfire burst from both sides of the road, catching the gang in a cross fire. The few who remained on their horses scrambled for protection.

"Might as well give up and make things easier on all concerned," Dan Roberts drawled. "It'll chap my hide if I have to come get you."

"You hear that, boys? I don't think you want on the cap'n's bad side." Luke scanned the brush.

"Luke? That you?"

What the…? The familiar voice shouldn't be here.

Maybe his imagination was playing tricks. "Who wants to know?"

"It's me, little brother."

"Great day in the morning!"

"Heard you might have your hands full with this gang."

Relief unbent a few of the kinks in his gut. "Cap'n, you and Duel are welcome to join the fun."

"Ooh, you got us shaking in our boots," Frenchie hurled from his hiding place.

Creede joined the discussion. "I figure it's three against six or more of us. Don't think you're big enough."

"Wrong thing to say," Luke muttered.

Foster's boys were not only smelly, they were flat stupid. Dan and Duel could outfight a grizzly. Not that Luke was any slouch.

He crept toward the clump of mesquites. A twig snapped, stealing the surprise. Creede whirled. The bullet caught Luke's arm, jarring the Colt from his grasp.

Searing pain ran up his neck. He took a flying leap into the half-breed's chest.

Grunts came from both when they hit the ground.

Luke grabbed for the man's throat and squeezed as Creede gouged his eyes. Sharp pain took his breath. He couldn't see. He only knew he had to hang on for dear life. Rocks and thorns penetrated his shirt in the rolling struggle.

All of sudden, Creede's hand slipped. Luke spied his Colt through a faint haze.

He lunged for it and put the muzzle to the half-breed's forehead. Rage swept through him. For a brief heartbeat, he fought the urge to send the man to his fate.

"Do it." Hate glistened in Creede's dark eyes. "Go ahead."

"No." Luke shifted and hauled him up. "It's too good for you."

Several hundred yards away, Dan had assembled the other members of the gang. They sat in the road in a circle. He guarded them while Duel tied their hands.

"Got another one." Luke shoved Creede forward. "Don't know where you came from, brother, but I'm happy to see you. That goes for you too, Dan."

Roberts returned the grin. "Thought I taught you better than to try to whip a nest of outlaws single-handed. You trying to get your job back or something?"

Blood soaked Luke's sleeve. He clenched his jaw and took note of the shot-up group. None of the faces were ugly enough to be Frenchie's. A branch snapped off to his right. Whipping off his bandana and looping it around the wound, he tied it with his teeth and gave chase.

One horse. One rider. Glory listened with bated breath. It didn't sound like Soldier. The paint had an unusual canter. And Luke would be whistling some silly tune. A flurry whipped the air. She knew Patience made a beeline for the window.

"It's only Dr. Dalton." Squirt's dejection matched her own.

True to his word, he came to check on Mama. Dedicated and professional described the esteemed doctor. She harbored no grudge for his opinion.

That she'd never see again was a given.

Baby Ethan sucked greedily on the bottle.

"The girls and I will make ourselves scarce," Jessie said.

"I won't hear of it." Mama's firm tone brooked no argument. "You're our guests."

"Mama's right." Glory laid a hand on her arm. "Please."

Dr. Dalton rapped on the front door.

"Won't you come in?" Ruth greeted him.

The sounds indicated she'd shown him into the parlor.

"Has your mother been ill?" Jessie asked.

"I'm afraid so. But she's better now."

"Patience, will you dry dishes for me?" The pump squeaked as Hope filled a pan and put it on the stove.

"I can't. I promised Marley Rose and Lily I'd show them Miss Minnie's kittens." The chair scooted on the floor. "Take my hand, girls, and come with me," she ordered imperiously.

Wouldn't you know? Few things changed. Glory rose. "I'll do it. Lord knows I need to feel useful."

"How long…without sight, I mean?" Jessie's question lingered quietly in the room.

"My vision has gotten progressively worse over the last three months. Total blindness came about four days ago."

"I have to say I'm amazed at your courage." Glory sensed that Jessie put Ethan on her shoulder and patted his back. "If it were me, I'd probably crawl in bed and pull the sheet over my head. How do you find the strength?"

"My sisters should take a lot of credit, for in bed is exactly where I wanted to stay. And Luke…" Recollections of their lovemaking swirled in her head. "He had quite a few pearls of wisdom."

"Patience spoke of Luke asking you to wed him."

Glory grinned wryly. "More than once in fact. I couldn't accept."

"Forgive me for being too forward—may I ask why not?"

"It's rather complicated."

"Don't you love him?"

*Oh yes, more than life…*in ways no one suspected.

"My knees go weak with wanting. Love? It's fair to say Luke occupies every nook and cranny in my heart. I've never known such a man."

Nor would she ever again. Her charmer was one of a kind.

Baby Ethan gave a resounding burp.

"There. That should make you all better," Jessie crooned before she continued. "Then why deny yourself?"

"He doesn't feel the same."

She had no illusions. She was simply a problem Luke thought he could solve. Something broken in need of fixing. Nothing more. And he deserved something better than a blind wife. Two good reasons. Hotness stung her eyes. She couldn't strap him with that. He had dreams to fulfill.

"I'm sorry to butt in," Hope interrupted. "I disagree. I've watched how Luke lights up when he looks at Glory. He can't hide it. She's wrong."

"One thing I've discovered…my brother-in-law has no half measures. When Luke truly cares, he does so with every ounce of his being. He latches on to people with the same fierce loyalty that he embraces ideals. I suppose that's what makes him so tender and compassionate. Duel and Luke got that from their father, may he rest in peace." Jessie's voice caught.

"Judging from the fine sons Walt McClain raised, he must've been a fine man." The heated water sizzled as Hope poured it into the dish tub. Glory fumbled for the drying cloth.

"My life is better for having known such a special person. I viewed him as a father. Since he married my mother after she came to live with us, he filled those shoes in every way."

Glory threw down the cloth and moved for the door. "I can't stand this infernal waiting another second!"

"Where are you going?"

"To find them. I have to. Maybe I can help."

The swirl of baby scents enveloped Glory when Jessie took her arm.

"You'd be more of a hindrance, dear. It could make things worse for Luke. You wouldn't want that."

"A few weeks ago, I'd be out there looking for him." And daring anyone to stop her.

❧

This thumb-twiddling made an old woman of Glory as the day wore on. Every one of her frayed nerves had snapped.

They should've heard something by now. Bad news was better than silence.

Middle afternoon approached, best she could figure. She dared not consider what might've gone wrong.

Patience had selected a book to read and wandered down to the creek. Her charges snoozed peacefully on a floor pallet.

The click of knitting needles blended with the rhythm of the rocking chair in the parlor where she and the other three women had gathered. She envied Hope and Mama's ability to busy their hands with mending and knitting.

Sewing had never appealed much. Except when she'd sewn Luke's trousers. Had he known of her inept abilities? she wondered. The fond memory of the way his clothes felt to the touch renewed the stabbing pain.

Strange she'd not realized the depth of her love sooner. Tragedy had to open her eyes.

Wasted days—weeks—and minutes.

A foolish, stupid mistake. A whole passel of them.

Moisture left her mouth, making swallowing difficult. Luke had been the one—the suitor of whom she'd dreamed.

Glory stood at the window. The wispy lace curtains, yellowed from two decades of hanging, brushed the back of her hand as she stared with unseeing eyes into the distance. "Mama, why don't you lie down for a nap? Dr. Dalton stressed not to overdo. If anyone comes, we'll wake you."

"I am a little tired, dear. Perhaps a few winks before the supper hour."

Ruth's steps became faint and disappeared altogether beyond the soft click of the bedroom door.

"I do hope Mama takes care of herself," Hope said. "When I think how close we came to losing her, I get terrified."

"Your mother is a lovely woman."

Hope paused from her knitting. "You're beautiful as well."

"I wish I could have half her refinement." Jessie stopped

rocking. "Shoot, I'm plain ol' me. Duel claims about all a body can hope for is to live your days with no regrets. Where you can look deep in your heart and know you are all you can be. That's what brings real peace."

Glory considered the theory that expanded on Horace's perception. When a body found the image on the water, he'd better have sense enough to know what he saw.

Skipping rocks across every silent pond, creek, and mud puddle she encountered had seemed a preoccupation of hers in the past. She'd destroyed everything good, not even sparing a moment to consider the importance of a whip-poor-will call in the flush of early morning.

And she especially overlooked the warmth of family who accepted her for who she was and loved her in spite of it.

An easy, carefree life didn't ensure happiness. She saw that now. Challenges and hardship carved the full measure of a person.

Nor did bliss come from hanging your hat on a star.

When the thing she most desired waltzed into her life, she'd spurned it because she'd demanded perfection, nay, been unwilling to settle for less.

She'd denied herself and Luke. Ice formed around her heart.

Even should a miracle snatch him from harm, he'd turned from her. Albeit with good reason.

"Strange, isn't it, how we can never see the true picture of our lives until we can no longer see?" she murmured to no one in particular.

The glassy lake reflected a meddling charmer with teasing glints in his eyes.

Regrets? She could fill every cellar in the state with them and have plenty left over.

Glory cocked her head, listening. "Someone's coming."

Jessie's shallow breathing matched her own. "I wonder...?"

A horse galloped to the house.

Boots pounded across the porch.

Thirty

"UNCLE PETE, WHAT ON EARTH?" HOPE EXCLAIMED.

Glory's insides bumped over the raised ridges of too much worry. "Has something happened to Aunt Dorothy?"

"You ain't gonna believe this. You just ain't."

There seemed to be no letup. She cringed. "What? Tell us."

Standing as near as she was, Jessie's quick intake of air seemed to suck the life from Glory.

"Luke? Have you word of Duel or Luke?" Jessie asked.

"Who the heck is Duel?"

"I'm sorry, Uncle Pete." Glory had trouble remembering her own name these days. "This is Jessie McClain. Her husband, Duel, is Luke's brother. They arrived this morning bringing sad news of their father's death. After hearing about Luke's fix, Duel rode to help."

"I'm right proud to know you, Mrs. McClain. I shouldn't have barged in here like this. What in blazes kind of trouble is Luke in?"

"It's a long story, but he found the outlaw gang that's got Santa Anna in an uproar."

"You don't say?"

"What brought you out this way, Uncle Pete?" Hope prodded.

"Well, you girls know how I been digging for treasure?"

"You found the gold?" Hope gripped Glory's arm.

"Nope, something better…water."

"You found water?" That would make him rich. Glory was happy folks wouldn't scorn him anymore.

"Yep, when I wasn't even looking for it. And guess where?" A second's silence passed. "On Day land. You'll have your own water well."

"Praise be," said Ruth from the doorway. "At last something good for a change to break the string of bad."

Glory pried Hope's fingers loose and tried to bite back the disappointment. In the grand scheme of things, she had to look at finding water in a positive light, but for the life of her she wished for something of a more personal nature.

Starting with the rakish, teasing baritone of a certain heart-stealer. What she would give to hear it!

✑

The forty-five filled Luke's hand while the sound of blood gushing through his veins created a roar in his ears. Nothing except the dogged purpose in his soul spurred him forward.

He brushed aside a curtain of desert willow, taking note of an agarita shrub's broken limb. He leaned to examine it. When he rose, he came face-to-face with the unexpected muzzle of gray steel. The cold metal pressed into his cheek.

"Imagine this. I couldn't have planned our last little meeting better, not in a hundred years." Vince Foster's soft tone belied the evil lurking beneath.

"I always figured you for the boss man."

"You've reached the end of your ride, Ranger McClain." The man laughed. "Uh-oh, I plumb forgot, you lost your job. That's right. Now, you're a wanted man. Folks in Santa Anna will pin a medal on me for killing poor ol' Mrs. Tucker's murderer."

Luke ignored the icy pinpricks. He answered evenly, "What makes you so sure you'll be the one left breathing?"

"This guarantees it." Foster poked him harder. "And

probably because I'm doing the holding of it. Yep, McClain, my finger is about to put a hole in your skull a whole mess of lawmen sons a bitches could pass through at full gallop."

"Way I see it, we have an equal chance."

"I've been counting. Reckon I heard six shots from your Colt. You done spent all your bargaining chips."

Coldness spread in waves. Luke knew he'd lost the tally. Maybe Foster was right. Or maybe not. He reckoned King of the Bluffers had one more hand to deal.

"First, mind telling me why you have it in for me? You must have a reason. Do I know you?"

"Remember Willie Foster?"

Why hadn't he connected the name? An oversight for sure. How could he forget that bloodthirsty demon? Though this one had more age on him, the two shared the same shifty eyes, hateful sneer, and devil soul.

He measured the man who wore hate like a heavy overcoat. Foster's eyes widened, anticipating his victory, positive he had the upper hand. The man would be dead wrong on that last part. Luke gripped the Colt tighter. Shot or no, he'd give him a heck of a fight.

"Willie? Willie who? Maybe you oughta refresh my memory. I've come across a bunch of cutthroats in the last five years. Which sorry piece of scum was he?"

"The one you ambushed and fed to the crows. My boy."

"Oh, that murdering piece of scum. The one who unloaded his pistol in the gut of a new recruit, barely nineteen."

Foster shrugged. "Willie had the right to survive just like everybody else. A man's gotta do what he's gotta."

"I'm curious. Before you walk me to the gates of hell, I'd like to know why you framed Jack Day."

"Make any difference?"

"Humor a dying man."

Vince Foster brushed away a horsefly that landed on his ear. He shifted the plug of chewing tobacco in his mouth.

"Reckon no harm in telling since you'll be dead. Jack caught Willie in his root cellar. Ran my boy off his land. That taste of revenge was mighty sweet. But not as satisfying as getting you out of the way."

The most twisted thinking he'd ever heard—to frame and kill for a son who'd never had a decent care for a living soul.

"And Mad Dog Perkins? I suppose that was your handiwork, too?" Luke's gaze never wavered from Foster's. He only needed a small opening.

"Had to. You were hot on his trail. Didn't want to take a chance you might beat the truth out of him."

If he meant to act, he'd best do it now.

Six shots spent? Or five? The next second would tell.

With a quick jerk of his arm, Luke raised the pistol. In planned precision, he cocked and fired into Boss Man's belly. For all his hot air, Foster's reflexes were a second slow. The bullet flew wide above Luke's head.

The gang leader wore a surprised look. Blood stained the hand he'd placed over his stomach a dark red.

"Seems I had one left." Luke knelt. "Reckon you ain't much in the way of adding and subtracting, Foster."

He untied the bandana from Foster's neck and pressed it to the wound.

"Go to hell!"

Life ebbed from the man in final, gasping breaths.

Luke closed the lids over eyes that would never have another innocent in their sights again.

Through a haze, he felt a presence. Arms lifted him up.

"Nothing more you can do for him, little brother."

"Damn! What a waste."

Duel clasped him tight, patting his back. "He's not worth it. Remember, he made his choices."

Luke was tired and felt old. "You're right. What I can't understand… Foster's hate ruined so many lives."

"No figuring some people. I'm lucky if I can make heads or tails about myself. Jessie says I'm clear as muddy water."

"Good ol' Jess. How is she?"

"You can ask her yourself. She's at the Day farm. Along with Marley Rose, Lily, and baby Ethan."

Luke's brain appeared to be in a fog. He stepped back for a better view. Surely this was a dream. He thought he heard mention of...

"The Days? Who in tarnation is Ethan? And what in hell are you doing here anyway?"

"Whoa, hoss. One at a time."

Luke took an exasperated breath and adopted a more reasonable tone. "May I ask why you're at the Day farm?"

"Looking for you. Bad news, Luke...Pop died."

Pain and sadness flowed over him. He turned to stare into the distance. "I've been meaning to come for a visit. Things kept getting in the way. I never got to tell him..."

"Pop knew what was in your heart. We didn't always have to speak it. You were his favorite, you know."

Luke whirled. "He never let on. I thought he favored you." Strange how a person kept secrets. "What happened?"

"He went fast, no suffering. Fell down a ravine. We buried him beside Ma. I'm sorry."

"When?"

"Three weeks ago. We had a hard time tracking you down. If it hadn't been for the Rangers in Waco, we'd still be hunting you. Ever hear of contacting your family once in a blue moon?"

The thought had crossed his mind. Carrying feelings for your brother's wife didn't exactly make going home an option. Luke suddenly realized he hadn't thought of Jessie in a long while. Not since Glory had taken her place.

"Well, I've been sorta busy." He squinted up. He was glad Duel would never know his sin. "I'm assuming Ethan is your newest addition. How many kids call you Papa now?"

"Only six. There's been a lull in Jessie finding strays."

"Have mercy!"

"You'd better get busy, little brother. By the way, I met Glory. A special woman. If you don't marry her, I'll know you're crazy."

"That would just confirm everyone's suspicions."

"She's in love with you, you know."

Not very likely. Stabbing pain rose from the depths of his heart. He could never make up for what he did.

"After the way I spoke to her most recently, I'm the last person she'd want to have any dealings with."

"We'll see." Duel slapped his back. "Let's go home."

"Not before I exchange Miss Gut Twister for Soldier."

❧

"They're here," Patience screeched.

The parlor gathering stampeded for the door.

Glory stumbled over a foot. Her pulse raced as Luke's face swam in her memory. Someone took her hand. The snort of horses came closer when they stepped onto the porch.

This cursed blindness!

"Oh no," Hope murmured.

"What?" Was he dead? She pictured his lanky form draped lifeless across Soldier's back.

"He's been shot!"

The squawk from Patience shot an arrow through Glory's heart.

"Who?" She forced the question through stiff lips.

"Mr. Luke, that's who."

Dear Mother Mary! Her worst fears had come to pass. Ice formed in her veins.

"Mr. Luke, you've been shot. And it wasn't even Glory this time."

"Nope, Punkin. The shooter didn't have quite the aim your sister has. He wasn't near as pretty either."

A squeak of leather as a body slid from the saddle, the pound of footsteps, and Glory found herself swept up…into the arms of her cowboy.

Only she didn't mind. Not one bit.

A big smile curved her mouth as a rainbow formed inside

that dark place where her fears dwelt. The only concern on her mind was that he'd vanish on the breeze.

"Miss me?"

Even if the host of flutters had subsided, the thickness in her throat made speaking difficult. She nodded, holding on tight.

"Hey, don't spring a leak now. I can't handle tears."

"I've been so worried."

"That makes two of us. What makes you think you can go traipsing after murderers in the dead of night in a storm?"

"I had Horace with me."

A husky gravel lent itself to the joking tone. "Not that I'm ungrateful, but don't let it happen again. I won't have you risking your neck to save my sorry hide. You understand, lady?"

Luke's soft breath disturbed the wispy hair beside her ear. The charmer hadn't lost his touch. She found the tendrils weren't the sole things he disturbed. A mass of tingles made her wonder if another storm had passed by. Lightning bolts were said to bring this measure of electrified awareness.

Another nod gave him the answer he sought. Yet, she knew she'd do it all again should the need arise.

Saving her perfect stranger was something worthwhile and noble—a calling she wouldn't ignore.

"Wunkle Wuke! Me. Hold me."

Glory gathered from the jerks below that Marley Rose tugged on his pant leg.

"Hey there, Peanut. You're next on my list."

"Put me down," Glory protested. "You shouldn't be lifting me with a wound."

Patience came out the door. "Mr. Luke, who shot you?"

"Well, Punkin. Let's just say he won't ever do it again."

Back on her own feet, Glory patted his back and stomach. "Where are you bleeding?"

"Shoot, it's only a scratch. And nowhere near the vital parts the last bunch were."

A flush filled her cheeks with warmth. He'd never let sleeping dogs lie.

"It's his arm, dear," Ruth Day said. "Luke, come in and we'll get that bandaged. In fact, I want you all to wash up for supper. Won't hear a word of a soul leaving."

"Yes, ma'am. Duel, Cap'n Dan, you'd best pay attention. These ladies serve up some of the best darn food you ever sank your teeth into."

Satisfied Luke wouldn't lose his arm to infection, Glory allowed the relief she'd held at bay. They'd finished the evening meal and gotten the dishes out of the way. She couldn't refuse his request for a moonlight stroll. Well, she could've, but didn't. Their shoulders brushed as they walked. Her arm looped comfortably through the crook of his elbow, she leaned more fully into his presence. The essence of all that was her dearest dream brought a heady glow.

"Forgive me for what I said to you. I had to get you away from there. Scared the holy Moses out of me when I saw you."

"You were despicable. I thought you hated me. Until your kiss. A man who put that much tenderness in a kiss couldn't believe the words he used."

"I had good reason. My plan worked though."

She jabbed a finger in his shoulder, making sure it was the uninjured one. "You should've told me what was going on."

"I couldn't take a chance. Besides, I know your mulish disposition. Boy, do I know it!"

"What's that supposed to mean?"

"Not a thing, darling."

The cigar band on her left hand bespoke his love.

Even if he dared not trust himself with the word.

While everyone had busied with meal preparations, she'd fumbled beneath her bed for the remembrance that made sense of everything—their yesterdays and their tomorrows.

Now on his arm, she wished for a mere second of sight. The soft, silver moonlight probably played in his brown hair. Maybe even creating a halo at the crown, an idea she found quite ludicrous. This man called McClain was no angel. That fact she found most comforting. A heavenly being couldn't make her this delirious. She believed she'd take Luke any way she could get him, whether tarnished or saintly.

"Captain Dan and I leave at dawn for the Texas State Penitentiary at Huntsville."

They stopped walking. She felt a tad lost when he released her arm and they leaned on the corral fence. A froggie clan set loud clamors down by the creek. Their efforts motivated the crickets and night owls, enlivening the air.

"Am I dreaming?"

Luke couldn't take his eyes off her. She represented everything he'd ever wanted or needed. It didn't seem possible he'd returned to where his soul had found such contentment.

This was the only place he'd felt truly whole.

Where he belonged.

And where he knew his name was safely tucked inside someone's heart. A rare thing to find.

"I surely hope I'm not sleepwalking. If so, I never want to wake up." He drank his fill of the vision he'd tried so hard to walk away from. He pressed his lips to her forehead. His next words came barely louder than a whisper. "Nope, you're real all right."

His gaze lit on the cigar band encircling her finger. That she saw fit to wear such an inadequate token of his affection released warmth in him. Beside his Glory, all other women paled.

Including Jessie, which he never thought possible. None of the old familiar ache had come over him when he came face-to-face with her this afternoon. He realized the feelings had been mere infatuation.

"You know, I gave up on having my papa home. When this thief stole my sight, I had no hope of granting his last wish."

"Then I shall take extra pleasure in making it happen."

"My family owes you more than we can ever repay."

"No more than my debt to you for saving my hide, pretty lady. You don't suffer from a shortage of courage."

"You deeply touched our lives. We'll not be the same. Not Mama, Hope, Patience...or myself."

"Pretty good for a nosy meddler, huh?"

"McClain, are you mocking me?" She turned. "You are!"

"No harm in poking a little fun."

"You're mocking...and you're staring. I can feel it."

Soft rays outlined her curved moist mouth. Luke took her face between his palms. Playful nibbles along the bottom lip brought the whimper he'd sought.

Teasing suddenly had the appeal of a sack of gourds.

He wanted to taste her fully with nothing held back.

The crush of his lips on hers set his heart hammering. It threatened to jump from its lodging and take up company with hers.

"*Have mercy*," he murmured weakly into her hair.

Glory struggled equally, it seemed, resting her forehead on his chin.

The sampling had shaken them both evidently. He took the hand that bore his token, tracing it with his finger. He couldn't trust himself to speak yet. A strange tremble ran the length of him. He simply let her tender inner spirit and the outward beauty of her features feed the hope inside his hungry soul.

When he could speak, the words came haltingly, as if spoken by someone who had only learned to make the sounds.

"The night I left here, I swore I'd not return. It appeared useless. You spurned my offers at every turn. I saw no need to risk further trampling of my pride."

Glory opened her mouth to speak. He shushed her with a finger over her lips.

"Not yet. Let me finish. Please?" He took a gulp of air. "I'm not esteemed or professional, which appear to be two qualities you most seek in a mate. Anyhow, not in the way of the good doctor. My admirable qualities are a bit harder to spot and covered with rust. But I believe with all my heart and soul I can make you never regret a day of knowing me. You'll make me the happiest man in the world if you say yes."

Luke knelt amid the sharp rocks and thorny weeds. He lifted her hand to his lips.

"Miss Glory Marie Day, will you be my wife? To share with me all the riches I may possess, pitiful few they are… And to bear my children?" Then, he added in a rush, "And to never shoot me again, not even in a fit of desperation."

Her silence scared him.

When she opened her mouth to speak, he stopped her. "Please, don't say anything. Not tonight. Think about this and then give me your answer."

Thirty-one

Glory sat on the porch steps, contemplating her life and the challenges that brought her to this place. She leaned to scratch the soft fur of Miss Minnie and babies who cavorted at her feet. Five days had passed since Luke proposed again. He hadn't let her answer that night—told her to think it over until he brought her father home.

The only reply she wanted to give wouldn't be fair to the man who'd given her sunbeams, rainbows, and...a toothbrush.

Did he truly know what he asked?

The faint rumble of a wagon interrupted her thoughts. Her ears perked up. The unmistakable sound of a horse team turned onto their land.

"Mama, come quick!"

The screen door creaked. "Oh, dear heavens!"

"Is it them, Mama? Is it Papa and Luke?"

"I do believe so, daughter." She put her head inside. "Girls, your father"—and then, her voice becoming quiet, her words filled with doubting disbelief—"has come home."

But whether breathing or in a pine box? They'd taken so long. Glory wondered what it would do to her mother should Luke have failed. "Do you see him?"

"Luke's on the seat." A strangled sob caught in Hope's throat. "Someone is lying in back."

Mother Mary, they'd let him die in prison!

Stabbing pain created a hollow crater where her heart had been. Barely aware, she heard the rig come to a stop a few yards away.

"Papa! It's Papa," Patience screamed, flying past her.

Great sobs rocked her mother. "My Jack."

"Is it him?" Glory asked.

"See for yourself." Luke lightly brushed her cheek with a knuckle, and helped her down the steps.

"Great day in the morning! Ain't it fine to be home?"

Although the voice had long been absent, and the effects of illness had robbed it of a vibrant timbre, Glory had no trouble recognizing it.

"I can't believe it's really you."

"In the flesh. Come and hug your old papa."

Amid hugs, tears, and more happiness than they had a right to, they settled Jack Day into the bed he shared with Mama.

While the rest busied with cooking, cleaning, and a dozen other little details that required tending to, Glory perched beside him. She smoothed the covers over his thin frame. He seemed a mere shadow of the robust man she adored, lost beneath the quilts.

She didn't know how long before the good Lord would take him. But he'd come home at last. That fact brought a measure of peace. They'd make the time he had restful and full of every ounce of pampering he could hold.

He took her palm, his frail grip shaking. "You don't know how I prayed for this moment. I lay awake nights thinking I'd never see this land again. Or be with Mama and my girls."

Thickness lodged in the back of her throat. "We…I missed you. When you left, you took our sunshine."

How could she ever have harbored such anger for him?

"For me too, Glory."

"I've heard people speak of prison and how awful it is."

"Believe everything you've heard and multiply it by three. Don't be sad, it's behind me now."

"I wish we'd have known what Foster did. If Penelope Tucker had—"

"Shh! Don't speak ill of the dead." He had changed from the man she knew. Instead of turning his heart to stone, prison made him forgive. "Having a hand in creating my children has to rate as my single best accomplishment. I love Hope and Patience dearly, but I've always been a bit partial to you, Glory. I knew I could count on you to keep things going. You have the same steel in your spine I once had. McClain told me how hard you worked making this possible. That was a brave thing you did, trailing that outlaw and spying on them."

"McClain exaggerates. I was scared stiff." And mad afterward that Foster would plan such a heinous act against the people she loved.

"Daughter, a healthy dose of fear keeps our blood pumping. You showed bravery despite facing every nightmare you ever had. You spat on it, daring it come get you. I couldn't be more proud."

"Horace Simon deserves most of the credit."

"Nothing much changed about you. You're modest to a fault. You know, I like that fellow McClain. Me and him had a nice long talk."

Stillness came, the kind that warned of loss.

"Luke's a fine man." The cigar band encircling her finger reminded her how honorable.

"He asked for your hand. I said I'd be proud to give my girl to him."

"You didn't!"

"Sure the hell did. What's wrong with that?"

"Because…" She struggled for a logical reason, yet none came to mind. At least none she wanted to share.

"I thought you liked the man."

"I… Yes, I suppose he's better than most."

"You don't want to marry him?"

"It's not that cut-and-dried."

"On account of your blindness? Glory, you need someone to take care of you."

When did a body know the difference between a want and a need? Which was necessary and which an extravagance? Having a want tip the scales of the fine balance could destroy the love between a man and a woman. She would make any sacrifice to prevent that. Her selfish desires had already brought enough destruction.

"Luke deserves more than a burdensome wife. If I can't carry my share of the load, we should go separate ways."

Somehow, she'd have to forget the stranger who'd shown her the beauty of life and made her believe she could reach for the stars and hold them in her grasp.

She had to let the man with the key go…if she could.

※

Luke's breath caught when the silken-haired beauty slipped into the barn.

The first rays of dawn cast an eerie light through the doorway behind her. He hadn't slept a wink for thinking of the answer he meant to have before morning passed.

Funny how one little word could bring sun rays or the darkest, most desolate midnight.

She lifted the feed bucket and scooped up oats for the animals. The sway to Glory's walk brought indecent images into his head. She could do that to a man and not even half try. His gaze followed each line of the curved hips that made him forget how badly the dangerous thoughts scorched him.

Soldier and the white mule sat up and said howdy as she rubbed them between the ears after giving each a portion.

He'd do some nuzzling, too, for less than a little oats.

Envy still rifled through him when she took the pitchfork and thrust it into the hay. The bending movement stretched the britches tight across her backside, outlining her long legs with painstaking clarity.

Have mercy! Hot blood flooded his groin.

"Luke?"

Her upturned face swept to the loft. She had heard his subtle movement.

"Yep, I confess."

"I felt someone watching me."

On the climb down, he marveled at her uncanny sensing ability. She seemed to grasp mere thought in the same way her hand did.

"Caught me red-handed." As he faced her, his voice turned husky.

"Not all I took unaware, it appears."

Damn! He flung his hands across the tight front of his trousers.

"For someone with no sight, you can darn sure see good."

"What? Mr. George catching a mouse? I heard the scurry and the satisfied meow."

Dunce, he called himself, releasing the hold. "Oh, that."

"My goodness, what did you think I meant?"

"Nothing. Nothing at all." Lifting a loose curl, he rolled it around his fingers. The satiny texture cast a balm around the ache inside that only she could fix.

"I thought you left—went home to Tranquillity to visit your father's grave." Glory seemed a mite breathless.

"Not much I can do for him now. I will soon though. I wanted to be close in case you needed me for something." *Anything, any reason to be near her.* "Or in case you might want to talk. How's Jack?"

"Considering the arduous trip...his time grows short."

"I'm sorry I couldn't give you more." He caressed the delicate lines of her face before slipping to the long column of her neck.

"I must look a fright." She fussed with her hair.

"Darlin', I've seen you at your best, your worst, and

everything in between. You happen to be an exceptional, very beautiful lady."

"Trying to turn a girl's head with all this sweet talk?"

"Is it working?"

A rosy blush colored her face. The flustered, disarming smile fed his fancies. Yet, it was her slightly parted mouth he found he had no resistance to.

She came easily, her trim waist a snug fit in his palms. Through the thin, worn shirt, her breasts nestled against the hardness of his chest.

He pressed his lips to hers, knowing if he wasted one second it would be way too long.

A groan crept from the place he discovered he never wanted to leave, a paradise where no one could run him off with a stick. Well, wouldn't make any never mind to him if they tried, he'd only come back. She hadn't reached for the Winchester yet, or stabbed him, so he reckoned he must stand a chance.

However, dying in her arms had certain merit too. No other place he'd rather be, he reckoned. She already knew how he wanted his tombstone to read.

When at last he dragged his lips from her sweetness, he could barely speak. "Have mercy! Please. Or I'll have to make an honest woman of you."

"Before I give my answer, I have to know some things." Glory ran her tongue with maddening slowness across white teeth.

"Fair enough." It was agree to that or carry her to a bed of hay.

Both ideas brought repercussions.

"Understand, I won't ask you to give up your intention of becoming a full-fledged lawman again."

Strange how the importance of the Ranger's job that he once ate, slept, and breathed ranked far down the list.

And the silver badge he once would've died for?

Law work wasn't everything. He could learn to farm. Hell, he'd consider himself the luckiest man ever born if he could spend the rest of his days waking up with her beside him!

"It's my choice. Sure as I stand here, I want you more than I ever wanted anything."

"What if you find out later you've made a terrible mistake? What if you grow to resent having to shoulder the full load? What if—"

Luke kissed the end of her saucy nose. "My father, God rest his soul, believed we were given a knotted rope when we're born. As we pass through life, each lesson we learn we untie a knot. Maybe, with a little luck, by the time we die, we've gotten all the kinks straightened out." He cupped her face between his hands, tilting it up. "I figure both of us still have a few left and I can't think of anyone I'd rather untie my knots with."

"My goodness, that's the dearest thing I ever heard. I regret I won't have the pleasure of meeting Walt McClain. I would've liked that."

"Darling, I will be your eyes if you'll teach me how to see inside here." He gently placed a hand over her heart.

"I have to say you mount interesting arguments."

"Listen to me. Nothing on this earth will make me happier than if you'll quit all this worry and say yes. Take my love and cherish it as I'll do yours."

"Love? Are you saying...?" Tears sparkled in the depths of her stonewashed gaze.

"I don't think I stuttered." He pulled her into the circle of his arms. "You're my one and only, Glory. My love, my life, my all. Now, madam, what is your answer to that?"

She sucked in a deep breath. "I do. I will, for all eternity."

Thirty-two

ON AUGUST 20, 1881, WITH PAPA BY HER SIDE, GLORY became Mrs. Luke McClain. She brought a sizeable piece of property to the marriage; land that she hoped made up for the property Luke had sacrificed for her family.

"It's about time," Squirt had declared. "If you weren't gonna marry him, I was."

At least she could depend on baby sis to liven the solemn ceremony.

Hope tried to shush her, but she'd have none of that. "I mean it too. And, sister, if you don't get a move on, I'll set my cap for Alex O'Brien."

Horace came to say goodbye. "I gotta go. I'm a Texas Ranger now. Captain Roberts is waiting for me. Pa is real mad, but I don't care. I'm finally somebody." He whispered in her ear, "Remember, Mr. Luke has the key that can unlock any door."

Two days later, Glory lay wrapped in Luke's arms in a bed in Fort Worth. Sleep had long since vanished.

Lovemaking with a new husband had a way of stealing the need for rest. In fact, it reduced all else to trivial indulgence.

The hotel's finest bridal suite held a lot of unfamiliar noises and scents, none of the frightening variety. She was safe. And even had they lain in the midst of the loudest, raging storm, she would have no trouble distinguishing the sound of Luke's quiet breathing. His presence had a way of filling her so completely, it left no room for fear of any sort.

Outside Hotel Alexander, the wind howled, slamming the beginnings of a rain shower against the windowpane.

Once upon a time, when she believed such a wind signaled ill will and danger, the noise would've sent foreboding through her bones. Not now.

She smiled and rolled toward Sir Cowboy, Prince of Charmers, letting the barest tips of her fingers trail across the broad expanse of his chest. Never would she tire of touching the man who magically turned ashes of dreams into a life of promise, complete with more bliss than she could imagine. He'd shown her the lady already inside and given everything he possessed for little more than the light in her eyes.

"Umm...I suppose we should get dressed or...we'll miss that mysterious appointment."

"You'd better stop or I'll say to hell with it and give you another lesson in the fine art of wifely pleasures."

The rakish threat aroused another slew of tingles. When he rose on an elbow, brushed aside her hair to ply her earlobes and neck with hot caresses, tiny pinpricks of excitement marched as one army with a single purpose.

"Me?" The breathy question stole softly from her lips.

"Yep, it's your fault. See what you started?"

"What can be so all-fired important we can't miss it?"

Luke gave her a lingering kiss, leaving the taste of him in her mouth. "Sorry to disappoint, darlin'. Get dressed now. Can't be late."

The springs squeaked when he sat on the side. Glory threw back the sheet. Only after she heard a loud groan did she remember she didn't wear a stitch of anything. Amazing how fast a woman in love shed her modesty. She would hide nothing from her helpmate.

They were one heart, one body, one soul forevermore.

He'd best not look if he didn't want an eyeful, that's all she had to say.

She reached for the water pitcher, filled the ceramic bowl, and dipped the washcloth. Wringing it, she encountered the smooth metal ring on her finger. Luke had insisted on replacing the token she'd worn. *With something more proper,* he'd said, grinning. She missed that simple cigar band. It symbolized the purity and depth of their commitment in ways expensive gold bands failed.

Her mind flew to the time they'd spoken of epitaphs and tombstones.

She lived, she died, end of story?

Hardly. She would carve the words *Here lies Glory Day McClain, who had the greatest love the world has ever known.*

Glory listened to the click of the latch closing behind them as they left the office of the renowned eye specialist. Soft rain muffled her heels on the wooden sidewalk. Luke took her elbow and steered her toward the hotel. His unusual quiet flung old fears to the surface.

If only she could see the truth on his face!

"Have the regrets I warned you of already begun?"

Permanent blindness, Dr. Smith had told them. No surprise to her. She'd accepted such a verdict. Her stomach twisted with dread. Would he not want the damaged goods he'd gotten?

Perhaps the depth of her disability had not sunk in until he'd heard it from a learned man of science.

How could she, in all faith, hold him?

Luke helped her carefully manage the hotel steps a few doors down. "Lady, I have not one qualm. I will take you with sight or blind, with shoes or barefoot, makes no difference. Dr. Smith's opinion doesn't change the fact that I happen to love you."

Brimming tears of happiness swept aside the last of her doubts. "Then why did you drag us here?"

"Santa Anna's esteemed sawbones."

"You spoke with Ted Dalton?" The image of the two men conversing brought a smile. He must truly have tender feelings for her to consult the man he envied.

"That so hard to believe? I have nothing against Dalton. He can't flirt with your affections now. Well, he can, but he'd better not if he knows what's best for him. Mrs. McClain, you are legally bound to me, lock, stock, and barrel. I can afford to be generous."

"But why did he advise you to seek out an eye specialist? He said himself my sight would never return."

"I wanted to make absolutely sure. He hinted there might be a speck of hope. And if I could do something... I just wanted to leave no stone unturned, that's all."

Mr. Fix-It at work again. She thought she'd broken him of the habit. A happy grin spread over her face. You could lead a horse to water, but you couldn't make him drink.

Didn't matter. Nothing could dampen her mood. Her husband could be as imperfect as he wished.

Luke was hers to cherish.

She had that in writing on her heart.

He'd never leave.

Except when he had law work to do. A smile touched her lips. Santa Anna should have a sheriff before long. Luke just didn't know it yet. He had no monopoly on fixing things. He had no idea the can of worms he'd opened.

But in the meantime, while she was breaking him in, she meant to give him more lessons in reading her mind.

The strong arm around her waist heated the embers they'd had to hurriedly bank earlier. A change in the steady rhythm of his heart against her shoulder promised another ride on the magic carpet of the man called McClain.

She broke into a faster walk.

Dear Reader:

History bears witness to the places I mention in this story. Camp Colorado was one in a line of forts stretched across Texas that protected settlers from the Indians. Forts were largely responsible for taming the West. Camp Colorado was commissioned and built in 1856 on the Colorado River. Due to a malaria outbreak, however, it was moved in 1857 to north of the town of Coleman. It served the area well until federal troops abandoned it in 1861. The site then became the property of Henry Sackett.

The town of Santa Anna was settled in the early 1870s under the name "The Gap" because it sat between twin mesas in central Coleman County. The mountainous range became known as the home of the Comanche war chief Santanna. In 1879, settlers filed a petition to open a post office and they chose to rename the town Santa Anna.

Bead Mountain also exists. It was an old Indian burial ground. People in the area began referring to it by that name because heavy rains would wash beads out of the ground. It's also rumored to be haunted by spirits of the earliest Americans.

Then, of course, the Texas Rangers—those fearless men who gave their all. No job was too large or too small. They tackled whatever was asked of them and gave 100 percent to seeing it done. Much has been unjustly attributed to them—a swaggering walk, a dead shot, a man who bragged. In truth, Walter Prescott Webb said it best: "A real Ranger has been a very quiet, deliberate, gentle person who could gaze calmly into the eye of a murderer, divine his thoughts, and anticipate his action, a man who could ride straight up to death." Their feats stand as testament to the great state of Texas.

The Rangers continue to exist and they are just as courageous as their earlier counterparts who helped lay down the creed they live by today. Texas Rangers are synonymous with justice, compassion, and dedication. In this story, Luke was a simple man who embodied overwhelming duty. He was a man who "kept on coming" despite the odds. I hope you agree.

Best,
Linda Broday

About the Author

At a young age, Linda Broday discovered a love for story-telling, history, and anything pertaining to the Old West. Cowboys fascinate her. There's something about Stetsons, boots, and tall, rugged cowboys that get her fired up. A *New York Times* and *USA Today* bestselling author, Linda has won many awards, including the prestigious National Readers' Choice Award and the Texas Gold Award. She resides in the Texas Panhandle on the Llano Estacado.

Also by Linda Broday

Texas Redemption

Bachelors of Battle Creek
Texas Mail Order Bride
Twice a Texas Bride
Forever His Texas Bride

Men of Legend
To Love a Texas Ranger
The Heart of a Texas Cowboy
To Marry a Texas Outlaw

Texas Heroes
Knight on the Texas Plains
The Cowboy Who Came Calling